W9-BAJ-560

Praise for Michael Robotham's

L O S T

"Simply terrific. If you haven't already discovered Robotham . . . then now's the time." —*The Globe and Mail* (Toronto)

"Robotham spins an agreeably complex plot, and he has an eye for peripheral details." —*Entertainment Weekly*

"*Lost* is a whip-cracking thriller, gritty, authentic and crisply written, and with a plot that has more twists in it than a strand of barbed wire." —*Adelaide Advertiser*

"Robotham has done perhaps his best work with his characters. . . . They have the shine and feel of real people." —*Rocky Mountain News*

"*Lost* works because Robotham doesn't allow his hero to wave a magic wand and restore his life to order. Ruiz must work at finding answers, and at every turn, he is confronted by people who want him dead." —*The Orlando Sentinel*

"*Lost* begins with a bang. . . . Robotham takes his readers on a hair-raising journey through London's underworld. . . . Just when you think you have the story figured out, Robotham takes a turn, leaving you unsure of how things will be resolved until the very last page." —*Library Journal* (starred)

Michael Robotham
LOST

Michael Robotham is a former journalist. He lives in Sydney, Australia.

www.michaelrobotham.com

Also by Michael Robotham

SUSPECT

L O S T

Michael Robotham

A novel

VINTAGE CRIME/BLACK LIZARD

Vintage Books

A Division of Random House, Inc.

New York

FIRST VINTAGE CRIME/BLACK LIZARD EDITION, MAY 2007

Copyright © 2005 by Bookwrite Pty. Ltd.

All rights reserved. Published in the United States by Vintage Books, a division of
Random House, Inc., New York. Originally published in hardcover in the United
Kingdom by Little, Brown, a division of Time Warner Book Group UK, London, in
2005, and subsequently in hardcover in the United States by Doubleday,
a division of Random House, Inc., New York, in 2006.

Vintage is a registered trademark and Vintage Crime/Black Lizard and colophon
are trademarks of Random House, Inc.

This is a work of fiction. Names, characters, businesses, organizations, places,
events, and incidents either are the product of the author's imagination or are used
fictitiously. Any resemblance to actual persons, living or dead, events,
or locales is entirely coincidental.

The Library of Congress has cataloged the Doubleday edition as follows:
Robotham, Michael, 1960–
Lost : a novel / Michael Robotham.—1st ed.
p. cm.
1. Police—England—London—Fiction. 2. Boys—Crimes against—Fiction.
3. Missing children—Fiction. 4. Recovered memory—Fiction.
5. London (England)—Fiction. 6. Amnesia—Fiction.
I. Title.
PR6118.O26L67 2005
813'.6—dc22   2005045568

Vintage ISBN: 978-0-307-27548-6

www.vintagebooks.com

Printed in the United States of America
10 9 8 7 6 5 4 3 2 1

For my mother and father

acknowledgments

I wish to thank the usual suspects, such as my agent, Mark Lucas, and my different publishers around the world who have helped me to find the heart of *Lost*. They share my gratitude along with those who toil in the background bringing books to life.

Again I am indebted to Vivien, a passionate reader, stern critic, bedroom psychologist, gentle reviewer and mother to my children, who has lived with my characters and my sleepless nights. Last time I said a lesser woman would have slept in the guest room. I was wrong. A lesser woman would have banished *me* to the guest room.

Wealth lost, something lost;

Honor lost, much lost;

Courage lost, all lost.

GERMAN PROVERB

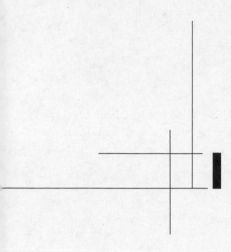

The Thames, London

I remember someone once telling me that you know it's cold when you see a lawyer with his hands in his *own* pockets. It's colder than that now. My mouth is numb and every breath is like slivers of ice in my lungs.

People are shouting and shining flashlights in my eyes. In the meantime, I'm hugging this big yellow buoy like it's Marilyn Monroe. A very fat Marilyn Monroe, after she took all the pills and went to seed.

My favorite Monroe film is *Some Like It Hot* with Jack Lemmon and Tony Curtis. I don't know why I should think of that now, although how anyone could mistake Jack Lemmon for a woman is beyond me.

A guy with a really thick mustache and pizza breath is panting in my ear. He's wearing a life vest and trying to peel my fingers away from the buoy. I'm too cold to move. He wraps his arms around my chest and pulls me backward through the water. More people, silhouetted against the lights, take hold of my arms, lifting me onto the deck.

"Jesus, look at his leg!" someone says.

"He's been shot!"

Who are they talking about?

People are shouting all over again, yelling for bandages and plasma.

A black guy with a gold earring slides a needle into my arm and puts a bag over my face.

"Someone get some blankets. Let's keep this guy warm."

"He's palping at one-twenty."

"One-twenty?"

"Palping at one-twenty."

"Any head injuries?"

"That's negative."

The engine roars and we're moving. I can't feel my legs. I can't feel anything—not even the cold anymore. The lights are also disappearing. Darkness has seeped into my eyes.

"Ready?"

"Yeah."

"One, two, three."

"Watch the IV lines. Watch the IV lines."

"I got it."

"Bag a couple of times."

"OK."

The guy with pizza breath is puffing really hard now, running alongside the gurney. His fist is in front of my face, pressing a bag to force air into my lungs. They lift again and square lights pass overhead. I can still see.

A siren wails in my head. Every time we slow down it gets louder and closer. Someone is talking on a radio. "We've pumped two liters of fluid. He's on his fourth unit of blood. He's bleeding out. Systolic pressure dropping."

"He needs volume."

"Squeeze in another bag of fluid."

"He's seizing!"

"He's seizing. See that?"

One of the machines has gone into a prolonged cry. Why don't they turn it off?

Pizza breath rips open my shirt and slaps two pads on my chest.

"CLEAR!" he yells.

The pain almost blows the top of my skull clean off.

He does that again and I'll break his arms.

"CLEAR!"

I swear to God I'm going to remember you, pizza breath. I'm going to remember exactly who you are. And when I get out of here I'm coming looking for you. I was happier in the river. Take me back to Marilyn Monroe.

I am awake now. My eyelids flutter as if fighting gravity. Squeezing them shut, I try again, blinking into the darkness.

Turning my head, I can make out orange dials on a machine near the bed and a green blip of light sliding across a liquid crystal display window like one of those stereo systems with bouncing waves of colored light.

Where am I?

Beside my head is a chrome stand that catches stars on its curves. Suspended from a hook is a plastic satchel bulging with a clear fluid. The liquid trails down a pliable plastic tube and disappears under a wide strip of surgical tape wrapped around my left forearm.

I'm in a hospital room. There is a pad on the bedside table. Reaching toward it, I suddenly notice my left hand—not so much my hand as a finger. It's missing. Instead of a digit and a wedding ring I have a lump of gauze dressing. I stare at it idiotically, as though this is some sort of magic trick.

When the twins were youngsters, we had a game where I pulled off my thumb and if they sneezed it would come back again. Michael used to laugh so hard he almost wet his pants.

Fumbling for the pad, I read the letterhead: St. Mary's Hospital, Paddington, London. There is nothing in the drawer except a Bible and a copy of the Koran.

I spy a clipboard hanging at the end of the bed. Reaching down, I feel a sudden pain that explodes from my right leg and shoots out of the top of my head. Christ! Do not, under any circumstances, do that again.

Curled up in a ball, I wait for the pain to go away. Closing my eyes, I take a deep breath. If I concentrate very hard on a particular point just under my jawbone, I actually feel the blood sliding back and forth beneath my skin, squeezing into smaller and smaller channels, circulating oxygen.

My estranged wife, Miranda, is such a lousy sleeper that she said my heart kept her awake because it beat too loudly. I didn't snore or wake with the night terrors, but my heart pumped up a riot. This has been listed among Miranda's grounds for divorce. I'm exaggerating, of course. She doesn't need extra justification.

I open my eyes again. The world is still here.

Taking a deep breath, I grip the bedclothes and raise them a few inches. I still have two legs. I count them. One. Two. The right leg is bandaged in layers of gauze taped down at the edges. Something has been written in a felt-tip pen down the side of my thigh but I can't read what it says.

Farther down I can see my toes. They wave hello to me. "Hello toes," I whisper.

Tentatively, I reach down and cup my genitals, rolling my testicles between my fingers.

A nurse slips silently through the curtains. Her voice startles me. "Is this a very private moment?"

"I was . . . I was . . . just checking."

"Well, I think you should consider buying that thing dinner first."

Her accent is Irish and her eyes are as green as mown grass. She presses the call button above my head. "Thank goodness you're finally awake. We were very worried about you." She taps the bag of fluid and checks the flow control. Then she straightens my pillows.

"What happened? How did I get here?"

"You were shot."

"Who shot me?"

She laughs. "Oh, don't ask me. Nobody ever tells me things like that."

"But I can't remember anything. My leg . . . my finger . . ."

"The doctor should be here soon."

She doesn't seem to be listening. I reach out and grab her arm. She tries to pull away, suddenly frightened of me.

"You don't understand—I *can't* remember! I don't know how I got here."

She glances at the emergency button. "They found you floating in the river. That's what I heard them say. The police have been waiting for you to wake up."

"How long have I been here?"

"Eight days . . . you were in a coma. I thought you might be coming out yesterday. You were talking to yourself."

4

"What did I say?"

"You kept asking about a girl—saying you had to find her."

"Who?"

"You didn't say. Please let go of my arm. You're hurting me."

My fingers open and she steps well away, rubbing her forearm. She won't come close again.

My heart won't slow down. It is pounding away, getting faster and faster like Chinese drums. How can I have been here eight days?

"What day is it today?"

"October the third."

"Did you give me drugs? What have you done to me?"

She stammers, "You're on morphine for the pain."

"What else? What else have you given me?"

"Nothing." She glances again at the emergency button. "The doctor is coming. Try to stay calm or he'll have to sedate you."

She's out of the door and won't come back. As it swings closed I notice a uniformed policeman sitting on a chair outside the door, with his legs stretched out like he's been there for a while.

I slump back in bed, smelling bandages and dried blood. Holding up my hand I look at the gauze bandage, trying to wiggle the missing finger. How can I not remember?

For me there has never been such a thing as forgetting, nothing is hazy or vague or frayed at the edges. I hoard memories like a miser counts his gold. Every scrap of a moment is kept as long as it has some value.

I don't see things photographically. Instead I make connections, spinning them together like a spider weaving a web, threading one strand into the next. That's why I can reach back and pluck details of criminal cases from five, ten, fifteen years ago and remember them as if they happened only yesterday. Names, dates, places, witnesses, perpetrators, victims—I can conjure them up and walk through the same streets, have the same conversations, hear the same lies.

Now for the first time I've forgotten something truly important. I can't remember what happened and how I finished up here. There is a black hole in my mind like a dark shadow on a chest X-ray. I've seen those shadows. I lost my first wife to cancer. Black holes suck everything into them. Not even light can escape.

Twenty minutes go by and then Dr. Bennett sweeps through the curtains. He's wearing jeans and a bow tie under his white coat.

"Detective Inspector Ruiz, welcome back to the land of the living and high taxation." He sounds very public school and has one of those foppish Hugh Grant fringe haircuts that falls across his forehead like a dinner napkin on a thigh.

Shining a penlight in my eyes, he asks, "Can you wiggle your toes?"

"Yes."

"Any pins and needles?"

"No."

He pulls back the bedclothes and scrapes a key along the sole of my right foot. "Can you feel that?"

"Yes."

"Excellent."

Picking up a clipboard, he scrawls his initials with a flick of the wrist.

"I can't remember anything."

"About the accident."

"It was an accident?"

"I have no idea. You were shot."

"Who shot me?"

"You don't remember?"

"No."

This conversation is going around in circles.

Dr. Bennett taps the pen against his teeth, contemplating this answer. Then he pulls up a chair and sits on it backward, draping his arms over the backrest.

"You were shot. One bullet entered just above your gracilis muscle on your right leg leaving a quarter-inch hole. It went through the skin, then the fat layer, through the pectineus muscle, just medial to the femoral vessels and nerve, through the quadratus femoris muscle, through the head of the biceps femoris and through the gluteus maximus before exiting through the skin on the other side. The exit wound was far more impressive. It blew a hole four inches across. Gone. No flap. No pieces. Your skin just vaporized."

He whistles impressively through his teeth. "You had a pulse but you were bleeding out when they found you. Then you stopped breathing. You were dead but we brought you back."

He holds up his thumb and forefinger. "The bullet missed your femoral artery by this far." I can barely see a gap between them. "Oth-

6

erwise you would have bled to death in three minutes. Apart from the bullet we had to deal with infection. Your clothes were filthy. God knows what was in that water. We've been pumping you full of antibiotics. Bottom line, Inspector, you are one lucky puppy."

Is he kidding? How much luck does it take to get shot?

I hold up my hand. "What about my finger?"

"Gone, I'm afraid, just above the first knuckle."

A skinny looking intern with a crewcut pokes his head through the curtains. Dr. Bennett lets out a low-pitched growl that only underlings can hear. Rising from the chair, he buries his hands in the pockets of his white coat.

"Will that be all?"

"Why can't I remember?"

"It's not really my field, I'm afraid. We can run some tests. You'll need a CT scan or an MRI to rule out a skull fracture or hemorrhage. I'll call neurology."

"My leg hurts."

"Good. It's getting better. You'll need a walker or crutches. A physiotherapist will come and talk to you about a program to help you strengthen your leg." He flips his bangs and turns to leave. "I'm sorry about your memory, Detective. Be thankful you're alive."

He's gone, leaving a scent of aftershave and superiority. Why do surgeons cultivate this air of owning the world? I know I should be grateful. Maybe if I could remember what happened I could trust the explanations more.

So I should be dead. I always suspected that I would die suddenly. It's not that I'm particularly foolhardy but I have a knack for taking shortcuts. Most people only die once. Now I've had two lives. Throw in three wives and I've had more than my fair share of living. (I'll definitely forgo the three wives, should someone want them back.)

My Irish nurse is back again. Her name is Maggie and she has one of those reassuring smiles they teach in nursing school. She has a bowl of warm water and a sponge.

"Are you feeling better?"

"I'm sorry I frightened you."

"That's OK. Time for a bath."

She pulls back the covers and I drag them up again.

"There's nothing under there I haven't seen," she says.

"I beg to differ. I have a pretty fair recollection of how many women have danced with old Johnnie One-Eye and unless you were that girl in the back row of the Shepherd's Bush Empire during a Yardbirds concert in 1961, I don't think you're one of them."

"Johnnie One-Eye?"

"My oldest friend."

She shakes her head and looks sorry for me.

A familiar figure appears from behind her—a short, square man, with no neck and a five-o'clock shadow. Campbell Smith is a Chief Superintendent, with a crushing handshake and a no-brand smile. He's wearing his uniform, with polished silver buttons and a shirt collar so highly starched it threatens to decapitate him.

Everyone claims to like Campbell—even his enemies—but few people are ever happy to see him. Not me. Not today. I remember him! That's a good sign.

"Christ, Vincent, you gave us a scare!" he booms. "It was touch and go for a while. We were all praying for you—everyone at the station. See all the cards and flowers?"

I turn my head and look at a table piled high with flowers and bowls of fruit.

"Someone shot me," I say, incredulously.

"Yes," he replies, pulling up a chair. "We need to know what happened."

"I don't remember."

"You didn't see them?"

"Who?"

"The people on the boat."

"What boat?" I look at him blankly.

His voice suddenly grows louder. "You were found floating in the Thames shot to shit and less than a mile away there was a boat that looked like a floating abattoir. What happened?"

"I don't remember."

"You don't remember the massacre?"

"I don't remember the fucking boat."

Campbell has dropped any pretense of affability. He paces the room, bunching his fists and trying to control himself.

"This isn't good, Vincent. This isn't pretty. Did you kill anyone?"

"Today?"

"Don't joke with me. Did you discharge your firearm? Your service pistol was signed out of the station armory. Are we going to find bodies?"

Bodies? Is that what happened?

Campbell rubs his hands through his hair in frustration.

"I can't tell you the crap that's flying already. There's going to be a full inquiry. The Commissioner is demanding answers. The press will have a fucking field day. The blood of three people was found on that boat, including yours. Forensics says at least one of them must have died. They found brains and skull fragments."

The walls seem to dip and sway. Maybe it's the morphine or the closeness of the air. How could I have forgotten something like that?

"What were you doing on that boat?"

"It must have been a police operation—"

"No," he declares angrily, all pretense of friendship gone. "You weren't working a case. This wasn't a police operation. You were on your own."

We have an old-fashioned staring contest. I own this one. I might never blink again. Morphine is the answer. God, it feels good.

Finally Campbell slumps into a chair and plucks a handful of grapes from a brown paper bag beside the bed.

"What is the last thing you remember?"

We sit in silence as I try to recover shreds of a dream. Pictures float in and out of my head, dim and then sharp: a yellow life buoy, Marilyn Monroe . . .

"I remember ordering a pizza."

"Is that it?"

"Sorry."

Staring at the gauze dressing on my hand, I marvel at how the missing finger feels itchy. "What was I working on?"

Campbell shrugs. "You were on leave."

"Why?"

"You needed a rest."

He's lying to me. Sometimes I think he forgets how far back we go. We did our training together at the Police Staff College, Bramshill. And

I introduced him to his wife, Maureen, at a barbecue thirty-five years ago. She has never completely forgiven me. I don't know what upsets her most—my three marriages or the fact that I pawned her off on someone else.

It's been a long while since Campbell called me buddy and we haven't shared a beer since he made Chief Superintendent. He's a different man. No better or no worse, just different.

He spits a grape seed into his hand. "You always thought you were better than me, Vincent, but I got promoted ahead of you."

You were a brownnoser.

"I know you think I'm a brownnoser." (*He's reading my mind.*) "But I was just smarter. I made the right contacts and let the system work for me instead of fighting against it. You should have retired three years ago, when you had the chance. Nobody would have thought any less of you. We would have given you a big send-off. You could have settled down, played a bit of golf, maybe even saved your marriage."

I wait for him to say something else but he just stares at me with his head cocked to one side.

"Vincent, would you mind if I made an observation?" He doesn't wait for my answer. "You put a pretty good face on things considering all that's happened, but the feeling I get from you is . . . well . . . you're a sad man. But it's something more than that . . . you're angry."

Embarrassment prickles like heat rash under my hospital gown.

"Some people find solace in religion and others have people they can talk to. I know that's not your style. Look at you! You hardly see your kids. You live alone . . . Now you've gone and fucked up your career. I can't help you anymore. I told you to leave this alone."

"What was I supposed to leave alone?"

He doesn't answer. Instead he picks up his hat and polishes the brim with his sleeve. Any moment now he's going to turn and tell me what he means. Only he doesn't; he keeps on walking out the door and along the corridor.

My grapes have also gone. The stalks look like dead trees on a crumpled brown-paper plain. Beside them a basket of flowers has started to wilt. The begonias and tulips are losing their petals like fat fan dancers and dusting the top of the table with pollen. A small white card embossed with a silver scroll is wedged between the stems. I can't read the message.

Some bastard shot me! It should be etched in my memory. I should be able to relive it over and over again like those whining victims on daytime talk shows who have personal-injury lawyers on speed dial. Instead, I remember nothing. And no matter how many times I squeeze my eye shut and bang my fists on my forehead it doesn't change.

The really strange thing is what I imagine I remember. For instance I recall seeing silhouettes against bright lights; masked men wearing plastic shower caps and paper slippers, who were discussing cars, pension plans and football results. Of course this could have been a near-death experience. I was given a glimpse of Hell and it was full of surgeons.

Perhaps if I start with the simple stuff, I may get to the point where I can remember what happened to me. Staring at the ceiling, I silently spell my name: Vincent Yanko Ruiz; born December 11, 1945. I am a Detective Inspector of the London Metropolitan Police and the head of the Serious Crime Group (Western Division). I live on Rainville Road, Fulham . . .

I used to say I would pay good money to forget most of my life. Now I want the memories back.

2

I only know two people who have been shot. One was a chap I went through police training college with. His name was Angus Lehmann and he wanted to be first at everything—first in his exams, first to the bar, first to get promoted . . .

A few years back he led a raid on a drug factory in Brixton and was first through the door. An entire magazine from a semiautomatic took his head clean off. There's a lesson in that somewhere.

A farmer in our valley called Bruce Curley is the other one. He shot himself in the foot when he tried to chase his wife's lover out the bedroom window. Bruce was fat with gray hair sprouting from his ears and Mrs. Curley used to cower like a dog whenever he raised a hand. Shame he didn't shoot himself between the eyes.

During my police training we did a firearms course. The instructor was a Geordie with a head like a billiard ball and he took against me from the first day because I suggested the best way to keep a gun barrel clean was to cover it with a condom.

We were standing on the live firing range, freezing our bollocks off. He pointed out the cardboard cutout at the end of the range. It was a silhouette of a crouching gun-wielding villain with a white circle painted over his heart and another on his head.

Taking a service pistol the Geordie crouched down with his legs apart and squeezed off six shots—a heartbeat between each of them—every one grouped in the upper circle.

Flicking the smoking clip into his hand, he said, "Now I don't expect any of you to do that but at least try to hit the fucking target. Who wants to go first?"

Nobody volunteered.

"How about you, condom boy?"

The class laughed.

I stepped forward and raised my revolver. I hated how good it felt in my hand. The instructor said, "No, not like that, keep both eyes open. Crouch. Count and squeeze."

Before he could finish the gun kicked in my hand, rattling the air and something deep inside me.

The cutout swayed from side to side as the pulley dragged it down the range toward us. Six shots, each so close together they formed a ragged hole through the cardboard.

"He shot out his arsehole," someone muttered in astonishment.

"Right up the Khyber Pass."

I didn't look at the instructor's face. I turned away, checked the chamber, put on the safety catch and removed my earplugs.

"You missed," he said triumphantly.

"If you say so, sir."

I wake with a sudden jolt and it takes a while for my heart to settle. I look at my watch—not so much at the time but the date. I want to make sure I haven't slept for too long or lost any more time.

It's been two days since I regained consciousness. A man is sitting by the bed.

"My name is Dr. Wickham," he says, smiling. "I'm a neurologist."

He looks like one of those doctors you see on daytime chat shows.

"I once saw you play rugby for Harlequins against London Scottish," he says. "You would have made the England team that year if you hadn't been injured. I played a bit of rugby myself. Never higher than seconds . . ."

"Really, what position?"

"Outside center."

I figured as much—he probably touched the ball twice a game and is still talking about the tries he *could* have scored.

"I have the results of your MRI scan," he says, opening a folder. "There is no evidence of a skull fracture, aneurysms or a hemorrhage." He glances up from his notes. "I want to run some neurological tests to help establish what you've forgotten. It means answering some questions about the shooting."

"I don't remember it."

"Yes, but I want you to answer regardless—even if it means guessing. It's called a forced-choice recognition test. It forces you to make choices."

I think I understand, although I don't see the point.

"How many people were on the boat?"

"I don't remember."

Dr. Wickham reiterates, "You have to make a choice."

"Four."

"Was there a full moon?"

"Yes."

"Was the name of the boat *Charmaine*?"

"No."

"How many engines did it have?"

"One."

"Was it a stolen boat?"

"Yes."

"Was the engine running?"

"No."

"Were you anchored or drifting?"

"Drifting."

"Were you carrying a weapon?"

"Yes."

"Did you fire your weapon?"

"No."

This is ridiculous! What possible good does it do? I'm guessing the answers.

Suddenly, it dawns on me. They think I'm faking amnesia. This isn't a test to see how much I remember—they're testing the validity of my symptoms. They're forcing me to make choices so they can work out what percentage of questions I answer correctly. If I'm telling the truth, pure guesswork should mean half of my answers are correct. Anything significantly above or below fifty percent could mean I'm trying to "influence" the result by deliberately getting things right or wrong.

I know enough about statistics to see the objective. The chance of someone with memory loss answering only ten questions correctly out of fifty is less than five percent.

Dr. Wickham has been taking notes. No doubt he's studying the distribution of my answers—looking for patterns that might indicate something other than random chance.

Stopping him, I ask, "Who wrote these questions?"

"I don't know."

"Guess."

He blinks at me.

"Come on, Doc, true or false? I'll accept a guess. Is this a test to see if I'm faking memory loss?"

"I don't know what you mean," he stammers.

"If I can guess the answer, so can you. Who put you up to this—Internal Affairs or Campbell Smith?"

Struggling to his feet, he tucks the clipboard under his arm and turns toward the door. I wish I'd met him on the rugby field. I'd have driven his head into a muddy hole.

Swinging my legs out of bed, I put one foot on the floor. The linoleum is cool and slightly sticky. Gulping hard on the pain, I slide my forearms into the plastic cuffs of the crutches.

I'm supposed to be using a walker on wheels but I'm too vain. I'm not going to walk around in a chrome cage like some geriatric in a post office queue. I look in the cupboard for my clothes. Empty.

I know it sounds paranoid but they're not telling me everything. Someone *must* know what I was doing on the river. Someone will have heard the shots or seen something. Why haven't they found any bodies?

Halfway down the corridor I see Campbell talking to Dr. Wickham. Two detectives are with them. I recognize one of them: John Keebal. I used to work with him until he joined the Met's Anti-Corruption Group, otherwise known as the Ghost Squad, and began investigating his own.

Keebal is one of those coppers who call all gays "fudge-packers" and Asians "Pakis." He is loud, bigoted and totally obsessed with the job. When the *Marchioness* riverboat sank in the Thames, he did thirteen death-knocks before lunchtime, telling people their kids had drowned. He knew exactly what to say and when to stop talking. A man like that can't be all bad.

"Where do you think you're going?" asks Campbell.

"I thought I might get some fresh air."

Keebal interrupts, "Yeah, just got a whiff of something myself."

I push past them heading for the lift.

"You can't possibly leave," says Dr. Wickham. "Your dressing has to be changed every few days. You need painkillers."

"Fill my pockets and I'll self-administer."

Campbell grabs my arm. "Don't be so bloody foolish."

I realize I'm shaking.

"Have you found anyone? Any . . . any bodies?"

"No."

"I'm not faking this, you know. I really can't remember."

He steers me away from the others. "I believe you, Vincent, but you know the drill. The IPCC has to investigate."

"What's Keebal doing here?"

"He just wants to talk to you."

"Do I need a lawyer?"

Campbell laughs but it doesn't reassure me like it should. Before I can weigh up my options, Keebal leads me down the corridor to the hospital lounge—a stark, windowless place, with burnt-orange sofas and posters of healthy people. He unbuttons his jacket and takes a seat, waiting for me to lever myself down from my crutches.

"I hear you nearly met the grim reaper."

"He offered me a room with a view."

"And you turned him down?"

"I'm not a good traveler."

For the next ten minutes we shoot the breeze about mutual acquaintances and old times. He asks about my mother and I tell him she's in a retirement village.

"Some of those places can be pretty expensive."

"Yep."

"Where you living nowadays?"

"Right here."

The coffee arrives and Keebal keeps talking. He gives me his opinion on the proliferation of firearms, random violence and senseless crimes. The police are becoming easy targets and scapegoats all at once. I know what he's trying to do. He wants to draw me in with a spiel about good guys having to stick together.

Keebal is one of those police officers who adopt a warrior ethic as though something separates them from normal society. They listen to politicians talk about the war on crime and the war on drugs and the war on terror and they start picturing themselves as soldiers fighting to keep the streets safe.

"How many times have you put your life on the line, Ruiz? You think any of the bastards care? The left call us pigs and the right call us Nazis. Sieg, sieg, oink! Sieg, sieg, oink!" He throws his right arm forward in a Nazi salute.

I stare at the signet ring on his pinkie and think of Orwell's *Animal Farm*.

Keebal is on a roll. "We don't live in a perfect world and we don't have perfect police officers, eh? But what do they expect? We have no fucking resources and we're fighting a system that lets criminals out quicker than we can catch them. And all this new-age touchy-feely waa-waa bullshit they pass off as crime prevention has done nothing for you and me. And it's done nothing for the poor misguided kids who get caught up in crime.

"A while back I went to a conference and some lard-arse criminologist with an American accent told us that police officers had no enemies. 'Criminals are not the enemy, crime is,' he said. Jesus wept! Have you ever heard anything so stupid? I had to stop myself giving this guy a slap."

Keebal leans in a little closer. I smell peanuts on his breath.

"I don't blame coppers for being pissed off. And I can understand when they pocket a little for themselves, as long as they're not dealing drugs or hurting children, eh?" He puts his hand on my shoulder. "I can help you. Just tell me what happened that night."

"I don't remember."

"Am I correct in assuming, therefore, you cannot identify the person who shot you?"

"You would be correct in that assumption."

My sarcasm seems to light a fire under Keebal. He knows I'm not buying his we're-all-alone-in-the-trenches bullshit.

"Where are the diamonds?"

"What diamonds?"

He tries to change the subject.

"No. No. Stop! What diamonds?"

He shouts over me. "The decks of that boat were swimming in blood. People died but we haven't found any bodies and nobody has been reported missing. What does that suggest to you?"

He makes me think. The victims probably had no close ties or they were engaged in something illegal. I want to go back to the diamonds, but Keebal has his own agenda.

"I read an interesting statistic the other day. Thirty-five percent of offenders found guilty of homicide claim amnesia of the event."

More bloody statistics. "You think I'm lying."

"I think you're bent."

I reach for my crutches and swing onto my feet. "Since you know all the answers, Keebal, you tell me what happened. Oh, that's right— you weren't there. Then again—you never are. When real coppers are out risking their lives, you're at home tucked up in bed watching reruns of *The Bill*. You risk nothing and you persecute honest coppers for standards that you couldn't piss over. Get out of here. And next time you want to talk to me you better come armed with an arrest warrant and a set of handcuffs."

Keebal's face turns a slapped-red color. He does lots of preening and flexing as he walks away, yelling over his shoulder. "The only person you got fooled is that neurologist. Nobody else believes you. You're gonna wish that bullet did the job."

I try to chase them down the corridor, hopping on one crutch, and screaming my head off. Two black orderlies hold me back, pinning my arms behind me.

Finally, I calm down and they take me back to my room. Maggie gives me a small plastic cup of syrupy liquid and soon I'm like Alice in Wonderland shrinking into the room. The white folds of the bedclothes are an arctic wasteland.

The dream has a whiff of strawberry lip gloss and spearmint breath—a missing girl in a pink-and-orange bikini. Her name is Mickey Carlyle and she's wedged in the rocks in my mind like a spar of driftwood, bleached white by the sun—as white as her skin and the fine hairs on her forearms. She is four feet tall, tugging at my sleeve, saying, "Why didn't you ever find me? You promised my friend Sarah that you'd find me."

She even says it in the same voice that Sarah used when she asked me for an ice-cream cone. "You promised me. You said I could have one if I told you what happened."

Mickey disappeared not far from here. You might even be able to see Randolph Avenue from the window. It's a solid, redbrick canyon of mansion blocks built as cheap Victorian housing, but now the flats cost hundreds of thousands of pounds. I could save for ten years or two hundred and never afford to buy one.

I can still picture the lift, an old-fashioned metal cage that rattled and twanged between the landings. The stairs wrapped around the lift shaft, turning back and forth as they rose. Mickey grew up playing on those stairs, holding impromptu concerts after school because the acoustics were so good. She sang with a lisp because of the gap in her front teeth.

Three years have passed since then. The world has tuned out her story because there are other crimes to titillate and horrify—dead beauty queens, the war on terror, sportsmen behaving badly . . . Mickey hasn't gone away. She is still here. She is like the ghost who sits opposite me at every feast and the voice inside my head when I fall asleep. I know she's alive. I know it deep down inside, where my guts are tied in knots. I know it but I can't prove it.

It was the first week of the summer holidays, three years ago when she entered my life. Eighty-five steps and then darkness; she vanished. How can a child disappear in a building with only five floors and eleven flats?

We searched every one of them—every room, cupboard and crawl space. I even checked the same places over and over again, somehow expecting her to suddenly be there, despite all the other searches.

Mickey was seven years old with blond hair, blue eyes and a gap-toothed smile. She was last seen wearing a bikini, a white headband, red canvas shoes, and carrying a striped beach towel.

Police cars had blocked the street outside and the neighbors were organizing searches. Someone had set up a trestle table with jugs of ice water and bottles of cordial. The temperature reached 30°C at nine o'clock that morning and the air smelled of hot bitumen and exhaust fumes.

A fat guy in baggy green shorts was taking photographs. I didn't recognize him at first but I knew him from somewhere. Where?

Then it came back to me, like it always does. Cottesloe Park—an Anglican boarding school in Warrington. His name was Howard Wavell, a baffling, unfortunate figure, who was three years behind me. My memory triumphs again.

I knew Mickey hadn't left the building. I had a witness. Her name was Sarah Jordan and she was only nine years old but she knew what she knew. Sitting on the bottom stair, sipping from a can of lemonade, she brushed mousy brown hair from her eyes. Tiny crosses clung to her earlobes like pieces of silver foil.

Sarah wore a blue-and-yellow swimsuit, with white shorts, brown sandals and a baseball cap. Her legs were pale and spotted with insect bites pink from her scratching. Too young to be body conscious, she swung her knees open and closed, resting her cheek against the coolness of the banister.

"My name is Detective Inspector Ruiz," I said, sitting next to her. "Tell me what happened again."

She sighed and straightened her legs. "I pressed the buzzer, like I said."

"Which buzzer?"

"Eleven. Where Mickey lives."

"Show me which button you pressed."

She sighed again and walked across the foyer through the large front door. The intercom was just outside. She pointed to the top button. Pink nail varnish had been chipped off her fingernails.

"See! I know what number eleven is."

"Of course, you do. What happened then?"

"Mickey's mum said Mickey would be right down."

"Is that exactly what she said? Word for word?"

Her brow furrowed in concentration. "No. First she said hello and I said hello. And I asked if Mickey could come and play. We were going to sunbathe in the garden and play under the hose. Mr. Murphy lets us use the sprinkler. He says we're helping him water the lawn at the same time."

"And who is Mr. Murphy?"

"Mickey says he owns the building, but I think he's just the caretaker."

"Mickey didn't come down."

"No."

"How long did you wait?"

"Ages and ages." She fans her face with her hand. "Can I have an ice cream?"

"In a minute . . . Did anyone come past you while you were waiting?"

"No."

"And you didn't leave these steps—not even to get a drink . . ."

She shook her head.

". . . or to talk to a friend, or to pat a dog?"

"No."

"What happened then?"

"Mickey's mum came down with the trash. Then she said, 'What are you doing? Where's Mickey?' And I said, 'I'm still waiting for her.' Then she said she came down ages ago. Only she never did because I've been here the whole time . . ."

"What did you do then?"

"Mickey's mum told me to wait. She said not to move, so I sat on the stairs."

"Did anyone come past you?"

"Only the neighbors who helped look for Mickey."

"Do you know their names?"

"Some of them." She counted quietly on her fingers and listed them. "Is this a mystery?"

"I guess you could call it that."

"Where did Mickey go?"

"I don't know, sweetheart, but we're going to find her."

3

Professor Joseph O'Loughlin has arrived to see me. I can see him walking across the hospital parking lot with his left leg swinging as if bound in a splint. His mouth is moving—smiling, wishing people good morning and making jokes about how he likes his martinis shaken not stirred. Only the Professor could make fun of Parkinson's disease.

Joe is a clinical psychologist and looks exactly like you'd expect a shrink to look—tall and thin with a tangle of brown hair like some absentminded academic escaped from a lecture hall.

We met a few years back during a murder investigation when I had him pegged as a possible killer until it turned out to be one of his patients. I don't think he mentions that in his lectures.

Knocking gently on the door, he opens it and smiles awkwardly. He has one of those totally open faces with wet brown eyes, like a baby seal just before it gets clubbed.

"I hear you're suffering memory problems."

"Yeah, who the fuck are you?"

"Very good. Nice to see you haven't lost your sense of humor."

He turns around several times trying to decide where to put his briefcase. Then he takes a notepad and pulls up a chair, sitting with his knees touching the bed. Finally settled, he looks at me and says nothing—as though I've asked him to come because there's something on my mind.

This is what I hate about shrinks. The way they create silences and have you questioning your sanity. This wasn't my idea. I can remember my name. I know where I live. I know where I put the car keys and parked the car. I'm tickety-boo.

"How are you feeling?"

"Some bastard shot me."

Without warning his left arm jerks and trembles. Self-consciously, he holds it down.

"How's the Parkinson's?"

"I've stopped ordering soup at restaurants."

"Very wise. Julianne?"

"She's great."

"And the girls?"

"They're growing up."

Swapping small talk and family stories has never been a feature of our relationship. Usually, I invite myself around to Joe's place for dinner, drink his wine, flirt with his wife and shamelessly milk him for ideas about unsolved cases. Joe knows this, of course—not because he's so bloody clever but because I'm so transparent.

I like him. He's a privately educated, middle-class pseud but that's OK. And I like Julianne, his wife, who for some reason thinks she can marry me off again because my track record shouldn't be held against me.

"I take it you met my boss."

"The Chief Superintendent."

"What did you make of him?"

Joe shrugs. "He seems very professional."

"Come on, Prof, you can do better than that. Tell me what you really think."

Joe makes a little "Tsh" sound like a cymbal. He knows I'm challenging him.

Clearing his throat, he glances at his hands. "The Chief Superintendent is a well-spoken career police officer, who is self-conscious about his double chins and colors his hair. He is asthmatic. He wears Calvin Klein aftershave. He is married with three daughters, who have him so tightly wrapped around their little fingers he should be dipped in silver and engraved. They are vegetarians and won't let him eat meat at home so he eats meals at the station canteen. He reads P. D. James novels and likes to think of himself as Adam Dalgleish, although he doesn't write poetry and he's not particularly perceptive. And he has a very irritating habit of lecturing rather than listening to people."

I let out a low, admiring whistle. "Have you been stalking this guy?"

Joe suddenly looks embarrassed. Some people would make it sound like a party trick but he always seems genuinely surprised that he knows even half this stuff. And it's not like he plucks details out of the air. I could ask him to justify every statement and he'd rattle off the answers. He will have seen Campbell's asthma puffer, recognized his aftershave, watched him eat and seen the photographs of his children . . .

This is what frightens me about Joe. It's as if he can crack open someone's head and read the contents like tea leaves. You don't want to get too close to someone like that because one day they might hold up a mirror and let you see what the world sees.

Joe is thumbing through my medical notes, looking at the results of the CT and MRI scans. He closes the folder. "So what happened?"

"A rifle, a bullet, usual story."

"What's the first thing you do recall?"

"Waking up in here."

"And the last thing?"

I don't answer him. I've been wracking my brain for two days—ever since I woke up—and all I can come up with is pizza.

"How do you feel now?"

"Frustrated. Angry."

"Because you can't remember?"

"Nobody knows what I was doing on the river. It wasn't a police operation. I acted alone. I'm not a maverick. I don't go off half-cocked like some punk kid with 'Born to Lose' tattooed on my chest . . . They're treating me like a criminal."

"The doctors?"

"The police."

"You could be reacting to not being able to remember. You feel excluded. You think everyone knows the secret except you."

"You think I'm paranoid."

"It's a common symptom of amnesia. You think people are holding out on you."

Yeah, well that doesn't explain Keebal. He's visited me three times already, making false charges and outrageous claims. The more I refuse to talk, the harder he bullies.

Joe rolls his pen over his knuckles. "I once had a patient, thirty-five years old, with no history of neurological or psychiatric disorders. He slipped on an icy pavement and hit his head. He didn't lose consciousness or anything like that. He bounced straight up onto his feet and kept walking—"

"Is there a point to this story?"

"He didn't remember falling over. And he no longer knew where he was going. He had totally forgotten what happened in the previous twelve hours, yet he knew his name and recognized his wife and kids. It's called transient global amnesia. Minutes, hours or days disappear. Self-identification is still possible and sufferers behave normally otherwise but they can't remember a particular event or a missing period of time."

"But the memories come back, right?"

"Not always."

"What happened to your patient?"

"At first we thought he'd only forgotten the fall, but other memories had also gone missing. He didn't remember his earlier marriage, or a house he'd once built. And he had no knowledge of John Major ever being Prime Minister."

"It wasn't all bad then."

Joe smiles. "It's too early to say if your memory loss is permanent. Head trauma is only one possibility. Most recorded cases have been preceded by physical and emotional stress. Getting shot would qualify. Sexual intercourse and diving into cold water have also triggered attacks."

"I'll remember not to shag in the plunge pool."

My sarcasm falls flat. Joe carries on. "During traumatic events our brains radically alter the balance of our hormones and neurochemicals. This is like our survival mode—our fight-or-flight response. Sometimes when the threat ends, our brains stay in survival mode for a while—just in case. We have to convince your brain it can let go."

"How do we do that?"

"We talk. We investigate. We use diaries and photographs to prompt recollections."

"When did you last see me?" I ask him suddenly.

He thinks for a moment. "We had dinner about four months ago. Julianne wanted you to meet one of her friends."

"The publishing editor."

"That's the one. Why do you ask?"

"I've been asking everyone. I call them up and say, 'Hey, what's new? That's great. Listen, when did you last see me? Yeah, it's been too long. We should get together.' "

"And what have you discovered?"

"I'm lousy at keeping in touch with people."

"OK, but that's the right idea. We have to find the missing pieces."

"Can't you just hypnotize me?"

"No. And a blow on the head doesn't help either."

Reaching for his briefcase, his left arm trembles. He retrieves a folder and takes out a small square piece of cardboard, frayed at the edges.

"They found this in your pocket. It's water damaged."

He turns his hand. Spit dries on my lips.

It's a photograph of Mickey Carlyle. She's wearing her school uniform and grinning at the camera with her gappy smile like she's laughing at something we can't see.

Instead of confusion I feel an overwhelming sense of relief. I'm not going mad. This *does* have something to do with Mickey.

"You're not surprised."

"No."

"Why?"

"You're going to think I'm crazy, but I've been having these dreams."

Already I can see the psychologist in him turning my statements into symptoms.

"You remember the investigation and trial?"

"Yes."

"Howard Wavell went to prison for her murder."

"Yes."

"You don't think he killed her?"

"I don't think she's dead."

Now I get a reaction. He's not such a poker face after all.

"What about the evidence?"

I raise my hands. My bandaged hand could be a white flag. I know all the arguments. I helped put the case together. All of the evidence pointed to Howard, including the fibers, bloodstains and his lack of an alibi. The jury did its job and justice prevailed; justice polled on one day in the hearts of twelve people.

The law ruled a line through Mickey's name and put a full stop after Howard's. Logic agrees but my heart can't accept it. I simply cannot conceive of a world that Mickey isn't a part of.

Joe glances at the photograph again. "Do you remember putting this in your wallet?"

"No."

"Can you think why?"

I shake my head but in the back of my mind I wonder if perhaps I wanted to be able to recognize her. "What else was I carrying?"

Joe reads from a list. "A shoulder holster, a wallet, keys and a pocketknife . . . You used your belt as a tourniquet to slow the bleeding."

"I don't remember."

"Don't worry. We're going to go back. We're going to follow the clues you left behind—receipts, invoices, appointments, diaries. We'll retrace your steps."

"And I'll remember."

"Or learn to remember."

He turns toward the window and glances at the sky as though planning a picnic. "Do you fancy a day out?"

"I don't think I'm allowed."

He takes a letter from his jacket pocket. "Don't worry—I booked ahead."

Joe waits while I dress, struggling with the buttons on my shirt because of my bandaged hand.

"Do you want some help?"

"No." I say it too harshly. "I have to learn."

Keebal watches me as I cross the foyer, giving me a look like I'm dating his sister. I resist the urge to salute him.

Outside, I raise my face to the sunshine and take a deep breath. Planting the points of my crutches carefully, I move across the parking lot and see a familiar figure waiting in an unmarked police car. Detective Constable Alisha Kaur Barba (everyone calls her Ali) is studying a textbook for her sergeant's exam. Anybody who commits half that stuff to memory deserves to make Chief Constable.

Smiling at me nervously, she opens the car door. Indian women have such wonderful skin and dark wet eyes. She's wearing tailored trousers and a white blouse that highlights the small gold medallion around her neck.

Ali used to be the youngest member of the Serious Crime Group. We worked on the Mickey Carlyle case together, and she had the makings of a great detective until Campbell refused to promote her.

Nowadays she works with the DPG (Diplomatic Protection Group), looking after ambassadors and diplomats, and protecting witnesses. Perhaps that's why she's here now—to protect me.

As we drive out of the parking lot, she glances at me in the mirror, waiting for some sign of recognition.

"So tell me about yourself, Detective Constable."

A furrow forms just above her nose. "My name is Alisha Barba. I'm in the Diplomatic Protection Group."

"Have we met before?"

"Ah—well—yes, Sir, you used to be my boss."

"Fancy that! That's one of the three great things about having amnesia: apart from being able to hide my own Easter eggs, I get to meet new people every day."

After a long pause, Ali asks, "What's the third thing, Sir?"

"I get to hide my own Easter eggs."

She starts to laugh and I flick her on the ear. "Of course I remember you. Ali Baba, the catcher of thieves."

She grins at me sheepishly.

Beneath her short jacket I notice a shoulder holster. She's carrying a gun—an MP5 A2 carbine, with a solid stock. It's strange seeing her carrying a firearm because so few officers in the Met are authorized to have one.

Driving south past Victoria through Whitehall, we skirt parks and gardens that are dotted with office workers eating lunch on the grass—healthy girls with skirts full of autumn sunshine and fresh air and men dozing with their jackets under their heads. Turning along Victoria Embankment, I glimpse the Thames, sliding along the smooth stone banks.

Waxing and waning beneath lion-head gargoyles, it rolls beneath the bridges past the Tower of London and on toward Canary Wharf and Rotherhithe.

Ali parks the car in a small lane alongside Cannon Street Station. There are seventeen stone steps leading down to a narrow gravel beach slowly being exposed by the tide. On closer inspection the beach is not gravel but broken pottery, bricks, rubble and shards of glass worn smooth by the water.

"This is where they found you," Joe says, sliding his hand across the horizon until it rests on a yellow navigation buoy, streaked with rust.

"Marilyn Monroe."

"I beg your pardon?"

"It's nothing."

Above our heads the trains accelerate and brake as they leave and enter the station across a railway bridge.

"They say you lost about four pints of blood. The cold water slowed down your metabolism, which probably saved your life. You also had the presence of mind to use your belt as a tourniquet."

"What about the boat?"

"That wasn't found until later that morning, drifting east of Tower Bridge. Any of this coming back?"

I shake my head.

"There was a tide running that night. The water level was about six feet higher than it is now. And the tide was running at about five knots an hour. Given your blood loss and body temperature that puts the shooting about three miles upstream . . ."

Give or take about a thousand different variables, I think to myself, but I see where he's coming from. He is trying to work backward.

"You had blood on your trousers, along with a mixture of clay, sediment and traces of benzene and ammonia."

"Was the boat engine running?"

"It had run out of fuel."

"Did anyone report shots being fired on the river?"

"No."

I stare across the shit-brown water, slick with leaves and debris. This was once the busiest thoroughfare in the city, a source of wealth, cliques, clubs, boundary disputes, ancient jealousies, salvage battles and folklore.

Nowadays, three people can get shot within a few miles of Tower Bridge and nobody sees a thing.

A blue-and-white police launch pulls into view. The sergeant is wearing orange overalls and a baseball cap, along with a life vest that makes his chest look barrel shaped. He offers his hand as I negotiate the gangway. Ali has donned a sun hat as though we're off for a spot of fishing.

A tourist boat cruises past, sending us rocking in its wake. Camcorders and digital cameras record the moment as though we're part of London's rich tapestry. The sergeant pushes back on the throttle and we turn against the current and head upstream beneath Southwark Bridge.

The river runs faster on the inside of each bend, rushing along smooth stone walls, pulling at boats on their moorings, creating pressure waves against the pylons.

A young girl with long black hair rows under the bridge in a single scull. Her back is curved and her forearms slick with perspiration. I follow her wake and then raise my eyes to the buildings and the sky above them. High white clouds are like chalk marks against the blue.

The Millennium Wheel looks like something that should be floating in space instead of scooping up tourists. Nearby a class of schoolchildren sit on benches, the girls dressed in tartan skirts and blue stockings. Joggers ghost past them along Albert Embankment.

I can't remember if it was a clear night. You don't often see stars in London because of light and air pollution. At most they appear as half a dozen faint dots overhead or sometimes you can see Mars in the southeast. On a cloudy night some stretches of the river, particularly opposite the parks, are almost in total darkness. The gates are locked at sunset.

A century ago people made a living out of pulling bodies from the Thames. They knew every little race and eddy where a floater might bob up. The mooring chains and ropes, the stationary boats and barges that split the current into arrowheads.

When I first came down from Lancashire I was posted with the Thames Water Police. We used to pull two bodies a week out of the river, mostly suicides. You see the wannabes all the time, leaning from bridges, staring into the depths. That's the nature of the river—it can carry away all your hopes and ambitions or deliver them up unchanged.

The bullet that put a hole in my leg was traveling at high velocity:

a sniper's bullet fired from long range. There must have been enough light for the shooter to see me. Either that or he used an infrared sight. He could have been anywhere within a thousand yards but was probably only half that distance. At five hundred yards the angle of dispersion can be measured in single inches—enough to miss the heart or the head.

This was no ordinary contract killer. Few have this sort of skill. Most hit men kill at close range, lying in wait or pulling alongside cars at traffic lights, pumping bullets through the window. This one was different. He lay prone, completely still, cradling the stock against his chin, caressing the trigger . . . A sniper is like a computer firing system, able to calculate distance, wind speed, direction and air temperature. Someone had to train him—probably the military.

Scanning the broken skyline of factories, cranes and apartment blocks, I try to picture where the shooter was hiding. He must have been above me. It can't have been easy trying to hit targets on the water. The slightest breeze and movement of the boat would have caused him to miss. Each shot would have created a flash, giving away his position.

The tide is still going out and the river shrinks inward, exposing a slick of mud where seagulls fight for scraps in the slime and the remnants of ancient pylons stick from the shallows like rotting teeth.

The Professor looks decidedly uncomfortable. I don't think speed or boats agree with him. "Why were you on the river?"

"I don't know."

"Speculate."

"I was meeting someone or following someone . . ."

"With information about Mickey Carlyle?"

"Maybe."

Why would someone meet on a boat? It seems an odd choice. Then again, the river at night is relatively deserted once the dinner-party cruises have finished. It's a quick escape route.

"Why would someone shoot you?" asks Joe.

"Perhaps we had a falling out or . . ."

"Or what?"

"It was a mopping-up operation. We haven't found any bodies. Maybe we're not supposed to."

Christ, this is frustrating! I want to reach into my skull and press my fingers into the gray porridge until I feel the key that's hidden there.

"I want to see the boat."

"It's at Wapping, Sir," replies the sergeant.

"Make it so."

He spins the wheel casually and accelerates, creating a wave of spray as the outboard engine dips deep into the water and the bow lifts. Spray clings to Ali's eyelashes and she holds her flapping hat to her head.

Twenty minutes later, a mile downstream from Tower Bridge, we pull into the headquarters of the Marine Support Unit.

The motor cruiser *Charmaine* is in dry dock, propped upright on wooden beams and surrounded by scaffolding. At first glance the forty-foot inland cruiser looks immaculate, with a varnished wooden wheelhouse and brass fittings. A closer inspection reveals the shattered portholes and splintered decking. Blue-and-white police tape is threaded around the guardrails and small white evidence flags mark the various bullet holes and other points of interest.

Ali explains how the *Charmaine* had been reported stolen from Kew Pier in West London fourteen hours after I was found. She rattles off the engine size, range and top speed. She knows I appreciate facts.

A SOCO (scene of crime officer) in white overalls emerges from the wheelhouse and crouches near the stern. Running a tape measure across the deck, she makes a note of the measurement and adjusts a surveyor's theodolite mounted on a tripod beside her.

Turning, she shields her eyes from the sun behind us, recognizing the sergeant.

"This is DC Kay Simpson," he says, making the introductions.

Only in her thirties, she has short-cropped blond hair and inquisitive eyes. She keeps staring at me like I'm a ghost.

"So what exactly are you doing now?" I ask, self-consciously.

"Trajectories, impact velocity, yaw angle, the point of aim, distances, margin for error and blood patterns—" She stops in mid-sentence when she realizes that she has left us all behind. "I'm trying to work out how far away the shooter must have been, as well as his elevation and how often he missed his target."

"He hit me in the leg."

"Yes, but he could have been aiming at your head." She adds the word "Sir" as an afterthought, just in case I'm offended. "The shooter used Boat Tail Hollow Point ammunition with a velocity of 2,675 feet per second. They're not widely available commercially but nowadays you can source almost anything from Eastern Europe."

A thought occurs to her. "Would you mind helping me, Sir?"

"How?"

"Can you lie on the deck just here?" She points to her feet. "Half on your side, with your legs stretched out, one just crossing the other." Letting go of my crutches I let her move me into position like an artist's model.

As she leans over me I get a sudden image of another woman bending to brush her lips against mine. The air twitches and the picture is gone.

DC Simpson takes the tripod and angles it down toward my legs. A bright red beam of light reflects on my trousers above my bandaged thigh.

Pure fear rushes through me and suddenly I'm screaming at her to get down. Everyone! Get down! I remember the red light, a dancing red beam that signaled death. I lay in darkness, doubled over in pain as the beam moved back and forth across the deck, searching for me.

Nobody seems to have noticed me screaming. The sound is inside my head. They're all listening to the DC.

"The bullet came down from here, entered your thigh here, exited and lodged in the deck. It nudged against your femur and tumbled end-on-end, which is why the exit wound was so large."

She walks several paces away and uses a tape measure to check the distance between the side rail and another bullet hole. "For years people have debated whether momentum or kinetic energy is the best means of determining the striking power of a bullet. The answer is to merge the two parameters of bodies in motion. We have software programs that can tell us—based on measurements—the distance traveled by a particular bullet. In this case we're looking at 430 yards, with a two percent margin for error. Once we know the location of the shooting we can reconstruct the trajectory and find out where the shooter was hiding."

She looks down at me as though I should have an answer ready for her. I'm still trying to slow my heart rate.

"Are you OK, Sir?"

"I'm fine."

Joe is crouching next to me now. "Maybe you should take it easy."

"I'm not a fucking invalid!"

Instantly I want to take it back and apologize. Everyone is uncomfortable now.

DC Simpson helps me stand.

"How much more can you re-create of what happened?" I ask.

She seems quite pleased with the question.

"OK, this is where you were initially shot. Someone else got hit and fell on top of you. Traces of their bone and blood were found in your hair."

She sits down and drags herself backward until her back is braced against the side rail.

"One of the main clusters of bullets is this one." She points to the deck near her legs. "I believe you pulled yourself back here to get cover but more bullets went through the sides and hit the deck. You were too exposed, so—"

"I rolled across the deck and took cover behind the wheelhouse."

Joe looks at me. "You remember?"

"No, but it makes sense." Even as I answer I realize that part of it must be memory.

The DC scrambles across the deck to the far side of the wheelhouse. "This is where you lost your finger. You wanted to look inside or to see where the shooting was coming from. You were badly wounded. You hooked your fingers over the ledge around the porthole and raised yourself up. A bullet came through the glass and your finger disappeared."

Dried blood stains the wall, leaking around exit holes in the splintered wood.

"We found twenty-four bullet holes in the vessel. The sniper fired only eight of them. He was very controlled and precise."

"What about the others?"

"The rest were 9mm rounds."

My Glock 17 self-loading pistol was signed out of the station armory on September 22 and still hasn't been found. Maybe Campbell is right and I shot someone.

DC Simpson continues with her hypothesis. "I think you were dragged over the railing at the stern with the help of a boat hook which tore one of your belt loops. You vomited just here."

"So I must have been in the water first—before I was shot?"

"Yes."

I look at Joe and shake my head. I can't remember. Blood—that's all I can see. I can taste it in my mouth and feel it throbbing in my ears.

I look at the DC and my voice catches in my throat. "You said someone died, right? You must have tested the blood. Was it . . . I mean . . . did it belong to . . . could it have been . . . ?" I can't get the words out.

Joe finishes the question and answers it all at once.

"It wasn't Mickey Carlyle."

Back in the car, we edge through Tobacco Dock, past a gray square of water surrounded by warehouses. I can never tell if these new housing developments are gentrification or reclamation—most of them were derelict before the developers arrived. The dockside pubs have gone, replaced by fitness centers, cybercafés and juice bars selling shots of wheatgrass.

Farther from the river, squeezed between the Victorian terraces, we find a more traditional café and take a table by the window. The walls are decorated with posters of South and Central America, and the air smells of boiled milk and porridge.

Two gray plump women run the dining room—one taking orders and the other cooking.

Fried eggs stare up from my plate like large jaundiced eyes, along with a blackened sausage and a twisted mouth of bacon. Ali has a vegetarian sandwich and pours the tea from a stainless steel teapot. The brew is a dark shade of khaki, thick with floating leaves.

A local school has just broken for lunch and the street is full of Asian teenagers eating buckets of hot chips. Some of them smoke by the phone box while others swap headphones, listening to music.

Joe tries to stir his coffee with his left hand and stalls, switching to the right. His voice cuts through the sound of metal knives scraping on crockery. "Why did you think Mickey might have been on the boat?"

Ali's ears prick up. She's been asking herself the same question.

"I don't know. I was thinking about the photograph. Why would I carry it—unless I wanted to recognize her? It's been three years. She won't look the same."

Ali glances from me to the Professor and back to me again. "You think she's *alive?*"

"I didn't imagine all this." I motion to my leg. "You saw the boat. People died. I know it has something to do with Mickey."

I haven't touched my food. I don't feel hungry anymore. Perhaps the Professor is right—I'm trying to right the wrongs of the past and ease my own conscience.

"We should get back to the hospital," he says.

"No, not yet, I want to find Rachel Carlyle first. Maybe she knows something about Mickey."

Joe nods in agreement. It's a good plan.

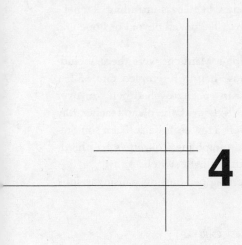

4

The autumn leaves swirl across Randolph Avenue, collecting against the steps of Dolphin Mansions. The place still looks the same, with a white-trimmed arch over the entrance and bronze letters sandblasted into the glass above the door.

Ali taps impatiently on the steering wheel with short manicured fingernails. The place unnerves her. We both remember a different time of year, the haste and noise and sullen heat, the shock and sadness. Joe doesn't understand but must sense something. Shuffling through leaves, we cross the road and climb the front steps. The bottom buzzer automatically opens the door between nine and four every day. Standing in the foyer, I glance up the central stairwell as though listening for a distant echo. Everything passes up and down these stairs—letters, furniture, food, newborn babies and missing children.

I can remember the names and faces of every resident. I can draw lines between them on a whiteboard showing relationships, contacts, employment history, movements and alibis for when Mickey disappeared. I remember it not like yesterday but like I remember the meal I just ordered and failed to eat, the fried eggs and lean bacon.

Take Rachel Carlyle, for instance. The last time I saw her was at the memorial service for Mickey a few months after the trial.

I arrived late and sat at the back, feeling like I was intruding. Rachel's soft, drugged sobs filled the chapel and she looked devoid of hope and tired of living.

Some of the neighbors from Dolphin Mansions were there, including Mrs. Swingler, the cat lady, whose hairdo resembled one of her tabbies curled on top of her head. Kirsten Fitzroy had her arm over Rachel's shoulders. Next to her was S. K. Dravid, the piano teacher. Ray Murphy, the caretaker, and his wife were a few seats back. Their son Stevie sat between them, twitching and mumbling. Tourette's had hardwired his movements to be quicker than a light switch.

I didn't stay for the whole service. I slipped outside, pausing to look at the plaque waiting to be blessed.

MICHAELA LOUISE CARLYLE

1995–2002

*We didn't have time to say goodbye, my Angel, but you're
only a thought away.*

There were no lessons to be learned, no logic or plot to be raked over, no moral comfort to be gained. According to the trial judge, her death had been pointless, violent and put into context.

I interviewed Howard Wavell a dozen times after that, hoping he might give up Mickey's burial place, but he said nothing. Periodically, we investigated new leads, excavating a garden in Pimlico and dredging the pond in Ravenscourt Park.

I haven't talked to Rachel since then but sometimes, secretly, I have found myself parked outside Dolphin Mansions, staring out the windshield, wondering how a child disappears in five stories and eleven flats.

The old-fashioned metal lift rattles and twangs between the landings as it rises to the top floor. I knock on the door of number 11 but there's no answer.

Ali peers through the leadlight panels and then lowers herself onto one knee and pushes open the hinged mail flap.

"She hasn't been home for a while. There are letters piled up on the floor."

"What else can you see?"

"The bedroom door is open. There is a dressing gown hanging on a hook."

"Is it light blue?"

"Yes."

I remember Rachel wearing the robe, sitting on the sofa, cradling the telephone.

Her forehead was pasty with perspiration and her eyes fogged. I had seen the signs before. She wanted a drink—she *needed* a drink—a steadier to get her through.

"Seven years old. That's a great age."

She didn't respond.

"Did you and Mickey get on well?"

She blinked at me in bafflement.

"I mean did you ever fight?"

"Sometimes. No more than normal."

"How often do you think normal families fight?"

"I don't know, Inspector. I only see normal families in TV sitcoms."

She looked at me steadily, not with defiance but with a sure knowledge that I was following the wrong line of questioning.

"Does Mickey hang out with anyone in particular in the building?"

"She knows everyone. Mr. Wavell downstairs, Kirsten across the hall, Mrs. Swingler, Mr. Murphy, Dravid on the ground floor. He teaches piano . . ."

"Is there any reason why Mickey might have wandered off?"

"No." One bra strap slid down her shoulder and she tugged it back. It slid down again.

"Could someone have wanted to take her?"

She shook her head.

"What about her father?"

"No."

"You're divorced?"

"Three years."

"Does he see Mickey?"

She squeezed a ball of soggy tissues in her fist and again shook her head.

My marbled notebook rested open on my knee. "I need a name."

She didn't reply.

I waited for the silence to wear her down but it didn't seem to affect her. She had no nervous habits like touching her hair or biting her bottom lip. She was totally enclosed.

"He would never hurt her," she pronounced suddenly. "And he's not silly enough to take her."

My pen was poised over the page.

"Aleksei Kuznet," she whispered.

I thought she was joking. I almost laughed.

Here was a name to conjure with; a name to tighten the throat and loosen the bowels; a name to speak softly in quiet corners with fingers crossed and knuckles rapping on wood.

"When did you last see your ex-husband?"

"On the day we divorced."

"And what makes you so sure he didn't take Mickey?"

She didn't miss a beat. "My husband has a reputation as a violent and dangerous man, Inspector, but he is not stupid. He will never touch Mickey or me. He knows I can destroy him."

"And how exactly can you do that?"

She didn't have to answer. I could see my reflection in her unblinking stare. She believed this. There was absolutely no doubt in her mind.

"There's something else you should know," she said. "Mickey has a panic disorder. She won't go outside by herself. Her psychologist says she is agoraphobic."

"But she's only a—"

"Child? Yes. People don't expect it, but it happens. Even the thought of going to school used to make her sick. Chest pains, palpitations, nausea, shortness of breath . . . Most days I had to walk her right to the classroom and pick her up from the same place."

The tears almost came again, but she found a place to put them. Women and tears—I'm no good with them. Some men can just wrap their arms around a woman and soak up the hurt, but that's not me. I wish it were different.

Rachel seemed too damaged to hold herself together but she wasn't going to break in front of me. She was going to show me how strong she could be. I didn't doubt it. Any woman who walked away from Aleksei Kuznet needed courage beyond words.

"Have you remembered something?" asks Joe, close to me now.

"No. I'm just daydreaming."

Ali looks over the banister. "Maybe one of the neighbors knows where Rachel is. What about the one with the cats?"

"Mrs. Swingler."

A lot of the neighbors have moved on since the tragedy. The Murphys were managing a pub in Dartford and Kirsten Fitzroy, Rachel's best friend, had moved to Notting Hill. Perhaps tragedy permeates a place like a smell you can't get rid of.

Taking the lift to the first floor, I knock on Mrs. Swingler's door. Resting on my crutches, I hear her coming down her hallway. Long strings of colored beads threaded into her hair gently clack as she moves. The door opens a crack.

"Hello, Mrs. Swingler, do you remember me?"

She peers at me aggressively. She thinks I'm a health inspector from the local council, come to take away her cats.

"I was here a few years ago—when Mickey Carlyle disappeared. I'm looking for Rachel Carlyle. Have you seen her?"

The smell coming from inside is a fetid stench, part feline and part human. She finds her voice. "No."

"When did you last see her?"

She shrugs. "Weeks back. She must have gone on holidays."

"Did she tell you that?"

"No."

"Have you seen her car parked outside?"

"What sort of car does she drive?"

I think hard. I don't know why I remember. "A Renault Estate."

Mrs. Swingler shakes her head, making the beads clack.

The hallway behind her is crammed with boxes and chests. I notice a small movement, then another, as though the shadows are shifting. Cats. Everywhere. Crawling out of boxes and drawers, from under the bed and on top of wardrobes. Dark shapes leak across the floor, gathering around her, rubbing against her pale legs and nipping her ankles.

"When did you last see me?"

She looks at me oddly. "Last month . . . you was in and out of here all the time."

"Was I with anyone?"

She glances at the Professor suspiciously. "Is your friend trying to be funny?"

"No. He has just forgotten a few things."

"You were seeing *her* upstairs, I suppose."

"Do you know why?"

Her laugh rasps like a violin. "Do I look like your social secretary?"

She's about to shut the door but thinks of something else. "I remember you now. You was always looking for that little girl got murdered. It's her fault, you know."

"Whose fault?"

"People like her shouldn't have kids if they can't control them. I don't mind my taxes going to sick kiddies in hospitals and to fix the roads but why should I pay for single mothers, sponging on welfare and spending their money on cigarettes and booze?"

"She didn't need handouts."

Mrs. Swingler hitches up her caftan. "Once an alkie, always an alkie."

I step toward her. "You think so?"

Suddenly she's less sure of her ground.

"I'll be sure to tell my mother. One day at a time, eh?"

The Professor pulls the cage door closed and the lift jerks into motion. When we reach the foyer, I turn back toward the stairs. I have searched this building dozens of times—in reality and in dreams—but I still want to search it again. I want to take it apart, brick by brick.

Rachel is missing. So are the people who left bloodstains on the boat. I don't know what any of it means but a twitch of the brain, a nervous shudder and something like instinct tells me to worry.

It's getting late. Streetlights are beginning to blink and taillights glow. We skirt along the side path and reach the rear garden—a narrow rectangle of grass surrounded by brick walls. A child's wading pool lies upturned in the shadows and outdoor furniture has been stacked outside a shed.

Beyond the rear fence is Paddington Recreation Ground where muddy puddles dot the turf. To the left is a lane with garages, while to the right, across half a dozen walls, is the Macmillan Estate, a drab, postwar council housing estate. There are ninety-six flats, with laundry hanging from the balconies and satellite dishes bolted to the walls.

This is the spot where Mickey and Sarah used to sunbathe. Above is the window Howard watched them from. On the day Mickey disappeared I came to the garden to find some shade and quiet. I knew then that she hadn't just wandered off. And a child doesn't accidentally go missing in a five-story mansion block. It felt like a kidnapping or something worse.

Missing children, you see, no good news can come of them. Dozens disappear every day, mostly runaways or throwaways. A seven-year-old is different because the only possibilities are the stuff of nightmares.

I crouch gingerly and stare into the pond where ornamental carp are lazily circling. I have never understood why people keep fish. They're indifferent, expensive, covered in scales and have such a fragile hold on their lives. My second wife, Jessie, was like that. We were married for six months and then I went out of fashion faster than male thongs.

As a kid I bred frogs. I used to collect the spawn from a pond on our farm and keep them in a forty-four-gallon drum cut down the middle. Baby frogs are cute but put a hundred of them in a bucket and you have a squirming, slippery mass. They finished up invading the house. My stepfather told me I was "fantastic" at raising tadpoles. I'm assuming he didn't mean "fantastic" in a good way.

Ali is standing next to me. She pushes hair behind her ears. "You thought she might already be dead on that first day."

"I know."

"We hadn't done background checks and SOCO hadn't arrived. There were no bloodstains or suspects, but you still had a bad feeling."

"Yes."

"And right from the outset you noticed Howard. What was it about him?"

"He was taking photographs. Everyone else in the building was searching for Mickey but he went back to get his camera. He said he wanted to have a record."

"A record?"

"Of all the excitement."

"Why?"

"So he could remember it."

5

By the time I get back to the hospital it's almost dark. The whole place has a sour smell like the dead air in closed-up rooms. I have missed a physiotherapy session and Maggie is waiting to change my bandages.

"Somebody took some pills from the pharmacy cart yesterday," she says, cutting the last of the bandages. "It was a bottle of morphine capsules. My friend is in trouble. They think it's her fault."

Maggie isn't accusing me but I know there's a subtext. "We're hoping the capsules might turn up. Maybe they were misplaced."

She withdraws, walking backward, the tray with bandages and scissors held before her.

"I hope your friend doesn't get into too much trouble," I say.

Maggie nods, turns and is gone without a sound.

Lying back, I listen to the carts and gurneys rattling to distant rooms and someone waking from a nightmare with a scream. Four times during the evening I try to phone Rachel Carlyle. She's still not home. Ali has promised to run her name and vehicle through the Police National Computer.

There's nobody in the corridor outside my room. Maybe the weasels from the ACG have grown tired of watching me.

At 9:00 p.m. I call my mother at Villawood Lodge. She takes a long while to answer the phone.

"Were you sleeping?" I ask.

"I was watching TV." I can hear it buzzing in the background. "Why haven't you come to see me?"

"I'm in the hospital."

"What's wrong with you?"

"I hurt my leg, but I'm going to be fine."

"Well if it's not serious you should come to see me."

"The doctors say I have to be here for another week or so."

"Do the twins know?"

"I didn't want to bother them."

"Claire sent me a postcard from New York. She went to Martha's Vineyard last weekend. And she said Michael might be doing a yacht transfer to Newport, Rhode Island. They can catch up with each other."

"That's nice."

"You should call them."

"Yes."

I ask her a few more questions, trying to make conversation, but she isn't concentrating on anything except the TV. Suddenly, she starts sniffling. It feels like her nose is right in my ear.

"Good night, Daj." That's what I call her.

"Wait!" She presses her mouth to the phone. "Yanko, come and see me."

"I will. Soon."

I wait until she hangs up. Then I hold the receiver and contemplate calling the twins—just to make sure they're OK. It's the same call I always imagine making but never do.

I imagine Claire saying, "Hi, Dad, how are you doing? Did you get that book I sent you? No, it's not a diet book; it's about lifestyle . . . cleansing your liver, purging toxins . . ." Then she invites me around for a vegetarian dinner that will purge more toxins and clear entire rooms.

I also imagine calling Michael. We'll get together for a beer, swapping jokes and talking football like a normal father and son. Only there is nothing normal about any of this. I'm imagining someone else's life. Neither of my children would waste a phone conversation, let alone an evening, on their father.

I love my children fit to bust—I just don't understand them. As babies they were fine, but then they turned into teenagers who drove too fast, played music too loud and treated me like some fascist conspirator because I worked for the Metropolitan Police. Loving children is easy. Keeping them is hard.

I fall asleep watching a vacation program on TV. The last thing I remember is seeing a woman with a permanent smile drop her sarong and dive into a pool.

Some time later the pain wakes me. There's a lethal swiftness in the air, like the vortex left behind by a passenger jet. Someone is in the room with me. Only his hands are in the light. Draped over the knuckles are polished-silver worry beads.

"How did you get in here?"

"Don't believe everything you read about hospital waiting lists."

Aleksei Kuznet leans forward. He has dark eyes and even darker hair combed in rigid lines back from his forehead and kept there with hair gel and willpower. His other most notable feature is a pink puckered circle of scar tissue on his cheek, wrinkled and milky white. The watch on his wrist is worth more than I earn in a year.

"Forgive me, I didn't ask after your welfare. Are you well?"

"Fine."

"That is very pleasing news. I am sure your mother will be relieved."

He's sending me a message.

Tiny beads of perspiration gather on my fingertips. "What are you doing here?"

"I have come to collect."

"Collect?"

"I seem to remember we had an arrangement." His accent is classic public-school English—perfect yet cold.

I look at him blankly. His voice hardens. "My daughter—you were to collect her."

I feel as though some snippet of the conversation has passed me by. "What do you mean? How could I collect Mickey?"

"Dear me, wrong answer."

"No, listen! I can't remember. I don't know what happened."

"Did you see my daughter?"

"I don't think so. I'm not sure."

47

"My ex-wife is hiding her. Don't believe anything else."

"Why would she do that?"

"Because she's a cruel heartless bitch, who enjoys turning the knife. It can feel like a jousting stick."

The statement is delivered with a ferocity that lowers the temperature.

Regaining his calm, he tugs at the cuffs of his jacket. "So I take it you didn't hand over the ransom."

"What ransom? Who wanted the ransom?"

My hands are shaking. The uncertainty and frustration of the past few days condenses down to this moment. Aleksei *knows* what happened.

Tripping over the words, I plead with him to tell me. "There was a shooting on the river. I can't remember what happened. I need you to help me understand."

Aleksei smiles. I have seen the same indolent, foreknowing expression before. The silence grows too long. He doesn't believe me. Bringing a hand to his forehead, he grips the front of his skull as though trying to crush it. He's wearing a thumb ring—gold and very thick.

"Do you always forget your failures, Inspector?"

"On the contrary, they're normally the only things I remember."

"Somebody must take responsibility for this."

"Yes, but first help me remember."

He laughs wryly and points at me with his hand. His right index finger is aimed at my head and his gold thumb ring is like the hammer of a gun. Then he smoothly turns his hand and frames my face within a backward "L".

"I want my daughter or I want my diamonds. I hope that's clear. My father told me never to trust Gypsies. Prove him wrong."

Even after Aleksei has gone I can feel his presence. He's like a character from a Quentin Tarantino film with an aura of violence held barely in check. Although he hides behind his tailored suits and polished English accent, I know where he comes from. I knew kids just like him at school. I can even picture him in his cheap white shirt, clunking shoes and oversize shorts, taking a beating at lunchtimes because of his strange name and his peasant-poor clothes and his strange accent.

I know this because I was just like him—an outsider—the son of a Romany Gypsy, who went to school with *ankrusté* (small balls of dough flavored with caraway and coriander) instead of sandwiches, wearing a painted badge on my blazer because we couldn't afford to buy a stitched one.

"Beauty cannot be eaten with a spoon," my mother would tell me. I didn't understand what she meant then. It was just another one of her queer sayings like, "One behind cannot sit on two horses."

I survived the beatings and the ridicule, just like Aleksei. Unlike him I didn't win a scholarship to Charterhouse, where he lost his Russian accent. None of his classmates were ever invited home and the food parcels his mother sent—with their chocolate dates, gingerbread and milk candy—were kept hidden. How do I know these things? I walked in his shoes.

Aleksei's father, Dimitri Kuznet, was a Russian émigré who started with a single flower barrow in Soho and cultivated a small empire of pitches around the West End. The turf war left three people dead and five unaccounted for.

On Valentine's Day in 1987 a flower seller in Covent Garden was nailed to his barrow, doused in kerosene and set alight. We arrested Dimitri the following day. Aleksei watched from his upstairs bedroom as we led his father away. His mother wailed and screamed, waking half the neighborhood.

Three weeks before the trial Aleksei left school and took over the family business alongside Sacha, his older brother. Within five years Kuznet Brothers controlled every flower barrow in central London. Within a decade it held sway over the entire cut-flower industry in Britain with more influence over prices and availability than Mother Nature herself.

I don't believe the urban myths or bogeyman stories about Aleksei Kuznet but he still frightens me. His brutality and violence are by-products of his upbringing; an ongoing act of defiance against the genetic hand that God dealt him.

We might have both started off the same, suffering the same taunts and humiliation, but I didn't let it lodge like a ball of phlegm in my throat and cut off oxygen to my brain.

Even his brother disappointed him. Perhaps Sacha was too Russian and not English enough. More likely Aleksei disapproved of his cocaine parties and glamour-model girlfriends. A teenage waitress was found floating facedown in the swimming pool after one such party, with semen in her stomach and traces of heroin in her blood.

Sacha didn't face a jury of twelve. Only four men were needed. Dressed in balaclavas they broke into his house one night, smothered his wife, and took Sacha away. Some say Aleksei had him strung up by his wrists and lowered into an acid bath. Others say he took off his head with a wood-splitting ax. For all anyone knows Sacha's still alive, living abroad under a different name.

For Aleksei there are only two proven categories of people in the world—not the rich and the poor or the good and the evil or the talkers and the doers. There are winners and losers. Heads or tails. His universal truth.

———

Under normal circumstances, better circumstances, I try not to dwell on the past. I don't want to envisage what might have happened to a child like Mickey Carlyle or to the other missing children in my life.

But ever since I woke up in the hospital I can't stop myself going back there, filling in the missing hours with horrible scenarios. I see the Thames littered with corpses that bob along beneath the bridges and tumble in the wake of passing tourist boats. I see blood in the water and guns sinking into the silt.

I look at my watch. It's 5:00 a.m. That's when predators do their hunting and police come knocking. Human beings are more vulnerable at that hour. They wake and wonder, pulling the covers close around them.

Aleksei mentioned a ransom. He and Keebal both knew about the diamonds. I must have been there—on the ransom drop. I wouldn't have gone ahead without proof of life. I must have been sure.

Against the quietness comes commotion—people running and shouting. I can hear a fire alarm.

Maggie appears in the door. "There's been a gas leak. We're evacuating the hospital. I'll get a wheelchair—I don't know how many are left."

"I can walk."

She nods approval. "We're taking the sickest patients first. Wait for me. I'll come back."

In the same breath she has gone. Police and fire sirens wail against the glass. The sound is soon masked by gurneys rattling down the corridors and people shouting instructions.

After twenty minutes the noise level abates and the minutes stretch out. Maybe they've forgotten me. I once got left behind on a school field trip to Morecambe Bay. Someone decided to dare me to walk the eight miles across the mudflats from Arnside to Kents Bank. People drown out there all the time, getting lost in the fog and trapped by the incoming tides.

Of course, I wasn't foolish enough to take up the dare. I spent the afternoon in a café eating scones and clotted cream, while the rest of the class studied waders and wildfowl. I convinced everyone that I'd made it. I was fourteen at the time and it almost got me expelled from Cottesloe Park but for the rest of my school days I was famous.

My aluminum crutches are beside the door. Swinging my legs out of bed, I hop sideways until my fingers close around the handles and my upper arms slip into the plastic cuffs.

Leaving the room, I look down a long straight corridor to a set of doors and through the glass panels I see another corridor reaching deeper into the building. There is a faint smell of gas.

Following the exit signs I start walking toward the stairs, glancing into empty rooms with messed-up bedclothes. I pass an abandoned cleaner's cart. Mops and brooms sprout from inside like seventies rock stars.

The stairs are in darkness. I look over the handrail, half expecting to see Maggie on her way up. Turning back I catch sight of something moving at the far end of the corridor, the way I've come. Maybe they're looking for me.

Retracing my steps, I push open closed doors with a raised crutch.

"Hello? Can you hear me?"

Behind green-tinted Perspex I find a surgery with a bloodstained paper sheet crumpled on the operating table.

The nursing station is deserted. Files are open on the counter. A mug of coffee is growing cold.

I hear a low moan coming from behind a partition. Maggie is lying motionless on the floor with one leg twisted under her. Blood covers her mouth and nose, dripping onto the floor beneath her head.

A muffled voice makes me turn. "Hey, man, what you still doing here?"

A fireman in a full face mask appears in the doorway. The breathing apparatus makes him look almost alien but he's holding a spray can in his hand.

"She's hurt. Quick. Do something."

He crouches next to Maggie, pressing his fingers against her neck. "What did you do to her?"

"Nothing. I found her like this."

I can just see his eyes behind the glass but he's looking at me warily. "You shouldn't be here."

"They left me behind."

Glancing above my head, he stands suddenly and pushes past me. "I'll get you a wheelchair."

"I can walk."

He doesn't seem to hear me. Less than a minute later he reappears through a set of swinging doors.

"What about Maggie?"

"I'll come back for her."

"But she's hurt—"

"She'll be fine."

Nursing the aluminum crutches across my lap, I lower myself into the chair. He sets off at a jog down the corridor, turning right and then left toward the main lifts.

His overalls are freshly laundered and his heavy rubber boots slap on the hard polished floor. For some reason I can't hear the flow of oxygen into his mask.

"I can't smell gas anymore," I say.

He doesn't respond.

We turn into the main corridor. There are three lifts at the far end. The middle one is propped open by a yellow maintenance sign. He picks up the pace and the wheelchair rattles and jumps over the linoleum.

"I didn't think it would be safe to use the lifts."

He doesn't answer or slow down.

"Maybe we should take the stairs," I repeat.

He accelerates, pushing me at a sprinter's pace toward the open doors. The blackness of the shaft yawns like an open throat.

At the last possible moment I raise the aluminum crutches. They brace across the doors and I slam into them. Air is forced out of my lungs and I feel my ribs bend. Bouncing backward, I twist sideways and roll away from the chair.

The fireman is doubled over where the handle of the wheelchair has punched into his groin. I scramble up and pull his arm through the wheel of the chair. Spinning it a half turn, I jam his wrist against the frame. Another quarter turn will snap it like a pencil.

He is flailing now, trying to reach me with his other fist. I keep twisting away from him, with the chair between us.

"Who are you? Why are you doing this?"

Cursing and struggling, his mask is nearly off. Suddenly, he changes his point of attack and sinks his fist into my damaged leg, grinding his knuckles into the bandaged flesh. The pain is unbelievable and white spots dance in front of my eyes. I spin the wheelchair sideways, trying to escape. At that same moment I hear the crack of his wrist breaking. He groans.

Both of us are on the floor. He launches a kick at my chest, sending me backward. My head slams against the wall. Up on his knees, he grips me by the back of my shirt with his good hand and tries to drag me toward the lift shaft. I kick at the floor with my one good leg and wrap my fingers around the harness on his jacket. I'm not letting go.

Exhaustion is slowing us down. He wants to kill me. I want to survive. He has strength and stamina. I have fear and bloody-mindedness.

"Listen, Tarzan, this isn't working," I say, sucking in air between each word. "The only way I'm going down that hole is if you go with me."

"Go to hell! You broke my fucking wrist!"

"And someone shot me in the leg. You see me crying?"

Somewhere below us an engine grinds into motion. The lifts are moving. He glances up at the numbers above the door. Scrambling to his feet, he stumbles down the corridor, carrying his busted wrist as though it's already in a sling. He is going to escape down the stairs. There is nothing I can do.

Reaching for my shirt pocket I feel for the small yellow tablet. My fingers are too large for such a delicate task. I have it now, squeezed between my thumb and forefinger . . . now it's on my tongue.

The adrenaline leaks away and my eyelids flutter like moth wings on wet glass. Someone wants me dead. Isn't that strange?

I listen to the lifts rise and the murmur of voices. Pointing down the corridor, I mumble, "Help Maggie."

6

There are police patrolling the corridors, interviewing staff and taking photographs. I can hear Campbell berating some poor doctor about hampering a police investigation. He makes it sound like a hanging offense.

The morphine is wearing off and I'm shaking. Why would someone want to kill me? Maybe I witnessed a murder on the river. Maybe I shot someone. I don't remember.

Campbell opens the door and I get a sense of déjà vu—not about the place but the conversation that's coming. He takes a seat and gives me one of his ultra-mild smiles. Before he can speak I ask about Maggie.

"She's in a room downstairs. Someone gave her a broken nose and two black eyes. Was it you?"

"No."

He nods. "Yeah, that's what she said. You want to tell me what happened?"

I go through the whole story—telling him about "Fireman Sam" and the wheelchair sprint down the corridor. He seems happy enough with the details.

"What did the cameras pick up?"

"Sod all. He blacked out the lenses with spray paint. We got one image from the nursing station but no face behind the mask. You didn't recognize him?"

"No."

He looks disgusted.

"I'm convinced this has something to do with Mickey Carlyle," I tell him. "Someone sent a ransom demand. I think that's why I was on the river—"

"Mickey Carlyle is dead."

"But what if we got it wrong?"

"Bullshit! We got it right."

"There must have been proof of life."

Campbell knows about this. He's known all along.

"IT'S A HOAX!" he rasps. "Nobody believed any of it except you and Mrs. Carlyle. A grieving mother I can understand—but you!" His fingers curl and uncurl. "You were the officer in charge of a successful murder prosecution yet you chose to believe a hoax that cast doubt on the outcome. First you ordered a DNA test and then you went off half-cocked like some maverick Hollywood vigilante and got yourself shot."

Campbell is close now. I can see the dandruff in his eyebrows. "Howard Wavell murdered Mickey Carlyle. And if that sick, perverted, murdering son of a bitch walks free because of you, there won't be a police officer in the Met who will ever work with you again. You're finished."

A deep continuous vibration has built up inside me, like the sound of a ship's engine deep within a hull.

"We *have* to investigate. People died on that boat."

"Yeah! For all I know, you shot them!"

My resolve is disintegrating. I don't know enough details to argue with him. Whatever happened on the river was my fault. I stirred up something poisonous and nobody wants to help me.

Campbell is still talking. "I don't know what you did, Vincent, but you made some serious enemies. Stay away from Rachel Carlyle. Stay away from this. If you jeopardize Wavell's conviction—if I hear so much as a mouse fart from you—your career is finished. That's a cast-iron fucking guarantee."

He's gone then, storming down the corridor. How long was I unconscious, eight days or eight years? Long enough for the world to change.

• • •

The Professor arrives, his cheeks red from the cold. He hovers in the doorway as though waiting for an invitation. Behind him I see Ali sitting on a chair. She is now officially my shadow.

There are metal detectors being installed in the lobby and my medical personnel are being screened. Maggie isn't among them. I am responsible.

Although I've been over it a dozen times with detectives, I don't mind talking to Joe about the attack because he asks different questions. He wants to know what I heard and smelled. Was the guy breathing heavily? Did he sound scared?

I take him on a guided tour, showing him where the fight took place. Ali stays two paces away from me, scanning the corridors and rooms.

Leaning on my crutches, I watch Joe do his mad professor routine, pacing out distances, crouching on the floor and studying angles.

"Tell me about the gas leak."

"One of the delivery drivers noticed the smell first but they couldn't find the source. Someone opened up a valve on one of the feeder pipes from the gas tanks near the loading docks."

Joe kicks at the ground as though trying to make it even. I can almost see his mind moving forward and backward as he tries to reconstruct what happened.

Out loud now, he says, "He knew his way around the hospital but he didn't know which room you were in. Once he evacuated the floors there was nobody to ask."

Joe turns and strides down the corridor. I struggle to keep up without overbalancing. He stops beneath a CCTV camera and reaches toward it as if holding a spray can. "He must have been about six two."

"Yeah."

He continues to the nursing station, eyes darting over the long narrow counter and kitchenette. There are clipboards hanging on a wall. Each one corresponds to a patient.

"Where did you find Maggie?"

"On the floor."

Joe drops to his knees and then lies down, with his head toward the sink.

"No, she was lying this way, with her head almost under the desk."

Jumping to his feet, he stands facing the clipboards and half closes his eyes. "He was looking at the clipboards to find your room number."

"How do you know?"

Joe crouches and I follow his outstretched finger. There are two black smudges on the baseboard made by the heels of the fireman's boots. "Maggie came up the corridor. She was coming back to get you. He heard her coming and he stepped back to hide . . ."

I can picture Maggie bustling up the corridor, admonishing herself for being late.

"As she passed the doorway, she turned her head. He struck her with his elbow across the bridge of her nose." Joe tumbles to the floor and lies where she fell. "Then he went to your room but you had already gone."

All this sounds reasonable.

"There is something I don't understand. He could have killed me right away, here in the corridor, but he collected a wheelchair and tried to push me down the lift shaft."

Still lying on the floor, Joe points past my shoulder at the CCTV camera. "It's the only one he didn't black out."

"It didn't matter, he wore a mask."

"Psychologically it made a big difference. Even with his face hidden, he didn't want to star in a home movie. The footage was evidence against him."

"So he took me out of view."

"Yes."

Joe is thinking out loud now, unaware of his twitches and trembles. I follow him down the corridor to the stairs. He pauses, puzzled by something.

"The gas leak was part of both plans," he announces.

"Both plans?"

"One for outside and one for inside . . ."

I don't understand. Joe motions for me to follow him and waits for me to climb two flights of stairs. We reach a heavy fire door and emerge onto a barren rectangle of bitumen, the rooftop of the hospital. A gust of wind slaps me in the face and Joe grabs my shirtfront to steady me. A big-bellied gray sky hangs overhead.

Circular ducts and metal air-conditioning plants punctuate the bitumen. A low brick wall with white capping stones marks the outside edge of the building. A wire security fence is attached, curling inward before being topped with barbed wire.

Joe slowly walks the perimeter, occasionally glancing at surrounding buildings as though adjusting his internal compass. When he reaches the northeast corner of the building, he leans close to the fence. "You see that park down there—the one with the fountain?" I follow his gaze. "That's the evacuation meeting point. Everyone was supposed to meet there when they emptied the hospital. You were supposed to be with them. There is no way they could have known you were going to be left inside."

We are both on the same page now. "Perhaps he was supposed to hide in my room and kill me when I came back."

"Or they were going to kill you outside."

Joe drops onto his haunches, studying the thin layer of soot on the capping stones. It's the same black film that settles on everything in London until the next shower. Three penny-size circles smudge the surface. Joe swings his eyes to the ground where two larger smudges appear beneath the wall.

Someone knelt here and rested a tripod on the wall—a lone sniper with a finger on the trigger and his eyelashes brushing the lens, studying the park below. The hair on my forearms is standing on end.

Fifteen minutes later the rooftop has been sealed off and a SOCO team is at work, searching for clues. Campbell is smarting about being shown up by a clinical psychologist.

Joe takes me downstairs to the canteen—one of those sterile food halls with tiles on the floor and stainless steel counters. Cedric, the guy in charge, is a Jamaican with impossibly tight curls and a laugh that sounds like someone cracking nuts with a brick.

He brings us coffee and pulls a half bottle of Scotch from the pocket of his apron. He pours me a slug. Joe doesn't seem to notice. He's too busy trying to fill in the missing pieces.

"Snipers have very little emotional investment in their victims. It's like playing a computer game."

"So he could be young?"

"And isolated."

True to form, the Professor is more interested in why than who; he wants an explanation while I want a face for my empty picture frame, someone to catch and punish.

"Aleksei Kuznet visited me last night. I think I know why I was in the river. I was following a ransom."

Joe doesn't bat an eyelid.

"He wouldn't tell me the details, but there must have been proof of life. I must have believed Mickey was still alive."

"Or wished it."

I know what he's saying. He doesn't think I'm being rational.

"OK, let's ask ourselves some questions," he says. "If Mickey is alive, where has she been for the past three years?"

"I don't know."

"And why would anyone wait three years to post a ransom demand?"

"Maybe they didn't kidnap her for ransom, not at first."

"OK. If not for ransom, why?"

I'm struggling now. I don't know. "Maybe they wanted to punish Aleksei."

It doesn't sound convincing.

"It sounds like a hoax to me. Someone close to the family or to the original investigation knew enough to convince desperate people that Mickey might still be alive."

"And the shootings?"

"They had a falling out or someone got greedy."

It sounds so much more rational than my theory.

Joe takes out his notebook and starts drawing lines on the page as if playing hangman.

"You grew up in Lancashire, didn't you?"

"What's that got to do with anything?"

"I'm just asking a question. Your stepfather was an RAF pilot in the war."

"How do you know that?"

"I remember you telling me."

"Bullshit!"

A ball of anger forms in my throat. "You're just itching to get inside my head, aren't you? The Human Condition—isn't that what you call it? You got to watch out for that bastard."

"Why do you keep dreaming about missing children?"

"Fuck you!"

"Maybe you feel guilty."

I don't answer.

"Maybe you blocked it out."

"I don't block things out."

"Did you ever meet your real father?"

"You're going to have trouble asking questions with your jaw wired shut."

"A lot of people don't know their fathers. You must wonder what he's like; whether you look like him or sound like him."

"You're wrong. I don't care."

"If you don't care, why won't you talk about it? You were probably a war baby—born just afterward. A lot of fathers didn't come home. Others were stationed overseas. Children get lost . . ."

I hate that word "lost." My father didn't go missing. He isn't lying in some small part of France that will forever be England. I don't even know his name.

Joe is still waiting. He's sitting there, twirling his pen, waiting for Godot. I don't want to be psychoanalyzed or have my past explored. I don't want to talk about my childhood.

I was fourteen years old the first time my mother sat down and told me about where I came from. She was drunk, of course, curled up on the end of my bed, wanting me to massage her feet. She told me the story of Germile Purrum, a Gypsy girl, with a "Z" tattooed on her left arm and a black triangle sewn into her rags.

"We looked like bowling balls with sticky-out ears and frightened eyes," she said, nursing a drink between her breasts.

The prettiest and the strongest Gypsy girls were sent to the homes of the officers in the SS. The next group were used in camp brothels, gang-raped to break them in and often sterilized because the Roma were considered unclean.

My mother was fifteen when she arrived at Ravensbrück, the largest concentration camp for women in the Reich. She was put to work in the camp brothel, working twelve hours a day.

She didn't go into details but I know she remembered every one of them.

"I think I'm pregnant," she slurred.

"That's not possible, Daj."

"I haven't had my monthly days."

"Have you been to see the doctor?"

She looked at me crossly. "Esther tried to make me bleed."

"Who is Esther?"

"A Jewish angel . . . but you clung to my insides. You didn't want to leave. You wanted so much to live."

Daj was talking about *me*. I knew this part of the story.

She was three months pregnant when the war ended. She spent another two months looking for her family, but they were all gone—her twin brothers, her mother, her father, aunts, uncles, cousins . . .

At a displaced persons camp near Frankfurt, a young British immigration officer called Vincent Smith told her she should emigrate. The United States and England were taking refugees if they had identity papers and skills. Germile had neither.

Because nobody would take a Gypsy she lied on the application form and said she was Jewish. So many had perished it was easy to get identity papers in someone else's name. Germile Purrum became Sofia Eisner, aged nineteen instead of sixteen, a seamstress from Frankfurt—a new person for a new life.

I was born in a rain-swept English town in a county hospital that still had blackout curtains on the windows. She didn't let me die. She didn't say, "Who needs another white-haired German bastard with cold blue eyes?" And even when I rejected her milk, puking it down her open blouse (another sign, perhaps, that I was more of him than her), she forgave me.

I don't know what she saw when she looked in my eyes: the enemy, perhaps, or the soldiers who raped her. I looked as though I owned the world, she said. As though everything in creation would be recast or rearranged to suit me.

I don't know who I am now. I am either a miracle of survival or an abomination. I'm part German, part Gypsy, part English, one-third evil, one-third victim and the other third angry. My mother used to say I was a gentleman. No other language has such a word to describe a man. It's a paradox. You can't claim to be such a thing but you hope others see you that way.

I look up at Joe and blink away the past. I've been talking all this time.

His voice is softer than mine. "You're not responsible for your father's sins."

Yeah, right! I'm angry now. Why did he start me out on this? I don't want any of his airy-fairy, touchy-feely, Pollyanna-pass-the-tissues psychological crap.

We sit in silence. I'm through with talking. My nightmares march in jackboots and are best left alone.

Joe stands suddenly and begins to pack his briefcase. I don't want him to go now.

"Aren't we going to talk about the ransom?"

"You're tired. I'll come and see you tomorrow."

"But I remembered some of the details."

"That's good."

"Isn't there something you can tell me; something I should be doing?"

He looks at me quizzically. "You want some advice?"

"Yes."

"Never go to a doctor whose office plants have died."

Then he's gone.

7

When Mickey disappeared I didn't sleep for the first forty-eight hours. If a missing child isn't found within the first two days the chances of her being found alive diminishes by forty percent. Within two weeks it is down to less than ten percent.

I hate statistics. I read somewhere that the average person uses 5.9 sheets of toilet tissue when they wipe their arse. It proves nothing and helps no one.

Here are some more figures. There were six hundred volunteers scouring the streets and eighty officers going door to door. The sense of urgency bordered on violence. I wanted to kick open doors, shake trees and chase every child from the parks and pavements.

We checked alibis, stopped motorists, interviewed tradesmen and tracked down visitors to Dolphin Mansions in the previous month. Every resident was interviewed. I knew which of them beat his spouse, slept with prostitutes, lied about sickies, owed money to bookies and cultivated marijuana in a box under her bed.

There had been sixty-five unconfirmed sightings of Mickey and four confessions (including someone claiming to have sacrificed her to the pagan god of the forest). We had also been offered the services of twelve psychics, two palm readers and a guy calling himself the Wizard of Little Milton.

The closest we came to a confirmed sighting was by an elderly couple at Leicester Square tube station on Wednesday evening. Mrs. Esmerelda Bird wasn't wearing her glasses and her husband, Brian, didn't get close enough to see the girl clearly. There were twelve CCTV cameras at the station but the angles were wrong and the footage such poor quality it resolved nothing and risked derailing the entire investigation if we made it public.

Already the search had become a media event. TV vans blocked Randolph Avenue, beaming pictures to boxes within boxes, so that people who had never met Mickey could look up from their breakfast cereal and fleetingly adopt her.

Purple ribbons were tied to the railings outside Dolphin Mansions. Some were threaded with flowers and photographs of Mickey. There were pictures of her displayed on building sites, lampposts and shop windows.

The sex offenders' register threw up 359 names for Greater London. Two dozen of them either lived in or had some link to the area. Every name was cross-checked, every detail compared and contrasted, looking for those ley lines of human connection that thread the world together.

Unfortunately, this took time and the tyranny of the clock was absolute. It ticked away with a mechanical heart. A minute doesn't become any longer just because a child is missing. It only feels that way.

After two days I went home for just long enough to shower and change my clothes. I found Daj snoring at the kitchen table with her head between her arms and a Siamese cat curled up on her lap. A glass of vodka was wedged between her fingers. Her first drink every day was always a revelation, she said, the juice of angels copulating in flight. Gin was too English and whiskey too Scottish. Port made her teeth and gums go crimson. And when she vomited it looked like black currants shat out by sparrows.

Daj had become more like a Gypsy as she grew older (and drunker), reverting to type; wrapping herself in layers of the past like the layers of her petticoats. She drank to forget and to deaden the pain. She drank because her demons were thirsty.

I had to prise her fingers from the glass before I carried her to bed. The Siamese slid off her lap and settled like liquid filling a puddle. As I pulled the bedclothes over her, she opened her eyes.

"You'll find her won't you, Yanko?" she slurred. "You'll find that little girl. I know what it's like to lose someone."

"I'll do the best I can."

"I can see *all* the lost children."

"I can't bring them back, Daj."

"Close your eyes and you'll see her."

"Shush now. Go to sleep."

"They never die," she whispered, accepting my kiss on her cheek. A month later she went into the retirement home. She has never forgiven me for abandoning her, but that's the least of my sins.

The hospital room is dark. The corridors are dark. The world outside is dark except for the streetlights, shining on parked cars that are covered in icy white fur.

Ali is asleep in a chair beside my bed. Her face is ashen with weariness and her body held stiffly. The only light is from the TV flickering in the corner.

Her eyes open.

"You should have gone home."

She shrugs. "They have cable here."

I glance at the TV. They're showing an old black-and-white film—*Kind Hearts and Coronets* with Alec Guinness. The overacting is more obvious with the sound turned down.

"I'm not obsessed, you know."

"What do you mean, Sir?"

"I'm not trying to bring Mickey Carlyle back from the dead."

Ali brushes hair from her eyes. "Why do you think she's alive?"

"I can't explain."

She nods.

"You were sure about Howard once."

"Never completely." I wish I could explain but I know I'll sound paranoid. Sometimes I think there is only one person in the world who I know didn't kidnap Mickey—and that's me. We conducted more than 8,000 interviews and took 1,200 statements. It was one of the largest, most expensive abduction investigations in British policing history but still we couldn't find her.

Even now, periodically, I come across posters of Mickey stuck on lampposts and building sites. Nobody else seems to note her features or stare at her wistfully but I can't help it. Sometimes, in the dark hours, I even have conversations with her, which is strange because I never really talked to Claire, my own daughter, when she was Mickey's age. I had more in common with my son because we could talk about sports. What did I know about ballet and Barbie dolls?

I know more about Mickey than I did about Claire. I know she liked glitter nail polish, strawberry-flavored lip gloss and MTV. She had a treasure box with polished pebbles, painted clay beads and a hair clip that she told everyone was decorated with diamonds instead of chips of glass.

She loved to sing and dance and her favorite driving song was "Row, row, row your boat gently down the stream and if you see a crocodile don't forget to scream." I used to sing the same song to Claire at bedtime and chase her giggling around the room until she dived under the covers.

Maybe this is guilt I'm feeling. It's something I know a lot about. I have lived with it, been married to it and watched it float beneath an ice-covered pond. Guilt I'm an expert at. There are other missing children in my life.

"Are you OK?" asks Ali, reaching over to rest her hand on the bed next to me.

"Just thinking."

She puts an extra pillow behind my back and then turns away, bending over the sink and splashing water on her face. My eyes are now graded to the darkness.

"Are you happy?"

She casts her face back to me, surprised by the question.

"What do you mean?"

"Do you like working for the DPG? Is it what you wanted to do?"

"I wanted to be a detective. Now I chauffeur people around."

"But you're going to sit your sergeant's exam."

"They'll never put me in charge of an investigation."

"Did you always want to be a police officer?"

She shakes her head. "I wanted to be an athlete. I was going to be the first British-born Sikh sprinter to compete at the Olympics."

"What happened?"

"I couldn't run fast enough." She laughs and stretches her arms above her head until her joints crack. Then she looks at me sideways along her cheek. "You're going to keep investigating this, aren't you, despite what the Chief Super says?"

"Yes."

A streak of lightning breaks through the gloom outside the window. The flash is too far away for me to hear the thunder.

Ali clicks her tongue against the roof of her mouth. She's trying to make a decision. "I'm owed a few weeks long-service leave. Maybe I could help, Sir."

"No. Don't jeopardize your career."

"What career?"

"Seriously, you don't owe me any favors."

She glances at the TV. The gray square of light reflects in her eyes.

"You probably think this sounds pretty wet, Sir, but I've always looked up to you. It's not easy being a woman in the Met but you never treated me any differently. You gave me a chance."

"They should have promoted you."

"That's not your fault. When you get out of here, maybe you should come and stay with me . . . in the spare room. I can keep you safe. I know you're going to say no, Sir, because you think you don't need my help or you're worried about getting me in trouble, but don't just dismiss the idea. I think it's a good one."

"Thank you," I whisper.

"What did you say?"

"I said thank you."

"Oh! Right. Jolly good."

Ali wipes her hands on her jeans and looks relieved. Another streak of lightning paints the room white, taking a snapshot of the moment.

I tell her to go home and rest because in a few hours I'm leaving the hospital. Despite Keebal's efforts, I'm not under arrest. The police are here to protect me, not to hold me. I don't care what the doctors say or what Campbell Smith might do. I want to go home, collect my diary and find Rachel Carlyle.

From now on, I'm not going to rely on my memory coming back. It might never happen. Facts, not memories, solve cases. Facts, not memories, will tell me what happened to Mickey Carlyle. They say a bad cop can't sleep because his conscience won't let him and a good cop can't sleep because there's still a piece of the puzzle missing.

I don't think I'm a bad cop. Maybe I'll find that out, too.

8

Dr. Bennett is walking backward down the corridor in his Cuban-heeled cowboy boots.

"You're not supposed to leave. This is madness. Think about your leg."

"I feel fine."

He puts his hand over the button for the lift. "You're under police protection, you can't leave."

I pretend to stumble and he reaches out to catch me. At the same moment I stab the walking stick against the down arrow. "Sorry, Doc, but I've arranged my own protection." I motion to Ali, who's carrying my belongings in a plastic bag. That's all I want to take out of here.

For the first time since the shooting I feel like my old self. I'm a detective not a victim. Members of the staff begin appearing in the corridor. Word is spreading. They've come to say goodbye. I shake hands and mumble "Thank you" while I wait for the lift to arrive.

The doors open and Maggie emerges. She looks like a jovial panda with black eyes and a bandaged nose. I don't know what to say to her.

"Were you going to leave without saying goodbye?"

"No."

Ali produces a bunch of flowers and Maggie beams, throwing her arms around me, crushing the blooms against my chest. I've been a pain in the arse and managed to put her in a hospital bed but she still wants to hug me. I'll never understand women.

Downstairs, rocking on a walking stick, I cross the foyer. My leg is getting stronger and if I concentrate really hard I look like someone with a pebble in his shoe rather than a bullet wound. More nurses and doctors wish me good luck. I'm a celebrity—the detective who survived an assassination attempt. I want my fifteen minutes of fame to be over.

The place is crawling with police officers, guarding the entrances and rooftops. They're wearing black body armor and carrying automatic weapons. None of them knows what to do. They're supposed to be guarding me but now I'm leaving.

Ali leads the way, taking me through an exit door and down concrete stairs to the parking garage. As I cross toward her car, I notice John Keebal leaning against a pillar. He doesn't approach. Instead he cracks a peanut and drops the shells into a neat pile at his feet.

Briefly leaving Ali, I walk over to him.

"Are you visiting a sick granny or waiting for me?"

"Thought I'd give you a ride home but I guess you're covered," he replies, giving Ali the once-over. "Bit young for you, isn't she?"

"That'd be none of your business."

We look at each other for a few moments and Keebal grins. I'm getting too old for these swinging-dick contests.

"What exactly do you want?"

"I thought you might invite me back to your place."

"Couldn't you get a warrant?"

"Seems not."

What a nerve! He can't convince a judge to let him search my house and then expects me to say yes anyway. It's all part of building a case. If I say no Keebal will say I'm being uncooperative. Fuck him!

"Listen, under normal circumstances, you know I'd happily let you come over. If I'd known I'd have cleaned up the place and bought a cake but I haven't been home in a few weeks. Maybe some other time."

I pivot on the walking stick and rejoin Ali.

She raises an eyebrow. "I didn't know he was a friend of yours."

"You know how it is—everyone is worried about me."

I slip into the backseat of a black Audi. Ali takes the wheel and the car swings through bends and beneath a boom gate before emerging into the sunshine. She doesn't say a word on the drive. Instead her eyes flick between her mirrors and the road ahead. She purposely drops her speed and accelerates, weaving between traffic, checking to see if we're being followed.

Ali rummages on the seat next to her and tosses me a bulletproof vest. We argue over whether I'm going to wear it or not. I can see her losing patience with me.

"Sir, with all due respect, you either wear this vest or I will put a bullet in your other leg and drive you back to the hospital."

Looking at her eyes in the mirror, I don't doubt her for a second. There are too many women in my life and none of the fringe benefits.

We drive south through Kensington and Earls Court, past the tourist hotels and fast-food joints. The playgrounds are dotted with mothers and toddlers playing on brightly colored swings and slides.

Rainville Road runs alongside the Thames, opposite the Barn Elms Wildfowl Reserve. I like living by the river. Of a morning I can look out of my bedroom window at the expanse of sky and pretend I don't live in a city of seven million.

Ali parks at the front of the house, scanning the riverside pavement and the houses on the opposite side of the street. Out of the car, she moves quickly up the stairs, using my key to unlock the front door. Having searched the rooms, she comes back to me.

With her arm around my waist, I hobble inside. A mound of unopened letters, bills and junk mail has collected on the front mat. Ali scoops it all up in her arms. I haven't time to sort them out now. We have to leave quickly. Dumping the letters in a shopping bag, I walk through the house, trying to resurrect my memories.

I know this place by heart but there is nothing reassuring in the familiar. The dimensions seem the same, the colors and the furniture. The kitchen benches are clear except for three coffee mugs in the sink. I must have had company.

The kitchen table is littered with scraps of orange plastic, masking tape and squares of polystyrene foam cut with a serrated knife. I must have been wrapping something. Foam dust looks like fake snow on the floor.

My diary is beside the telephone—open on September 25, a Sunday. I was shot in the early hours of Monday morning. Tucked into the spine is an invoice for a classified advertisement in *The Sunday Times*. The text is in my handwriting:

> *Tuscan Villa Wanted: to sleep 6. Pool preferable. Patio. Garden. Short drive from Florence. Sept/Oct. Two-month booking.*

I paid for the advertisement by credit card four days before the shooting. Why would I want to rent a Tuscan villa?

I don't recognize the cell-phone number printed at the bottom. Picking up the receiver, I punch the numbers. A metallic voice tells me the number is unavailable. I can leave a message. It beeps. I don't know what to say and I don't want to leave my name. It might not be safe.

I hang up and flick backward through the diary, skimming over final reminders for unpaid bills and dental appointments. There must be other clues. One name stands out—Rachel Carlyle. I met her six times in the ten days prior to the shooting. Hope rises in me like a wave.

Going farther back through the pages, I look at the previous month. On the second Thursday in August I wrote a name: Sarah Jordan—the girl who waited on the front steps for Mickey to arrive. I don't remember meeting Sarah. How old would she be now—twelve, maybe thirteen?

Ali is upstairs trying to pack some clothes for me. "Do you have any spare sheets?" she calls.

"Yeah. I'll get them."

The linen cupboard is in the hallway near the laundry. I lean my walking stick against the door and reach up with both hands.

A sports bag is jammed at the back of the shelf. I pull it out and drop it to the floor until I find the sheets. Only then does it dawn on me. I stare down at the bag. I know there's a lot I have forgotten but I can't recall owning such a bag.

Easing myself onto one knee, I peel back the zipper. Inside there are four bright-orange packages. My hands are steady as I tear open the tape and peel back the plastic. A second layer is underneath and inside there is a black velvet pouch. Diamonds spill out onto my hand, tumbling into the crevices between my fingers.

Ali is coming down the stairs. "Did you find those sheets?"

There's no time to react. I look up at her, unable to explain. My voice sounds hoarse.

"Diamonds! It must be the ransom!"

Ali's hands are steady as she breaks ice from the freezer and drops it into my glass of whiskey. She makes herself a cup of coffee and slides onto the bench seat opposite me, waiting for an explanation.

I don't have one. I feel as if I'm lost in a strange place, surrounded by countries on the map I can't even name.

"They must be worth a fortune."

"Two million pounds," I whisper.

"How do you know that?"

"I have no idea. They belong to Aleksei Kuznet."

Fear clouds her eyes like the onset of fever. She knows the stories. I can imagine them being told after lights-out at probationer training.

Again I notice the scraps of plastic on the floor and dusting of foam. I wrapped the packages here; four identical bundles, each lined with polystyrene and wrapped in fluorescent plastic. They were meant to float.

Diamonds are easy to smuggle and hard to trace. They can't be picked up by sniffer dogs or tracked with serial numbers. Selling them isn't a problem. There are plenty of buyers in Antwerp or New York who deal in "blood" diamonds from dubious places like Angola, Sierra Leone and the Congo.

Ali leans forward, resting her forearms on the table. "What's the ransom doing here?"

"I don't know." What was it that Aleksei said to me at the hospital: "I want my daughter or I want my diamonds."

"We have to hand them in," insists Ali.

The trailing silence goes on too long.

"You can't be serious! You're not going to keep them!"

"Of course not."

Ali is staring at me. I hate the way I look in her eyes—diminished, undermined. She turns her head away, as though she doesn't want to see the mess I've made of my life. Is this why Keebal wanted a search warrant and the "fireman" tried to kill me?

The doorbell rings. Both of us jump.

Ali is on her feet. "Quick! Hide them! Hide them!"

"Calm down, you get the door."

There are certain rules in policing that I learned very early on. The first is never to search a dark warehouse with an armed cop whose nickname is "Boom-Boom." And the second is to take your own pulse first.

Using my forearm I scoop the bundles into the bag and notice beads of moisture left on the smooth surface of the table. The packages have been in water.

I hear Keebal's voice! He's standing in the front hall, silhouetted against the light. Ali turns back toward me, her eyes wide with alarm.

"I bought a cake," he announces, holding up a shopping bag.

"You better come in then."

With her back to him, Ali looks at me incredulously.

"Will you put the kettle on please, Ali," I say, putting my hand on the small of her back and guiding her across to the sink.

"What are you doing?" she whispers, but I'm already turning back to Keebal.

"How do you take your tea?"

"Just a splash of milk."

"We have none, I'm afraid."

He holds up a carton of long-life milk. "I think of everything."

Ali sets out the cups, keeping out of the way because her hands are shaking. Keebal finds a sports bag sitting on a chair.

"Just toss it on the floor," I say.

He picks up the handles and swings the bag beneath his feet. Ali's hands are suspended over the teacups, frozen there.

"So what do you think happened, Ruiz? Even if you're telling the truth and you can't remember, you must have a theory."

"Nothing as concrete as a theory."

Keebal glances at his shoes, which are resting on the sports bag. He leans down and brushes a speck of dirt from one polished toe.

"You want my theory," I say, attracting his attention. "I think this has something to do with Mickey Carlyle."

"She died three years ago."

"We didn't find her body."

"A man went to prison for her murder. That makes her dead. Case closed. You resurrect her and you better be God Almighty because otherwise you're in big trouble."

"But what if Howard is innocent."

Keebal laughs at me. "Is that your theory! What do you want to do—set a pedophile free from prison? You sound like his defense lawyer. Remember what you're paid to do—protect and serve. You're doing just the opposite if you let Howard Wavell walk out of prison."

A few token rays of sunshine have settled on the paving stones in the garden. We sit in silence for a while, finishing our tea and leaving the cake uneaten. Eventually, Keebal rises to his feet and puts the sports bag on the chair where he found it. He glances around the kitchen and then at the ceiling as if trying to penetrate the wood and plaster with X-ray vision.

"You think your memory is going to come back?" he asks.

"I'll keep you posted."

"Do that."

After he's gone Ali lowers her head onto the table in a mixture of relief and despair. She's scared, but not in a cowardly way. She doesn't understand what's happening.

I take the bag and drop it beside the front door.

"What are you doing?" she asks.

"We can't leave it here."

"But it almost got you killed," she says without flinching.

Right now I can't think of a better plan. I have to keep going. My only way out is to gather the pieces.

"What if you don't remember?" she whispers.

I don't answer. When I contemplate failure every scenario finishes with the same unpalatable truth. I put men in prison. I don't go there.

9

My clothes are in a suitcase in the trunk of Ali's car along with the shopping bag full of the unopened mail. The diamonds are there, too. I have never had two million pounds. I've never had a Ferrari either or a wife who could tie knots in cherry stems with her tongue. Maybe I should be more impressed.

The Professor is right, I have to follow the trail—the invoices, phone calls and diary appointments. I have to retrace my steps until I find the ransom letters and the proof of life. I wouldn't have delivered a single stone without them.

Sarah Jordan lives around the corner from Dolphin Mansions. Her mother answers the door and remembers me. Behind her Mr. Jordan is double-parked on the sofa with the *Racing Post* on his stomach and the TV blaring.

"Sarah won't be long," she says. "She's just gone to pick up a few things from the supermarket. Is everything all right?"

"Fine."

"But you talked to Sarah a few weeks ago."

"It's just a follow-up."

The supermarket is only around the corner. I leave Ali at the house and go looking for Sarah, happy to stretch my legs. The brightly lit aisles are stacked with cartons and half-empty boxes creating an obstacle course for shopping carts.

On my second circuit, I see a young girl in a long coat lurking at the far end of the aisle. She glances in both directions and then stuffs chocolate bars into her pockets. Her right arm is pressed against her side, holding something else beneath her coat.

I recognize Sarah. She's taller, of course, having lost her puppy fat. Light brown bangs fall across her forehead and her fine straight nose is dusted with freckles.

I glance up at the surveillance camera bolted to the ceiling. It is pointing down the aisle away from her. Sarah knows the blind spots.

Wrapping the coat around her, she walks toward the checkout and puts a box of breakfast cereal and a bag of marshmallows on the conveyor belt. Then she picks up a magazine and flicks through the pages, looking disinterested as the cashier deals with the customer ahead of her.

A young mother and toddler join the queue. Sarah looks up and notices me staring at her. Immediately she looks away and counts the loose change in her hand.

The store security guard, a Sikh wearing a bright blue turban, has been watching her through the window, hiding behind the posters for "red spot" specials. He marches through the automatic doors with one hand on his hip as though reaching for a nonexistent gun. The light behind him creates a halo around his turbaned head: the Sikh Terminator.

Sarah doesn't realize until he grabs hold of her arm and bends it behind her back. Two magazines tumble from beneath her coat. She twists from side to side and screams. Everything stops—the cashier chewing her pink bubble gum, a shelf stacker on a stepladder, the butcher slicing ham . . .

A frozen chicken korma is burning my fingers. I can't remember picking it out of the freezer. I push past the queue and hand it to the cashier. "Sarah, I told you to wait for me."

The security guard hesitates.

"I'm sorry about this. We didn't have a basket." I reach into Sarah's pockets and take out the chocolate bars, placing them on the conveyor belt. Then I pick up the magazines from the floor and find a packet of biscuits tucked into the waistband of her jeans.

"She was trying to steal those," protests the guard.

"She was holding them. Take your hands off her."

"And who the fuck are you?"

My badge flips open. "I'm the guy who's going to charge you with assault if you don't let her go."

Sarah reaches inside her coat and takes a box of tea bags from an inner pocket. Then she waits while the cashier scans each item and packs them into a plastic bag.

I take hold of the shopping bag and she follows me through the automatic doors. The manager intercepts us. "She's not welcome here. I don't want her coming back."

"She pays, she comes," I say, as I pass him and walk into the bright sunshine.

For a fleeting moment I think Sarah might run, but instead she turns and holds out her hand for her groceries.

"Not so fast."

She shrugs off her overcoat revealing khaki jeans and a T-shirt.

"It's a bit of a giveaway." I motion to the coat.

"Thanks for the advice." Her voice is full of fake toughness.

"You want a cold drink?"

She balks. She's waiting for a lecture on the evils of shoplifting.

I hold up the shopping bag. "You want this stuff, you have a cold drink."

We go to a juice bar on the corner and take a table outside. Sarah orders a banana smoothie before eyeing up the muffins. I get hungry watching her eat.

"You saw me a few weeks ago."

She nods.

"What did we talk about?"

She gives me an odd look.

"I had an accident. I've forgotten a few things. I was hoping you could help me remember them."

Sarah glances at my leg. "You mean like amnesia?"

"Something like that."

She takes another mouthful of muffin.

"Why did I come and see you?"

"You wanted to know if I ever cut Mickey's hair or counted the coins in her money box."

"Did I say why?"

"No."

"What else did we talk about?"

"I dunno. Stuff, I guess."

Sarah glances down at her shoes, stubbing the toe against the legs of the chair. The sun is pitched high and sharp, like the last hurrah before winter.

"Do you ever think about Mickey?" I ask.

"Sometimes."

"So do I. I guess you have lots of new friends now."

"Yeah, some, but Mickey was different. She was like an . . . a . . . a . . . appendix."

"You mean appendage."

"Yeah—like a heart."

"That's not really an appendage."

"OK, like an arm, real important." She drains her smoothie.

"You ever see Mrs. Carlyle?"

Sarah runs her fingers around the rim of her glass, collecting froth. "She still lives in the same place. My mum says it'd give her the creeps living where someone got killed but I reckon Mrs. Carlyle stays for a reason."

"Why's that?"

"She's waiting for Mickey. I'm not saying that Mickey is gonna come home, you know. I just figure Mrs. Carlyle wants to know where she is. That's why she goes to prison every month and visits him."

"Visits who?"

"Mr. Wavell."

"She visits him!"

"Every month. My mum says there's something sick about that. Gives her the creeps."

Sarah reaches across the table and turns my wrist so she can read the time. "I'm in heaps of trouble. Can I have my stuff now?"

I hand her the plastic shopping bag and a ten-quid note. "If I catch you shoplifting again, I'll make you mop supermarket floors for a month."

She rolls her eyes and is gone, pedalling furiously on her bicycle, carrying her coat, the bag of groceries and my frozen chicken korma.

The idea of Rachel Carlyle visiting Howard Wavell in prison sends chills through me. A grooming pedophile and a grieving parent—it's wrong, it's sick, but I know what she's doing. Rachel wants to find Mickey. She wants to bring her home.

I remember something she said to me a long while ago. Her fingers were tumbling over and over in her lap as she described a little routine she had with Mickey. "Even to the post office," they would say to each other, as they said goodbye and hugged.

"Sometimes people don't come back," said Rachel. "That's why you should always make your goodbyes count."

She was trying to hold on to every detail of Mickey—the clothes she wore, the games she played, the songs she sang; the way she frowned when she talked about something serious or a hiccupping laugh that made milk spurt out of her nose at the dinner table. She wanted to remember the thousands of tiny details and trivia that give light and shade to every life—even one as short as Mickey's.

Ali meets me at the juice bar and I tell her what Sarah said.

"You're going to go and see Howard, aren't you, Sir?"

"Yes."

"Could he have sent the ransom demand?"

"Not without help."

I know what she's thinking, although she won't say anything. She agrees with Campbell. Every likely explanation has the word "hoax" attached, including the one where Howard uses a ransom demand to win his appeal.

On the drive to Wormwood Scrubs we cross under the Westway into Scrubs Lane. Teenage girls are playing hockey on the playing fields, while teenage boys sit and watch, captivated by the blue pleated skirts that swirl and dip against muddy knees and moss-smooth thighs.

Wormwood Scrubs Prison looks like a film set for a 1950s musical, where the filth and grime have been scrubbed off for the cameras. The twin towers are four stories high and in the center is a huge arched door impregnated with iron bolts.

I try to picture Rachel Carlyle arriving here to visit Howard. In my mind I see a black cab pull up in the forecourt and Rachel sliding out, never letting her knees separate. She walks carefully over the cobble-stones, wary of turning her ankle. Glamour hasn't been bred into her, despite her family's money.

The visitors center is located to the right of the main gate in a set of temporary buildings. Wives and girlfriends have already started to gather, some with children who fidget and fight.

Once inside they are searched and asked for proof of identity. Their belongings are stored in lockers and gifts are vetted in advance. Anyone wearing clothes that too closely match the prison uniform is asked to change.

Ali gazes up at the Victorian façade and shivers.

"You ever been inside?"

"Once or twice," she replies. "They should tear the place down."

"It's called a deterrent."

"Works on me."

Leaving her for a moment, I open the trunk and retrieve the dia-monds. I can fit two packages in the inside pockets of my overcoat and two more in the outer pockets. I put the coat on the seat beside her.

"I want you to stay with the car and look after the diamonds."

She nods. "You want to wear the vest?"

"I think I'm safe enough in prison."

Crossing the road, I show my badge at the visitors center. Ten minutes later I climb two flights of stairs and emerge into a large room with a long continuous table divided down the middle by a partition. Visitors stay on one side and prisoners on the other. Knees can't touch or lips meet. Physical contact is restricted to holding hands or lifting young children over the divide.

Heavy boots echo in the corridors as the cons are brought in. Each visitor hands over a docket and has to wait until the prisoner is in place before being admitted.

I watch a young prisoner greet his wife or girlfriend. He kisses her hand and doesn't want to let it go. They both lean forward as though trying to breathe the same air. His hand reaches under the table.

Suddenly, the screws seize her chair and wrench it backward. Falling to the floor, she shields her swollen belly. She's pregnant, for Christ's sake. He only wants to feel his baby, but there's no sign of empathy from the screws.

"DI Ruiz, you can't stay away."

The Governor appears beside me. Barrel-chested and balding, he's in his late forties. Finishing a sandwich, he dabs at his lips with a paper napkin, missing egg yoke on his chin.

"So what brings you back?"

"It must be the ambience."

He laughs roughly and glances through the Perspex screen at the reunions.

"How long since I was here last?"

"Don't you remember?"

"Old age, I'm getting forgetful."

"About four weeks ago; you were interested in that woman who comes to see Howard Wavell."

"Mrs. Carlyle."

"Yeah. She's not here today. She comes every month and tries to bring the same gifts: kiddie catalogs. That sick fuck better not get an appeal!"

I try to picture Howard sitting opposite Rachel. Did she reach across the partition and take his hand? I even feel a pang of jealousy and imagine his eyes traveling down the V-neck of her blouse. We live in a sick sick world.

"I need to talk to him."

"He's in segregation."

"Why?"

The Governor picks at his fingernails. "Like I told you before, nobody expected him to live this long. He killed Aleksei Kuznet's little girl! That's a death sentence whichever way you look at it."

"But you've managed to protect him."

He laughs wryly. "You could say that. He was only here four days before someone ran a razor blade across his throat. He spent the next month in the hospital wing. Nobody's touched him since then so I figure Aleksei must want him alive. Howard doesn't care."

"What do you mean?"

"Like I told you before, he keeps refusing to take his insulin. Twice in the last six months he's lapsed into a diabetic coma. If he can't be bothered why should Her Majesty, eh? I'd let the bastard die."

The Governor senses I don't agree with him. He sneers. "Contrary to popular opinion, Inspector, I'm not here to play nursemaid to prisoners. I don't hold their hands and say, 'You poor things, you had a lousy childhood or a crap lawyer or a hanging judge.' A dog on a leash could do what I do."

(With a lot more compassion no doubt.)

"I still need to see him."

"He wasn't listed for visitors today."

"But you can bring him up."

The Governor grunts softly to a senior guard, who picks up a phone, setting the chain of command into motion. Somewhere deep in the intestines of this place someone will fetch Howard. I can picture him lying on a narrow cot, smelling the sourness of the air. The future is a scary business when you're a pedophile in prison. It's not next summer's holiday or a long weekend in the Lake District. The future stretches from when you wake up until you go to sleep again. Sixteen hours can seem like a lifetime.

Visiting time has almost ended. Howard pushes against the tide, walking as though his legs are shackled. He gazes around the room, looking for his visitor, perhaps expecting Rachel.

More than forty years on I can still recognize him as the fat kid from school, who changed behind a towel and chain-smoked on an asthma puffer. He was almost a semi-tragic figure but not quite so tragic as Rory McIntyre, a sleepwalker who did a high dive off the third-floor balcony in the early hours of Foundation Day. They say that sleepwalkers wake up in midair but Rory didn't make a sound. Nor did he make a splash. He always was a good diver.

Howard takes a seat and doesn't seem surprised by the sound of my voice. Instead he stops, arches his neck and swivels his head like an old tortoise. I step in front of him. He blinks at me slowly.

"Hello, Howard, I want to talk to you about Rachel Carlyle."

He smiles little by little but doesn't answer. A scar runs from one side of his throat to the other, just beneath his chins.

"She comes to see you. Why?"

"You should ask her."

"What do you talk about?"

He glances at the screws. "I don't have to tell you anything. My appeal application is next Thursday."

"You're not getting out of here, Howard. Nobody wants to set you free."

Again he smiles. Certain people don't seem to match their voices. Howard is like that. It is pitched too high, as though laced with helium, and his pale face seems disconnected from his body like a white balloon moving gently in a breeze.

"We can't all be perfect, Mr. Ruiz. We make mistakes and we deal with the consequences. The difference between you and me is that I have my God. He will judge me and get me out of here. Do you ever wonder who is judging you?"

He seems confident. Why? Maybe he knows about the ransom demand. Any suggestion Mickey might still be alive would automatically grant him a retrial.

"Why does Mrs. Carlyle come here?"

He raises his hands in mock surrender and lowers them again. "She wants to know what I did with Mickey. She's worried I might die before telling anyone."

"You're messing up your insulin injections."

"Do you know what it's like to go into a diabetic coma? First my breathing becomes labored. My mouth and tongue are parched. My blood pressure falls and my pulse accelerates. I get blurred vision, then pain in my eyes. Finally, I slip into unconsciousness. If they don't reach me quickly enough, my kidneys will fail completely and my brain will be permanently damaged. Soon after that I will die."

He seems to revel in these details, as if looking forward to it.

"Did you tell her what happened to Mickey?"

"I told her the truth."

"Tell me."

"I told her that I'm not an innocent man but I am innocent of this crime. I have sinned but not committed *this* sin. I believe in the sanctity of human life. I believe all children are gifts from God, born pure and innocent. They only act with hate and violence because we teach them hate and violence. They are the only ones who can truly judge me."

"And how are the children going to judge you?"

He goes silent.

Sweat rings beneath his arms have spread out and merged, plastering his shirt to his skin so that I can see every freckle and mole. There's something else on his back, beneath the fabric. Something has discolored the material, turning it yellow.

Howard has to look over his right shoulder to see me. He grimaces slightly. At that same moment, I force him forward across the table. Deaf to his squeals that are muffled against my forearm, I lift his shirt. His flesh is like pulped melon. Angry wounds crisscross his back, weeping blood and yellow crystalline scum.

Prison guards are running toward us. One of them puts a handkerchief over his mouth.

"Get a doctor," I yell. "Move!"

Commands are shouted and phone calls are made. Howard is screaming and thrashing like he's on fire. Suddenly, he lies still, with his arms stretched across the table.

"Who did this to you?"

He doesn't answer.

"Talk to me. Who did this?"

He mumbles something. I can't quite hear him. Leaning closer, I pick up the words, "Suffer the little children to come unto me and forbid them not . . . never yield to temptation . . ."

There is something tucked inside the sleeve of his shirt. He doesn't stop me pulling it free. It's the wooden handle of a skipping rope, threaded with a twelve-inch strand of fencing wire. Self-flagellation, self-mutilation, fasting and flogging—can someone please explain them to me?

Howard shrugs my hand away and gets to his feet. He won't wait for a doctor and he doesn't want to talk any more. He shuffles toward the door, with his flapping shoes, yellow skin and shallow breathing. At the last possible moment he turns and I'm expecting one of those pleading, kicked-dog looks.

Instead I get something different. This man whom I helped lock away for murder; who flays himself with fencing wire, who every day is spat upon, jeered, threatened and abused . . . this man looks sorry for *me*.

Eighty-five steps and ninety-four hours—that's how long Mickey had been missing when I served a search warrant on number 9 Dolphin Mansions.

"Surprise. Surprise," I said as Howard opened the door. His large eyes bulged slightly and his mouth opened but no sound came out. He was wearing a pajama top, long shorts with an elasticized waist and dark brown loafers that accentuated the whiteness of his shins.

I started like I always did—telling Howard how much I knew about him. He was single, never married. He grew up in Warrington, the youngest of seven children in a big loud Protestant family. Both his parents were dead. He had twenty-eight nieces and nephews and was godfather to eleven of them. In 1962 he was hospitalized after a traffic accident. A year later he suffered a nervous breakdown and became a voluntary outpatient at a clinic in north London. He had worked as a storeman, a laborer, a painter and decorator, a van driver and now a gardener. He went to church three times a week, sang in the choir, read biographies, was allergic to strawberries and took photographs in his spare time.

I wanted Howard to feel like he was fifteen and I had just caught him jerking off in the showers at Cottesloe Park. And no matter what excuses he offered, I'd know he was lying. Fear and uncertainty—the most powerful weapons in the known world.

"You left something out," he mumbled.

"What's that?"

"I'm a diabetic. Insulin shots, the whole business."

"My uncle had that."

"Don't tell me—he gave up chocolate bars and started jogging and his diabetes went away. I hear that all the time. That and, 'Christ, I would just die if I had to stick a needle in myself every day.' Or this is a good one, 'You get that from being fat don't you?' "

People were trooping past us, wearing overalls and gloves. Some carried metal boxes with photographic equipment and lights. Duckboards had been laid like stepping-stones down the hall.

"What are you looking for?" he asked softly.

"Evidence. That's what detectives do. It's what we use to support a case. It turns hypothesis into theories and theories into cases."

"I'm a case."

"A work in progress."

That was the truth of it. I couldn't say what I was looking for until I found it—clothing, fingerprints, binding material, videos, photographs, a seven-year-old girl with a lisp . . . any of the above.

"I want a lawyer."

"Good. You can use my phone. Afterward we'll go outside and hold a joint press conference on the front steps."

"You can't take me out there." The television cameras were lined up along the pavement like metal Triffids, waiting to lash out at anyone who left the building.

Howard sat down on the staircase, holding on to the banister for support.

"I can smell bleach."

"I was cleaning."

"My eyes are watering, Howard. What were you cleaning?"

"I spilled some chemicals in my darkroom."

There were scratches on his wrists. I pointed to them. "How did you get those?"

"Two of Mrs. Swingler's cats got loose in the garden. One of your officers left the door open. I helped her get them back."

He listened to the sound of drawers being opened and furniture moved.

"Do you know the story of Adam and Eve, Howard? It was the most important moment in human history, the telling of the first lie. That's what separates us from the other animals. It has nothing to do with humans thinking on a higher plane or having easily available credit. We lie to each other. We deliberately mislead. I think you're a truthful person, Howard, but you're providing me with false information. A liar has a choice."

"I'm telling you the truth."

"Do you have any secrets?"

"No."

"Did you and Mickey have a secret?"

He shook his head. "Am I under arrest?"

"No. You're helping us with our inquiries. You're a very helpful man. I noticed that right from the beginning when you were taking photographs and printing flyers."

"I was showing people what Mickey looked like."

"There you go. Helpful. That's what you are."

The search took three hours. Surfaces were dusted, carpets vacuumed, clothes brushed and sinks dismantled. Overseeing the operation was George Noonan, a veteran scene of crime investigator who is almost albino with his completely white hair and pale skin. Noonan seems to resent searches where he doesn't have a body to work with. For him death is always a bonus.

"You might want to see this," he said.

I followed him down the hallway to the sitting room. He had sealed off all sources of light by blacking out windows and using masking tape around the edges of the doors. He positioned me in front of the fireplace, closed the door and turned off the light.

Darkness. I couldn't even see my feet. Then I noticed a small pattern of droplets, glowing blue-green on the carpet.

"They could be low-velocity bloodstains," explained Noonan. "The hemoglobin in blood reacts to the luminol, a chemical that I sprayed on the floor. Substances like household bleach can trigger the same reaction but I think this is blood."

"You said low velocity?"

"A slow bleeder—probably not a stab wound."

The droplets were no bigger than bread crumbs and stopped abruptly in a straight line.

"There used to be something here—possibly a carpet or a rug," he explains.

"With more blood on it?"

"He may have tried to get rid of the evidence."

"Or wrapped up a body. Is there enough to get DNA?"

"I believe so."

My knee joints creaked as I stood. Noonan turned on the light.

"We found something else." He held up a pair of child's bikini briefs sealed in a plastic evidence bag. "There don't appear to be traces of blood or semen. I won't be sure until I get it back to the lab."

Howard had waited on the stairs. I didn't ask him about the blood-stains or the underwear. Nor did I query the 86,000 images of children on his computer hard drive or the six boxes of clothing catalogs—all featuring children—beneath his bed. The time for that would come later.

Howard's world had been turned upside down and emptied like the contents of a drawer yet he didn't even raise his head as the last officer left.

Emerging onto the front steps, I blinked into the sunshine and turned to the cameras. "We have served a search warrant at this address. A man is helping us with our inquiries. He is not under arrest. I want you to respect his privacy and leave the residents of this building alone. Do not jeopardize this investigation."

A barrage of questions came from beyond the cameras.

"Is Mickey Carlyle still alive?"

"Are you close to making an arrest?"

"Is it true you found photographs?"

Pushing through the crowd I walked to my car, refusing to answer any questions. At the last moment, I turned back and glanced up at Dolphin Mansions. Howard peered from the window. He didn't look at me. Instead he stared at the TV cameras and realized, with a growing sense of horror, that they weren't going to leave. They were waiting for *him*.

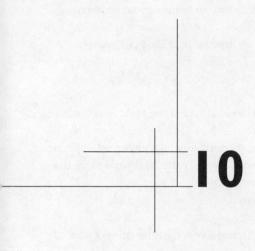

10

Emerging from the prison, I get a sudden, stultifying sense of déjà vu. A black BMW pulls up suddenly, the door opens and Aleksei Kuznet steps onto the pavement. His hair is dark and wet, clinging to his scalp as though glued there.

How did he know I was here?

A bodyguard appears behind him, the sort of paid thug who bulks up in prison weight rooms and settles arguments with a tire iron. He has Slavic features and walks with his left arm swinging less freely than his right because of the gun beneath his armpit.

"DI Ruiz, are you visiting a friend?"

"I could ask you the same question."

Ali is out of the car and running toward me. The Russian reaches inside his coat and for a moment I have visions of all hell breaking loose. Aleksei flashes a look and the situation defuses. Hands are withdrawn and coats are buttoned.

Ali's aggressive demeanor amuses Aleksei and he spends a moment examining her face and figure. Then he tells her to run along because he doesn't need cookies today.

Ali glances at me, waiting for a signal. "Stretch your legs. I won't be long."

She doesn't go far, just to the other side of the square, where she turns and watches.

"Forgive me," Aleksei says, "I didn't mean to insult your young friend."

"She's a police officer."

"Really! They take all colors nowadays. Has your memory returned?"

"No."

"How unfortunate."

His eyes rove over mine with an aloof curiosity. He doesn't believe me. He glances around the square.

"Do you know that nowadays there is a digital shotgun microphone that can pick up a conversation in a park or a restaurant from more than a thousand feet away?"

"The Met isn't that sophisticated."

"Maybe not."

"I'm not trying to trap you, Aleksei. Nobody is listening. I honestly can't remember what happened."

"It is very simple—I gave you 965 one-carat or above, superior-quality diamonds. You promised to pick up my daughter. I made myself perfectly clear—I don't pay for things twice."

His phone is ringing. Reaching into his jacket, he pulls out a sleek cell phone, smaller than a cigarette box, and reads the text message.

"I am a gadget geek, Inspector," he explains. "Someone stole my phone recently. Of course, I reported it to the police. I also called the thief and told him what I would do to him."

"Did he return your property?"

"It makes no difference. He was very apologetic when I saw him last. He couldn't actually tell me this in his own words. His vocal cords had burned off. People should mark acid bottles more carefully."

Aleksei's eyes ghost across the cobblestones. "You took my diamonds. You were going to keep my investment safe."

I think of my overcoat on the seat of Ali's car. If only he knew!

"Is Mickey still alive?"

"You tell me!"

"If there was a ransom demand, there must have been proof of life."

"They sent strands of hair. You organized the DNA tests. The hair belonged to Mickey."

"That doesn't prove she's alive. The hair could have come from a hairbrush or a pillow; it could have been collected three years ago. It could have been a hoax."

"Yes, Inspector, but you *were* sure. You staked your life on it."

I don't like the way he says "life." He makes it sound like a worthless wager. Panic spikes in my chest.

"Why did you believe me?"

He blinks at me coldly. "Tell me what choice I had."

Suddenly, I recognize his dilemma. Whether Mickey was alive or dead made no difference—Aleksei *had* to provide the ransom. It was about saving face and grasping at straws. Imagine a one-in-a-thousand chance of getting her back. He couldn't ignore it. How would it look? What would people say? A father is supposed to cling to impossible dreams. He must keep his children safe and bring them home.

Maybe it's this knowledge but I feel a sudden rush of tenderness toward Aleksei. Almost as quickly I remember the attack at the hospital.

"Somebody tried to kill me yesterday."

"Well, well." He makes a little church with his fingers. "Perhaps you took something from them."

It's not an admission.

"We can discuss this."

"Like gentlemen?" He's teasing me now. "You have an accent."

"No, I was born here."

"Maybe so, but you still have an accent."

He takes a long thin paper tube of sugar from his pocket and tears it open.

"My mother is German."

He nods and pours the sugar on his tongue. "Zigeuner?" It's the German word for Gypsy. "My father used to say Gypsies were the eighth plague of Egypt."

The insult is delivered without any sense of malice.

"Do you have children, Detective?"

"Twins."

"How old are they?"

"Twenty-six."

"You see much of them?"

"Not anymore."

"Maybe you forget how it feels. I am thirty-six now. I have done things I am not particularly proud of but I can live with that. I sleep like a baby. But let me tell you—I don't care how much someone has in the bank, until they have a child they have nothing of value. Nothing!"

He scratches at the scar on his cheek. "My wife turned against me a long time ago but Michaela was always going to be half mine . . . half of me. She was going to grow up and make up her own mind. She was going to forgive me."

"You think she's dead?"

"I let you convince me otherwise."

"I must have had a good reason."

"I hope so."

He turns to leave.

"I'm not your enemy, Aleksei. I just want to find out what happened. What do you know about the sniper? Does he work for you?"

"Me?" He laughs.

"Where were you on the night of September 25?"

"Don't you remember? I have an alibi. I was with you."

He swivels and signals to the Russian who's been waiting like a dog tied to a post. I can't let him leave. He *has* to tell me about Rachel and the ransom demand. I grab his arm and twist it outward until his back arches and he drops to his knees. My walking stick clatters to the pavement.

Pedestrians and prison visitors turn to watch. It strikes me how vaguely ridiculous I must look—making an arrest with a walking stick. Vanity still matters.

"You're under arrest for withholding information from a police investigation."

"You're making a big mistake," he hisses.

"Stay down!"

A shape materializes behind me and the warm metal of a gun brushes the base of my skull. It's the Russian, massive, filling the space like a statue. Suddenly, his attention shifts. Ali is standing with her feet apart in a half crouch and her gun pointed at his chest.

Still holding Aleksei's arms, I put my face close to his ear.

"Is this what you want? Are we all going to shoot each other?"

"Nyet!" he says. The Russian takes a step back and slips the gun into its holster. He looks closely at Ali, memorizing her face.

I'm already steering Aleksei toward the car. Ali walks backward behind me, watching the Russian.

"Call Carlucci," Aleksei yells. Carlucci is his lawyer.

Pushing his head down, he sits in the backseat. I slide in alongside him. My overcoat is hanging over the seat in front of us. Ali hasn't said a word but I know her mind is working faster than ever.

"You're going to be sorry," mutters Aleksei, peering past me out the window. "You said no police. We had a deal."

"Help me then! Someone shot me that night. I suffered something called transient global amnesia. I can't remember what happened."

His tongue rolls around his mouth like he's sucking on the idea.

"Go to hell!"

Frank Carlucci is already at the Harrow Road Police Station when we arrive. Small, tanned and very Italian, his face is wrinkled like a walnut except for around his eyes. A surgeon has been at work.

He scuttles up the stairs beside me, demanding to speak with his client.

"You can wait your turn. He has to be processed."

Ali has stayed in the car. I turn back toward her. "Look after my coat."

"What do you want me to do?"

"Find the Professor. Tell him I need him. Then look for Rachel. She must be somewhere."

Ali's face is full of questions. She's not sure if I know what I'm doing. I try to muster a confident smile and turn back to Aleksei.

As we enter the charge room the place falls silent. I swear I can actually hear the indoor plants growing and ink drying on paper. That's how quiet things get. These people were once my friends and colleagues. Now they avoid my eyes or ignore me completely. Maybe I died on the river and just don't realize it yet.

I leave Aleksei in an interview room with Carlucci. My heart is pounding and I want to pull myself together. First up I call Campbell. He's in a meeting at Scotland Yard so I leave a message on his voice mail. Twenty minutes later he comes storming through the front door looking for a cat to kick.

He finds me in the corridor.

"ARE YOU COMPLETELY INSANE?"

I put this down as a rhetorical question. "Would you mind keeping your voice down?"

"What?"

"Please keep your voice down. I have a suspect in the interview room."

Calmer this time: "You arrested Aleksei Kuznet."

"He knows about the ransom demand. He's withholding information."

"I told you to stay away from this."

"People were shot. Mickey Carlyle might still be alive!"

"I've heard enough of this. I want you back in the hospital."

"No, Sir!"

He lets out a deep growl like a bear coming out of a cave. "Surrender your badge, Detective. You're suspended!"

Along the corridor a door opens and Frank Carlucci emerges followed by Aleksei. Carlucci yells and points at finger at me. "I want that officer charged."

"Fuck you! You want a piece of me? Outside!"

It's like someone hits a panic button inside me and I'm consumed by a bloodred rage. Campbell has to hold me back. I'm fighting at his arms.

Aleksei turns slowly and smiles. His physical smoothness is remarkable.

"You have something of mine. Like I said, I don't pay for things twice."

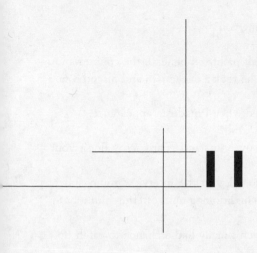

I have been sitting in silence in an interview room, having finished my tea and eaten the ginger-nut biscuits. The room smells of fear and loathing. Maybe it's me.

Given a choice, Campbell would have had me arrested. Instead he wants me taken back to the hospital because he can't guarantee my safety. In reality, he wants me out of the way.

Almost instinctively my fingers find the morphine capsules. My leg is hurting again but maybe it's my pride. I don't want to think about anything for a while. I want to forget and float away. Amnesia isn't such a bad thing.

This is where I interviewed Howard Wavell for the first time. He had been holed up in his flat for three days with people buzzing on the intercom and the media camped outside. Most people would have disappeared by then—gone to stay with friends or family—but Howard wouldn't risk bringing the circus with him.

I remember him standing at the front counter, arguing with the desk sergeant. He rocked from one foot to the other, glancing over his shoulder. The short sleeves of his shirt stretched tight over his biceps and the buttons pulled across his stomach.

"They put dog shit through my mailbox," he said, incredulously. "And someone threw eggs at my windows. You have to stop them."

The desk sergeant regarded him with an exhausted authority. "Are you reporting a crime, Sir?"

"I'm being threatened."

"And who exactly is threatening you?"

"Vigilantes! Vandals!"

The sergeant pulled an incident pad from beneath the counter and slid it across the bench top. Then he took a cheap pen and placed it on the pad. "Write it down."

Howard looked almost relieved when I made an appearance.

"They attacked my flat."

"I'm sorry. I'll send someone over to stand guard. Why don't you come and sit down."

He followed me along the corridor to the interview room and I pulled his chair nearer to the air-conditioning unit, offering him a bottle of water.

"I'm glad you're here. We haven't really had a chance to catch up. It's been a long time."

"I guess," he said, sipping at the water.

Acting like we were old friends I started reminiscing about school and some of the teachers. With a little prompting, Howard added his own stories. There is a theory about interrogations that once suspects begin talking easily about any particular topic it is harder for them to stop talking about other topics that you raise or for them to suddenly start lying.

"So tell me, Howard, what do you think happened to Mickey Carlyle? You must have given it some thought. Everyone else seems to be trying to figure it out. Do you think she just walked out of the front door without anyone seeing her or was she abducted? Maybe you think aliens whisked her away. I've heard every bizarre theory you can imagine over the past seven days."

Howard frowned and moistened his lips with the tip of his tongue. A pigeon landed on the ledge outside, beside the air-conditioning unit. Howard gazed at the bird as though it might have brought him a message.

"At first I thought she might just be hiding, you know. She used to like hiding under the stairs and playing in the boiler room. That's what I thought last week but well, now, I don't know. Maybe she went to sell cookies or something."

"There's a possibility I hadn't considered."

"I didn't mean to sound flippant," he said clumsily. "That's how I first met her. She knocked on my door selling Girl Scout cookies—only she wasn't wearing a uniform and the cookies were homemade."

"Did you buy any?"

"Nobody else was going to—they were burned to a crisp."

"So why did you?"

He shrugged. "She showed a bit of initiative. I got nieces and nephews . . ." The statement tailed off.

"I thought you might have a sweet tooth. Sugar and spice and all things nice, eh?"

A wave of pale pink shaded his cheeks and his neck muscles tightened. He couldn't tell if I was inferring something.

Changing focus, I took him back to the beginning, asking him to explain his movements in the hours before and after Mickey disappeared. His blinds had been drawn that Monday morning. None of his workmates saw him mowing the covered reservoir at Primrose Hill. At one o'clock the police searched his flat. He didn't go back to work. Instead he spent the afternoon outside, taking photographs.

"You didn't go to work on Tuesday morning?"

"No. I wanted to do something to help. I printed up a photograph of Mickey to put on a flyer."

"In your darkroom?"

"Yes."

"What did you do after that?"

"I did some washing."

"This is Tuesday morning, right? Everyone else is out searching and you're doing your laundry."

He nodded uncertainly.

"There used to be a rug on the floor in your sitting room." I showed him a photograph—one of his own. "Where is this rug now?"

"I threw it away."

"Why?"

"It was dirty. I couldn't get it clean."

"Why was it dirty?"

"I spilled some potting compost on it. I was making hanging baskets."

"When did you throw it away?"

"I don't remember."

"Was it after Mickey disappeared?"

"I think so. Maybe."

"Where did you throw it?"

"In a Dumpster off the Edgware Road."

"You couldn't find one closer?"

"Dumpsters get filled up."

"But you work for the council. There must have been dozens of trash cans you could have used."

"I . . . I didn't think . . ."

"You see how it looks, Howard. You cleaned up your flat, you took out the rug, the place smelled of bleach—it looks like you might be hiding something."

"No, I just cleaned up a bit. I wanted the flat to look nice."

"Nice?"

"Yeah."

"Have you ever seen these before, Howard?" I held up a pair of girl's panties enclosed in a plastic evidence bag. "They were found in your laundry bag."

His voice tightened. "They belong to one of my nieces. They stay with me all the time—my nieces and nephews . . ."

"Do they sleep over?"

"In my spare room."

"Has Mickey Carlyle ever been in your spare room?"

"Yes. No. Maybe."

"Do you know Mrs. Carlyle very well?"

"Only to say hello when I see her on the stairs."

"She a good mother?"

"I guess."

"A good-looking woman."

"She's not really my type."

"Why's that?"

"She's kind of abrupt, you know, not very friendly. Don't tell her I said that; I don't want to hurt her feelings."

"And you prefer?"

"Um, you know, it's not a sexual thing. I don't know really. Hard to say."

"You got a girlfriend, Howard?"

"Not just now."

He made it sound like he had one for breakfast with his coffee.

"Tell me about Danielle."

"I don't know any Danielle."

"You have photographs of a girl called Danielle—on your computer. She's wearing bikini bottoms."

He blinked once, twice, three times. "She's the daughter of a former girlfriend."

"She's not wearing a top. How old is she?"

"Eleven."

"There's another girl pictured with a towel over her head, lying on a bed. She's only wearing a pair of shorts. Who is she?"

He hesitated. "Mickey and Sarah were playing a game. They were putting on a play. It was just a bit of fun."

"Yeah, that's what I figured." I smiled reassuringly.

Howard's hair was plastered to his head and every so often a drop of perspiration leaked into his eyes, making him blink. Opening a large yellow envelope, I pulled out a bundle of photographs and started laying them out side by side, row after row. They were all shots of Mickey—two hundred and seventy of them—pictures of her sunbathing in the garden with Sarah, others of them playing under a sprinkler, eating ice-cream cones and wrestling on his couch.

"They're just photographs," he said defensively. "She was very photogenic."

"You said 'was,' Howard. Like you don't think she's still alive."

"I didn't mean . . . you're . . . you're trying to make out I'm . . . I'm . . . a . . ."

"You take pictures, Howard, it's obvious. Some of these are very good. You're also in the church choir and you're an altar boy."

"An altar server."

"*And* you teach Sunday school."

"I help out."

"By taking kids away on day trips—to the beach or to the zoo?"

"Yes."

I made him look closely at a photograph. "She doesn't look very comfortable posing in a bikini, does she?" I put another photograph in front of him . . . then another.

"It was just a bit of fun."

"Where did she get changed?"

"In the spare room."

"Did you take photographs of her getting changed?"

"No."

"Did Mickey ever stay overnight with you?"

"No."

"Did you ever leave her alone in your flat?"

"No."

"And you wouldn't take her outside without permission."

"No."

"You didn't take her to the zoo or for any day trips?"

He shook his head.

"That's good. I mean, it would have been negligent, wouldn't it, to leave such a young child alone or to let her play with photographic chemicals or with sharp implements?"

He nodded.

"And if she cut herself you might have to explain this to her mother. I'm sure Mrs. Carlyle would understand. Accidents happen. Then again, you wouldn't want her getting angry and stopping Mickey from seeing you. So maybe you wouldn't tell her. Maybe you'd keep it a secret."

"No, I'd tell her."

"Of course you would. If Mickey cut herself, you'd have to tell her mother."

"Yes."

I picked up a blue folder and slid a sheet into view, running my finger down several paragraphs and then tapping it thoughtfully with my index finger.

"That's very good, Howard, but I'm puzzled. You see we found traces of Mickey's blood on your sitting-room floor as well as in the bathroom and on one of your towels."

Howard's jaw flapped up and down and his voice grew strident. "You think I did something—but I didn't."

"So tell me about the blood."

"She cut her finger. She and Sarah were making a tin-can phone but one of the cans had a sharp edge. I should have checked it first. It wasn't a deep cut. I put a Band-Aid on it. She was very brave. She didn't cry . . ."

"And did you tell her mother?"

He looked down at his hands. "I told Mickey not to. I was scared Mrs. Carlyle might stop her coming over if she thought I was negligent."

"There was too much blood for a cut finger. You tried to clean it all up but the rug was too stained. That's why you threw it away."

"No, not blood. Soil from the hanging baskets—I spilled some."

"Soil?"

He nodded enthusiastically.

"You said you never took Mickey on an excursion. We found fibers from her clothes in your van."

"No. No."

I let the silence stretch out. Howard's eyes were filled with a mixture of fear and regret. Suddenly, he surprised me by speaking first. "You remember Mrs. Castle . . . from school? She used to take us for ballroom dancing lessons."

I remembered her. She looked like Julie Andrews in *The Sound of Music* (after she left the convent) and featured in every fifth-form boy's wet dreams except perhaps for Nigel Bryant and Richard Coyle who batted for the other side.

"What about her?"

"I once saw her in the shower."

"Getaway!"

"No, it's true. She was using the dean's shower and old Archie" (the sports master) "sent me to pick up a starter pistol from the staff quarters. She came out of the shower drying her hair and didn't see me until it was too late. She let me look. She stood there and let me watch her drying her breasts and pulling on her tights. Afterward she made me promise not to tell anyone. I would have been the most famous kid at school. All I had to do was tell that story. I could have saved myself a dozen beatings and all those taunts and jibes. I could have been a legend."

"So why didn't you?"

He looked at me sadly. "I was in love with her. And it didn't matter that she wasn't in love with me. I loved her. It was *my* love story. I don't expect you to understand that but it's true. You don't have to be loved back. You can love anyway."

"What does this have to do with Mickey?"

"I loved Mickey, too. I would never have hurt her . . . not on purpose."

His pale green eyes were filled with tears. When he couldn't blink them away he wiped them with his hands. I felt sorry for him. I always did.

"It's important that you listen to me right now, Howard. I'll let you talk later." I pulled my chair closer so that we were sitting knee to knee. "You're a middle-aged guy, never married, living alone, spending all his spare time with children, taking pictures of them, giving them ice-cream cones, taking them on outings . . ."

His cheeks darkened but his lips stayed white and narrow. "I have nieces and nephews. I take pictures of them, too. There's nothing wrong with that."

"And you collect kiddie clothing catalogs and magazines?"

"It's not against the law. They're not pornographic. I want to be a photographer, a children's photographer . . ."

Getting to my feet I moved behind him. "Here's the thing I can't understand, Howard. What do you see in little girls? No hips, no breasts, no experience. They're straight up and down. I can understand the sugar and spice and all things nice stuff—girls smell nicer than boys, but Mickey had no curves. The adolescent good fairy hadn't sprinkled that magic dust in her eyes that made her eyelids flutter and her body develop. What do you see in little girls?"

"They're innocent."

"And you want to take that away from them?"

"No. Never."

"You want to hold them . . . to touch them."

"Not like that. Not in a dirty way."

"Mickey must have laughed at you. The creepy old guy across the hall."

Louder this time: "I never touched her!"

"Do you remember *To Kill a Mockingbird*?"

He paused, looking at me curiously.

"Boo Radley was the scary guy who lived in the basement across the road. All the kids were frightened of him. They threw stones on his roof and dared each other to go into his yard. But in the end it's Boo Radley who saves Scout and Jem from the real villain. He becomes the hero. Is that what you were waiting for, Howard—to rescue Mickey?"

"You don't know me. You don't know anything about me."

"Oh, yes I do. I know exactly what you are. There's a name for peo-

ple like you: grooming pedophiles. You pick out your victims. You iso-
late them. You befriend their parents. You slowly work your way into
their lives until they trust you—"

"No."

"What did you do with Mickey?"

"Nothing. I didn't touch her."

"But you wanted to."

"I just took pictures. I would never hurt her."

He was about to say something else but I raised my hand and
stopped him.

"I know you're not the sort of guy who would have planned to hurt
her. You're not like that. But sometimes accidents happen. They aren't
planned. They get out of hand . . . you saw her that day."

"No. I didn't touch her."

"We found her fingerprints and fibers from her clothes."

He kept shaking his head.

"They were in your van, Howard. They were in your bedroom."

Reaching over his shoulder, I jabbed my finger at each of the different girls in his photographs.

"We're going to find your 'models,' Howard, this one and this one
and this one. And we're going to ask these girls what you did to them.
We're going to find out if you touched them and if you took any other
sorts of photographs."

My voice had grown low and harsh. I leaned against him, shoulder
to shoulder, forcing him sideways off his chair. "I'm not leaving you alone,
Howard. We're in this together—like Siamese twins, joined at the hip,
but not up here." I tapped my head. "Help me understand."

He turned slowly toward me, searching my eyes for sympathy. Then
suddenly, he toppled backward, scurrying to the corner of the room
where he crouched, covering his head with his arms.

"DON'T HIT ME! DON'T HIT ME!" he screamed. "I'll tell you
what you want—"

"What are you doing?" I hissed.

"NOT MY FACE, DON'T HURT MY FACE."

"Stand up! Cut this out!"

"PLEASE . . . NOT AGAIN . . . AAAARGH!"

I opened the door and called for two uniforms. They were already
coming down the corridor.

"Pick him up. Make him sit in his chair."

Howard went limp. It was like trying to pick up spilled jelly. Each time they tried to lift him onto a chair he slid to the floor, quivering and moaning. The uniforms looked at each other and back to me. I knew what they were thinking.

Finally we left him there, lying beneath the table. I turned back in the doorway. I wanted to say something. I wanted to tell him that it was just the beginning.

"You can't bully me," he said softly. "I'm an expert. I've been bullied all my life."

———

Sitting in the same interview room, three years on, it's still not over. My cell phone is ringing.

The Professor sounds relieved. "Are you OK?"

"Yeah, but I need you to come and get me. They want to send me back to the hospital."

"Maybe it's a good idea."

"Are you going to help me or not?"

Shifts are changing at the station. The evening crews are coming on watch. Campbell is somewhere upstairs, shuffling paper or whatever else justifies his salary. Slipping along the corridor past the charge room, I reach a door to the rear parking lot. A blast of cold wind ushers me outside.

Gears on the electric gate grind into motion. Hiding in the shadows, I watch an ambulance pull through the opening. It's coming to pick me up. The gates are shutting again. At the last possible moment I step through the closing gap. Turning right, I follow the pavement and turn right twice more until I'm back on the Harrow Road. Slow lines of traffic puncture the darkness.

There's a pub called the Greyhound on the Harrow Road—a smoky, nicotine-stained place with a jukebox and a resident drunk in the corner. I take a table and a morphine capsule. By the time the Professor arrives I'm floating on a chemical cloud. The Greeks had a god called Morpheus—the god of dreams. Who said studying the classics was a waste of time?

Joe pokes his head through the door and looks around nervously. Maybe he's forgotten how authentic pubs used to look before the Continental café culture turned them into white-tiled waiting rooms serving overpriced cooking lager.

"Have you taken something?"

"My leg was hurting."

"How much are you taking?"

"Not enough."

He waits for a better explanation.

"I started on about two hundred milligrams but lately I've been popping them like Tic Tacs. The pain won't go away. I function better if I don't have to think about the pain."

"The pain?" He doesn't believe me. "You're a mess! You're jumpy and anxious. You're not eating or sleeping."

"I'm fine."

"You need help."

"No! I need to find Rachel Carlyle."

The statement is harsh and abrupt. Joe swallows some uneasy thoughts and drops the subject. Instead, I tell him about visiting Howard and arresting Aleksei Kuznet. He looks at me in disbelief.

"He wouldn't tell me about the ransom."

"What ransom?"

Joe doesn't know about the diamonds and I'm not going to tell him. It won't add to his understanding and I've already put Ali in danger. Nothing has become any clearer in the past few hours but at least I have a goal—to find Rachel.

"How did Aleksei find you?"

"I don't know. He didn't follow me from the hospital and nobody knew I was going to Wormwood Scrubs. Maybe someone called him from the prison."

I close my eyes and replay events. I'm totally flying but can still think straight. Snatches of conversation drift back to me.

"God is going to set me free." That's what Howard said.

If Howard sent the ransom demand why did he wait so long? He could have set up a hoax during his trial or at any stage since then. He would have needed help from the outside. Who?

The Home Office keeps a record of all visitors to Her Majesty's prisons. Howard's eldest sister visits him every few months, traveling down from Warrington and staying overnight at a local B & B. Apart from her there's only been Rachel.

In the first few months after his conviction he received bundles of fan mail. Many of the letters were from women who fell in love with his lonely countenance and his crime. One of them, Bettina Gallagher, a legal secretary from Cardiff, is a notorious pinup among the lifers. She sends pornographic photographs of herself and has twice been engaged to death row inmates in Alabama and Oklahoma.

Howard is allowed one free postage-paid letter a week but can buy more stationery and stamps from the prison shop. Each prisoner is also given a unique PIN number he must use when using the telephone. Pedophiles and child molesters can dial only approved numbers. Letters and calls are monitored.

These details rattle in the emptiness. I can't see Howard arranging a ransom drop—not from inside a prison cell.

"Give your eyes a chance," my stepfather used to say when we were looking for newborn lambs on frosty nights. White on white is difficult to see. Sometimes you have to look past things before you really see them.

There used to be a really good comedian who called himself Nosmo King. I watched this guy for years and didn't realize where the name came from. NO SMOKING. Nosmo King. That's why you have to keep your eyes open. The answer can be right in front of you.

The Professor has opened his briefcase and pulled out a photograph album. The cover is frayed and silverfish have given it a mottled finish along the spine. I recognize it from somewhere.

"I went to see your mother," he says.

"You did what!"

"I went to see her."

My teeth are clenched. "You had no right."

Ignoring me, he runs his fingers over the album cover. Here it comes—the search backward, the probing of my childhood, my family and my relationships. What does it prove? Nothing. How can another human being have any appreciation of my life and the things that shaped me?

"You don't want to talk about this."

"No."

"Why?"

"Because you're poking your nose into my business—you're screwing with my head."

It takes me a moment to realize that I'm shouting at him. Thankfully, there's nobody around except the barman and the sleeping drunk.

"She doesn't seem very happy in the nursing home."

"It's a fucking retirement village."

He opens the album. The first photograph is of my stepfather, John Francis Ruiz. A farmer's son from Lancashire, he's dressed in his RAF uniform, standing on the wing of a Lancaster bomber. Already losing his hair, his high forehead makes his eyes seem bigger and more alive.

I remember that photograph. For twenty years it stood on the mantelpiece beside a silver jubilee picture frame and one of those tacky snowballs of St. Paul's Cathedral.

John Ruiz went missing over Belgium on July 15, 1943, while on his way to bomb a bridge in Ghent. The Lancaster was hit by German fighters and exploded in midair, dropping like a fiery comet.

"Missing in action. Presumed dead," the telegram said. Only he wasn't dead. He survived a German POW camp and came home to discover that the "future" he had fought so hard to protect had run off and married an American catering corps sergeant and moved to Texas. Nobody blamed her, least of all him.

And then he met Sofia Eisner (or Germile Purrum), a "Jewish" seamstress with a newborn son. She was striding down the hill from Golders Green, between two young friends, their arms locked together, laughing.

"Don't forget now," shouted the eldest of them. "We're going to meet the men we're going to marry tonight."

At the cinema at the bottom of the hill they came across a group of young men waiting in the queue. One of them wore a single-breasted jacket with notched lapels and three buttons.

Germile whispered to her friends, "Which one's mine?"

John Ruiz smiled at her. A year later they were married.

Joe turns another page of the album. The sepia images seem to have soaked into the paper. There is a photograph of the farm—a plowman's cottage with small leadlight windows and doors so low my stepfather had to duck his head to get through them. My mother filled the rooms with bric-a-brac and souvenirs, managing to convince herself they were heirlooms of her vanished family.

Outside the plowed fields were milk-chocolate brown and smoke fluttered like a ragged white flag from the chimney. In late summer wheels of hay dotted the hillsides like spilled lozenges.

I can still smell the mornings sometimes—the burned toast, strong tea and the talcum powder my stepfather sprinkled between his toes before pulling on his socks. As he closed the door the dogs barking excitedly, dancing around his feet.

I learned all about life and death on the farm. I snipped the scrotums of newborn lambs and pulled out the testes with my teeth. I put my forearm deep in a mare, feeling for the dilation of the cervix. I killed calves for the freezer and buried dogs that were more like siblings than working animals.

There aren't any photographs of everyday workings on the farm. The album records only special occasions—weddings, births, christenings and anniversaries.

"Who's this?" Joe points to a picture of Luke, who is wearing a sailor's suit and sitting on the front stairs. His blond cowlick stands up like a flag fall on an old-fashioned taxicab meter.

The lump forming in my throat feels like a tumor. Covering my mouth with my fingers, I try to stop the alcohol and morphine from talking but words leak out through my open pores.

Luke was always small for his age but he compensated for it by being loud and annoying. Most of the time I was at boarding school so I only saw him during the holidays. Daj would tell me to keep an eye on him and at the same time she'd tell Luke to stop bugging me because he constantly wanted to play Old Maid and to look at my football cards.

In the depths of winter when it snowed I used to go tobogganing down Hill Field, starting off near the front door and finishing at the pond. Luke was too young so he rode on a toboggan with me. Several hillocks along the way would throw us in the air and he squealed with laughter, clinging to my knees.

The track leveled off toward the end and a mesh fence sagged between posts having been hit so many times by braced feet.

My stepfather had gone into town to get a thermostat for the boiler. Daj was trying to hand dye my bedsheets a darker color to hide the semen stains. I can't remember what I was doing. Isn't that strange? I can remember every other detail with the clarity of a home movie.

At bath time we noticed him missing. We used a spotlight powered by the tractor engine to search the pond but the hole in the ice had closed over.

I lay awake that night, trying to will Luke into being. I wanted him to be lying in his bed, snuffling in his sleep and twitching like a dog dreaming of fleas.

They found him in the morning beneath the ice. His face was blue, his lips bluer. He was wearing hand-me-down trousers and hand-me-down shoes.

I watched from my bedroom window as they laid him on a sheet and tucked another beneath his chin. The ambulance had mud-streaked arches and open doors. As they lifted the stretcher I went flying out of the front door, screaming at them to leave my brother alone. My stepfather caught me at the gate. He picked me up and hugged me so hard I could barely breathe. His face was gray and prickly. His eyes were blurred with tears.

"He's gone, Vince."

"I want him back."

"We've lost him."

"Let me see."

"Go back inside."

"Let me see."

His chin was pressing into my hair. Daj had fallen to her knees beside Luke. She screamed and rocked back and forth, rubbing her fingers through his hair and kissing his closed lids.

She would hate me now. I knew that. She would hate me forever. It was my fault. I should have been looking after him. I should have helped him count his football cards and played his childish games. Nobody ever blamed me; nobody except me. I knew the truth. It had been my fault. I was responsible.

"We lost him," my stepfather had said.

Lost? You lose something down the back of the sofa or through a hole in your pocket; you lose your train of thought or you lose track of time. You don't lose a child.

I wipe the wetness from my eyes and look at the Professor. I've been talking all this time. Why did he start me on this? What does he know about guilt? He doesn't have to look at it every day in the mirror or scrape whiskers off its soapy skin or see it reflected in his mother's eyes. I turned Daj into an alcoholic. She drank with the ghosts of her dead family and her dead son. She drank until her hands shook and her world smeared like lipstick on the edge of a glass. Alcoholics don't have relationships—they take hostages.

"Please leave this alone," I whisper, wanting him to stop.

Joe closes the photograph album. "Your memory loss was the result of psychological trauma."

"I was shot."

"The scans showed no injuries or bruising or internal bleeding. You didn't get a bump on the head. You didn't lose particular memories; you blocked them out. I want to know why."

"Luke died more than forty years ago."

"But you think about him every day. You still wonder if you could have saved him just like you wonder if you could have saved Mickey."

I don't answer. I want him to stop talking.

"It's like having a film inside your head, isn't it, eh? Playing on a continuous loop, over and over—"

"That's enough."

"You want to be riding down the icy hill with Luke sitting between your knees. You want to hold on tightly to him and drive your boots into the snow, making sure the toboggan stops in time—"

"Shut up! Just shut the fuck up!"

On my feet now, I'm standing over him. My finger is pointed between his eyes. The barman reaches behind the counter for a phone or a metal pipe.

Joe hasn't moved. Christ, he's cool. I can see my reflection—desolate and hollow—mirrored in his eyes. The anger leaks away. My cell phone is rattling on the table.

"Are you OK?" asks Ali. "I heard about what happened at the station."

Bile blocks my throat. I finally get the words out. "Have you found Rachel?"

"No, but I think I've found her car."

"Where?"

"Someone reported it abandoned. It was towed away from Haverstock Hill about a fortnight ago. Now it's at a car pound on Regis Road. You want me to check it out?"

"No, I'll go."

I look at my watch. It's nearly six. Car pounds stay open all night. It's not about the revenue, of course, it's about keeping the city moving. If you believe that I could sell you the Tower of London.

Finishing my beer, I grab my things. The Professor looks ready to wave me off.

"You're coming, too," I tell him. "You can drive, just keep your mouth shut."

12

Camden Car Pound looks like a World War II prison camp with razor wire on the fences and spotlights around the perimeter. It even has a wooden hut where a lone security guard has his polished boots propped on a desk with a small TV perched between his knees. I hammer on the window and his head snaps around. Swinging his feet to the floor, he hoists his trousers. He has a baby face and spiked hair. A nightstick in a leather pouch sways on his belt.

"My name is Detective Inspector Ruiz. You have a vehicle here that was towed from a street on Haverstock Hill two weeks ago."

His eyes flick up and down, sizing me up. "You here to collect it?"

"No. I'm here to inspect it."

He glances at the Professor, wondering why his left arm is trembling. What a pair we make—Hopalong Cassidy and Pegleg Pete.

"Nobody told me you was coming. I should have been told. You gonna pay the towing fee?"

"We're not taking the vehicle. We're just looking at it."

Something stirs behind him. An Alsatian uncurls and seems to self-inflate until it stands as high as the desk. The dog growls and the guard hisses a command.

"Don't mind him. He won't hurt you."

"You'll make sure of it."

There must be a hundred cars on the lot, each with a number and grid reference. It takes the guard several minutes to find the details of Rachel's Renault Estate.

The reference says the car was found on Lyndhurst Road with the keys in the ignition and the doors unlocked. Someone had stolen the stereo and one of the seats.

He directs us across the pound, which is divided into painted squares. Rachel's car is beaded with rain and the internal light doesn't work when I open the door. I reach inside and trigger it manually.

There is no front passenger seat. The space is empty except for a dark blanket bundled on the floor. Carefully lifting the blanket I find a bottle of water, chocolate bars and a hand-held periscope.

"Someone was meant to lie on the floor, out of sight," says Joe.

"Rachel must have delivered the ransom. Someone went with her."

We're both thinking the same thing—was it me? Campbell called me a vigilante. Aleksei said no police, which means there were no surveillance teams in cars, on motorbikes or in the air.

"If I were delivering a ransom, what would I make sure of?"

"Proof of life!" says Joe.

"Yes, but apart from that—when I was physically carrying the ransom, what would I be sure of?"

Joe shrugs. I answer for him. "Backup. I would have wanted someone following me, at least from a distance. And I would have made sure they didn't lose me."

"How?"

"A tracking device." I would have put one in the car and another with the ransom.

The universe suddenly shrinks to one thought. That's how Aleksei found me at the prison. And that's why Keebal wanted to search the house. One of the bundles of diamonds must have a transmitter.

Ali!

———

One ring, two rings, three rings . . .

"Pick up the phone. Pick it up now!" I wait several seconds. She's not answering.

I try her home number. Pick up the phone, Ali. Please.

"Hello." (Thank God.)

"What did you do with my coat?"

"It's here."

"Stay right there! Lock the door. Stay away from the windows."

"What's wrong?"

"Please, Ali, just do as I say. There's a tracking device with the diamonds. That's how Aleksei found me."

The traffic suddenly melts away. Joe has his foot down, weaving through backstreets, taking shortcuts across garage forecourts and parking lots. God knows where he learned to drive like this. He's either an expert or a complete amateur who's going to put us through a plate-glass window.

"What diamonds? What are you talking about?" he yells.

"Just shut up and drive."

Ali is still on the phone.

"I might be wrong about the transmitter," I tell her. "Just relax."

She's already ahead of me—ripping open the packages. I can hear her breaking open the blocks of foam. I know what she's going to find. Radio transmitters can weigh less than eighty grams and have a battery life of three, maybe four weeks. My kitchen floor was dusted with polystyrene foam and scraps of plastic. I hollowed out the foam with a knife.

"I found it."

"Disconnect the battery."

Joe is yelling at me. "You have Aleksei Kuznet's diamonds! Are you crazy?"

The car swerves suddenly into Albany Street and he brakes hard, pulling us around a line of traffic. He accelerates again and we leap over a speed bump.

Ali lives in a run-down, crumbling neighborhood in Hackney, on a narrow street of soot-blackened warehouses and barred shop windows. She's still on the phone.

"Where are you now?"

"Close. Are the lights turned off?"

"Yes."

In the background I hear a doorbell ringing.

"Are you expecting anyone?"

"No."

"Don't answer it."

Ten . . . twenty . . . thirty seconds pass. Then comes the sound of breaking glass.

"Someone just smashed a door panel," says Ali, her voice thick with fear. The burglar alarm is sounding.

"Are you armed?"

"Yes."

"Just give them the diamonds, Ali. Don't take any risks."

"Yes, Sir. I can't talk anymore. Hurry!"

The phone goes dead.

The next few minutes are the longest I can remember. Joe has his foot hard on the floor, braking around the corners and running red lights. Weaving onto the wrong side of the road, he accelerates past three buses and forces oncoming cars off the road.

Wrenching the wheel, he puts us into a half spin, sliding around a tight bend. I'm thrown against the door and the phone smacks my ear. I'm calling the police, telling them there's an officer in trouble.

"It's the next on the left . . . about halfway down."

There are terraced houses on either side of the road. The streetlights have turned everything yellow, including the pebble-dash façades and net curtains.

Ali's place is ahead of us. The burglar alarm is still ringing. The car brakes and I'm out of the door hobbling in a half run toward the house. Joe is yelling at me to slow down.

The front door gapes darkly. Pressing my back to the outside wall, I glance inside. I can see the hallway and the stairs to the upper floor. Sliding sideways, I move inside, letting my eyes get used to the darkness.

I have visited Ali's house once before. It was years ago. We sat outside on her roof garden, drinking beer and resting our feet on a skylight. Everything was painted gold by the sunset and I remember thinking that maybe London *was* the new Babylon after all. The thought disappeared in the darkness.

There's a living room just off the left and a dining room farther along the hall. The kitchen is at the rear. I can see moonlight coming through the window and no sign of a telltale silhouette.

The shrill alarm is shredding my senses. Running my fingers along the wall, I search for the control panel. The alarm will be linked to the main electric supply and have a backup twelve-volt battery with an anti-tamper switch.

Joe puts his hand on my shoulder and nearly gets flattened with a walking stick. Shouting to be heard, I tell him to go back outside, find the alarm bell and pull it off the wall.

"What with?"

"Use your imagination."

He disappears and I search the kitchen and sitting room. A streetlight is shining outside and I can see Joe crossing the road with a tire iron. Hoisting himself onto a brick wall, he takes a swing at the alarm bell. Twice more he hits the box and suddenly the alarm falls silent. The change is so dramatic it feels like the air pressure has dropped.

Climbing the stairs, I step onto the next landing. For all my opposition to firearms, I wish I had one now. My gun is somewhere at the bottom of the river or fenced on the black market.

Reaching the first door I pause and listen. I can only hear my heartbeat. Then, in the stillness, I pick up another sound, someone breathing. Pressing my ear against the door, I wait, trying to hear the sound again.

Weighing my walking stick, I reach for the door handle and push it open. The darkness is more intense than the dimness behind me.

Here, too, I wait.

I hear metal shaking . . . springs. It's a tremble born of dependency rather than fear. Reaching forward, I flick the light switch. Ali is perched on her bed, her MP5 A2 carbine pointing directly at my chest.

We gaze into each other's eyes. She blinks at me slowly and lets out a long slow breath. "You were lucky I didn't shoot you."

"I had it covered."

Pulling open my shirt, I show her the bulletproof vest.

The Professor slumps in a chair, his hands gripping the armrests. The last few minutes have drained his reserves. Ali pours him a glass of water. He takes it with his right hand—the steady one.

"Where did you learn to drive like that?"

"At Silverstone," he replies. "I won an advanced driving course at a school trivia night."

"Michael Schumacher eat your heart out."

Ali has barricaded the front door and is moving through the rooms, checking to see if anything is missing. Whoever broke in triggered the alarm and then fled.

"Did you see anyone?"

"No."

"Where are the diamonds?"

Ali opens a drawer. "I put them where a girl puts anything personal—with her underwear."

Four velvet pouches are tucked inside. She opens one of them and diamonds spill through her fingers onto the duvet. Sometimes when you see an excess of something rare and beautiful it begins to pale. Diamonds are different. They always take your breath away.

I can hear police sirens approaching. Ali goes downstairs to meet them. I don't expect there'll be fingerprints or physical evidence left behind but we'll go through the motions of making statements and dusting for prints. Joe still doesn't understand how the ransom ended up with Ali. I relate the whole story about the linen cupboard and the scraps of plastic on my kitchen floor.

I have to admire his sense of priorities. Instead of being frightened or angry, he sits on Ali's bed and studies the remnants of the packages, the bright orange plastic, white foam and electrical tape. The transmitter is the size of a matchbox with twin wires separated from a smaller battery unit.

"Why are they packed like this?"

"I think they were meant to float."

"So you took the diamonds to the river."

"I don't know. This type of transmitter sends out a signal every ten seconds and is picked up by a receiver. Unlike a satellite tracking device the transmitter has a limited range—about three miles in the city and six miles in the countryside."

"How accurate is it?"

"Down to within fifty yards."

If Rachel acted as the ransom courier and I went with her, I would have arranged for someone to follow us, tracking the signals. Aleksei had the most to gain. They were *his* diamonds and it was *his* daughter.

Joe weighs the transmitter in his hands. "But how did the ransom wind up in your cupboard? Something must have gone wrong."

"Tell me about it! I got shot."

"No, but think about it. You were in the hospital for two weeks. If Aleksei knew you had the diamonds, he could have taken them back at any time. Instead he waited."

"Perhaps he wanted someone else to find them first—like Keebal."

Almost immediately, I try to push the thought away. I'm not a believer in conspiracy theories and I have nothing against Keebal except the job he does—spying on his colleagues—but someone tipped him off about the diamonds. It must have been Aleksei. Are they working together or feeding off each other?

The Professor is still studying the packaging as if trying to re-create the dimensions.

"What do we do now?" asks Ali, returning upstairs.

"We take advantage of this." I toss her the transmitter.

She grins. We're both singing from the same song sheet. "Are you thinking Intercity Express?"

"Nah, it's too fast." I look at my watch. "The printing presses are just starting to run at Wapping. Some of those newspaper trucks drive all the way to Cornwall."

Bon voyage!

13

Condensation drips steadily down the dormer window creating rainbow patterns on the windowsill. What day is it? Thursday. No, it's Friday. Lying in bed, I listen to the delivery trucks, pneumatic drills and workmen shouting to each other. This is London's dawn chorus.

Against my better judgment I let Ali bring me here last night—to her parents' house in Millwall. We couldn't stay at her flat—not after what happened.

Ali's parents were both asleep when we arrived and exhaustion drove me to bed soon afterward. Ali showed me the spare room and left a fresh towel and cake of soap on the end of the bed like at some fancy B & B.

This must be Ali's old room. The shelves and tops of bookcases are crammed with elephants of all description, ranging from tiny blown-glass figurines to a large furry mammoth guarding the wooden chest at the end of the bed.

There's a light knock on the door. "I brought you a cup of tea," says Ali, pushing the door open with her hip. "I also have to change the dressing on your leg."

She's wearing a dressing gown with a frayed cord and an elephant sewn into the pocket. Her bare feet are out-turned slightly, which splays her knees and puts me in mind of a penguin, which is strange considering she moves so gracefully.

"How did you sleep?"

"Great."

She knows I'm lying. Sitting next to me, she sets out scissors, bandages and surgical tape. For the next fifteen minutes I watch her unwrapping and rewrapping my thigh.

"These stitches are nearly ready to come out."

"Where did you learn first aid?"

"I have four brothers."

"I thought most Indian lads were pretty peaceful."

"They don't *start* the fights."

She cuts off the last strip of tape and wraps it around my leg. "Does it hurt, today?"

"Not so much."

She wants to ask about the morphine but changes her mind. As she leans forward to retrieve the scissors, her dressing gown falls open and I glimpse her breasts beneath a T-shirt. The nipples are dark, sharp peaks. Immediately, I feel guilty and look away.

"So what are you going to do with the diamonds?" she asks.

"Hide them somewhere safe." I glance around the room. "You seem to like elephants."

She smiles self-consciously. "They bring good luck. That's why their trunks are raised."

"What about that one?" I point to the woolly mammoth, which has a lowered trunk.

"An ex-boyfriend gave that to me. He's also extinct."

She picks up the scraps of bandages and straightens a lace doily on the bedside table. "I had a call this morning about Rachel Carlyle." She pauses and my hopes soar. "She suffered some sort of nervous breakdown. A night watchman found her sitting in a stolen car on some wasteland in Kilburn."

"When was this?"

"On the morning you were pulled from the river. The police took her to the hospital—the Royal Free in Hampstead."

Rather than joy I feel relief. Up until now I have tried not to think of who might have been on the boat. The longer Rachel remained missing, the harder this had become.

"Was she interviewed?"

"No. The police didn't talk to her at all."

This is Campbell's doing. He won't investigate anything associated with Mickey Carlyle because he's frightened of where it might lead. It's not a cover-up if you don't lift the covers in the first place. Plausible deniability is a coward's defense.

"They searched Rachel's flat and found your messages on her answering machine. They also found a set of your clothes. They don't want you anywhere near her—not so close to Howard's appeal."

"Where is Rachel now?"

"She checked out ten days ago."

Someone close to Campbell must have told Ali these things, a detective who worked on the original investigation. It was probably "New Boy" Dave King, who has always fancied her. We call him "New Boy" because he was the newest member of the Serious Crime Group, but that was eight years ago.

"How is your boyfriend?"

She screws up her face. "That would be none of your business."

"He's a good lad, Dave. Very fit looking. I think he must work out."

She doesn't respond.

"He's not the sharpest quill on the porcupine but you could do a lot worse."

"He's not really for me, Sir."

"Why's that?"

"Well for one thing his legs are skinnier than mine. If he can *fit* into my pants he can't *get* into my pants."

She keeps a completely straight face for about fifteen seconds. Poor Dave. She's far too sharp for him.

Downstairs in the kitchen I meet Ali's mother. She's barely five feet tall, dressed in a bright green sari that makes her look like a bauble on a Christmas tree.

"Good morning, Inspector, welcome to our home. I trust you slept well." Her dark eyes seem to be smiling at me and her accent is incredibly proper as though I'm someone important. She doesn't even know me.

"Fine, thank you."

"I have prepared you breakfast."

"I normally eat breakfast closer to lunch."

Her look of disappointment makes me regret the statement. She doesn't seem bothered. She is already clearing the table from the first sitting. Some of Ali's brothers still live at home. Two of them run a garage in Mile End, one is an accountant and the other is at university.

A toilet flushes at the rear of the house and Ali's father appears moments later dressed in a British Rail uniform. He has a salt-and-pepper beard and a bright blue turban. Shaking my hand, he bows his head slightly.

"You are welcome, Inspector."

Ali appears, dressed in jeans and a sweatshirt. Her father swallows his disappointment.

"We're all British now, Babba," she says, kissing him on the forehead.

"Outside these walls, yes," he replies. "In this house you are still *my* daughter. It's bad enough that you cut your hair."

Ali is supposed to wear a sari when she visits her parents. I saw her once, looking self-consciously beautiful, wrapped in orange-and-green silk. She was on her way to a cousin's wedding. I felt strangely envious. Instead of being caught between two cultures she seemed to straddle them.

"Thank you for letting me stay like this," I say, trying to change the subject.

Mr. Barba rocks his head from side to side. "That's quite all right, Inspector. My daughter has explained everything . . ."

Somehow I doubt that.

"You are very welcome. Sit. Eat. I must apologize for leaving."

He takes a lunch box and thermos from the kitchen bench. Mrs. Barba walks him to the front door and kisses his cheek. Whistling steam billows from the kettle and Ali begins making a fresh pot of tea.

"You'll have to forgive my parents," she says. "And I should warn you about the questions."

"Questions?"

"My mother is very nosey."

A voice answers from the hallway. "I heard that."

"She also has ears like a bat," whispers Ali.

"I heard that, too." Mrs. Barba appears again. "I'm sure you don't talk to *your* mother like this, Inspector."

I feel a stab of guilt. "She's in a retirement home."

"And I'm sure it's very nice."

Does that mean expensive?

Mrs. Barba puts her arms around Ali's waist. "My daughter thinks I spy on her just because I come to clean her house once a week."

"I don't need you to clean."

"Oh, yes! And if you are Queen and I am Queen, who is to fetch the water?"

Ali rolls her eyes. Mrs. Barba directs a question at me. "Do you have any children, Inspector?"

"Two."

"You're divorced, aren't you?"

"Twice. I'm trying for third time lucky."

"That is sad for you. Do you miss your wife?"

"Yes, but my aim is improving."

The joke doesn't make her smile. She puts a fresh cup of tea in front of me. "Why didn't your marriage work out?"

Ali looks horrified. "You don't ask questions like that, Mama!"

"That's all right," I say. "I don't really know the answer."

"Why not? My daughter says you are very clever."

"Not in matters of the heart."

"It's not hard to love a wife."

"I could love one, I just couldn't hold on to her."

Without realizing how it happens, I'm telling her how my first wife, Laura, died of breast cancer at thirty-eight and my second wife, Jessie, left me when she realized that marriage wasn't just for the weekend. Now she's in Argentina filming a documentary about polo players and most likely shagging one of them. And my current wife, Miranda, packed her bags because I spent more time in the office than I did at home. It sounds like a soap opera.

Mrs. Barba picks up on the melancholy note in my voice when I talk about Laura, who should have been my childhood sweetheart because then I would have known her longer than fifteen years. We deserved more. *She* deserved more.

One thing leads to another and soon I'm telling her about the twins—

how Claire is dancing in New York and every time I see her disfigured toes I feel like arresting everyone at the New York City Ballet; and the last I heard from Michael he was crewing on charter yachts in the Caribbean.

"You don't see much of them."

"No."

She shakes her head and I wait for a lecture on parental responsibility. Instead, she pours another cup of tea and begins talking about her children and her faith. She doesn't see any difference between races or genders or religions. Humanity is all the same except in some countries where life is held more lightly and hatred gets a hearing.

Ali apologizes again for her mother when we get outside.

"I thought she was very nice."

"She drives me crazy."

"Wanna swap?"

We have changed vehicles since yesterday. Ali has borrowed a car from one of her brothers. I know it is part of her training—never using the same vehicle or driving the same route two days in a row. People spend years learning this stuff. I wonder what happens to them afterward. Are they frightened of the world just like Mickey Carlyle?

Edging through the traffic, north along the Edgware Road, I feel a sense of expectation. The uncertainty could end today. Once I find Rachel she'll tell me what happened. I might not *remember* but I'll know.

We cross a railway bridge and turn right into an industrial area, full of car-repair shops, wrecker yards, spray painters and engineering workshops. Pigeons pick at the trash behind a café.

The road runs out and we pull up on a patch of wasteland littered with rusting drums, broken chimney pots, fence posts and scaffolding. An abandoned freezer, pockmarked by stones, rises above the weeds.

"This is where they found Rachel. She was sitting in the passenger seat of a stolen car," says Ali, studying an ordinance survey map on her lap. "The car was reported missing the previous evening from a multi-story parking garage in Soho."

The skies have cleared and the sun is shining strongly, reflecting off the puddles. Climbing out of the car, I walk toward the freezer, moving gingerly across the broken ground. The nearest factory or warehouse is fifty yards away. London is littered with sites like this one. People imagine high-density living with every spare foot being utilized, but there are thousands of empty warehouses, vacant blocks and patches of waste ground.

I don't know what I expected to find. Answers. Witnesses. Something familiar. Everybody leaves a trail. The ridiculous thing is, I can't look at a vacant lot without thinking what crops might grow there. I'm in the middle of a vast city and I'm thinking about barley and rapeseed.

"Why can't I remember any of this?"

"You might never have been here," says Ali. "Rachel abandoned her car three miles from here."

"I would have followed her."

"How?"

"I don't know."

Finding the smoothest path through the weeds and rubble, she moves ahead of me until we reach a wire fence. Beyond are railway tracks—the Bakerloo line. The ground trembles as a train rattles past.

Turning left at the fence, we come to a pedestrian footbridge over the tracks. The platforms of Kilburn Station are partially visible to the north. The dual tracks have weeds growing at the edges and rubbish has collected in the ditches.

It's a good location to drop a ransom. Quiet. The factories and warehouses would have been empty at night. There are major roads leading north and south. The railway line runs east-west. Ten minutes traveling in any direction would put someone miles away.

"I need you to get hold of the incident logs from the local police stations," I tell Ali. "I want to know everything that happened that night within a two-mile radius—burglaries, assaults, parking tickets, broken streetlights, whatever you can find."

"What are you looking for?"

"I'll tell you when I find it."

• • •

The Royal Free Hospital in Hampstead is less than half a mile from where Rachel's car was abandoned and three miles from where she was found. Ali waits outside while I go through the main doors.

The receptionist is in her fifties with reddish-brown hair pinned tightly to her skull. She might be a nurse but it's hard to tell without a uniform.

"I'm Detective Inspector Ruiz. I need some information about a woman who was treated here two weeks ago." I notice her name tag and add, "Thank you very much, Joanne."

She straightens and touches her hair.

"Her name is Rachel Carlyle. She was brought in by the police."

Joanne is leaning on her elbows, looking at me.

"Perhaps you should check on the computer," I suggest.

Blushing slightly, she turns to the keyboard. "I'm afraid Miss Carlyle is no longer a patient."

"Why was she admitted?"

"I'm afraid I can't give you that sort of information."

"What day did she check out?"

"Let me see . . . September 29."

"Do you know where she went?"

"Well, there is an address . . . I'm not sure . . ."

I know what she's going to say. She's going to ask for some official identification or a letter of authority. I no longer have a badge.

Then I notice her staring at my hands, in particular my Gypsy ring. It's fourteen-karat yellow gold, mounted with a champagne colored diamond. According to Daj it belonged to my grandfather, although I don't know how she knows this or how she managed to recover it from Auschwitz.

People are superstitious about Gypsies. My mother used to play on it. At school fetes and local fairs she would set down her cloth-covered table and shuffle the tarot cards, telling fortunes at a few quid a time. Private readings were conducted in the cottage parlor, with the curtains drawn and incense stinking the air.

"The dead come back through children," Daj would say. "They steal their souls."

None of this crap about Gypsy curses and fortune-telling impressed me but sometimes when I interview a suspect, I notice them grow suddenly anxious when they see my ring. They look just like Joanne does now.

Her eyes move to my left hand—the one missing a finger.

"A bullet did that," I say, holding it up for her. "Sometimes I think the finger is still there. It itches. You were going to give me the address."

She shudders slightly. "I think her father might have signed her out. Sir Douglas Carlyle."

"Don't bother about the address. I know where he lives."

Sir Douglas Carlyle is a retired banker and a descendant of Robert the Bruce, King of Scotland. I interviewed him during the original investigation and he didn't seem to like me very much. Then again, he didn't have much time for Rachel either. The two of them hadn't spoken in eleven years—ever since she dropped out of university, embraced the politics of the left, and disowned him for being rich and titled.

Rachel did everything she could to provoke him, working part-time for homeless shelters, housing cooperatives and environmental groups, saving the world one tree at a time. However, the real sword in her father's side was marrying Aleksei Kuznet, a foreigner and a flower seller.

The thing that struck me about Sir Douglas was his equanimity and patience. He remained convinced that one day Rachel would come back to him. Now it seems he may have been right.

Parking out front of the large house in Henley, I self-consciously check my appearance in the side mirror. Titled people make me feel uncomfortable. I could never be a class warrior. A large white fountain dominates the garden, surrounded by paths that radiate between flower beds and angular patches of lawn.

I can hear laughter coming from outside and the gentle *thwack* of ball on racquet. There are wild cries of exultation and breathless moans of despair. Either someone is playing tennis or it's the soundtrack to a sixties blue movie.

The tennis court at the side of the house is hidden behind fences draped with ivy. We follow a path and emerge at a pagoda beside the courts, where trays of cold drinks have been set out on the table. Two couples are on court. The men are my age, sporting expensive suntans and muscled forearms. The women are younger and prettier, wearing miniskirts and midriff tops that show off their flat stomachs.

Sir Douglas is about to serve. With his aggressive countenance and eagle nose, he makes a social game look serious.

"Can I help you?" he asks, irritated by the interruption. Then he recognizes me.

"I am sorry to trouble you, Sir Douglas, I am looking for Rachel."

Angrily, he slams the ball into the side fence. "I really can't be dealing with this now."

"It's important."

He troops off the court with his playing partner, who brushes past me as she reaches for a zip-up jacket to stay warm. She towels her face and neck. It's a very long neck. I read about Sir Douglas's divorce from Rachel's mother.

"This is Charlotte," he says.

She beams. "You can call me Tottie. Everyone does. I've been Tottie forever."

I can see that.

Sir Douglas waves to the far end of the court. "And those are friends of ours." He shouts to them: "Why don't you go and get ready for lunch? We'll meet you inside."

The couple wave back.

Sir Douglas looks even fitter than I remember, with one of those deep suntans you see on sailing types and Australians. You could cut off his arm and the tan would go all the way through.

"Is Rachel here?"

"What makes you think that?" He's testing me.

"You collected her from the hospital ten days ago."

He plays an imaginary backhand. "I don't know if you recall, Inspector, but my daughter has never liked me very much. She thinks the Establishment is some sort of criminal society like the Mafia and that I am the Godfather. She doesn't believe in titles or privilege or the education that I paid for. She thinks there is only dignity in being poor and has swallowed the popular mythology of the working class being full of decent hardworking people possessed of piety and common sense. Breeding, however, is a curse."

"Where is she?"

He drinks from a glass of lemonade and looks at Tottie. Why do I get the impression I'm about to be fed a plate of bullshit?

"Perhaps you should go inside sweetheart," he says. "Tell Thomas he can clear these things away."

Thomas is the butler.

Tottie stands and stretches her long legs. She pecks him on the cheek. "Don't let it upset you, dear."

Sir Douglas motions us to the chairs, holding one for Ali.

"Do you know the hardest thing about being a father, Inspector? Trying to help your children *not* make the same mistakes as we did. You want to guide them. You want them to make certain decisions, marry certain people, believe certain things, but you can't make them go that way. They make their own decisions. My daughter chose to marry a gangster and a psychopath. She did it partly to punish me, I know that. I knew what sort of man Aleksei Kuznet was. It was bred into him. Like father, like son."

Sir Douglas slaps his racquet through the air again. "Oddly enough, I actually felt sorry for Aleksei. Only an innocent millionaire would have satisfied Rachel—and short of winning the lottery or finding buried treasure in one's back garden, there's no such thing."

I don't know where he's going with this but I try to keep the desperation out of my voice. "Just tell me where Rachel is."

He ignores the statement. "I have always felt sorry for those people who choose not to have children. They miss out on what it means to be human, to feel love in all its forms." His eyes have misted over. "I wasn't a very consistent father and I wasn't objective. I wanted Rachel to make me proud of her instead of realizing that I should *always* be proud of her."

"How is she?"

"Recovering."

"I need to speak to her."

"I'm afraid that won't be possible."

"You don't understand . . . there was a ransom demand. Rachel believed that Mickey was still alive. We both did. I need to find out why."

"Is this an official investigation, Detective?"

"There must have been proof. There must have been some evidence to convince us."

"I had a phone call from Chief Superintendent Smith. I don't know him well but he seems quite an impressive man. He alerted me to the fact that you might try to contact Rachel."

He is no longer looking at me. He could be talking to the trees for all I know. "My daughter has suffered a breakdown. Some very callous and cruel people took advantage of her grief. She has barely said a word since the police found her."

"I need her help—"

He raises his hand to stop me. "We have medical advice. She can't be upset."

"People have died. A serious crime has been committed—"

"Yes, it has. But now something good has happened. My daughter has come home and I'm going to protect her. I'm going to make sure nobody hurts her again."

He's serious. His eyes have a gleam of pure, unadulterated, idiotic determination. The whole conversation has had a ritualistic quality. I even expect him to say, "Maybe next time," as though nothing would be simpler or more obvious than coming back another day.

Warm, melting undulations of fear ripple through me. I can't leave without talking to Rachel; too much is at stake.

"Does Rachel know that before Mickey disappeared you applied for custody of your granddaughter?"

He flinches now. "My daughter was an alcoholic, Inspector. We were concerned for Michaela. At one point Rachel fell in the bathroom and my granddaughter spent the night lying next to her on the floor."

"How did you find out about that?"

He doesn't answer.

"You were spying on her."

Again he doesn't respond. I've known about the custody application from the start. If Howard hadn't emerged as such a strong suspect I would have investigated it further and confronted Sir Douglas.

"How far would you have gone to protect Mickey?"

Angry now, he exclaims, "I didn't kidnap my granddaughter, if that's what you're suggesting. I wish I had—maybe then she would still be alive. Whatever happened in the past has been forgiven. My daughter has come home."

He stands now. The conversation is over.

On my feet, I swing toward the house. He tries to intercept me but I brush him aside and begin yelling.

"RACHEL!"

"You can't do this! I demand you leave!"

"RACHEL!"

"Leave my property this instant."

Ali tries to stop me. "Perhaps we should leave, Sir."

Sir Douglas tackles me in front of the conservatory. With his tanned forearms and sinewy legs, he's surprisingly strong.

"Let it go, Sir," says Ali, taking hold of my arms.

"I have to see Rachel."

"Not this way."

At that moment Thomas appears, wearing an apron over a pressed white shirt. He's carrying a silver candlestick like a club.

Suddenly the whole scene registers as being vaguely ridiculous. In Clue there is a candlestick among the possible murder weapons but, surprisingly, not a butler among the suspects. Blaming the staff is just another lousy cliché.

Thomas is standing over me now, while Sir Douglas brushes mud and grass clippings from his shorts. Ali takes my arm and helps me up, steering me toward the path.

Sir Douglas is already on the phone, no doubt complaining to Campbell. Turning, I shout, "What if you're making a mistake? What if Mickey is still alive?"

Only the birds answer back.

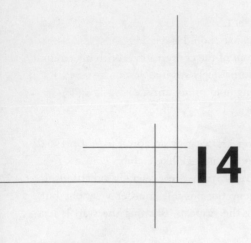

14

Fumbling in my pocket, I take out a morphine capsule and swallow it dry, feeling it catch in my throat. Twenty minutes later I'm peering through pale translucent gauze. The car seems to float between the red lights and people drift along the pavements like leaves on a river.

A conga line of buses comes to a stuttering halt. My stepfather died at a bus stop in Bradford in October 1995. He had a stroke on his way to see a heart specialist. See what happens when buses don't run on time? He looked very distinguished in his coffin, like a lawyer or a businessman rather than a farmer. His remaining hair was plastered across his scalp and parted exactly in a manner he never managed in life. I copied it for a while. I thought it made me look more English.

Daj came to live in London after the funeral. She moved in with me and Miranda. The two of them were like oil and vinegar. Daj was the vinegar of course: balsamic—strong and dark. No matter how they were mixed together, they always separated and I was caught in between.

On the pavement, beneath a canvas awning, a young flower seller is enclosed by buckets of blooms. Tugging at the sleeves of her jumper, she covers her fists and hugs herself to keep warm. Aleksei employs a lot of refugees and immigrants on his flower stalls because they're cheap and grateful. I wonder what this girl dreams about when she goes to sleep at night in her bedsit hotel or shared house. Does she see herself as being blessed?

Tens of thousands of Eastern Europeans have washed up here from former Soviet satellite states that have declared themselves independent and then immediately begun to crumble. Sometimes it seems as if the whole of Europe is destined to tear itself apart, divided into smaller and smaller parcels until there isn't enough land left to sustain a language or a culture. Maybe we're all destined to become Gypsies.

Fury and fear are driving me. Fury at being shot and fear of not finding out why. I want to either remember or forget. I can't live in the middle. Either give me back the missing days or erase them completely.

Ali senses my despair. "Facts not memories solve cases. That's what you said. We just have to keep investigating."

She doesn't understand. Rachel had the answers. She was going to tell me what happened.

"He was never going to let you see her. We have to find another way."

"If I could get a message to her . . ."

Suddenly, the curious, chemical detachment lifts and a face floats into my thoughts—a woman with dark-brown hair and a birthmark that leaks across her throat like spilled caramel. Kirsten Fitzroy—Rachel's best friend and former neighbor.

Some women have a particular gaze from the day they are born. They look at you as though they know exactly what you're thinking and will always know. Kirsten was like that. In the days after Mickey disappeared she was the rock that Rachel clung to, shielding her from the media and making her meals.

Kirsten could get a message to her. She could find out what happened. I know she lives somewhere in Notting Hill.

"I can get the address," says Ali, pulling off the road. She punches speed dial on her cell phone, no doubt calling "New Boy" Dave.

Twenty minutes later we pull up outside a large whitewashed Georgian house in Ladbroke Square, overlooking the communal gardens. The surrounding streets are painted in candy colors and dotted with coffee shops and outdoor restaurants. Kirsten has moved up in the world.

Her flat is on the third floor, facing the street. I pause on the landing to get my breath back. That's when I notice the door is slightly ajar. Ali peers up and down the stairwell, automatically on edge.

Nudging the door open, I call Kirsten's name. No answer.

The lock has almost been torn off and splinters of wood lie inside the door. Farther along the hallway there are papers and clothes strewn haphazardly on the sea-grass matting.

Ali unclips her holster and motions for me to stay put. I shake my head. It's easier if I cover her back. She spins through the door and crouches, peering down the hallway to the kitchen. I enter behind her, facing in the opposite direction into the sitting room. Furniture is overturned and someone has filleted the sofa with a samurai sword. The stuffing spills out like the bloated intestines of a slain beast.

Rice-paper lampshades lie torn and crushed on the floor. Floating flowers are marooned in a dry bowl and a shoji screen is smashed into pieces.

Moving from room to room, we discover more wreckage. Foodstuffs, appliances and utensils litter the kitchen floor between upturned drawers and open cupboards. A chair lies broken. Someone has used it to search above the cabinets.

At first glance it looks more like an act of vandalism than a robbery. Then I notice several envelopes lying amid the destruction. The return addresses have been carefully torn off. There is no diary or address book beside the telephone. Someone has also cleared the corkboard of notes and photographs. Torn corners are all that remain, trapped beneath colored pins.

The morphine has left me with a sense of depleted reality. I go into the bathroom and splash water on my face. A towel and chemise are folded over the towel rail and a lipstick has fallen into the bath. Retrieving it, I unscrew the lid and stare at the pointed nub, holding it like a crayon.

Above the washbasin, tilted slightly downward, is a rectangular mirror with mother-of-pearl inlaid into the frame. I've lost weight. My cheeks are hollow and my eyes are deeply wrinkled at the edges. Or maybe it's someone else in the mirror. I have been replicated and imprisoned in a slightly different universe. The real world is on the other side of the glass. Already I can feel the opiate wearing off. I want to hold on to the unreality.

Returning the lipstick to a shelf, I marvel at the salves, pastes, powders and potpourri. From among them I can summon up Kirsten's fragrance and our first meeting at Dolphin Mansions the day after Mickey disappeared.

Tall and slim with tapered limbs, Kirsten's cream-colored slacks hung so low on her hips that I wondered what was holding them up. Her flat was full of antique armor and weaponry, including two samurai swords crossed on the wall and a Japanese warrior's helmet made from iron, leather and silk.

"They say it was worn by Toyotomi Hideyoshi," Kirsten explained. "He was the *daimyo* who unified Japan in the sixteenth century: the 'Age of Battles.' Are you interested in history, Detective Inspector?"

"No."

"So you don't believe we can learn from our mistakes?"

"We haven't so far."

She acknowledged my opinion without agreeing with it. Ali was moving through the flat, admiring the artifacts.

"What did you say you did?" she asked Kirsten.

"I didn't." Her eyes were smiling at the edges. "I manage an employment agency in Soho. We provide cooks, waitresses, hostesses, that sort of thing."

"Business must be good."

"I work hard."

Kirsten prepared us tea in a hand-painted Japanese teapot and ceramic bowls. We had to kneel at a table while she dipped a ladle into simmering water and beat the powdered tea like scrambled eggs. I didn't understand the elaborate ceremony. Ali seemed more in tune with the idea of meditation and "the One Mind."

Kirsten had lived at Dolphin Mansions for three years, moving in just a few weeks after Rachel and Mickey. She and Rachel became friends. Coffee buddies. They shopped together and borrowed each other's clothes. Yet apparently Rachel didn't confide in Kirsten about Aleksei or her famous family. It was one secret too far.

"Who would have thought . . . talk about Beauty and the Beast," Kirsten told me, when she learned the news. "All that money and she's living here."

"What would you have done?"

"I would have taken my share and gone to live in Patagonia—as far away as possible—and slept with a gun under my pillow for the rest of my life."

"You have a vivid imagination."

"Like I said, I've heard the stories about Aleksei. Everyone's got one, right? It's like the one about him playing blackjack in Las Vegas and this Californian dot-com millionaire comes over and tells him that he's sitting in his chair. Aleksei ignores him, so the Californian says, 'Listen, you limey faggot, I'm worth sixty million dollars and this is my goddamn chair.' So Aleksei takes a coin out of his pocket and says, 'Sixty million? I'll toss you for it.' "

She didn't expect anyone to laugh. Instead she let the silence stretch out. I wish my legs could have done the same.

She had an alibi for when Mickey disappeared. The caretaker, Ray Murphy, was fixing her shower. It had only taken him three attempts, she said.

"What did you do afterward?"

"I went back to sleep." She looked at me quizzically and then added: "Alone."

Twenty years ago I would have said she was flirting, but I knew she was making fun of me. Being older and wiser doesn't help the ego. Youth and beauty rule the world.

Returning to the sitting room, I find Ali going through the contents of the toppled bookcase. Whoever did this opened every book, box file and photograph album. Diaries, address books, computer disks and photographs were taken. This wasn't a robbery, it was a search. They were looking for Kirsten. They wanted the names of friends and contacts—anyone who might know her.

"We should call this in, Sir."

"Yes."

"What do you want me to say?"

"Tell them the truth. We found a break-in."

We wait downstairs for the uniforms to arrive, sitting on the front steps and going over possible scenarios. Misty rain has started falling. It settles on Ali's hair and the weave of her coat.

Across the road a handful of muddy boys spill from a Range Rover with football boots hanging from laces and socks pushed down around their ankles.

Farther along the street, someone is waiting in a car. I wouldn't have noticed except for the flare of a cigarette lighter. It crosses my mind that Keebal has had me followed but almost immediately I consider another explanation. Maybe someone is waiting for Kirsten to come home.

I step out onto the pavement and stretch. The sun is trying to break through but keeps getting swallowed by fat putty-gray clouds. I begin to walk around the square. At first I'm heading away from the suspicious car but at the corner I turn and cross the street. I pause to read the plaque beneath a statue of a bronze horseman.

I turn again and set off. A pigeon takes flight in an awkward flurry. I'm walking toward the car now. I can just make out the silhouette of someone at the wheel.

I stay close to the gutter, keeping the line of vehicles between us. At the last possible moment I step alongside the Audi. Resting on the passenger seat is a photograph of Kirsten Fitzroy.

A burly, gray-haired man, gapes at me dumbfounded. I can see two bloated versions of myself in his sunglasses. I try to open the door. He reaches for the ignition and I yell at him to stop.

At that moment Ali arrives, slewing her car across the road to block his getaway. Finding reverse, he plants his foot and rubber shrieks on pavement. He slams into the car behind and then lurches forward, pushing the cars apart. Tires screech and smoke as he fires into reverse again.

Ali is out of the door with a hand on her holster. The driver sees her first. He raises a pistol, aiming at her chest.

Instinctively, I smash my walking stick across the windshield, where it explodes into shards of lacquered wood. The sound is enough to make him hesitate. Ali drops and rolls into the gutter. I spin the other way, falling fast and nowhere near as gracefully.

In the adjacent house, barely eighteen feet away, the door opens.

Two teenage girls appear, one of them pushing a bicycle. The pistol swings toward them.

I yell a warning, but they stop and stare. He won't miss from this range.

I glance across at Ali. She has her feet planted and arms outstretched, with the Glock in her right hand and her left hand cupped underneath.

"I can take him, Sir."

"Let him go."

She drops her arms between her thighs. The driver accelerates backward along the road, doing a handbrake turn at the end of the square, before swinging north into Ladbroke Grove.

Ali sits next to me in the gutter. The air stinks of burning clutch and rubber. The teenage girls have gone but curtains have opened and anxious faces are pressed to windows.

Ali wipes a smudge of gun oil from her fingers. "I could have taken him."

"I know."

"Why?"

"Because when they teach you how to shoot people, they don't teach you how to live with it."

She nods and a puff of breeze pushes hair across her eyes. She brushes it away.

"Did you recognize him?"

I shake my head. "He was waiting for Kirsten. Someone wants her very badly."

A Panda car rounds the corner and cruises slowly up the street. Two kids in uniform peer from side to side, looking for house numbers. Five minutes earlier they would have shat themselves or been shot. Thank heavens for small mercies.

Interviews must be conducted and statements taken. Ali fields most of the questions, giving a description of the car and driver. According to the computer the license plates belong to a builder's van in Newcastle. Someone has either stolen or copied them.

Under normal circumstances, the local CID would label the whole incident as road rage or call it a fail-to-stop accident. By normal circumstances, I mean if ordinary members of the public were involved instead of two police officers.

The Detective Sergeant, Mike Drury, is one of the young Turks from Paddington Green, who cut his teeth interviewing IRA and now Al Qaeda suspects. He looks up and down the street burying both hands in his pockets. His long nose sniffs the air as though he doesn't like the smell of it.

"So tell me again, why did you want to see Kirsten Fitzroy?"

"I'm trying to find a friend of hers—Rachel Carlyle."

"And why do you want to see her?"

"To catch up on old times."

He waits for something more. I'm not budging.

"Did you have a warrant?"

"I didn't need one. Her door was open when we arrived."

"And you went inside?"

"To make sure there wasn't a crime in progress. Miss Fitzroy might have been hurt. There was probable cause."

I don't like the tone of his questions. This is more like an interrogation than an interview.

Drury scribbles something in his notebook. "So you reported the break-in and then noticed the guy in the car."

"He seemed out of place."

"Out of place?"

"Yes."

"When you approached him, did you show him your badge?"

"No. I don't have my badge with me."

"Did you announce yourself as a police officer?"

"No."

"What *did* you do?"

"I tried to open the passenger door."

"So this guy was just sitting in a car, minding his own business, and you appeared from nowhere and tried to break into his car?"

"It wasn't like that."

Drury is playing devil's advocate. "He didn't know you were police officers. You must have scared the shit out of him. No wonder he took off—"

"He had a gun. He pointed it at my partner."

"Partner? I was under the impression that DC Barba worked for the Diplomatic Protection Group and is currently on holiday leave . . ." He consults his notebook. "And according to my information, you were suspended from all duties yesterday and are now the subject of an investigation by the Independent Police Complaints Commission."

I'm getting pretty pissed off with this guy. It's not just him—it's the whole attitude. Forty-three years on the force and I'm being treated as if I'm Charles Bronson making *Death Wish XV*.

In the old days there would have been sixty officers crawling all over this place—searching for the car, interviewing witnesses. Instead, I have to put up with this crap. Maybe Campbell's right and I should have retired three years ago. Everything I do nowadays is either against the rules or treading on someone's toes. Well, contrary to popular opinion, I haven't lost my edge. I'm still smarter than most scrotes and a damn sight cleverer than this prick.

"Ali can answer the rest of your questions. I have better things to do."

"You'll have to wait. I haven't finished," says Drury.

"Are you carrying a gun, DS?"

"No."

"What about handcuffs?"

"No."

"Well, if you can't shoot me and you can't shackle me—you can't keep me here."

15

The Professor lives in Primrose Hill, at the poor end of a leafy street where every house is worth seven figures and every car is covered in bird shit. The perverse symmetry appeals to me.

Joe answers the door on the second ring, dressed in corduroy trousers and an open-neck shirt.

"You look awful."

"Tell me about it! People keep wanting to shoot me."

Julianne appears behind him, looking like a woman plucked off a film poster. High cheekbones, blue eyes, perfect skin . . . In a soft voice, she announces, "You look terrible."

"So everyone keeps telling me."

She kisses me on the cheek and I follow her down the hall toward the kitchen. A toddler sits in a high chair, holding a spoon. Pureed apple is stuck to her cheeks and forehead. Charlie, aged eleven, is home from school and in charge of feeding.

"I'm sorry," I whisper to Julianne, suddenly embarrassed to barge in. "I didn't realize . . . you're all here."

"Yes, we have children remember?"

Joe wants to ask me what happened but he holds off for the sake of Charlie, who has a fascination with police stories—the more gruesome the better.

"Have you arrested anyone today?" she asks me.

"Why? Have you done something wrong?"

She looks horrified. "*No!*"

"Keep it that way."

Julianne hands me coffee. She notices my missing finger. "I guess it's official then—you're not the marrying kind."

Charlie is equally fascinated, leaning closer to examine the blunt stump where pink skin has puckered at the join.

"What happened?"

"I ate a hamburger too quickly."

"That's gross."

"I didn't taste a thing."

Julianne admonishes me. "Shush, you'll give her nightmares. Come on, Charlie, you have homework."

"But it's Friday. You said you'd take me shopping for new boots."

"We'll go tomorrow."

Her spirits soar. "Can I get heels?"

"Only if they're this high." She holds her thumb and forefinger an inch apart.

"Sick."

Charlie lifts the baby onto her hip, dips her head and tosses the bangs out of her eyes. Christ she looks like her mother!

Joe suggests we go to his study. I follow him up the stairs into a small room, overlooking the garden. A desk takes up most of the available space, squeezed between bookshelves and a filing cabinet. To the right on the wall is a corkboard, covered in notes, postcards and family photographs.

This is Joe's bolt-hole. If I lived with three women I'd want one, too, although mine would come with a bar fridge and a TV.

Joe scoops files off a chair and tidies his desk. I get the impression he's not so organized anymore. Maybe it's the Parkinson's.

"You've stopped using the walking stick," he observes.

"I broke it."

"I can lend you another one."

"That's OK. My leg is getting stronger."

For the next hour we pick over the wreckage of my day. I tell him about Sir Douglas and the attack outside Kirsten's flat. His face gives nothing away. It's like a blank page on one of his notepads. He once told me about something called a Parkinson's mask. Maybe this is it.

Joe begins drawing lines on the pad. "I've been thinking about the ransom."

"And what did you come up with?"

"There must have been an initial letter or an e-mail or a phone call. You mentioned DNA tests."

"On strands of hair."

"That first contact must have come as a tremendous shock. We have a dead girl, a man in prison for her murder, then suddenly a ransom demand arrives. What did you think?"

"I can't remember."

"But you can imagine. You can put yourself in the same position. What are you going to think when the ransom letter arrives?"

"It's a hoax."

"You've *never* been convinced of Howard's guilt."

"It still smells like a hoax."

"What would change your mind?"

"Proof of life."

"The letter contains strands of hair."

"I have it tested."

"What else?"

"I have everything analyzed—the ink, the handwriting, the paper—"

"Who does that?"

"The Forensic Science Service."

"But your boss refuses to believe you? He tells you to leave the case alone."

"He's wrong!"

"Nobody believes the letter except you and the girl's mother. Why do you believe?"

"It can't just be the hair. I need more proof."

"Like what?"

"A photograph or better still a video. And it has to include something time sensitive like the front page of a newspaper."

"Anything else?"

"Blood or skin tissue—something that can't be three years old."

"If there's no such proof, do you still go ahead with the ransom drop?"

"I don't know. It's too far-fetched."

"Maybe you want to catch the hoaxers."

"I wouldn't put Rachel in danger for that."

"So you must believe it."

"Yes."

"None of your colleagues agree with you. Why?"

"Perhaps the proof of life isn't conclusive."

Joe has turned his chair slightly away from me, so his gaze fixes me off center. Whenever I pause or falter, he finds a new question. It's like painting by numbers, working inward from the edges.

"Why would someone wait three years to post a ransom demand?"

"Maybe they didn't kidnap her for ransom—not at first."

"Why kidnap her then?"

I'm struggling now. According to Rachel, until Mickey disappeared nobody in England knew that Aleksei was her father. Sir Douglas Carlyle obviously did, but if he kidnapped Mickey he's hardly likely to send a ransom demand.

"So someone else took Mickey and we go back to the same question: Why wait three years?" says Joe.

Again, I don't know the answer. I'm guessing. "Either they didn't have her or they wanted to keep her."

"Why give her up now?"

I see where he's going now. The ransom makes no sense. What do I really imagine: that Mickey has been chained to a radiator for the past three years? It's not credible. She isn't sitting in a waiting room, rocking her legs beneath a chair, expecting to be rescued.

Joe is still talking. "There's another issue. If Mickey is still alive, we have to consider whether she wants to come home. Three years is a long time at the age of seven. She could have formed attachments, found a new family."

"But she wrote a letter!"

"What letter?"

The realization is like a sharp gust of wind. I remember this! A postcard in a child's hand—written in capital letters! I can recite the text:

DEAR MUMMY,
I MISS YOU VERY MUCH AND I WANT TO COME HOME.
I SAY MY PRAYERS EVERY NIGHT AND ASK FOR THE

SAME THING. THEY SAY THEY WILL LET ME GO IF YOU
SEND THEM SOMETHING. I THINK THEY WANT MONEY.
I HAVE £25 AND SOME GOLD COINS IN MY MONEY
BOX UNDER MY BED. PLEASE HURRY. I CAN SEE YOU
AGAIN SOON BUT ONLY IF YOU DON'T CALL THE
POLICE.

LOVE,
MICKEY

P.S. I HAVE BOTH MY FRONT TEETH NOW.

For a moment I feel like I might hug Joe. God, it's good to remember. It's better than morphine.

"What did you do with the postcard?" he asks.

"I had it analyzed."

"Where?"

"A private lab."

I can picture the postcard flattened under glass, being scanned by some sort of machine—a video spectral comparator. It can tell if any letters have been altered and what inks have been used.

"It looked like a child's handwriting."

"You don't sound certain."

"I'm not."

I remember a handwriting expert explaining to me how most children tend to write "R"s with the extender coming down from the intersection of the vertical line and the loop. This didn't happen on the postcard. And children also draw the capital "E" with a center line the same length as the upper and lower lines. And they cross their capital "J"s, whereas adults drop the line.

But the main clue came from the lines. Children have difficulty writing on blank paper. They tend to slew their writing down to the lower right corner. And they have trouble judging how much space words will use so they run out of room on the right-hand margin.

The ransom letter was perfectly straight.

"So it wasn't written by a child?" asks Joe.

"No."

My heart suddenly aches.

Joe tries to keep me focused. "What about the strands of hair?"

"There were six of them."

"Any instructions for the ransom?"

"No."

"So there must have been more letters . . . or phone calls."

"That makes sense."

Joe is still drawing on his pad, creating a spiral with a dark center. "The ransom packages were waterproof and designed to float. The orange plastic made them easier to see in the dark. Why were there four identical bundles?"

"I don't know. Maybe there were four kidnappers."

"They could have divided the diamonds themselves."

"You have a theory."

"I think the packages had to fit into something . . . or float through something."

"Like a drain."

"Yes."

I'm exhausted but exhilarated. It feels like my eyes have been partially opened and light is filtering inside.

"You can relax now," he says. "You did very well."

"I remembered the postcard."

"Yes."

"It mentioned Mickey's money box. It even gave a specific amount. Only someone very close to Mickey and Rachel would know something like that."

"A verifiable detail."

"It's not enough."

"Give it time."

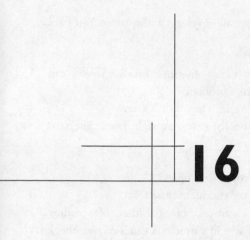

16

London has three private laboratories that do genetic testing. The biggest is Genetech Corporation on Harley Street. Although it's late Friday afternoon, the place is still open. The reception area has a granite counter, leather chairs and a framed poster that reads, PEACE OF MIND PATERNITY KITS. Isn't that an oxymoron?

The receptionist is a tall pale girl with straggly hair and a vacant face. She's wearing pearl earrings and has a plastic cigarette lighter tucked under her bra strap.

"Welcome to Genetech, how can I help you?"

"Do you remember me?"

She blinks slowly. "Um, well, I don't think so. Have you been here before?"

"I was hoping you might be able to tell me. My name is Detective Inspector Vincent Ruiz. I might have been here about a month ago."

"Did you order a test?"

"I believe so."

She doesn't bat an eyelid. I could be asking for a paternity test on Prince William and she'd act like it happens every day. She jots down my details and flicks at the keys of a computer. "Was it a police matter?"

"A private test."

"Yes, here it is—a DNA test. You wanted a comparison done on an earlier sample . . ." She pauses and gives a puzzled hum.

"What is it?"

"You also wanted us to analyze an envelope and a letter. You paid cash. Almost £450."

"How long did the tests take?"

"These were done in five days. It can sometimes take six weeks. You must have been in a hurry. Is there a problem?"

"I need to see the test results again. They didn't arrive."

"But you collected them personally. It says so right here." She taps the computer screen.

"You must be mistaken."

Her eyes fill with doubt. "So you want copies?"

"No. I want to speak to whoever conducted the tests."

For the next twenty minutes I wait on a black leather sofa, reading a brochure on genetic testing. We live in suspicious times. Wives check on husbands; husbands check on wives; and parents discover if their teenage children are taking drugs or sleeping around. Some things are safer left alone.

Eventually, I'm escorted upstairs, along sterile corridors and into a white room with benches lined with microscopes and machines that hum and blink. A young woman in a white coat peels off her rubber gloves before shaking hands. Her name is Bernadette Foster and she doesn't look old enough to have done her A levels let alone mastered these surroundings.

"You wanted to ask about some tests," she says.

"Yes, I need a fuller explanation."

Sliding off a high stool, she opens a filing cabinet and produces a bright-green folder.

"From memory the results were self-explanatory. I extracted DNA from strands of hair and compared this with earlier tests done by the Forensic Science Service, which I assume you provided."

"Yes."

"Both samples—new and old—belonged to a girl called Michaela Carlyle."

"Could the test be wrong?"

"Thirteen markers were the same. You're looking at one chance in ten billion."

Even though I'm expecting the news, I suddenly feel unsteady on my feet. Both samples were the same. This doesn't breathe air into Mickey's lungs or pump blood through her veins but it *does* prove that at some point, however long ago, the hair fell across her shoulders or brushed against her forehead.

Miss Foster looks up from her notes. "If you don't mind me asking, why did you ask us to do the test? We don't usually do police work."

"It was a private request from the girl's mother."

"But you're a detective."

"Yes."

She looks at me expectantly but then realizes I'm not going to explain. Referring back to the folder, she takes out several photographs. "Head hairs are usually the longest and have a uniform diameter. Uncut hair appears tapered but in this case you can see the cut tip from a hairdresser's scissors or clippers." She points to a photograph. "This hair hadn't been dyed or permed."

"Are you sure?"

"Positive."

"Can you tell her age?"

"No."

"Could she be alive?"

The question sounds too hopeful but she doesn't appear to notice. Instead she points to another highly magnified image. "When hair originates from a body in a state of decomposition a dark ring can sometimes appear near the root. It's called a postmortem root band."

"I can't see it."

"That makes two of us."

A second set of photographs show the postcard. The wording is just as I remember, with large block letters and completely straight lines.

"The envelope and card didn't tell us much. Whoever sent this didn't lick the stamp. And we didn't find any fingerprints." She shuffles through the photographs. "Why is everyone so interested in this case all of a sudden?"

"What do you mean?"

"We had a lawyer phone last week. He asked about forensic tests relating to Michaela Carlyle."

"Did he give his name?"

"No."

"What did you say?"

"I told him we couldn't comment. Our tests are confidential."

It may have been Howard's lawyer, which begs the question how did he know. Miss Foster returns the file to the cabinet. I seem to have exhausted my questions.

"Don't you want to know about the other package?" she asks.

My confusion lasts a fraction of a second—long enough to give myself away.

"You don't remember, do you?"

I feel a wave of heat down my neck.

"I'm sorry. I had an accident. I was shot." I motion to my leg. "I have no memory of what happened."

"Transient global amnesia."

"Yes. That's why I'm here—putting the pieces together. You have to help me. What was in the package?"

Opening a cupboard beneath the bench, she takes out a hard plastic box. Reaching inside she produces a transparent ziplock bag. It holds several triangles of pink-and-orange polyester. A bikini!

She turns it around in her fingers. "I did a little research. Michaela Carlyle was wearing a bikini like this when she disappeared, which I assume is why you asked us to analyze this."

"I assume so, too." My mouth is suddenly dry.

"Where did you get this?"

"I don't remember."

She hums knowingly. "So you can't tell me what's going on?"

"I can't, I'm sorry."

Reading something in my eyes, she accepts this.

"Is it Mickey's bikini?"

"We couldn't extract any DNA materials but we did find slight traces of urine and feces. Unfortunately, there isn't enough to analyze. I did, however, discover that it was part of a batch manufactured in Tunisia and sold through shops and catalogs in the spring of 2001. Three thousand units were imported and sold in the U.K.; five hundred were size seven."

Rapidly I try to process the information. A few triangles of polyester weave, size seven, don't constitute proof of life. Howard could have kept the swimsuit as a souvenir or someone else could have found one similar. The details were widely publicized. There was even a photograph of Mickey wearing the bikini.

Would this be enough to convince me that Mickey was still alive? I don't know. Would it convince Rachel? Absolutely.

Stifling a groan, I try to make my brain function. My leg has started to hurt again. It doesn't feel like part of me anymore. It's like I'm dragging around someone else's limb after a failed transplant.

Miss Foster takes me downstairs.

"You should still be in the hospital," she warns.

"I'm fine. Listen. Are there any more tests you can do . . . on the bikini?"

"What do you want to know?"

"I don't know—traces of hair dye, fibers, chemicals . . ."

"I can have another look."

"Thank you."

Every criminal investigation has loose ends. Most of them don't matter if you get a confession or a conviction; they're just white noise or static in the background. Now I keep going back to the original investigation looking for something we missed. All the unexplained details and unanswered questions rattle through my head when I should be sleeping.

We interviewed every resident of Dolphin Mansions. They all had an alibi except for Howard. He couldn't have known the exact contents of Mickey's money box—not unless she told him. Sarah told me she didn't know. Kirsten might have learned such a detail.

I need to see Joe again. He has the sort of brain that might be able to make sense of this. Somehow he can join random, unconnected details and make it look like dot-to-dot drawings that even a child could do.

I don't like calling him on a Saturday. For most people it's a family day. He picks up before the answering machine. I can hear Charlie laughing in the background.

"You had lunch?"

"Yeah."

"Already?"

"We have a baby remember—it's strained food and nursing home hours."

"Do you mind watching *me* eat?"

"No."

We arrange to meet at Peregrini's, an Italian restaurant in Camden Town where the Chianti is drinkable and the chef could have come straight from central casting with his walrus mustache and booming tenor voice.

I pour Joe a glass of wine and hand him a menu. He soaks up his surroundings, collecting information without even trying.

"So what made you choose this place?" he asks.

"Don't you like it?"

"No, it's fine."

"Well, the food is good, it reminds me of Tuscany and I know the family. Alberto has been here since the sixties. That's him in the kitchen. You sure you won't eat something?"

"I'll have pudding."

While we wait to order, I tell him about the DNA tests and the bikini. The likelihood of other letters is now obvious.

"What would you have done with them?"

"Had them analyzed."

"By the same lab."

"Maybe I didn't want anyone to know about the ransom demand. I would have put them somewhere safe . . . in case something happened to me."

Joe nods and stares into his wineglass. "OK, show me your wallet." He reaches across the table.

"I'm not worth robbing."

"Just give it to me."

He thumbs through the various pockets and pouches, pulling out receipts, business cards and the plastic that pays for my life. "OK, imagine for a moment that you don't know this person but you find his wallet on the ground. What does it tell you about him?"

"He doesn't carry much cash around."

"What else?"

This is one of Joe's psychological games. He wants me to play along. I pick up the receipts, which have dried into a clumped ball. The wallet was in the river with me. I peel them apart. Some are impossible to read but I notice half a dozen receipts for takeout food. I bought a pizza on September 24. When Joe came to see me in the hospital he asked me the last thing I remembered. I told him it was pizza.

Glancing at the table, I feel depressed. My life is piled in front of me. There are business cards from rugby mates; a discount voucher from some random shop; a reminder note from British Gas that my central heating needs servicing; a Royal Mail receipt for registered mail; my driver's license; a photograph of Luke . . .

It's a snapshot taken on the seafront at Blackpool. We were on a day trip and Daj is wearing a dozen petticoats and lace-up shoes. Her hair is hidden beneath a scarf and she is scowling at the photographer because my stepfather has asked her to smile. Luke is swinging from her hand and laughing. I'm in the background, staring at the bottom of one of my sandals as if I just stepped in something.

"You were always looking at the ground," Daj used to tell me. "And you still managed to fall over your own feet."

I remember that day. There was a talent competition on the pier. Hundreds of people were sitting in the sun listening to amateur Joe Blows singing songs and telling jokes. Luke kept tugging on Daj's hand, saying he wanted to sing. He was only four. She told him to be quiet.

Next thing we were watching this guy in a checked jacket and slicked-down hair pulling faces and telling jokes. He suddenly stopped because a little kid had walked right onto the stage. It was Luke with a blond cowlick and ice cream–stained shorts. This comedian made a big fuss about lowering the microphone so he could ask Luke a question.

"Well now, little boy, what's your name?"

"Luke."

"Are you here on a holiday, Luke?"

"No, I'm here with my mum."

Everyone laughed and Luke frowned. He couldn't work out why they were laughing.

"Why are you up here, Luke?"

"I wanna sing a song."

"What are you gonna sing?"

"I don't know."

They laughed again and I could have died, but Luke just stood there and stared, mesmerized by the crowd. Even when Daj dragged him off the stage and they all clapped, Luke didn't wave or acknowledge them. He just stared.

Joe is still sifting through the contents of my wallet. "Everyone leaves a trail," he says. "It isn't just scraps of paper and photographs. It's the impression we make on other people and how we confront the world."

He glances to his right. "You take that couple over there."

A man and a woman are ordering lunch. He's wearing a casual jacket and she's dressed in a classic A-line skirt and cashmere sweater.

"Notice how he doesn't look at the waiter when he's being told the specials. Instead he looks down as though reading from the menu. Now, his companion is different. She's leaning forward, with her elbows on the table and her hands framing her face. She's interested in everything the waiter says."

"She's flirting with him."

"You think so? Look at her legs."

A shoeless stockinged foot is raised and resting on her partner's calf. She's teasing him. She wants him to loosen up.

"You have to look at the whole picture," says Joe. "I know you can't remember things—not yet anyway. So you have to write things down or make mental notes. Flashes, images, words, faces, whatever comes to you. They don't make sense right now but one day they might."

A waitress arrives at the table with a plate of sardines.

"Compliments of the chef," she says.

I raise my glass to Alberto who is standing in the kitchen door. He thumps his chest like a gladiator.

Sucking fish oil from his fingers, Joe begins to focus on the bikini and who might have had it. Mickey was wearing very little when she disappeared and her beach towel became the most important piece of evidence against Howard.

All investigations need a breakthrough—a witness or a piece of evidence that turns theory into fact. In Mickey's case it had been her striped beach towel. A woman walking her dog had found it at East Finchley Cemetery. It was heavily stained with blood, vomit and traces of hair dye. Howard had no alibi for when Mickey disappeared and had been working at the cemetery in the days that followed.

A precipitin test confirmed the blood on the towel to be human— A negative, Mickey's group (along with seven percent of the population). The DNA tests were conclusive.

Without hesitation, I ordered a search of the flower beds and recently dug graves. We used ground-penetrating radar and Caterpillar diggers, as well as SOCO teams with hand spades and sieves.

Campbell went ballistic, of course. "You're digging up a fucking cemetery!" he yelled. I had to hold the phone six inches from my ear.

I took a deep breath. "I'm conducting a limited search, Sir. We have the cemetery records showing all the recently dug graves. Anything that doesn't match is worth investigating."

"What about the headstones?"

"We'll try not to touch them."

Campbell began listing all the people who had to sanction an exhumation, including a County Court Judge, the Administrator of Cemeteries and the Chief Medical Officer of Westminster Council.

"We're not snatching bodies or robbing graves," I reassured him.

Eighty feet of lawn and flower bed had been dug up by then. Paving stones were propped against walls and turf rolled into muddy faggots. Howard had helped plant the garden two months earlier for Westminster in Bloom, a flower competition.

Twenty-two other sites were also excavated within the cemetery. Although it sounds like a clever hiding place, it's not an easy thing to conceal a body in a graveyard. First you have to bury it without anyone noticing, most probably at night. And it doesn't matter if you believe in ghosts or not, very few people are comfortable in cemeteries after dark.

A media blackout covered the dig, but I knew it couldn't hold. Someone must have phoned Rachel and she turned up that first afternoon. Two police officers had to hold her back behind the police tape. She fought against their arms, pleading with them to let her go.

"Is it Mickey?" she yelled at me.

I pulled her to one side, trying to calm her down. "We don't know yet."

"You found something?"

"A towel."

"Mickey's towel?"

"We won't know until—"

"Is it Mickey's towel?"

She read the answer in my eyes and suddenly broke free, running toward the trench. I pulled her back before she reached the edge, wrapping my arms around her waist. She was crying then, with her arms outstretched, trying to throw herself into the hole.

There was nothing I could say to comfort her—nothing that would *ever* be able to comfort her.

Afterward, I walked her up to the chapel, waiting for a police car to take her home. We sat outside on a stone bench beneath a poster on the noticeboard, which said, CHILDREN ARE THE HOPE OF THE WORLD.

Where! Show me! You can want them, worry about them, love them with all your being, but you can't keep them safe. Time and accidents and evil will defeat you.

Somewhere in the restaurant kitchen a tray of glasses shatters on the floor. Diners pause momentarily, perhaps in sympathy, and then conversations begin again. Joe looks across the table, inscrutable as ever. He'll say it's the Parkinson's mask but I think he enjoys being impenetrable.

"Why the hair dye?" he asks.

"What do you mean?"

"You said there were traces of hair dye on the towel. If Howard snatched Mickey off the stairs and killed her in his flat, why bother dyeing her hair?"

He's right. But the towel might have been stained earlier. Rachel could have colored her hair. I didn't ask her. I can see Joe filing the information away for future reference.

My main course has arrived but I'm no longer hungry. The morphine is doing this to me—ruining my appetite. I roll the spaghetti around a fork and leave it resting on the plate.

Joe pours another glass of wine. "You said you had doubts about Howard. Why?"

"Oddly enough, it's because of something *you* once said to me. When we first met and I was investigating the murder of Catherine McBride, you gave me a profile of her killer."

"What did I say?"

"You said that sadists and pedophiles and sexual psychopaths aren't born whole. They're made."

Joe nods, impressed either by my memory or by the quality of his advice.

I try to explain. "Until we found Mickey's towel, the case against Howard was more wishful thinking than hard evidence. Not a single complaint had ever been made against him by a parent or a child in his care. Nobody had ever called him creepy or suggested he be kept away from children. There were thousands of images on his computer, but only a handful of them could be classed as questionable and none of them proved he was a pedophile. He had no history of sexual offenses, yet suddenly he appeared, a full-fledged child killer."

Joe peers at the wine bottle wrapped in raffia. "Someone can fantasize about children but never act. Their fantasy life can be rich enough to satisfy them."

"Exactly, but I couldn't see the progression. You told me that deviant behavior could be almost plotted on the axis of a graph. Someone begins by collecting pornography and progresses up the scale. Abduction and murder are at the very end."

"Did you find any pornography?"

"Howard owned a trailer that he claimed to have sold. We traced the location using gas and dry-cleaning receipts. It was at a campground on the South Coast. He paid the fees annually in advance. Inside there were boxes of magazines mostly from Eastern Europe and Asia. Child pornography."

Joe leans forward. His little gray cells are humming like a hard drive. "You're describing a classic grooming pedophile. He recognized Mickey's vulnerability. He became her friend and showered her with praise and presents, buying her toys and clothes. He took her photograph and told her how pretty she looked. Eventually, the sexual part of the 'dance' begins, the sly touches and play wrestling. Non-sadistic pedophiles sometimes spend months and even years getting to know a child, conditioning them."

"Exactly, they're extremely patient. So why would Howard invest all that time and effort into grooming Mickey and then suddenly snatch her off the stairs?"

Joe's arm trembles as if released from a catch. "You're right. A grooming pedophile uses slow seduction not violent abduction."

I feel relieved. It's nice to have someone agree with me.

Joe adds a note of caution. "Psychology isn't an exact science. And even if Howard is innocent—it doesn't bring Mickey back to life. One fact doesn't automatically change the other. What happened when you told Campbell about your doubts?"

"He told me to put my badge down and act like a real person. Did I think Mickey was dead? I thought about the blood on the towel and I said yes. Everything pointed to Howard."

"You didn't convict him—a jury did."

Joe doesn't mean to sound patronizing but I hate people making excuses for me. He drains his glass. "This case really got to you, didn't it?"

"Yeah, maybe."

"I think I know why."

"Leave it alone, Professor."

He pushes the wineglasses to one side and plants his elbow in the center of the table. He wants to arm wrestle me.

"You don't stand a chance."

"I know."

"So why bother?"

"It'll make you feel better."

"How?"

"Right now you keep acting as though I'm beating up on you. Well, here's your chance to get even. Maybe you'll realize that this isn't a contest. I'm trying to help you."

Almost immediately my heart feels stung. I notice the bitter yeasty odor of his medication and my throat constricts. Joe's hand is still waiting. He grins at me. "Shall we call it a draw?"

As much as I hate admitting it, Joe and I have a sort of kinship—a connection. Both of us are fighting against the "bastard time." My career is coming to a close and his disease will rob him of old age. I think he also understands how it feels to be responsible, by accident or omission, for the death of another human being. This could be my last chance to make amends; to prove I'm worth something; to square up the Great Ledger.

 **17**

It's dark by the time a black cab drops me at Ali's parents' place. She opens the door quickly and closes it again. A dustpan and brush rest on the floor amid broken pieces of pottery.

"I had a visitor," she explains.

"Keebal."

"How did you know?"

"I can smell his aftershave—Eau de Clan. Where are your parents?"

"At my Aunt Meena's house—they'll be home soon."

Ali gets the vacuum cleaner, while I dump the broken pottery in the trash can. She's wearing a sari, which seems to own her as much as she owns it. Scents of cumin, sandalwood and jasmine escape from the folds.

"What did Keebal want?"

"I'm being charged with breaching protocols. Police officers on leave are not allowed to undertake private investigations or carry a firearm. There's going to be a hearing."

"I'm sorry."

"Don't worry about it."

"No, this is my fault. I should never have asked you."

She reacts angrily. "Listen. I'm a big girl now. I make my own decisions."

"I think I should leave."

"No! This is not some glorious career I'm risking. I take care of ambassadors and diplomats, driving their spoiled children to school and their wives on shopping trips to Harrods. There's more to life."

"What else would you do?"

"I could do lots of things. I could set up a business. Maybe I'll get married . . ."

"To 'New Boy' Dave?"

She ignores me. "It's the politics that piss me off most—and guys like Keebal who should have been weeded out years ago, but instead they get promoted. He's a racist, chauvinist prick!"

I look at the broken vase. "Did you hit him?"

"I missed."

"Shame."

She laughs and I want to hug her. The moment passes.

Ali puts the kettle on and opens a packet of chocolate biscuits.

"I found out some interesting stuff today," she says, dipping a biscuit into her coffee and licking her fingers. "Aleksei Kuznet has a motor cruiser. He keeps it moored at Chelsea Harbour and uses it mainly for corporate hospitality. The skipper is Serbian. He lives on board. I could ask him some questions but I thought maybe we should tread softly."

"Good idea."

"There's something else. Aleksei has been selling a lot of stocks and shares in his companies. His house in Hampstead is also on the market."

"Why?"

"A friend of mine works for the *Financial Times*. She says Aleksei is liquidating assets but nobody knows exactly why. He's rumored to be highly leveraged and might need to pay off debts; or he could be getting ready to take over something big."

"Selling his house."

"It's been listed for the past month. Maybe we can dig up the basement and see where he buried his brother."

"I heard Sacha got disemboweled."

"That must have been before he went in the acid bath."

We laugh wryly, each aware of how apocryphal stories have just enough truth to keep them alive.

Ali has something else but she pauses, holding me in suspense. "I did some checking on Kirsten Fitzroy. Remember she told us she ran an employment agency in the West End? It operated from a building in Mayfair, leased by a company registered in Bermuda. The lease expired eight months ago and all the bills were paid. Since then any correspondence has been directed to a serviced office in Soho and then redirected to a Swiss law firm, which represents the beneficial owners, a Nevada-based company."

Corporate structures like this stand out like a dog's bollocks to everyone except DTI (Department of Trade and Industry) watchdogs. The only reason for them is to hide something or avoid paying taxes or escape liability.

"According to the neighbors the agency sometimes hosted private functions but mostly they hired staff out to short-term positions. The time sheets refer to cocktail waitresses, hostesses and waiters but there are no security numbers or tax records. Most were women and most had foreign-sounding names. Could be illegals."

It smells like something else to me—cleft cheeks, dewy thighs and hollows between elastic and skin. Sex and money! No wonder Kirsten could afford the antique armor and medieval swords.

Ali retrieves her notes and sits on the sofa, massaging her feet as she reads. "I did a property search on Kirsten's flat. She bought that place for only £500,000—half the market value—from a private company called Dalmatian Investments. The major shareholder of Dalmatian Investments is Sir Douglas Carlyle."

A frisson runs through me. "How do Kirsten and Sir Douglas know each other? And why was he so generous to her?"

"Maybe he was using her *services*," suggests Ali.

"Or she did him some other favor."

I might have misjudged Kirsten. It always struck me as odd her friendship with Rachel. They had very little in common. Rachel seemed determined to escape from her family's money and her privileged childhood, while Kirsten was equally devoted to moving up in the world and mixing in the right circles. She moved into Dolphin Mansions only weeks after Rachel did and the two became friends. They lived in each other's pockets, shopping, socializing and sharing meals.

Sir Douglas knew about Rachel collapsing drunk on the bathroom floor and Mickey spending the night lying next to her. He had a spy, a rat in the ranks, Kirsten. Half a million pounds is a lot of money for simply keeping watch on a neighbor. It's enough to make kidnapping a possibility and could also explain why someone wants to find Kirsten.

Ali collects my coffee cup. "I know you don't agree, Sir, but I still think it's a hoax."

"Motive?"

"Greed, revenge, getting Howard out of prison—could be any of them."

"Where does Kirsten come into it?"

"You said yourself she had the opportunity. She knew enough about the case and was close enough to Rachel to set up a hoax."

"But would she do it to her friend?"

"You mean the one she was spying on?"

We could argue all night and still not find an answer that fits the known facts.

"There's one more thing," says Ali, handing me a bundle of papers. "I managed to get hold of the incident logs for the night you were shot. It can be your bedtime reading."

The photocopied pages cover four square miles of north London between the hours of 10:00 p.m. and 3:00 a.m.

"I can tell you now there were five drug overdoses, three stolen cars, six burglaries, a carjacking, five hoax calls, a brawl at a bachelor party, a house fire, eleven complaints about ringing burglar alarms, a burst water main, minor flooding, a nurse attacked on her way home from work and an unexploded teargas shell found in a trash can."

"*How* many burglar alarms?"

"Eleven."

"In the one street?"

"Yes. Priory Road."

"Where was the burst water main?"

She consults the map and narrows her eyes. "On Priory Road. A row of shops got flooded."

"Can you find me the crew who repaired the water main?"

"You want to tell me why?"

"A man's allowed to have his secrets. What if I'm wrong? I don't want to destroy your delusions of my grandeur."

She doesn't even bother rolling her eyes. Instead she reaches past me and takes the phone.

"Who are you calling?"

"My boyfriend."

18

I dream of drowning—sucking watery mud into my lungs. There's a bright light and a chaos of voices against the darkness. My chest heaves vomit and brown water that runs from my nose, mouth and ears.

A woman appears, hovering over me. Her hips rest on mine and her hands press against my chest. She bends again and her lips touch mine. A pale birthmark leaks across her throat, spilling into the hollow between her breasts.

It takes me a long while to wake. I don't want to leave the dream. Opening my eyes, I get a sense of something that hasn't happened for a long while—not like this. I raise the covers a few inches to make sure I'm not mistaken. I should be embarrassed but feel somewhat elated. Any time I manage the one-gun salute these days is cause for celebration.

My euphoria doesn't last. Instead I think of Mickey and the ransom and the shootings on the river. There are too many missing pieces. There must have been other letters. What did I do with them? I put them somewhere safe. If something happened to me on the ransom drop, I would have wanted someone to know the truth.

There was a Royal Mail receipt in my wallet when Joe looked through it yesterday. I sent a registered letter to someone. Dragging my trousers off the chair, I tip the receipts onto the bed. The ink has almost washed away and I can only make out the postcode but it's enough.

Daj answers on the first ring and yells into the phone. I don't think she understands wireless technology and imagines I'm talking into a tin can.

"It's been three weeks. You don't love me."

"I've been in the hospital."

"You never call."

"I called you twice last week. You hung up on me."

"Piffle!"

"I was shot."

"Are you dying?"

"No."

"See! You're such a drama queen. Your friend came to see me—that psychologist chap, Professor O'Loughlin. He was very sweet. He stayed for tea . . ."

Throughout this guilt trip, she carries on a second conversation with someone in the background. *"My other son, Luke, is a god. A beautiful boy, blond hair . . . eyes like stars. This one breaks my heart."*

"Listen, Daj, I need to ask you a question. Did I post you something?"

"You never send me anything. *My Luke is such a sweet soul . . . Maybe you could knit him something. A vest to keep him warm.*"

"Come on, Daj. I want you to think really hard."

Something resonates in her. "You sent me a letter. You told me to look after it."

"I'm coming to see you now. Keep the letter safe."

"Bring me some dates."

The main building of Villawood Lodge looks like an old school, with gable roofs and gargoyles above the downspouts. The sandstone is just a façade and behind it is a seventies redbrick building, with aluminum window frames and cement roofing tiles.

Daj is waiting for me on the enclosed veranda. She accepts two kisses on each cheek and looks disappointed with only one box of dates. Her hands and fingers are moving constantly, brushing her arms as though something is crawling on her skin.

Ali tries to stay in the background but Daj looks at her suspiciously. "Who are you?"

"This is Ali," I say, making the introductions.

"She's very dark."

"My parents were born in India," explains Ali.

"Hmmmphf!"

I don't know why parents must embarrass their children. Maybe it's punishment for the mewling and puking and nights of broken sleep.

"Where is the envelope, Daj?"

"No, you talk to me first. You're going to take it and run away—just like last time." She turns to a group of elderly residents. "This is my son, Yanko! Yes, he's the policeman. The one who never comes to see me."

I feel my cheeks redden. Daj didn't just steal a Jewish woman's name—she adopted a whole demeanor.

"What do you mean, I ran away last time?"

She turns to Ali. "You see he never listens. Not even as a baby. Head full of fluff."

"When was I here last?"

"See! You've forgotten. It's been so long. Luke doesn't forget. Luke looks after me."

"Luke is dead, Daj. What day did I come?"

"Hmmphf! It was a Sunday. You had the newspapers and you were waiting for a call."

"How do you know?"

"The mother of that missing girl called you. She must have been very upset. You were telling her to be patient and wait for the call."

She returns to brushing her arms with her hands.

"I need to see that envelope."

"You won't find it unless I tell you where it is."

"I don't have time for this."

"You never have time. I want you to take me for a walk."

She's wearing her walking shoes and a warm coat. I take her arm and we shuffle along the white gravel path, moving in slow motion as her feet struggle to keep up with mine. A handful of residents are doing tai chi on the lawn. Elsewhere the gardeners are planting bulbs for the spring.

"How is the food?"

"They're trying to poison me."

"Have you been playing bridge?"

"Some of them cheat."

Even the half deaf can hear her.

"You really should make an effort, Daj."

"Why? We're all just waiting to die."

"It's not like that."

I stop and button up the top of her coat. Spidery wrinkles radiate from her lips but her eyes haven't aged. From a distance we are mother and son sharing an intimate moment. Up close we are a stuttering monosyllabic tragicomedy played out over fifty years.

"Can I have the envelope now?"

"After morning tea."

Inside we sit in the dining room and go through the ritual of stilted conversation served with jam and cream. The manager is wandering between the tables.

"Hello there! How lovely to see you. Isn't it nice to have your son here, Mrs. Ruiz? Maybe he'd like to come and hear Mr. Wilson's lecture on trekking in the Andes."

I'd rather be strung up and dunked headfirst into a vat of cold porridge.

Daj announces in a loud voice, "Yanko was always the strongest baby. I needed both hands to pull him away from the bottle. He didn't want the breast."

"Nobody wants to know that, Daj."

Louder this time: "His father was a Nazi, you know. Like Arnold Schwarzenegger's father." I feel my cheeks redden. She's on a roll. "I don't know if he looks like his father. There were so many of them. Maybe all their sperm got mixed up inside me."

The manager almost chokes and quickly makes her excuses before escaping. Her parting look reminds me of those my teachers used to give me when Daj came to Open Day.

With the tea grown cold and a token scone left on the plate, I go back to Daj's room and collect the envelope. On my way out I drop into the manager's office and write a check.

"You must love your mother very much," the secretary says.

I look at her impassively. "No. She's my mother."

• • •

Back in the car I open the large padded envelope. Inside are copies of the original postcard and envelope, along with the DNA tests and analysis of the ink, stationery and hair samples.

There is another letter in a plain plastic sleeve. Slipping my hand inside, I withdraw the note, blowing it open with my breath.

> *Dear Mrs. Carlyle,*
> *Your daughter is alive. She will remain so if you cooperate. Any mistakes and she will die. Her life is in your hands.*
>
> *We require two million pounds worth of superior quality cut diamonds, with no stone smaller than a carat. You will separate these stones into four velvet pouches. Each pouch must be taped to a square of quarter-inch-thick polystyrene foam and then double sealed in fluorescent plastic. Each package must be no more than 6 inches long, 2½ inches wide and ¾ inch deep. They are to be placed inside a 20-inch pizza box.*
>
> *Three days from now you will place an advertisement in* The Sunday Times *travel classifieds seeking to rent a Tuscan cottage. This will contain a cell-phone number for further communications.*
>
> *You must always answer the phone, Mrs. Carlyle. Only you. Anyone else picks up and Michaela dies.*
>
> *No negotiation will be possible. No excuses are acceptable. If the police are involved, you know the outcome.* YOU HAVE ONE CHANCE.

The letter is neatly typed and appears to have been laser printed. Although there is no attempt at childish handwriting this time, the emotional blackmail is just as great.

I placed the advertisement. I obtained the cell phone. I must have believed Mickey was still alive. Maybe it was the weight of evidence rather than conclusive proof that convinced me. We convicted Howard on circumstantial evidence and perhaps I resurrected Mickey on anecdotes and inferences.

"At least it's confirmation," says Ali, reading the DNA report.

"But it doesn't change the story. Campbell won't reopen the investigation or admit mistakes were made. The forensic experts, lawyers, police witnesses and politicians aren't going to backtrack on Howard's conviction."

"Do you blame them? Do you really want to set him free?"

"No."

"Well, why are we doing this, Sir?"

"Because I don't believe the ransom was a hoax. I think she's alive! Why else would I have risked everything?"

I stare across the road at a bus shelter where a young girl, barely twelve, looks longingly down the street for the 11:15 that won't arrive until 11:35.

This isn't about Howard. I don't care about reasonable doubt or innocence or guilt. I just want to find Mickey.

———

A storm is coming. The static electricity in the air lifts strands of hair on Ali's head and suspends them like invisible wires. Within minutes raindrops are bouncing off the windshield like marbles and the gutters are choked with leaves. Put it down to global warming or climate change, but I don't remember storms like this when I was younger.

The tires of the Vauxhall swish through the wet. Ali has a way of concentrating when she drives that brings to mind an arcade game. It's as though she expects someone to run a red light or step out from the pavement.

We cross Tower Bridge and turn east along the A2, passing through Blackheath and Shooters Hill before reaching Dartford. The storm has passed and the sky is low and gray. A cold wind picks up scraps of paper that swirl and dip along the pavements.

This is real English suburbia, with privet hedges and puddle-size birdbaths. I can even smell the lawn fertilizer and watch television three houses away through the picture windows.

The White Horse pub advertises all-day breakfasts but doesn't open until midday. Peering through the windows I see an empty bar, chairs stacked on tables, a vacuum cleaner squatting on claret carpet, a dartboard and a brass footrail along the base of the bar.

I circle around the back, Ali never more than a few feet away. The large wooden gate is shut but not locked. It leads to a bricked courtyard, full of silver kegs, with a motorbike and two cars, one of them marooned on bricks and painted camouflage green.

Just outside the door, a teenage boy, perhaps fifteen, is sitting on the hood of a car, cleaning a carburetor with an oily rag. His worn sneakers swing back and forth and his jaw moves constantly—biting off words, chewing them up and spitting them out.

Spying me, his head jerks. "FUKLEMICK!"

"Hello Stevie."

Sliding off the car he grasps my hand, pressing his ear to my wrist-watch. "Tickatock, tickatock."

Tourette's syndrome has turned him into a riot of twitches, cusses and screeches—"a human freak show," according to his father, Ray Murphy, the former caretaker at Dolphin Mansions.

I turn to Ali. "This is Stevie Murphy."

"S. Murphy. Smurfy. Smurf. Smurf." He barks the words like a seal.

Ali runs her fingers through his short-cropped hair and he purrs like a kitten.

"Is your dad inside?"

His head jerks. "FUKLEOFF! GONE!"

"Where's he gone?"

He shrugs.

Ray Murphy provided Kirsten with her alibi on the morning Mickey disappeared. According to both their statements, he was fixing her shower. A small man, slung low to the ground like a dachshund, I remember seeing Murphy fight at Wembley—top of the bill for the British bantamweight title. That must have been the early eighties.

I interviewed him twice during the original investigation. I thought he might have some ideas on how Mickey got out of the building.

"Same way as everyone else," he told me. "Through the front door."

"You think maybe her friend Sarah missed her."

"Kids don't always do what you want."

He was speaking from experience. His eldest boy, Tony, was in Brixton prison, doing five years for armed robbery.

Turning away from Stevie, I knock three times on the pub door. A chair scrapes and the door opens a few inches. A large woman with nicotine-colored hair, lacquered to concrete, regards me suspiciously. She is wearing a furry yellow pullover and black leggings that make her look like an oversize duckling.

"Mrs. Murphy?"

"You found him yet?"

"Excuse me?"

"You found my Ray? What slut is he shagging?"

Ali tries to sort out the confusion. "Are you saying that you haven't seen your husband?"

"No, shit, Miss Marple!"

She turns away from the door and waddles to her chair. The remains of breakfast cover the table and a TV perched on the counter is broadcasting images of a couple on a sofa, looking cheery and bright.

"I remember you," she says, not looking away from the screen. "You're that copper who looked for that little girl."

"Mickey Carlyle."

She gestures with her hand. "Stevie remembers. He doesn't forget things."

"Mickey ficky sticky licky," says Stevie, playing with the rhyme.

"Don't you be disgusting," scolds Mrs. Murphy. Stevie flinches and avoids her slap. He steps back and swivels his hips in an oddly adult dance.

The kitchen is small and cluttered. A strange collection of souvenirs and bric-a-brac decorates the mantelpiece, including a Donald Duck salt and pepper set, a boxing trophy and a signed photograph of Henry Cooper.

Stevie is still dancing while Mrs. Murphy has her eyes glued to the TV. I could be eighty before I get her undivided attention. I hit the standby button on the TV remote and Mrs. Murphy looks at me like I've turned off her life support.

"When did you last see Ray?"

"It's like I told them—September 24."

"Who did you tell?"

"The police! Twice I been down to see them, but they never believed me. They figured Ray had just taken off like before."

"Before?"

She wipes her eyes and glances at Stevie. Ali picks up on the signal.

"Perhaps we should go outside," she suggests. Stevie grins and hugs her around the waist.

"Just make sure he keeps his hands off you," says his mother, glancing forlornly at the blank TV.

When the door closes, Mrs. Murphy continues, "Ray could never keep his trousers buttoned. But ever since we got the pub he stayed home. He loved the White Horse . . ." The statement trails off.

"Being a caretaker must have paid pretty well to afford this place."

She bristles. "We bought it fair and square. An uncle left Ray some money."

"You ever meet this uncle?"

"He worked in Saudi Arabia. You don't pay taxes in Saudi Arabia. And Ray deserved it. He worked down them sewers for twenty years as a flusher. You know what that means? He shoveled shit. He worked knee-deep in the stuff, in the dark, with the rats. He used to come across huge nests of them, writhing like worms in a bucket."

"I thought he used to work on flood management."

"Yeah, later, but that's only after his back gave out. He helped Thames Water Board draw up plans in case a surge tide flooded London. People forget the Thames is a tidal river. Always was, always will be."

Her voice takes on a bitter tone. "When they built the Thames Flood Barrier they said surge tides weren't a problem no more. They got rid of Ray. He said they were idiots! Sea levels are rising and the southeast of England is sinking. You do the maths."

"What made him choose a pub?"

"You show me a man who doesn't want to own one."

"Most of them drink away the profits."

"Not my Ray—he hasn't touched a drop in sixteen years. He loved this place. Things were going OK, you know, until that bleedin' theme pub opened up the street. The Frog and Lettuce. What sort of name is that for a pub, eh? We were gonna do this place up and put on darts tournaments. Our Tony was going to arrange it. He knows lots of them professional players."

"How is Tony?"

She goes quiet.

"I was hoping to have a word with him."

"He's not here."

The answer is too abrupt. I glance toward the ceiling. The woman is like a fortune-telling ball—shake her up and the answer is written all over her face.

"He's done nothing wrong, my Tony. He's been a good boy."

"When did he get out?"

"Six months ago."

"You ever hear Ray mention Kirsten Fitzroy?"

The name slowly rings a bell.

"She was that uppity bird who lived in Dolphin Mansions. Had that scar on her neck . . ."

"A birthmark."

"Whatever," she says dismissively.

"She ever visit or telephone?"

"Ray wouldn't be shagging her. She's too skinny. He likes his women with some meat on their bones. That's where he'll be now—screwing some tart. He'll come home soon enough. Always does."

A car engine splutters and snarls outside. Stevie is peering under the hood while Ali sits behind the wheel, working the throttle. Somewhere on the floor above me a sash window opens and a string of invective fills the air, telling them to be quiet.

"Now that Tony is awake . . ." I say, maximizing her discomfort.

She plants both hands flat on the table, rises to her feet and clumps wearily up the stairs.

A few minutes later Tony emerges, wiry and loose-limbed in a dressing gown. He has shaved his head until only one tuft of hair remains, cut into a circle above the nape of his neck. With the tattoos on his forearms and ears that stick out like satellite dishes, he looks like an extra from an episode of *Star Trek*.

Like his father, Tony had been a promising fighter until he tried to apply some elements of the World Wrestling Federation to his boxing. The pageantry and phoney feuds might have been OK but when he started fixing fights he got into trouble. He came unstuck again when he tried to fix a darts tournament. He broke the fingers of a player who miscounted and won a game he was supposed to lose.

Tony opens the fridge and drinks from a carton of orange juice. Wiping his lips, he sits down. "I don't have to answer nothing. I don't even have to get out of bed for you."

"I appreciate you making the effort." The sarcasm is lost on him. "When did you last see your father?"

"Do I look like I keep a fucking diary?"

Reaching quickly across the table, avoiding the soggy cereal, I pin his forearm in my fist. "Listen you vicious little scumbag! You're still on parole. You want to go back inside? Fine. I'll make sure you're sharing a cell with the biggest, meanest faggot in the place. You won't have to get out of bed at all, Tony. He'll let you stay there *all* day."

I can see him eyeing a butter knife on the table but it's only a fleeting thought.

"It was about three weeks ago. I gave him a lift into South London and picked him up that afternoon."

"What was he doing?"

"I dunno. He wouldn't talk about it." Tony's voice rises. "None of this involves me, you know. Not a fucking thing."

"So you think he was up to something?"

"I don't know."

"But you know something, don't you? You got suspicions."

He chases spit around his mouth with his tongue, trying to decide what to tell me. "There's a guy I used to share a cell with at Brixton nick. Gerry Brandt. We called him Grub."

There's a name I haven't heard for a while.

Tony is still talking. "Never seen anyone sleep like Grub. Never. You'd swear he was dead half the time except his chest was moving up and down. Guys would be kicking off in their cells or getting beat up by screws but Grub would sleep through it all, drooling over himself like a baby. I'm telling you, that guy could *sleep*."

Tony takes another swig of orange juice. "Grub was only in for a few months. I hadn't seen him in years, you know, but about three months ago he turned up here looking like a playboy with a suntan and a suit."

"He had money?"

"Maybe on his back, but he was driving a heap of shit. Not worth stealing, not worth burning."

"What did he want?"

"I dunno. He didn't come to see me. He wanted to talk to the old man. I didn't hear what they were saying but they argued about something. My old man was spitting chips. Later he said Grub was looking for a job, but I know that's bullshit. Gerry Brandt don't wash glasses. He thinks he's a player."

"They were doing business."

Tony shrugs. "Fuck knows. I didn't even know they knew each other."

"When you shared a cell with this Gerry Brandt, did you ever mention your old man to him?"

"Might have said something. Cell talk, you know."

"And when your dad went up to London, what makes you think he was going to see Gerry?"

"I dropped him outside a boozer on Pentonville Road. I remember Grub talking 'bout the place. It was his local."

I take a photograph of Kirsten from my jacket pocket and slide it across the table. "Do you recognize her?"

Tony studies it for a moment. Lying comes easier than telling the truth, which is why he takes so long. He shakes his head. I believe him.

Back in the car I go over the details with Ali, letting her bounce questions off me. She is one of those people who reasons out loud whereas I work things out in my head.

"Do you remember someone called Gerry Brandt?"

She shrugs. "Who is he?"

"A nasty toerag with a toilet mouth and a taste for pimping."

"Charming."

"His name came up in the original investigation. When Howard was taking photographs outside Dolphin Mansions on the day Mickey disappeared, Gerry Brandt turned up in one of the shots—a face in the crowd. Later his name popped up again, this time on the sex offender's register. He had an early conviction for sex with a minor. Nobody read much into the sex charge. He was seventeen at the time and the girl was fourteen. They knew each other. We wanted to interview Gerry but we couldn't find him. He just seemed to vanish. Now he's turned up again. According to Tony, he came to see Ray Murphy three months back."

"It could be just a coincidence."

"Maybe."

Kirsten Fitzroy and Ray Murphy are both missing. Three years ago they provided each other with alibis when Mickey disappeared. She must have walked straight past Kirsten's door on her way downstairs to meet Sarah. Meanwhile, Sir Douglas Carlyle was paying Kirsten to keep watch on Rachel and gather evidence for a custody application. Perhaps he decided to go one step further and have his granddaughter kidnapped. It doesn't explain where she's been or why a ransom demand has arrived three years later.

Maybe Ali is right and it's all a hoax. Kirsten could have collected Mickey's hair from a pillow or a brush. She might have known about the money box. She could have concocted a plan to take advantage of the situation.

A chill wades through my skin like it's five o'clock in the morning. The Professor says coincidences are just two things happening simultaneously, but I don't believe that. Nothing twists a knife quicker than fate.

19

The Thames Water truck is parked halfway down Priory Road, facing south into the low sun. A foreman is standing beside it, sucking on a cigarette. He straightens up and adjusts his crotch. "This is my day off, it had better be important."

Not surprisingly, he looks like a man with nothing more important to do than play billiards with his mates at the pub.

Ali makes the introductions and the foreman grows more circumspect.

"Mr. Donovan, on September 26 you repaired a burst water main in this street."

"Why? Is someone complaining? We did nothing wrong."

Interrupting his excuses, I tell him I just want to know what happened.

Crushing the cigarette under his heel, he nods toward a dark stain of fresh bitumen covering thirty feet of road. "Looked like the Grand fucking Canyon, it did. Half this road got washed away. I ain't never seen a water main rupture like that one."

"How do you mean?"

He hitches up his trousers. "Well, you see, some of these pipes have been around for a hundred years and they're wearing out. Fix one and another one goes. Bang! It's like trying to plug a dozen holes when you only got ten fingers."

"But this one was different?"

"Yeah. Mostly they break on a join—the weakest point. This one just sort of blew apart." He presses his hands together and springs them open. "We couldn't reseal it. We had to replace twenty feet of pipe."

"Any idea what would have caused a break like that?" asks Ali.

He shakes his head and adjusts his crotch again. "Lew, a guy on our crew, used to be a sapper in the army. He reckoned it was some sort of explosion because of the way the metal got bent out of shape. He figured maybe a pocket of methane ignited in the sewers."

"Does that happen often?"

"Nope. Used to happen a lot. Nowadays they vent the sewers better. I heard about something similar to this a few years back. Flooded six streets in Bayswater."

Ali has been walking up and down the road, peering between her feet. "How do you know where the pipes are?" she asks.

"That depends," says Donovan. "A magnetometer can pick up iron and sometimes we need ground-probing radar, but in most cases you don't need any gizmos. The mains are built alongside the sewers."

"And how do you find those?"

"You walk downhill. The whole system is gravity fed."

Crouching down I run my fingers over a metal grate covering a drain. The bars are about three-quarters of an inch apart. The ransom had been wrapped very carefully. Each package was waterproof and designed to float. They were 6 inches long, 2½ inches wide and ¾ inch deep . . . just the right size.

Whoever sent the demand must have expected a tracking device. And the one place a transmitter or a global positioning system can't operate is below ground.

"Can you get me down in the drains, Mr. Donovan?"

"You're joking, right?"

"Humor me."

He rocks his hand back and forth. "Since 9/11 they been right edgy about the sewers. You take the Tyburn sewer—it runs right under the U.S. ambassador's residence and Buckingham Palace. The Tachbrook goes under Pimlico. You won't find 'em on maps—least not the maps they publish nowadays. And you won't even find the records in public libraries. They took 'em away."

"But it still must be possible. I can make an application."

"Yeah, I guess so. Might take a while."

"How long?"

He rubs his chin. "Few weeks, I guess."

I can see where this is going. The vast, moribund wheels of British bureaucracy will take my request and pass it between committees, sub-committees and working groups where it will be debated, deliberated upon, knocked about and run up the flagpole—and that's just to decide a form of words for the rejection.

Well, there is more than one way to skin a cat. There are three according to the Professor and he should know—he's been to medical school.

———

Nearly a decade ago in the battle over the Newbury bypass a man lived in a hole no wider than his shoulders for sixteen days. We had to dig him out but he could tunnel faster with his bare hands than a dozen men with picks and shovels.

Back then he called himself an eco-warrior, fighting the "earth rapists." The tabloids nicknamed him "Moley."

It takes Ali three hours and fifty quid in bribes to find his last known address—an abandoned warehouse in Hackney in one of those run-down areas that are hard to find unless you have a can of spray paint or need a "fix."

Driving slowly between soot-blackened factories and boarded-up shops, we pull up opposite a wasteland where kids have marked out football goals with their puffer jackets. Our arrival is noted. The message will be telegraphed through the neighborhood on whatever grapevine reaches under rocks and into holes.

"Maybe I should stay with the car," suggests Ali, "while it still has four wheels."

Ahead of us, a disused factory has soaked up layers of graffiti until one forms an undercoat for the next. To the right is a raised loading dock and large shutters. It includes a regulation doorway that has been covered with a sheet of corrugated iron. Levering it open, I step inside. Shafts of light slant through windows high up on the walls turning floating cobwebs into silver threads.

The ground floor is mostly empty, apart from discarded crates and boxes. Climbing to the second floor, I find a series of former offices, with broken plasterboard panels and exposed wires. One particular room, barely six feet square, has a narrow shelf with a blanket and a mattress stuffed with clothes. A pair of trousers hangs from a nail and cans of food are lined up on a beam. Resting on a box in the center of the room is a tin plate and a mug with a Batman logo.

I trip over an oil lamp on the floor and catch it before it breaks. The glass is warm. He must have heard me coming.

Around me the walls are plastered with sheets of newspaper and old election posters, forming a collage of faces from the news—Saddam Hussein, Tony Blair, Yasser Arafat and David Beckham. George W. Bush is dressed in desert fatigues holding a Thanksgiving turkey.

Another page has a picture of Art Carney along with an obituary. I didn't know Art Carney had died. I always remember him in *The Honeymooners* with Jackie Gleason. He was the neighbor upstairs. In this one episode he and Jackie are trying to learn golf from a book and Jackie says to him, "First you must address the ball." So Art gives it a wave and says, "Helloooo ball!"

At precisely that moment my fist punches through the newspaper and closes around a clump of filthy, matted hair. Dragging my arm forward, the paper shreds and a squealing, feral creature squirms at my feet.

"I didn't do it! It wasn't me!" cries Moley, as he rolls into a ball. "Don't hurt me! Don't hurt me!"

"Nobody is going to hurt you. I'm the police."

"Trespassing. You're trespassing. You got no right! You can't just come in here—you can't."

"You're squatting illegally, Moley, I don't think you have many rights."

He looks up at me with pale eyes in a paler face. His hair has been twisted into dreadlocks that hang down his neck like rattails. He's wearing cargo pants and a camouflage jacket with metal buckles and handles that look like ripcords for a nonexistent parachute.

Having coaxed him to sit on a packing case, he watches me suspiciously. I marvel at his makeshift furniture.

"I like your place."

"Keeps the rain off," he says, with no hint of sarcasm. His sideburns make him look like a badger. He scratches his neck and under his arms. Christ, I hope it's not contagious.

"I need to go into the sewers."

"Not allowed."

"But you can show me."

He shakes his head and nods at the same time. "No. No. No. Not allowed."

"I told you, Moley, I'm a police officer."

I light the oil lamp and set it on a box. Then I spread a map on the floor, smoothing the creases. "Do you know this place?"

I point to Priory Road but Moley stares at it blankly.

"It's near the corner of Abbot's Place," I explain. "I'm looking for a storm-water drain or a sewer."

Moley scratches his neck.

Suddenly, it dawns on me—he can't read a map. All his points of reference are below ground and he can't equate them to crossroads or landmarks above ground.

I take an orange from my pocket and put it on the map. It rolls several times and rocks to a stop. "You can show me."

Moley watches it intensely. "Follow the fall. Water finds the way."

"Yes, exactly, but I need your help."

Moley is still fixated by the orange. I hand it to him and he puts it into his pocket, zipping it closed. "You want to see where the devil lives."

"Yes."

"Just you."

"Just me."

"Tomorrow."

"Why not today?"

"I need to see Weatherman Pete. Pete will give us the forecast."

"What difference does it make in a sewer?"

Moley makes a whooshing sound like an express train. "You don't want to be down there when it rains. It's like God Himself pulled the chain."

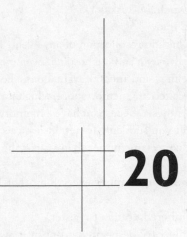

20

"Why are you so interested in the drains?" asks Joe. He motions me to sit with a mannered almost mechanical movement as though he's been practicing.

It's Monday morning and we're in his office, a private practice just off Harley Street. It's a Georgian house with black downspouts and white windowsills. The plaque on the door has a string of initials after his name, including a small round smiley face designed to make patients feel less intimidated.

"It's just a theory. The ransom was supposed to float."

"Is that all?"

"Ray Murphy used to work in the sewers. Now he's missing."

Joe's left arm jerks in his lap. There's a book lying open on his desk: *Reversing Memory Loss.*

"How's the leg?"

"Getting stronger."

He wants to ask me about the morphine but changes his mind. For a few seconds the silence spreads out like thick oil. Joe stands and sways for a moment, fighting for balance. Then he begins a slow, deliberate walk around the room, each step containing a struggle. Occasionally, he drifts to the right and has to straighten.

Glancing around his office, I notice that things are slightly askew—

the books on the shelves and files on the filing cabinet. He must be finding it harder to keep things tidy.

"Do you remember Jessica Lynch?" he asks.

"The U.S. soldier captured in Iraq."

"When they rescued her she had no recollection of any events from the time of the ambush until she awoke in an Iraqi hospital. Even months afterward, despite all the debriefings and mental evaluations, she still couldn't remember. The doctors called it a memory trace, which is completely different from amnesia. Amnesia means you have a memory but something traumatic happens and you suddenly forget. In Jessica's case her brain never allowed her to collect memories. It was like she was sleepwalking."

"So you're saying I might never remember everything that happened?"

"You might *never* have remembered. It didn't register."

He lets the news sink in while I try desperately to push it away. I don't want to accept an outcome like that. I *am* going to remember.

"Have you ever been involved in a ransom drop?" he asks.

"About fifteen years ago I helped run an operation to catch an extortionist. He threatened to contaminate baby food."

"So what do you plan for?"

"There are two types of drop—the long haul or the quick intervention. The long haul involves a complex set of instructions, making the courier jump through hoops, moving him around from A to B to C, stretching the resources of the police."

"And the alternative?"

"Well it starts off the same way, sending the courier back and forth between public phone boxes, on or off buses, swapping directions . . . then suddenly, somewhere along the way, something happens. They strike hard and fast, radically changing the plan."

"For example?"

"Back in the eighties a fellow called Michael Sams kidnapped a young estate agent, Stephanie Slater, and demanded a ransom. Stephanie's boss was the courier. It was a dark, foggy night in an isolated part of South Yorkshire. Sams left messages on telegraph poles and in public phone boxes. He moved the courier around like a chess piece through narrow country lanes until suddenly he stopped the car with a roadblock. The courier had to leave the money on a wooden tray on the edge of a bridge. Sams was down below. He pulled a rope, the tray fell down, and he escaped on a motor scooter along a muddy track."

"He got away?"

"With £175,000."

The Professor's eyes betray a glimmer of admiration. Like a lot of people he appreciates ingenuity but this wasn't a game. Michael Sams had already killed a girl.

"Would you have chosen Rachel to be the courier?"

"No."

"Why?"

"You can't expect to make rational decisions when it's your own child involved. They must have nominated Rachel. It's what I would have done in their shoes."

"OK, what else would you have done?"

"I would have prepared her. I would have gone over the different scenarios and tried to get her ready."

"How?" Joe points to an empty chair. "Imagine Rachel is sitting here now. How would you prepare her?"

I stare at the empty chair and try to picture Rachel. There were three coffee cups in my kitchen sink. Rachel was with me. Who else? Aleksei perhaps. They were *his* diamonds.

Closing my eyes I can see Rachel in black jeans and a gray pullover. Until now her appearance has melted into vagueness because of her pain but she's an attractive woman, rather bookish and sad. I can see why Aleksei was drawn to her.

She has her legs together and a soft leather satchel on her lap. Scraps of plastic and confetti-like foam are scattered on the kitchen floor.

"Remember, this is not a done deal," I say. "This is a negotiation."

She nods at me.

"They want you to follow blindly but we cannot let them dictate terms," I tell her. "You have to keep insisting on assurances that Mickey is alive. Keep asking for proof. Say you want to see her and speak to her."

"But they'll say we have the hair and bikini to prove it."

"And you'll say they prove nothing. You just want to be sure."

"What if they want me to drop the ransom somewhere?"

"Don't do it. Demand a straight exchange—Mickey for the diamonds."

"And if they don't agree?"

"It's no deal."

Her voice is as fragile as spun glass. "What if they don't bring Mickey? What if they want the diamonds first?"

"You say no."

"They'll kill her."

"No! They'll claim that she's alone or hungry or running out of air or water. They'll try to frighten and bully you—"

"But what if . . ." her voice catches, ". . . what if they hurt her?"

I can almost see the penny dropping.

She sobs. "They're going to kill her, aren't they? They'll never let her go because she can identify them . . ."

I cover her hands with mine and make her look at me. "Stop! Pull yourself together. Right now Mickey is their most valuable asset."

"And afterward?"

"That's why we have to dictate the terms and you have to be ready."

On my feet now, I stand behind her. "OK, let's practice what you're going to say." I pull out my cell phone and dial. The phone in front of her begins to ring. I nod toward it.

Uneasily she flips open the receiver. "Hello?"

"DITCH THE FUCKING WIRE!"

She looks up at me and stutters, "What . . . what . . . do you mean?"

"NOW, BITCH! DITCH THE WIRE OR I KILL MICKEY. RIGHT NOW."

"I'm not . . . I'm not wearing a wire."

"DON'T LIE TO ME. Dump it out the window."

"No."

"SHE'S DEAD. YOU HAD YOUR CHANCE."

"I'll do whatever you say. Anything. Please. I'm doing it . . ."

Rachel is shaking. I take the phone from her hands and terminate the call.

"OK, he didn't know you had a wire. He bluffed you. You should have called his bluff."

Rachel nods and takes a deep breath.

We go through the rehearsal again. I want her to be polite and forceful without being confrontational. Disagree but don't challenge. Delay.

"Tell them you're scared. You're new to this. You're nervous. They want control so let them think you're vulnerable."

For the next two hours we practice, going through the various scenarios. Realistically, I can only instill a handful of ideas. Over and over I repeat the same question. "What are you going to ask?"

"To *see* Mickey."

"When are you going to hand over the ransom?"

"When I *have* Mickey."

"That's right. When you're holding her by the hand."

I look into her eyes, hoping to see the same resolve that I witnessed at the first press conference after Mickey had gone missing when Rachel refused to break down or cry. I saw the same determination on the courthouse steps after the verdict when she read from a prepared statement.

"You don't have to go through with this," I remind her. Rachel doesn't blink or even breathe. Her fingers flutter against the buckles of the satchel.

On the edge of consciousness I hear a phone ringing. Joe leans across his desk and diverts the call. He looks at me expectantly, his left arm jerking like a broken fire hose.

"You remembered something."

I feel my stomach heave and settle again. "Not enough."

His arm has stopped shaking. His face assumes a pale blankness except for the brightness in his eyes. Life is one big mystery to him, an ever-shifting puzzle. Most people don't stop to think. Joe can't stop himself from thinking.

21

Ali has had her phone turned off all evening. Finally she calls me.

"Where have you been?"

"Working. I'm coming home now."

"Not on my account."

"I've been *working*."

Twenty minutes later she comes through the door, looking different. They say you can tell when a woman has had sex. Maybe I never did it well enough.

Ali has something for me. The Police National Computer confirmed that Gerry Brandt shared a prison cell with Tony Murphy four years ago. Brandt was released on parole two months before Mickey disappeared.

"And how's this for another coincidence," she says. "Tony Murphy got paroled six months ago—just in time to be involved in all this."

"How is 'New Boy' Dave?"

With just a hint of a smile: "He's a very happy bunny."

Although tired, she sits and goes through her notes. Gerry Brandt disappeared off radar screens the same month that Mickey went missing. Since then there have been no tax returns, social security payments, traffic fines, police cautions or overdue library books . . . He popped up again three months ago when he applied for welfare.

"So tell me, my clever young thing, does Mr. Brandt have a current location?"

"As a matter of fact he does," she says, holding up her hand. Between her fingers is a small piece of folded paper—an address in South London.

Bermondsey is one of those areas that has been raped twice—once by the Luftwaffe and then by architects in the seventies who put up Stalinesque tower blocks and concrete council estates. It's like seeing a set of healthy teeth riddled with fillings.

We pull up outside a big old white place, veiled in foliage. Beneath a pelmet of ivy, I see a small balcony supported by ornate brackets and above that a steep slate roof as dark and wet as a washed blackboard.

I look at my watch. It's just gone seven in the morning.

"Rise and shine, Princess."

A girl of about nineteen with tousled hair peers from the partially opened door. She's wearing a rugby sweater and a pair of cotton briefs. A tattoo peeps from beneath the waistband.

She looks at Ali's badge and unlocks the chain. Then we follow her down the hallway to the living room. Ali admonishes me silently for checking out the swaying arse.

Two more girls are asleep on the floor wrapped in each other's arms. Someone else of indeterminate sex is cocooned in a bedspread on the sofa. The air stinks of hash and stale cigarette smoke.

"Heavy night?"

"Not me, I don't drink," she says.

"We're looking for Gerry Brandt."

"He's upstairs."

She sits on a dining chair and rests her bare foot on the table to pick at a scab on her knee.

"Well maybe you'd like to go and tell him that we'd like a word," Ali replies.

The girl ponders this and then slides her foot off the table. She makes the stairs seem very steep. The dining room is plastered with cheap flyers for pub bands and there is a padded bench in the corner beneath a bar and weights. Through the door in the kitchen I see last night's takeout curry spilling out of the trash can.

The girl has returned. "Grub says he'll be a minute."

She goes into the bathroom and without bothering to fully close the door, sits on the toilet and urinates. After finishing, she brushes her teeth, watching me in the mirror. Another toilet flushes upstairs followed by the sound of a window opening. A few seconds later a figure drops past the kitchen window and lands in the yard.

I get a glimpse of his face and see pure unadulterated fear in his eyes.

By the time I reach the back door he has vaulted the fence and is sprinting up the rear lane. He is barefoot, wearing a cotton undershirt and faded track pants.

I do a stomach roll over the fence and land heavily on cobblestones. He's thirty yards in front of me, heading for a gate. I figure Ali has gone out the front, trying to cut him off.

The bastard leaps the gate almost without breaking his stride. My approach is to demolish it because it's slippery underfoot and I can't stop in time. He turns left, dodges an overflowing Dumpster and crosses the road, leaping a hedge as he cuts the corner into an adjoining road.

Give me twenty years and two good legs and I still couldn't catch this guy. I'm dropping farther behind, coughing up phlegm and seeing dots dance in front of my eyes.

A British Gas crew is digging a trench down one side of the street. The red clay is piled up next to the open pit. I make the jump easily enough, but I haven't looked for traffic. The silence of the electric motor is what deceives me. The milk truck has pulled out of a parking space and is only traveling a few miles per hour, but I'm in full flight and still in midair. I clip the front corner nearside mudguard and it feels like the entire New Zealand rugby team has driven me into the tarmac.

Rolling half a dozen times, I collide with the gutter and know my thigh is corked. What is it about my legs? People are just picking on me now!

Gerry is at the end of the road. He turns his head to look over his shoulder and at that moment is upended. Ali has driven her shoulder into his stomach, wrapped her arms around his waist and used his momentum to lift him up and throw him down. She drops her knees into his back and I can almost feel the air leaving his lungs.

She is sitting on him, trying to drag his arms behind his back to handcuff them. As she reaches to her belt for the cuffs, Gerry snaps his head back slamming into her chin. She almost loses her balance but she keeps her knees locked to his sides, trying to hold him down.

I'm on my feet, loping toward them. My leg is numb and next to useless.

Ahead of me Gerry has dragged himself up on all fours. Ali has her thighs locked around his waist and is riding him like a kid playing horsey with her father. She wraps her forearm around his neck, trying to compress his windpipe. Gerry is on his haunches, trying to stand. Now he's up. He's six one and more than two hundred pounds.

I can see what's going to happen. I can hear myself screaming at Ali to let go, but she's clinging tight. There is a low brick wall fronting the yard. It's only a foot high, with a straight edge.

He lines Ali up, holding her legs now. Then he looks directly at me. A strange noise, an animal sound comes from inside him. Then he falls backward. Every bit of their combined weight comes to bear across Ali's spine and the edge of the wall. She bends and she breaks.

No sound reaches me. I hear my own voice calling her name. The gas board workers are transfixed, standing in their cement-colored overalls as if suddenly turned to stone. I focus on one of them, yelling at him until his eyes shift from Ali and lock onto mine.

"Get an ambulance. Now!"

The pain in my leg is forgotten. Ali's body is draped over the wall. She hasn't moved. Fragments of light leap from the chrome on the parked cars and the tears in her eyes.

Kneeling beside her, she stares upward and I can see myself reflected in her corneas.

"I can't feel my legs," she whispers.

"Just stay where you are. Help is coming."

"I guess I fucked up pretty good."

"That was some tackle. Where did you learn to tackle like that?"

"Four brothers."

"What ever happened to Home Economics?"

She takes a ragged breath. God knows what's broken. I want to reach inside her body and hold her together.

"I wouldn't ask you normally, Sir, but can you brush the hair out of my eyes?"

I push the hair across her forehead and tuck it behind her ears.

"Maybe I'll take tomorrow off," she says. "I could catch the Eurostar and go shopping in Paris."

"Maybe I'll come with you."

"You hate shopping and you hate Paris."

"I know, but it's good to get away sometimes."

"What about Mickey?"

"We'll have found her by then."

There are no soft blankets to tuck under her chin or canteens of water she can sip. She isn't crying anymore. Her eyes are as serene as a deer's. I can hear the ambulance siren.

Gerry Brandt has long gone. He has left behind a trampled flower bed and a torn scrap of his undershirt trapped in Ali's fingers.

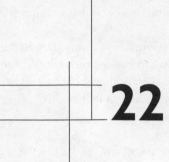

22

I hate hospitals. They're full of horrible diseases that end with "ia" and "oma." I know what I'm talking about. My first wife died in one of them, eaten away by cancer. Sometimes I wonder if the hospital didn't make her sicker than the disease.

It took two years for her to die but it seemed longer. Laura celebrated every day as a bonus but I couldn't do the same. It was like a slow torture, the endless, repetitive round of doctors' appointments, scans, drugs, bad news and cheerful smiles to hide the truth.

Claire and Michael were only thirteen but they handled it well enough. It was me who went off the rails. I disappeared and spent eighteen months driving aid trucks into Bosnia Herzegovina during the war. I should have been at home looking after my children instead of sending postcards. Maybe that's why they've never forgiven me.

They won't let me see Ali. The doctors and nurses move past me as if I'm a plastic chair in the waiting room. The triage nurse, Amanda, is plump and composed. When she speaks the words tumble out like paratroopers.

"You'll have to wait for the spinal surgeon. He won't be long. There are hot drinks and snacks in the machines. Sorry, I can't provide change."

"We've been waiting for six hours."

"Won't be long now," she says, counting rolls of bandages in a box.

Ali's family is listening to the conversation. Her father leans forward until his head rests on his folded arms. A gentle respectful man, he's like a torpedoed ship sinking beneath the waves.

Her mother is holding a paper cup of water, occasionally dipping her finger into the liquid and painting it across her eyelids. Three of her brothers are also in the waiting room and watch me with cold stares.

The stench of my own body odor rises from my shirt. It's the same BO smell that fills airline cabins when businessmen take off their jackets. Turning away from the nurse, I walk slowly back to my seat. As I pass Ali's father, I pause and wait for him to look up.

"I'm sorry this happened."

Out of politeness he shakes my hand.

"You were with her, Detective Inspector?"

"Yes."

He nods and looks past me. "What is a woman doing catching miscreants and criminals? That is men's work."

"She is a very fine police officer."

He doesn't reply. "My daughter was a very good athlete as a teenager. A sprinter. I once asked her why she wanted to run so fast. She said she was trying to catch up with the future—to see what sort of woman she was going to become." He smiles.

"You should be proud of her," I say.

He nods and shakes his head at the same time.

Moving past him, I slip into the toilet and douse my face with cold water. Taking off my shirt, I rub water under my arms, feeling it leak down to the belt of my trousers. Shutting the cubicle door, I lower the toilet lid and sit down.

This is my fault. I should have gone upstairs to find Gerry Brandt. I should have caught him before he escaped over the back fence. I can still see the look on his face as he held Ali's legs and fell backward, breaking her body against the wall. He knew what he was doing. Now I'm going to find him. I'm going to bring him in. And maybe, if I'm lucky, he might resist arrest.

. . .

The next moment my body jerks awake. I have fallen asleep in a toilet cubicle with my head against the wall. The knots in my neck feel like fists as I drag myself upward.

What day is it—Tuesday, no, Wednesday morning? It must be morning but it's dark. I don't even look at my watch.

My head starts to clear as I make it outside to the waiting room. My hair is matted on my forehead and my nose is crusted and dry.

The consultant is talking to Ali's family. Sick with fear I cross the room, zigzagging through rows of plastic chairs. Gloom seems to grow under the harsh strip lighting.

I hesitate for a moment, unsure whether to intrude, but the need to know is too great. As I reach the cluster of people, nobody looks up. The consultant is still talking.

"She has fractured two vertebrae and dislocated them, squeezing her spine like toothpaste in a tube. Until the bruising goes down we won't know for certain the extent of the paralysis or whether it's permanent. I have another patient, a jockey, who has similar injuries. He was thrown off a horse and landed on the running rail. He's doing very well and should walk again."

Sweat chills on my skin and the long empty corridors drop away in every direction.

"She's zonked out on painkillers but you can see her," he says, scratching his unshaved chin. "Try not to upset her." At that same moment his beeper sounds and concusses in my ears. He looks at Ali's parents apologetically and leaves in a clatter of shoes along the corridor.

I wait my turn outside Ali's room. I can't look at her parents' faces as they leave. Her mother has been crying and her brothers want someone to blame. There's nowhere to hide.

A wave of nausea ebbs inside me as I push open the door, taking several steps into the semidarkness. Ali is lying flat on her back, staring upward. A skeletal steel frame holds her neck and head in place, preventing her from turning.

I don't get too close, hoping to spare her my stench and ugliness. It's too late. She sees me in the mirror above her head and says, "Morning."

"Morning."

I glance about the room and take a chair. Gold bars of light leak through the curtains, falling across her bed.

"How are you feeling?" I ask.

"Right now I'm flying with Lucy and her diamonds. I don't feel a thing." She takes a breath, which is half a groan, and manages a smile. Tear trails have dried on either side of her eyes. "They say I need an operation on my spine. I'm going to get them to add a few inches. I've always wanted to be six feet tall."

She wants me to laugh but I can't manage more than a smile. Ali has gone quiet. Her eyes are closed. Silently, I stand to leave, but her hand reaches out and grabs my wrist.

"What did the doctor tell you?"

"They won't know for a few days."

Choking on the words: "Will I be able to walk?"

"They think so."

Her eyes squeeze shut and tears form in the delta of wrinkles.

"You'll be fine," I say, trying to sound convincing. "You'll be back at work in no time—all six feet of you."

Ali wants me to stay. I watch her sleeping until a nurse shoos me outside. It's almost midday. A dozen calls are waiting in my message bank—most of them from Campbell Smith.

Calling the operating room, I try to get the latest on Gerry Brandt, who is still missing. Nobody will talk to me. Finally I get through to the Senior Investigating Officer, who takes pity on me. There were three hundred Ecstasy tablets beneath the floorboards in Gerry Brandt's bedroom, as well as traces of speed in the S-bend of the upstairs toilet. Is that why he ran?

I arrive at the Harrow Road Police Station just before 2:00 p.m. and pass through a crowded front office where two motorists with bloodstained shirts are yelling about a traffic accident.

Campbell shuts the office door behind me. He looks every inch a chief-constable-in-waiting, with his arms behind him and a face stiffer than shirt cardboard.

"Jesus Christ, Ruiz! Two fractured vertebrae, broken ribs and a ruptured spleen—she could finish in a wheelchair. And where were you? Being run over by a fucking milk truck . . ."

I can hear them laughing down the hall. The worst of the jokes haven't started yet but that's only because Ali is so sick.

Campbell opens his top drawer and produces a sheet of typed paper. "I warned you. I told you to stay out of this."

He hands me a resignation letter. Mine. I am to retire immediately on health grounds.

"Sign this."

"What are you doing to find Gerry Brandt?"

"That's not your concern. Sign the letter."

"I want to help you find him. I'll sign the letter if you let me help find him."

Campbell grows indignant, huffing and puffing like a pantomime wolf. I can't see his eyes. They are hidden beneath eyebrows that crawl across his forehead, fleeing toward his ears.

I tell him about the ransom letters and the DNA tests, recounting what I've managed to piece together about the ransom drop. I know it sounds far-fetched but I'm getting closer. I just need help to follow the trail. Gerry Brandt had something to do with it.

Campbell shakes his head in disbelief. "You should hear yourself. You're obsessed."

"You're not listening. Someone kidnapped Mickey. I don't think Howard Wavell killed her. She's alive!"

"No! You listen to me. This is bullshit. Mickey Carlyle died three years ago. Answer me something—if someone kidnapped her, why did they wait three years before sending a ransom demand? It doesn't make sense because it isn't true."

He pushes my resignation letter back at me. "You should have retired when I gave you the chance. You're getting divorced. You hardly see your kids. You live alone. Look at you! Christ, you're a mess! I used to tell young detectives to model themselves on you, but now you're an embarrassment. You stayed on too long, Vincent—"

"No, don't ask me."

"You're over the hill."

"What hill? I didn't see any hill!"

"Sign the letter."

Turning my face to one side, I squeeze my eyes shut, blinking away the bitterness. The more I think about it, the angrier it makes me. I can feel it stirring in my guts, churning around like the pistons of a steam engine.

Campbell takes back the fountain pen and returns it to his drawer. "You give me no option. I regret to inform you that your commission with the London Metropolitan Police has been withdrawn. The Commissioner has decided you are a liability. He won't let you give evidence under the label of a serving officer."

"What do you mean give evidence?"

Campbell takes another letter from his desk drawer. This one is a subpoena.

"At ten o'clock this morning lawyers for Howard Wavell subpoenaed you to give evidence at his appeal hearing at midday tomorrow. They know about the ransom demand and the DNA test. They're going to argue that if a senior serving police officer approved the payment of a ransom for Michaela Carlyle we must believe she's still alive."

"How did they find out?"

"You tell me. They're also applying for bail. Howard Wavell could be out of prison by tomorrow afternoon."

Suddenly, I understand. My sacking will be part of the damage limitation. I'll be a maverick cop instead of a serving officer.

Breathing dies in the room. Campbell is still talking but I don't hear the words. I'm living ten seconds ahead of time or ten seconds behind. Meanwhile, a phone is ringing somewhere that nobody wants to answer.

23

Sitting low on worn springs in the front seat of the van, I peer through the windshield at the growing darkness. An Elvis doll on a suction cup dances to and fro on the dashboard.

Weatherman Pete is driving, with his woollen hat and walrus mustache. His jaw moves constantly on a wad of chewing gum that he retrieved from behind his ear.

In the back of the van are his four companions, who refer to themselves as "urban explorers." Barry, a Cockney, has only two front teeth and a complete absence of hair. He is arguing with Angus, a retired coal miner, about which heavyweight champion had the weakest jaw. Opposite them, Phil tries to join in the conversation but his stutter gives the others too much time to interrupt. The only quiet member of the crew is Moley, who sits on the floor of the van checking ropes and lamps.

"It's the last frontier," says Pete, talking to me. "Forty thousand miles of sewers, some of them hundreds of years old—it's a feat of engineering to rival the Suez Canal, but nobody gives your sewers a second thought. They just purge their poisons and flush them away."

"But why explore them?"

He gives me a disappointed look. "Did they ask Hillary why he climbed Everest?"

"Yeah, they did."

"OK. OK. Well these sewers are like Everest. They're the last frontier. You'll see. It's another world. Go down thirty feet and it's so quiet you can hear your pores opening and closing. And the darkness—it's unnatural. It's not like outside where if you wait your pupils dilate so that you can start making out shapes. Down there it's blacker than black."

Barry leans through from the back of the van. "It's like a lost city. You got streams, culverts, shelters, basements, grottoes, graves, crypts, catacombs, secret places that the government don't want nobody to know about. It's a different world. One layer burying the next, just like rock sediments. Whenever the great civilizations crumble—Egyptian, Hittite, Roman—the one thing they always leave behind is their sewers and latrines. A million years from now archaeologists are going to be digging up our fossilized turds, take my word for it."

"And a lot more besides," adds Angus. "We find all sorts of stuff—jewelry, false teeth, spectacles, flashlights, gold coins, hearing aids, harmonicas, shoes—"

"I once saw a full-grown p-p-p-p-pig," interrupts Phil. "Biggest p-p-p-porker you ever saw."

"Happy as a pig in shit, was he?" cackles Angus. Barry joins in until Weatherman Pete tries to raise the tone.

"You know what a tosher is?"

"No."

"Back in the eighteenth century they used to scour the sewers, panning the muck like you'd pan for gold. Imagine that! Then you had your gongfermers and rakers, who cleaned the sewers and repaired them. Nowadays they call them flushers. You might even hear some of 'em working tonight."

"Why do they work at night?"

"There's less shit flowing."

I wish I hadn't asked. Ray Murphy's wife had talked about him working as a flusher. Pete explains how teams of six men, with a ganger in charge, clear blockages by hauling silt out through the manholes.

"I know it sounds pretty antiquated but there's some high-tech stuff, too. They got these little boats—more like hovercrafts really—with cameras on 'em that film the inside of the sewers, looking for problems. You got to watch out for 'em. You don't want to get caught down there."

The van skids to a halt on loose gravel in a deserted parking lot. As the rear doors open, Moley climbs out first and hands me a pair of over-alls and waist-high waders. Next comes a safety harness and Sellafield gloves. Meanwhile, Weatherman Pete opens a yellow plastic suitcase and unfurls a retractable aluminum pole with a tripod and wind cups on the top.

"It's a portable weather station," he explains. "It gives me wind speed, wind direction, temperature, relative humidity, barometric pressure, so-lar radiation and precipitation. Everything gets fed into a computer." He opens a laptop and taps the keyboard. "Right now, you have a window of four hours."

Moley adds a safety helmet and an emergency breathing apparatus to my outfit. He scratches his armpits one last time before he shimmies into his waders.

"Any cuts? Cover them up with waterproof Band-Aids," says Barry, tossing a box toward me. "Weil's disease—you get that from rat urine. It gets into a cut and ends up in your brain."

He checks my harness. "Let me tell you what can go wrong down there: fire, explosions, asphyxiation, poisoning, infection and rats that can strip the flesh off your bones. Nobody knows we're down there, so we can't guarantee the sewers are vented. There could be pockets of methane, ammonia, hydrogen sulfide, benzene, CO_2 and gases I swear don't even have names yet. Don't touch your eyes or mouth with your gloves. Stick close to Moley. Nobody knows his way around like he does."

He clips a gas monitor onto my harness.

Weatherman Pete gives a thumbs-up and Moley levers open a man-hole cover, rolling it to one side. Then he lowers a safety lamp down the small circular shaft. Angus and Phil descend first, climbing down the iron rings. I'm squeezed between Barry and Moley.

The sewer is less than five feet high, forcing me to bend, and the air smells of feces and a putrid dampness. The brick walls curve at the sides and disappear into a shallow stream running down the center. Our shad-ows are distorted against the brickwork.

"Don't forget to put the seat down," says Angus, urinating against a wall.

Moley looks at me, the whiteness of his eyes glowing in the lamp-light. He doesn't say anything but I know he's giving me one last chance to go back.

Weatherman Pete rolls the manhole cover back into place, sealing us inside.

I suddenly feel nervous.

"How is he going to contact us if it rains?"

"The old-fashioned way," replies Barry. "He's going to pick up a manhole cover and drop it six inches. We'll hear it miles away."

Angus claps me on the shoulder. "So what do you think?"

"It doesn't smell so bad."

He laughs. "Come down here on Saturday morning. Friday is curry night."

Moley has moved off, wading along the stream. Barry falls in behind me, crouching more than most, as his ample frame is buttressed on all sides by the harness. Water swirls around my knees and the sweating bricks look almost silver in the flashlight beam.

"We call these snotsicles," says Barry, pointing out the stalactites brushing against our helmets.

Despite the cold I'm already starting to perspire. A hundred yards and a permanent shiver sets in. Every sound is magnified and it makes me edgy. I have been trying to weave Mickey into the various scenarios but it's getting harder.

Another part of me thinks of Ali in the hospital, staring at her crippled self in the mirror, wondering if she's ever going to walk again. I started this. I let her come along when she had far more to lose than I did. Now I'm wading in filth and shit and it seems appropriate. When you consider the state of my life, my career and my relationships, I belong down here.

"The place you showed us on the map. We're under it now," says Barry, his headlamp momentarily blinding me.

I glance up at a large opening and a side tunnel. The burst water main on the night of the ransom drop sent a thousand gallons a minute flooding through the streets and into the drains—enough to carry a ransom; maybe even enough to carry me.

"If something got washed down here, where would it finish up?"

"It's a top-down system. Operates on gravity," says Angus.

Moley nods in agreement.

"Go-go-go-got flushed away," stutters Phil.

Barry begins to explain. "These small local sewers feed into main sewers and the waste is then drawn off into one of five interceptory sewers that run west to east—all fed by gravity. The high-level sewer begins at Hampstead Hill and crosses Highgate Road near Kentish Town. Farther south you got two middle-level sewers. One begins close to Kilburn and runs under the Edgware Road to Euston Road, past Kings Cross. The second runs from Kentish Town under Bayswater and along Oxford Street. Then you got two low-level sewers, one under Kensington, Piccadilly and the City; and the other right under the Thames Embankment, following the northern bank of the river."

"Where do they all go?"

"To the sewage treatment works at Beckton."

"And the system gets flushed out by rainfall?"

He shakes his head. "The main sewers are built alongside old rivers that provide the water."

The only river I know that enters the Thames estuary from the north is the River Lea, which is a long way east of here.

"There are heaps of them," scoffs Angus. "You can't just wish a river away. You can cover 'em over or divert 'em into pipes but they'll keep flowing just the same as always."

"Where are they?"

"Well you got the Westbourne, the Walbrook, the Tyburn, Stamford Brook, Counter's Creek and the Fleet . . ."

Each of these names is familiar. There are dozens of streets, parks and estates named after them, but I had never equated them with ancient rivers. The fine hairs on my neck are standing on end. You hear stories about secret cities beneath cities; tunnels that took prime ministers to war cabinet rooms and passageways that carried mistresses for rendezvous with kings, but I had never imagined a world of water, unseen blind rivers, coursing beneath the streets. No wonder the walls are crying.

Moley wants us to keep moving. The tunnel goes straight on with occasional vertical shafts emptying into it from above creating mini-waterfalls. Keeping to the center of the stream, our boots slosh through the sediment and cold grayish water. Slowly the passages grow wider and taller and our shadows no longer stoop against the walls.

Tethered together we descend into a shaft and wade silently along a larger sewer. Occasionally we slide down cement slopes, splashing through several inches of stinking water. At other times we near the surface and faint beams of light angle through iron grates.

I try to imagine the ransom, divided and sealed in plastic, being carried through these tunnels, dropping over waterfalls, floating through crypts.

For another hour we walk, crawl and slide. Eventually, we emerge into a cavernous Victorian brick chamber supported by pillars and arches. It must be thirty feet high, although it's hard to tell in the darkness. White-green water seems to boil at my feet, plunging over a waterfall.

Everywhere there are rusty iron gratings and long chains hanging from the roof. A concrete weir, made up of two large spillways, divides the room. Foaming gouts of waste are swept away by a great culvert that intercepts the flow above the spillway.

Below it, down the sliding concrete weir, is a large empty concrete pool featuring huge hinged steel gates with counterweights on the top end to act like levers and seal the doors closed.

Angus sits on the edge of the spillway and takes a sandwich from his pocket, unwrapping the plastic film.

He motions with his sandwich. "That over there is the low-level interceptory sewer. It starts at Chiswick and runs east beneath the Thames Embankment to the Abbey Mills pumping station in east London. Everything gets diverted from here to the treatment works."

"Why the spillway?"

"Storms. You get a decent downpour in London and there's nowhere for the rain to go except into the drains. Thousands of miles of small local lines feed into the main sewers. First you get a gust of wind and then the whoosh!"

"Whoosh!" echoes Moley.

Angus picks a crumb off his chest. "The system can only accommodate a certain level of water. You don't want it backing up or the politicians would be knee-deep in shit in Westminster. I'm talking literally. So when the water reaches a certain level it spills over the weir and gets diverted through those gates." He points at the huge iron doors, which must each weigh about three tons. "They open like a valve when floodwaters come roaring over the weir."

"Where does it go?"

"Straight into the Thames at a good ten knots."

Suddenly another scenario emerges, swirling around me like the smell of almonds. The Thames Water foreman described the water main having "blown apart," creating a tremendous flood. This would have discouraged anyone from following the ransom and could also have served another purpose—to carry the packages over the weir.

"I need to get through those gates."

"You can't," says Moley. "They only open during floods."

"But you can get me there. You know where it comes out."

Moley scratches his armpits and rocks his head from side to side. My whole body has started to itch.

24

Weatherman Pete produces a high-pressure hose and hooks it up to a tap. The blast of water knocks me back a step. I turn around and around, getting pummeled by the spray.

The van is parked almost directly above an open manhole in Ranelagh Gardens in the grounds of the Royal Hospital Chelsea. The grand hospital buildings, painted by the rising sun, are just visible through the trees. Nearby, at Chelsea Barracks, I can hear the strains of a military band practicing.

These gardens are normally closed until 10:00 a.m. and I don't know how Weatherman Pete managed to get through the gates. Then I notice magnetic mats on the side of his van advertising the City of Westminster.

"I got dozens of them," he explains, rather sheepishly. "Come on, I'll show you what you want to see."

Shedding the overalls and waders, we seal them into plastic sacks and load up the van. Moley has changed into his camouflage uniform and blinks into the sunlight as though frightened it might do him permanent damage. The others are drinking tea from a flask and recounting the night's journey.

Piling into the van, I lean over the seat as Weatherman Pete drives along the narrow tarmac paths and waves at a trio of Chelsea pensioners on their morning walk. Pulling through the front gate, we circle the outer walls of the gardens until we reach the Thames.

Parking in the Embankment Gardens, I cross the road to Riverside Walk, overlooking the river. The Thames, caught between tides, smells like perfume after where I've been.

Pete joins me and glances across the brown slick of water. Clambering onto the wall, he hooks his arm around an iron lamppost and leans out over the muddy bank.

"There it is."

I follow his outstretched arm and notice a depression in the stone bank. A round metal door seals the entrance of a pipe that disappears underground. Water dribbles from the edge, forming a puddle in the mud.

"That's the Ranelagh Storm Relief Sewer. The door opens when it floods and closes again to stop the tide washing back into the sewer."

He turns and points past the hospital. "You were directly north of here. You followed the fall of the Westbourne River."

"Where does it come from?"

"It rises in West Hampstead and gets fed by five streams that join near Kilburn. Then it crosses Maida Vale and Paddington before flowing into Hyde Park where it fills the Serpentine. After that it disappears underground again, down William Street, under Cadogan Lane and Kings Road, past Sloane Square and finally beneath Chelsea Barracks."

"I can't see any water flowing."

"Most of it gets used by the sewer. You won't see this gate open unless they get surplus water in the system."

I don't hear the rest of his explanation. Instead I think of a story my stepfather told me about an old blind horse that fell into a dried-up well. The horse wasn't worth saving, so the farmer started shoveling earth into the well. But the old horse just shook off the dirt and stamped it down. More earth fell, and the old horse went right on stamping it down, slowly rising out of the darkness.

People have been trying to bury me but I keep stamping it down. Now I'm close to climbing out and, I promise you this, anyone holding a shovel will get a kick in the head.

I think I know what happened that night. I built a valuable boat and it floated away, sealed in plastic and buoyed by foam. The diamonds washed through Ranelagh sewer, pushed along by water from a busted main. Someone was waiting for the ransom; someone who knew his or her way around the sewers; someone like Ray Murphy.

Only now am I beginning to realize how angry I've been ever since I woke in the hospital with a gunshot wound, dreaming of Mickey Carlyle. This is far bigger than the sum of its parts. Clever, driven, cunning people have manipulated the emotions of a desperate mother and taken advantage of my own blinkered desire. Where has Mickey been all this time? I know she's alive. I can't explain why or point to the proof; I just know she belongs in the world on a morning like this.

Moley is taking batteries from the gas monitors and checking the harnesses. Angus and Barry have already gone—walking to the Underground station. It is almost seven in the morning.

"Can I drop you somewhere, DI?"

I think for a moment. I'm due in court at midday. I also want to visit Ali in the hospital. At the same time, having come this far, I don't want to stop searching. Facts not memories solve cases. I have to keep going.

"Maida Vale."

"Sure. Jump in."

The traffic seems to grow lighter as I get closer to Dolphin Mansions. My shoulders still ache from my journey in the sewers and I can smell the foulness in my nostrils.

Weatherman Pete drops me on the corner opposite the delicatessen and I walk the final seventy yards. Nestled in the lint of my trouser pocket are my last two morphine capsules. Every so often I reach inside and feel their smoothness with my fingertips.

The façade of Dolphin Mansions is in full sunshine. Stopping periodically, I study the gutters, looking for the openings and metal grates. I notice the camber of the road and where downspouts enter the ground.

Some of the mansion blocks have basement flats that are below street level. They have drains to take rainwater away and stop them from flooding.

I wait on the front steps until one of the residents leaves, nodding as they hold the door open for me. Then I glance up the central stairwell, checking I'm not being watched. Skirting the lift well, I discover the door leading to the basement. A low-wattage naked bulb suspended from the ceiling transforms the darkness. The stairs are narrow and steep and the walls are a mottled green where patches of damp have broken through the plaster.

Reaching the bottom of the stairs I try to put myself back in this place, three years ago. I remember searching the basement. Like every other room it was turned upside down. Along one wall, cut into an alcove, is a large disused boiler. It must be fifteen feet around, with meters, valves and pipes of every caliber. The square copper nameplate bears the inscription FERGUS & TATE. The floor is covered with half bags of plaster, cans of paint, offcuts of carpet and a Victorian gas lamp encased in bubble wrap.

Moving materials aside, I begin searching the floor.

A noise makes me turn. A young boy sits on the top step holding a plastic robot on his lap. His khaki trousers are stained with paint and his dark eyes peer at me suspiciously.

"Are you a stranger?" he asks.

"Yes, I suppose I am."

"My mum says I shouldn't talk to strangers."

"That's very good advice."

"She says I could get kidnapped. A girl got kidnapped from here— from right off the stairs. I used to know her name but I forgot. She's dead, you know. Do you think it hurts when you die? My friend Sam broke his arm when he fell out of a tree and he said it really hurt—"

"I don't know."

"What are you looking for?"

"I don't know that either."

"You'll never find my hiding place. She used to hide there, too."

"Who?"

"The girl who got kidnapped."

"Michaela Carlyle."

"You know her name! Do you still want to see it? You have to promise not to tell anyone."

"I promise."

"Cross your heart and hope to die, stick a needle in your eye."

I cross my heart.

Tucking his robot into his belt, the boy slides on his backside down the remaining stairs and steps past me toward the boiler. He disappears through a gap no wider than his shoulders where the curved side of the boiler doesn't quite touch the brickwork.

"Are you all right in there?"

"Yes," he replies, emerging again. He's holding a book in his hand. "That's my cubbyhole. Do you want to come in?"

"I don't think I'll fit. What have you got there?"

"A book. It used to be hers but it's mine now."

"Can I have a look?"

He hands it to me reluctantly. The front cover is tattered and chewed at the edges but I can still make out the illustration of a mother duck and ducklings. On the inside cover there is a large label with a scrolled border. Written on it is "Michaela Carlyle, 4½."

The story is about the five little ducks that go out one day, over the hills and far away. The mother duck says, "Quack, quack, quack, quack," but only four little ducks come back. The ducklings disappear one by one but on the final page they all return.

Handing the book back to him, I slide to my knees and put my head on the floor, peering into the gap between the boiler and the brickwork.

"It's dark in there."

"I have a light."

"Is that running water I can hear?"

"My dad says there's a river down there."

"Where?"

He gives me a thumbs-down and I look at his feet. A sudden chill rushes through me, like ice at the roots of my hair.

Dragging aside half bags of plaster and cement, I find a frayed square of carpet, folded twice. Pulling it back I reveal a metal grate with perpendicular bars embedded into the stone floor. Pressing my face close, I try to peer between them. My eyes follow the bricks downward, along walls that seem to be weeping black tears. I can hear water gurgling below as if filling a giant cistern.

The boy is still talking but I'm no longer listening. We should have found this three years ago. We weren't looking for tunnels and the noise of the search would have drowned out the sound of water.

"What's your name?"

"Timothy."

"Can I borrow your flashlight, Timothy?"

"Sure."

Although not powerful, it illuminates an extra six feet of the shaft. I can't see the bottom.

Hooking my fingers between the bars, I try to lift the grate. It's wedged into place. Looking around for a lever, I find an old blunt chisel with a broken handle. Sliding it into the gap between metal and stone, I work it from side to side, pushing it deeper. Then I force the chisel sideways, leaning my weight against it. The grate lifts just enough for me to squeeze my fingers beneath one edge. Christ it's heavy!

Timothy gives me a hand as we push it past vertical and let it drop with a clatter. He leans over and peers into the square black pit.

"Wow! Are you gonna go down there?"

I shine the flashlight into the hole. Instead of penetrating the darkness the light seems to bounce back at me. There are U-shaped handholds down one side.

"I'm a police officer," I tell the boy, taking my wallet from my pocket and giving him a business card. "Have you a watch, Timothy?"

"No."

"OK, do you know how long an hour is?"

"Yeah."

"If I haven't come to find you within an hour, I want you to give this card to your mum and ask her to call this number." I write down the Professor's details. "Tell him where I went. Do you understand?"

He nods.

Tucking the flashlight into my belt, I lower myself into the hole. Within a few feet I am soaking wet and the sound of running water is constant. The boy is still there. I can see his head silhouetted against the square of light.

"Go upstairs now, Timothy. Don't come down here again."

Fifteen feet down I pause, holding on to a metal rung with one hand and aiming the light below me. Nothing.

I descend farther, feeling the air grow colder, until my foot strikes something flat and hard. The light picks up a river rushing through a tunnel. A ledge seems to run along the edge, about ten inches above the water in both directions before the light beam disappears into the darkness. This is not a sewer. Large beams support the ceiling and the walls are worn smooth by the current.

I feel my way along the ledge by sliding each foot a few inches, expecting the stonework to collapse at any second and pitch me into the stream. I can pick up only small sections of the tunnel. Tiny yellow lights reflect back at me—the eyes of rats escaping along the ledge.

The moss on the walls is like slick black fur. Pressing my ear against the bricks I feel a slight vibration. Somewhere above my head is a road and traffic. The sound makes the tunnel seem alive, like some ancient, consumptive beast. Breathing. Digesting me.

Time and distance seem longer underground. I feel like I've been down here for hours yet I've probably only traveled a hundred yards. I don't know what I expected to find. Any evidence could never survive—not this long. The tunnel has been swept clean by seasonal downpours and storms.

I try to imagine someone taking Mickey through here. Unconscious she could have been lowered down the pit and then carried. Conscious she would have been terrified and too hard to control. Another possibility catches in my throat. What better way to dispose of a body? The river would sweep it away and the rats would pick it clean.

Shuddering, I push the thought aside.

Any kidnapping would have needed at least two people and remarkable preparation. Someone had to replace the grate and cover it with bags of plaster and cement.

My clothes cling to me and my teeth are chattering. Unlike the expedition with Moley, I'm not prepared for this. It was a stupid idea. I should go back.

Ahead of me the ledge suddenly stops and starts again. There is a four-foot gap where it has collapsed into the stream. I could try to jump it but even with two good legs I couldn't guarantee landing safely.

I kneel down and feel ahead with my fingers. There's a gap in the wall just above the level of the water. Rolling up my sleeve, I reach down, feeling for the bottom. The opening is two feet high and a similar width, channeling water away from the river. This could be one of the conduits that feed the sewers.

Lowering myself into the channel, water soaks my trousers and fills my shoes. My chest is submerged and my back scrapes against the roof. Holding the flashlight in my mouth, I crawl forward. The darkness pushes back at me.

Mud sticks to my knees and shoes. Three or four inches deep, I feel like I'm wiggling through it like an earthworm. The grunts and groans belong to me but echo back as though there's someone ahead of me . . . waiting. After fifteen feet the channel begins to slope downward, getting gradually steeper. My hands slip and I fall on my face into the water. The flashlight is submerged. Thank God it still works.

The steeper gradient and the force of the water behind me push me forward. If the tunnel gets any narrower I'll be wedged inside, trapped. My back scrapes against the ceiling. The water seems to be rising. Perhaps I'm being paranoid.

I slip again and shoot forward, pushing mud, gravel and water ahead of me. Convulsing and trying to retreat, I can't stop. My legs are useless. I rise over a hump and then feel myself in midair, falling. I land with a splash in water and muck. The smell is unmistakably a sewer. My first impulse is to vomit.

A poultice of dark mud covers my eyes. I scrape it off, trying to see, but the darkness is absolute. The flashlight is gone, either washed away or water-damaged.

Sitting up, I check that nothing is broken. My hands are shaking from the cold and I can't feel my fingers. Water cascades from the opening above my head. I have to get out of here.

Taking stock, I try to plot where I might be in relation to Dolphin Mansions. I can't read my watch so I don't know how long I've been down here. The ledge was narrow and my progress slow. I might only have traveled a few hundred yards. I heard traffic. I must have passed under a road. I listen again. Instead of a distant rumbling I feel a faint breeze against one cheek.

Standing too quickly, I smack my head against the roof and curse. Don't do that again. Crouching, I spread my palms against the curved brick wall and edge my way forward like a blind man in a maze. Occasionally, I pause and try to feel the breeze again. My mind wants to play tricks on me. Either the breeze disappears or seems to be coming from the opposite direction.

I can feel the desperation rising in me, scalding my esophagus. In the darkness I could plunge into a shaft and never get out. Maybe I should turn back.

Suddenly, a faint glow appears ahead of me. The shaft of light looks like a ghostly hologram in the center of the tunnel. I step inside and raise my face. I can see the sky through a rectangular grate. The edges are softened by turf spilling over the sides. I see football boots, shin guards and muddy knees. A handful of schoolboys and teachers are watching the game. Someone shouts, "Press forward." Someone else bellows, "Offside!"

Nearest to me a lone teenager appears to be reading a book.

"Help me!"

He looks around.

"I'm down here!"

He peers at the grate.

"Help me get out!"

Dropping to his knees, he puts an eye against the bars.

"Hey! What are you doing?"

"I'm a police officer."

I know it doesn't answer the question but it seems to be enough. He goes to fetch a teacher. I can hear him.

"Sir, there's someone in a hole over there. I think he might be stuck."

A new face appears at the grate, older and in charge.

"What are you doing down there?"

"Trying to get out."

More faces arrive and stand around the drain. The football game appears to have been forgotten. Most of the players are now scrabbling to get a look at "this guy stuck down a hole."

A crowbar is summoned from a car trunk. Turf is kicked away from the edges. The grate is pulled aside and strong hands reach inside. I emerge onto a patch of English autumn, blinking into the sunlight and wiping the remains of the sewer from my face.

Reaching into my sodden pocket I retrieve the last of the morphine capsules. Magically, the pain lifts and a wave of emotion passes over me. I don't normally like emotion. It's a wishy-washy, moist-eyed, soft-in-the-head state, good for postcoital bliss and rugby reunions, but you know something, I love these lads. Look at them, all dressed up in their school scarves, kicking a ball around the place. They look so cute. They even let me shower in the pavilion and someone lends me a shirt, tracksuit bottoms and a pair of sneakers. I look like a senior citizen on a power walk.

The Professor is summoned and finds me in the pavilion. Straight off he treats me like a patient, taking my face in his hands and holding my eyelids open.

"How many did you take?"

"The last two."

"Jesus!"

"I'm fine, really. Listen to me. I've been down there . . . in the river. We should have seen it years ago."

"What are you talking about?"

"I know how they got her out of Dolphin Mansions. She went down the hole—just like Alice in Wonderland."

I know I'm not making sense but Joe perseveres. Finally, I tell him the story but instead of getting excited he gets angry. He calls me stupid, foolhardy, rash and impulsive, but each of the criticisms is prefaced by the term "with all due respect." I've never been so politely told off.

I look at my watch. It's almost eleven o'clock. I'm due in court at midday.

"We can still make it."

"I have to stop off somewhere first."

"To change your clothes."

"To see a boy about a light."

25

The Royal Courts of Justice in the Strand are composed of a thousand rooms and three miles of hallways, most of them lined with dark wooden panels that soak up the light and add to the gloom. The architecture is Victorian Gothic because the courts are meant to intimidate the crap out of people, which they do.

For Eddie Barrett, however, it's just another stage. Striding along corridors, he pushes through doors and scatters the clusters of whispering lawyers. For a man with short legs and a bulldog swagger, he moves surprisingly quickly.

Barrett is to the legal profession what hyenas are to the African plains—a bully and a scavenger. He takes cases according to how much publicity they generate rather than the fees and he uses every legal loophole and ambiguity while grandly extolling the British judicial system as "the finest and fairest in the world."

In Eddie's mind the law is a flexible concept. It can be bent, twisted, flattened and stretched until it becomes whatever you want it to be. He can even make it disappear when turned sideways.

A dozen steps behind him comes Charles Raynor, QC, known as "The Rook" because of his black hair and beaked nose. He once made a former cabinet minister cry under cross-examination about his taste in women's underwear.

Eddie spies me and swaggers over. "Well, lookie see who's here—Inspector Roooeeeez. I hear all sorts of stories about you. I hear your wife is banging someone else—his dick, her pussy, making whoopee. I'd be pretty pissed if I caught my missus shagging her boss. For richer, for poorer, in sickness and in health, isn't that what they say? No mention there of giving it up for the firm's accountant."

My jaw clenches and I feel the red mist descending.

Eddie takes a step back. "Yeah, that's the temper I heard so much about. Have fun in court."

I know he's winding me up. That's what Eddie does—gets under people's skin, looking for the softest flesh.

Spectators are crammed into the public gallery and there are three full rows of press, including four sketch artists. The furnishings and fittings predate microphones and recording equipment so cables snake across the floor, pinned beneath masking tape.

I look around for Rachel, hoping she might be here. Instead I see Aleksei, who is watching me as though waiting for me to instantly disintegrate. To his left is the Russian and to the right a young black man with loose limbs and liquid eyes.

The Rook adjusts his horsehair wig and glances across at his adversary, Fiona Hanley, QC, a handsome woman, who reminds me of my second wife, Jessie, who has the same cool detachment and honey-colored eyes. Miss Hanley is busy shuffling papers and rearranging box files as though creating a mini-fortress around her. She turns and gives me an uncertain smile as though we might have met somewhere before (only about a dozen times).

"All rise."

Lord Connelly, the Chief Justice, enters and pauses, surveying the courtroom as though keeping watch over the pearly gates. He sits. Everybody sits.

Howard Wavell appears next, climbing the stairs into the dock. Gape-mouthed and gray, with his hair hanging limply across his forehead, he has a vague, forgetful frown as though he's lost his bearings. Eddie whispers something to him and they laugh. I'm seeing conspiracies everywhere.

Campbell thinks this has been Howard's plan from the very beginning. The ransom demand, the lock of Mickey's hair, her bikini—all were part of an elaborate hoax designed to cast doubt on his conviction and set him free.

I don't buy it because it begs the same question that Joe keeps asking me: Why wait three years?

Lord Connelly adjusts a lumbar cushion behind his back and clears his throat. He spends a moment studying the courtroom ceiling and begins.

"I have studied the defense submissions regarding the original trial of Mr. Wavell. While I am willing to agree with several of the points raised about the trial judge's summing up, on balance I don't feel they altered the outcome of the jury's deliberations. However, I am willing to hear oral arguments. Are you ready to proceed, Mr. Raynor?"

The Rook is on his feet, pushing his black gown along his forearms. "Yes, Your Honor, I will be seeking to introduce fresh evidence."

"Does this evidence address the grounds for appeal or the original offense?"

"The original offense."

Miss Hanley objects. "Your Honor, my learned friend seems intent on rerunning this trial even before being granted leave to appeal. We have been given a witness list with two dozen names. Surely he doesn't intend calling them all."

Lord Connelly looks at the list.

The Rook clarifies the situation. "It may be that we call only one witness, Your Honor. It very much depends upon what he has to say."

"I hope you're not embarking on a fishing expedition, Mr. Raynor."

"No, Your Honor, I can assure you that's not the case. I wish to call the Detective Inspector who was in charge of the original investigation into the disappearance of Michaela Carlyle."

Lord Connelly underlines my name on the list. "Miss Hanley, the overriding purpose of the Criminal Appeal Act is to further the interests of justice. It allows fresh evidence to be admitted by the prosecution and the defense. However, I warn you, Mr. Raynor, that I'm not going to allow you to rerun this trial."

Miss Hanley immediately makes an application for the proceedings to be heard in a closed court.

"Your Honor, there are issues involved that go beyond the immediate fate of Mr. Wavell. An important criminal investigation could be jeopardized if certain information is made public."

What investigation? Campbell is only interested in nailing me.

"Does this investigation involve Mr. Wavell?" asks Lord Connelly.

"Indirectly, it may do. I'm aware of the nature of the investigation but not the precise details. There is a media blackout in place."

The Rook puts his oar in, more out of habit than desire. "Justice must be seen to be done, Your Honor."

Lord Connelly rules in favor of the Crown and the public gallery and press benches are cleared. This is when the real arguments begin, full of phrases like "with all due respect" and "my learned friend" (legal shorthand for "you complete moron"). Then again, what do I know? The Rook and Miss Hanley could be the best of friends. They could be shagging each other's wigs off in chambers.

My name is called. I button my jacket on the walk to the witness box and unbutton it as I sit down.

The Rook looks up from his notes as if surprised that I've bothered showing. He rises slowly to his feet, drops his chin and tries to look at me through the top of his head. The first few questions are the easy ones—name, rank, years of experience as a police officer.

Miss Hanley is on her feet. "My learned friend seems to be placing great faith in the credibility of this witness. However, he has failed to mention that DI Ruiz was suspended as head of the Serious Crime Group several days ago and yesterday afternoon, following an internal disciplinary hearing, he was sacked. He is no longer a serving member of the London Metropolitan Police and is the subject of a criminal investigation—"

Lord Connelly motions her to sit down. "You'll get your opportunity to question the witness."

The Rook consults his notepad and then does something I don't expect. He takes me through the original investigation, getting me to restate the evidence against Howard. I talk about the photographs, the bloodstains, the missing carpet and Mickey's beach towel. He had the opportunity, the motive and the corrupted sexuality.

"At what point did Howard Wavell become a suspect in the original investigation?"

"Everyone who lived in Dolphin Mansions was immediately a suspect."

"Yes, but at what point did you focus your attentions upon Mr. Wavell?"

"He became of particular interest when he was seen acting suspiciously on the day Michaela disappeared. He also failed to provide an alibi."

"He failed to provide one or didn't have one?"

"He didn't have one."

"In what way was he acting suspiciously?"

"He was taking photographs of the search parties and people who had gathered outside Dolphin Mansions."

"Was there anyone else taking photographs?"

"There were several press photographers."

The Rook gives a wry smile. "So having a camera didn't automatically make someone a suspect?"

"A young girl was missing. Most of the other neighbors were helping look for her. Mr. Wavell seemed more interested in recording the event for posterity."

The Rook waits. He's letting everyone know that he expects a better answer.

"Prior to your seeing Howard Wavell at Dolphin Mansions that day had you ever come across him before?"

"We went to the same boarding school back in the sixties. He was a few years behind me."

"Did you know each other well?"

"No."

"As the officer in charge of the investigation, did you think about either stepping down or absenting yourself from interviews because of your past association?"

"No."

"Did you know Mr. Wavell's family?"

"I may have met one or two of them."

"So you don't remember going out with his sister?"

I pause, racking my brain.

The Rook smiles. "Perhaps you dated too many girls to remember."

Everyone cracks up. Howard laughs as hard as anyone.

The Rook waits for the laughter to subside. Almost in passing, he remarks, "Four weeks ago you took an envelope containing six hairs to a private laboratory in central London and asked for a DNA test to be carried out."

"Yes."

"Is that normal police procedure—using a private facility to conduct DNA tests?"

"No."

"I think I'm right in saying that the Forensic Science Service do DNA tests for the police."

"It was a private request not a police one."

He raises his eyebrows. "Unofficial? How did you pay?"

"Cash."

"Why?"

"I don't see how that's relevant—"

"You paid in cash because you didn't want a record of the transaction, isn't that the case? You didn't leave your address or phone number with the laboratory."

He doesn't give me a chance to answer, which is probably for the best. I'm dying here. Perspiration is leaking down my chest and settling in a pool at my navel.

"What exactly did you ask the technicians at Genetech to do for you?"

"I wanted them to extract DNA from the hair strands and compare it with the DNA of Michaela Carlyle."

"A girl who is supposed to be dead."

"Someone had sent a ransom demand to Rachel Carlyle alleging that her daughter was still alive."

"And you believed this letter?"

"I agreed to have the hair tested."

The Rook is more insistent. "You still haven't explained why you asked a private laboratory to conduct the test."

"It was a favor for Mrs. Carlyle. I didn't believe the hair would be a match for her daughter."

"You wanted to keep it a secret?"

"No. I was concerned that any official request would be misconstrued. I didn't want it perceived that I had doubts about the original investigation."

"You wanted to deny Mr. Wavell his right to natural justice?"

"I wanted to be sure."

The Rook walks back to the table and picks up a second sheet of paper, snapping it with his fingers as though calling the edges to attention.

Why doesn't he ask me the result of the DNA test? Perhaps he doesn't know the answer. If the hair didn't match Mickey's DNA profile, the ransom demand was more likely to be a hoax, weakening Howard's case.

The Rook begins again. "Subsequently, a second package was posted to Mrs. Carlyle. What did it contain?"

"A child's swimsuit."

"What can you tell us about this swimsuit?"

"It was a pink-and-orange bikini, similar to the one worn by Michaela Carlyle on the day she disappeared."

"Similar or the same one?"

"Forensic analysis couldn't produce a definitive answer."

The Rook is circling now. He has the face of a bird and the soul of a crocodile. "How many murders have you investigated, Detective?"

I shrug. "Upward of twenty."

"And how many missing children cases?"

"Too many."

"Too many to remember?"

"No, Sir." My eyes are locked on his. "I remember every last one of them."

The power of the statement throws him slightly. He turns back to the bar table, consulting his notepad.

"There must be a degree of pressure on the officer in charge of a high-profile investigation. A young girl is missing. Parents are scared. People want to be reassured."

"It was a thorough investigation. We didn't cut corners."

"No, quite right." He reads from a list. "Eight thousand interviews, 1,200 statements, more than a million man-hours . . . many of them focused on my client."

"We followed every important lead."

The Rook is leading me somewhere. "Were there any suspects that you didn't pursue?"

"Not if they were important."

"What about Gerry Brandt?"

I can feel myself hesitate. "He was a person of interest for a short time."

"And why did you discount him?"

"We made extensive inquiries—"

"You couldn't find him, isn't that the case?"

"Gerry Brandt was a known drug dealer and burglar. He had contacts within the criminal underworld who I believe helped hide him."

"This is the same man who was photographed outside Dolphin Mansions on the day Michaela disappeared?"

"That's correct, Sir."

He turns away from me now, addressing a wider audience. "A man with a previous conviction for sexually assaulting a minor?"

"His girlfriend."

"A sex offender who was seen outside Dolphin Mansions but you didn't regard him as being an important enough suspect to bother finding. Instead you focused your investigation exclusively on my client, a committed Christian, who had never been in trouble with the law. And when you obtained evidence that could suggest Michaela Carlyle might still be alive you sought to hide it."

"I made the results available to my superiors."

"But not to his defense."

"With all due respect, Sir, it's not my job to help defense lawyers."

"You're absolutely right, Mr. Ruiz. Your job is to establish the truth. And in this case you sought to hide the truth. You sought to ignore evidence or at worst conceal it, just as you ignored Gerry Brandt as a suspect."

"No."

The Rook sways back and forth on his heels. "Was the ransom demand a hoax, Detective Inspector?"

"I don't know."

"And are you willing to stake your career . . ." he corrects himself, ". . . your reputation and, more importantly, my client's freedom on the absolute conviction that Michaela Carlyle was murdered three years ago?"

There's a long pause. "No."

Even the Rook is taken by surprise. He pauses to compose himself. "So you believe she may still be alive?"

"When you don't find a body there is always a chance."

"And has that possibility become greater as a result of this ransom demand?"

"Yes."

"No further questions."

I don't look at Campbell or Eddie Barrett or Howard Wavell. I keep my eyes straight ahead as I walk out of the courtroom. Inside my jacket, pressed against my heart, a cell phone is vibrating.

Fumbling for the button, I take the call.

"I've just heard the news on the radio," says Joe. "They've found a body in the river."

"Where?"

"Somewhere near the Isle of Dogs."

This is how it looks: a bleak Thursday afternoon, a strong wind and water slapping against the pylons of Trinity Pier. A dredger squats low in the water, with skeletal arms held aloft and black pipes snaking across the decks. Spotlights have turned brown water into a murky white. Two water-police Zodiacs made of rubberized canvas with wooden bottoms fight the outgoing tide, dropping floating plastic pontoons in their wake.

The Professor parks on a slip road that comes to a dead end where the River Lea enters the Thames estuary. The river is two hundred yards wide at this point, with the Millennium Dome silhouetted against the porridgelike sky on the distant bank.

Halfway down the sloping metal ramp "New Boy" Dave steps away from a huddle of detectives. His shoulders are shaking and he's caught between wanting to spit in my face or smash it with his fists. This is about Ali.

"Fuck off! Just fuck off!" It's almost a wail. He pushes me in the chest, forcing me backward.

I want to say I'm sorry but the lump in my throat won't move. Instead I look over Dave's shoulder at the police divers preparing their tanks and equipment. "Who did they find?" The other detectives have circled like spectators at a playground fight. None of them want me here. I'm an outsider, a maverick, worse still a traitor. Joe tries to intervene. "Ali wouldn't want this. Just tell us who you found."

"Fuck you!"

As I try to step around Dave, he grabs me by my arm, swinging me hard into the brick-and-wire retaining wall. A kidney punch sends me down. He is standing over me looking wasted and wild. There's a trickle of blood down his chin where he's bitten his lip.

What happens next lacks a certain degree of elegance. I sink my fist into his groin and take hold. Dave groans in a high reedy voice and drops to his knees. I don't let go.

He raises his fists, wanting to pound me into the ground, but I squeeze even harder. He curls up in pain, unable to lift his head. My breath is hot on his cheek.

"Don't go bad on me, Dave," I whisper. "You're one of the good ones."

Letting him go, I ease myself up until I'm sitting against the wall, staring at the smooth darkness of the water. Dave drags himself alongside me, trying to get his breath back. Glancing at the other detectives, I tell them to leave us alone.

"Who did they find?"

"We don't know," Dave says, grimacing slightly. "The dredger sliced the body in half."

"Let me see it."

"Unless you can recognize this poor bastard from below the waist you're no use to anyone, especially me."

"How did he die?"

He pauses too long before he answers. "There is evidence of a gunshot wound." In the same breath, he arches his neck and looks past me. A coroner's van has pulled alongside the wharf. The back doors open. A stretcher slides from within.

"I didn't mean for Ali to get hurt—you know that."

He looks at his fists. "I'm sorry I hit you, Sir."

"That's OK."

"Campbell will go ape shit if he knows you're here."

"So don't tell him. I'll stay out of the way."

As the last rays of sunlight strike the towers of Canary Wharf, four divers tumble backward from the Zodiacs. Slick as seals, they disappear beneath the surface leaving barely a trace behind.

The officer in charge is short and barrel-chested, clad in a wet suit that makes him look as if he's carved from ebony. He swings an air tank into a boat and wipes both hands before offering one to me. "Sergeant Chris Kirkwood."

"Ruiz."

"Yeah, I know who you are."

"You got a problem talking to me?"

"Nah." He shakes his head. "I got other problems. Visibility is down to three feet and the current is running at four knots. Someone chained this bastard to a barrel of concrete. We're gonna need cutting gear." He swings another air tank into the boat.

"How long has he been in the water?"

"Most bodies eventually come up. Takes about five days at this time of year, but this guy was meant to stay down there. Usually a body stays together pretty good in the Thames. None of the marine life can chew through ligaments. I reckon chummy has been down there two, maybe three weeks . . ."

As he describes the process I can picture a body swaying beneath the water, white and waxlike, moving back and forth with the tide. Involuntarily, I shudder and reach for a morphine capsule. There are none left.

The closer of the Zodiacs rocks in the wake of a passing water taxi. I notice bubbles on the surface and a masked face emerges, with an upraised fist. A police-issue handgun is clenched in his gloved fingers.

The water ripples and sways. Something else is coming up. A rope appears in a second diver's hand and is hooked onto a winch. Suddenly, it feels like a cold grasping hand has taken hold of my heart. The air has condensed into water and the current is sucking me down.

Sergeant Kirkwood catches me as I fall. He has his arms under mine, pulling me back from the edge of the wharf. A box is found and I sit down. Joe is beside me, shouting at someone to get me a glass of water. I try to turn away but he holds my face.

My vision clears and I watch the first of the Zodiacs. The divers have hauled something from the water. The outboard engine rumbles and the Zodiac swings toward the wharf. A rope is thrown into willing hands and is looped around a pylon. The Zodiac is pulled closer.

Lying on the wooden base is a bloated, discolored torso hung with fronds of weed and wrack. It is barely recognizable as being human, yet I do recognize him; I recognize his name and his face and boxer's hands. And then I remember . . .

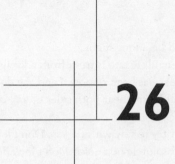

26

Deep inside my head doors and windows suddenly open. Files blow off desks, lights go on, photocopiers hum and phones ring. A closed office has suddenly come to life and the man hunched over his desk looks up from his hands and yells, Eureka!

Single frames and snapshot memories are put in order like a film being spliced together. I can picture scenes and hear dialogue. A phone is ringing. Rachel picks it up. The prerecorded message is a single question. One sentence: "Is my pizza ready?"

The phone goes dead. Rachel stares at me in disbelief.

"Don't worry—they'll call back."

We're sitting in my kitchen. Rachel is dressed in black jeans and a gray pullover. She has the dazed disbelieving air of a refugee who no more than an hour ago escaped over the border.

For the next three hours she doesn't move. She barely dares to breathe. Her hands are locked in a battle, each finger wrestling the others. I try to make her relax. I want her to conserve her energy.

Aleksei is nearby, waiting and watching with an animal quickness. Sometimes he wanders into my sitting room to make a call on his cell phone then he drifts back, regarding Rachel with a strange mixture of longing and disgust. The diamonds are packed and ready. They were delivered in a velvet-lined briefcase—965 stones, one carat or above, superior quality.

Aleksei is going to follow us—tracking the signals from the transmitter and a GPS beacon in Rachel's car.

"Nobody is going to know we're being followed," I reassure her. "Aleksei has promised to stay well away unless he gets a signal. I'm going to be with you. Just relax."

"How can I relax?"

"I know it's hard but it could be a long night."

Outside on the street, her Renault Estate is fresh from a local garage workshop. The front passenger seat has been removed and the doors reinforced. A hands-free phone will let me hear both sides of any conversation.

"Whatever happens you must try to stay with the car. Don't let them draw you away unless you have absolutely no choice. Don't look down at me. Don't talk to me. They might be watching. If I ask you a question and the answer is yes, I want you to tap the top of the steering wheel once. If the answer is no I want you to tap it twice. Do you understand?"

She nods.

Again, I deliver the most important message. "What are you going to ask?"

"To *see* Mickey."

"When are you going to hand over the ransom?"

"When I *have* Mickey."

"That's right. They want you to follow blindly but you have to keep insisting on assurances that Mickey is alive. Keep asking for proof—"

"They'll say the hair and bikini prove it."

"And you'll say they prove nothing. You just want to be sure."

"What if they want me to drop the ransom somewhere?"

"Don't do it. Demand a straight exchange—Mickey for the diamonds."

"And if they don't agree?"

"It's no deal."

At 11:37 p.m. the phone rings again. The caller is male but a voice-changing device has digitally altered his vowels and flattened the pitch.

He instructs Rachel to drive to the Hanger Lane Roundabout on the A40. She holds the cell phone in both hands, nodding rather than answering. She doesn't hesitate. She picks up the pizza box and walks to the door.

Aleksei follows, looking suddenly concerned. I don't know whether he wants to wish her luck or take her place. Maybe he's just worried about his diamonds. Farther down the street he opens a car door and I see the Russian behind the wheel.

Lying on the floor of Rachel's car, my shoulders are braced against the dashboard panel and my legs concertinaed toward the backseat. I can only see one side of her face. She looks straight ahead, with both hands on the wheel, as though retaking her driving test.

The caller has hung up.

"Just relax. We could put on some music."

She taps the steering wheel once.

I flip open the vinyl case of her CD collection. "I'm fairly easy to please—anything except Neil Diamond or Barry Manilow. I have a theory that ninety percent of deaths in nursing homes are caused by Neil Diamond and Barry Manilow."

She smiles.

I have a walkie-talkie clipped to my top pocket and a Glock 17 self-loading pistol in a holster under my left arm. The radio receiver tucked into my right ear is tuned to the same frequency as a handset in Aleksei's car.

I also have a dark blanket I can drag over myself at traffic lights or when vehicles pull alongside us.

"Remember not to look at me. If you have to park somewhere, try to avoid streetlights. Choose somewhere darker."

She taps the steering wheel once.

The cell phone rings again. She reaches down and presses the speaker button.

In the background a girl is crying. The male voice, still heavily distorted, screams at her to be quiet. Rachel flinches.

"You called the police, Mrs. Carlyle."

"No."

"Don't lie to me. Never lie to me. A detective visited you at work five days ago."

"Yes but I didn't invite him. I told him to leave."

"What else did you tell him?"

"Nothing."

"Don't insult my intelligence."

"I'm telling the truth. I swear. I have the ransom." Rachel's voice is shaking but she doesn't waver.

If this were a police operation we would be tracing the call, narrowing down the signal to the nearest transmitting tower. Then again, he's probably moving and he won't stay on the line for more than a few minutes at a time.

"I just need some assurance. I want to see Mickey," says Rachel. "I need to know she's OK, otherwise I don't think I can get through this—"

"SHUT THE FUCK UP! Don't try to bargain, Mrs. Carlyle."

"I'm not trying to be unreasonable. I just need to know she's—"

"Alive? Can't you hear her?"

"Yes, but . . . how do I know . . . ?"

"Well, let me see, I could cut out one of her big brown eyes and post it to you. Then again, maybe I should just run a knife across her pale pretty throat and send her head in a box. Then you can put it on the mantelpiece as a reminder of what a STUPID COW YOU ARE!"

Everything reels. I can see Rachel's chest heaving. For a long while she can't speak.

"Mrs. Carlyle?"

"I'm here."

"Are we clear?"

"Yes. Just don't hurt her."

"Listen very carefully. You get one chance at this. Disobey my instructions and I hang up. Argue with me and I hang up. You mess up and you won't hear from me again. You know what that means?"

"Yes."

"OK, let's do this one more time."

What does he mean by "one more time"? Has he done this before? Everything about his vocal tone and pace of his speech suggests he's not a first-timer. A cold draft of fear settles over me. Mickey's not coming home tonight. She's never coming home. And these people won't balk at killing Rachel. What was I thinking? It's too dangerous!

"Where are you now?"

"Ah, um, I'm getting close to the roundabout. It's just ahead of me."

"Circle the roundabout three times and then go back the way you came."

"Where to?"

"Prince Albert Road Roundabout near Regent's Park."

Roundabouts are open and hard to police. They're making her circle so they can check that she's not being followed. Hopefully, Aleksei will realize and hang back.

We're returning toward the West End now. From my hiding place, below the level of the windshield, I can only see the upper floors of buildings and the globes of streetlights. Ahead of us, above the Post Office Tower a blinking red light moves across the sky; a helicopter perhaps or a plane.

The phone line is still open. I raise my hand and make a talking motion. Rachel taps once on the steering wheel.

"Is Mickey OK?" she asks tentatively.

"For now."

"Can I speak to her?"

"No."

"Why did you wait so long?"

He doesn't answer. Then, "Where are you now?"

"Just passing the London Mosque."

"Turn right onto Prince Albert Road. Follow it around Regent's Park."

There is something about the voice. Even with the distortion I detect a slight accent, possibly South London or farther east. Beads of perspiration shine on Rachel's top lip. She licks them away and keeps her eyes fixed on the road.

"Get to Chalk Farm Road. Follow it north."

Through the windows I see the faintest wisps of clouds, engraved against the night sky by a half-moon. We must be climbing Haverstock Hill toward Hampstead Heath.

The caller begins naming crossroads and counting them down. "Belsize Avenue . . . Ornan Road . . . Wedderburn Road . . ." And then suddenly, "Turn left now. Now!"

My knees bang against the gear stick. Fifty yards farther, he yells, "STOP! Get out of the car. Bring the pizza."

"But where—?" pleads Rachel.

"Walk along the street and find the car that isn't locked. The keys are in the ignition. Leave the phone. There's another waiting for you."

"No. I can't—"

"DO AS YOU'RE TOLD OR SHE DIES!"

The phone goes dead. Rachel seems to be frozen in place, both hands still locked on the wheel.

"You OK?"

She taps the steering wheel once.

"You see anyone?"

She taps it twice.

"What about behind us?"

Two taps.

I ease myself upward, fighting the cramp in my legs. We're on a tree-lined street, with major intersections at each end. Branches shield the parked cars from above.

Rachel reaches for the door handle.

"Wait!"

"I have to go. You heard him."

He knew the crossroads. He was rattling off the distances. Either he's nearby or everything has been planned in advance. Can I take the risk of going with her?

"OK, I want you to take the ransom and walk along the street. When you find the car unlock the trunk."

She reaches into the backseat and retrieves the pizza box. The door opens. The interior light has been disconnected. Using a handheld periscope with a zoom lens, I watch her walk away from me, at the same time scanning the street for any movement. I punch the button on the two-way.

"Oscar Sierra this is Ruiz. Rachel is on foot. The target vehicle is changing. Be vigilant."

Rachel tries each car door and then moves on. She's getting farther and farther away from me. Far off I see the interior of a car light up. Rachel slips inside and picks up another cell phone. The door closes and the brake lights flare. It's now or never.

I'm out of the car. Running. My legs are stiff and wracked with cramps, making it hard to stay on my feet. Meanwhile the pavement is uneven and broken by tree roots.

A Vauxhall Vectra is pulling out ahead of me. Rachel spies me at the last minute in her rear mirror and slows down. I open the trunk and tumble heavily inside, pulling the lid closed until it jams hard on my fingers but doesn't lock shut.

We're moving again. I'm curled up in a ball, with my cheek pressed against the nylon floor mat and my heart pounding. The wheel arches amplify the sound of the tires on the road and I can hear nothing else.

I feel for the earpiece. It's fallen out and is dangling down on my chest. Putting it back into my ear, I hear Aleksei yelling in Russian. They don't know which car to follow. There are two vehicles leaving the street—a BMW turning south down Fitzjohn's Avenue and the Vectra turning north.

They're trying to contact me. The walkie-talkie is digging into my chest. I lever myself upward and pull it free. There's no response when I depress the talk button. I must have broken the two-way when I rolled into the car.

Aleksei won't know which vehicle to follow until the cars are far enough apart for the transmitter to identify which one is carrying the ransom. By then he risks losing us completely.

I can't help. Instead I concentrate on creating a mental map of north London in my head, trying to calculate which turns we make and the direction we're heading. The minutes and miles tick by.

The weight of the trunk is keeping it closed until we hit a pothole, when it tries to jump open. I raise my head and try to peer through the narrow gap. The only thing visible is the light gray tarmac and occasional flashes of headlights.

Through the earpiece I can monitor Aleksei and the Russian. The BMW has been discounted. Now they're heading toward Kilburn, relying solely on the signal from the diamonds.

Rolling onto my back, I keep one hand on the lid of the trunk and feel along the inside walls until I locate the internal light. The bulb feels smooth in my fingertips and I twist it free from the socket.

Several times the car stops and does a U-turn. Either Rachel is lost or they're still making her jump through hoops. She's driving faster now. The streets are emptier.

The car crosses a speed hump and suddenly stops. Is this it? I slide my gun from its holster and cradle it on my chest.

"Hey, Lady, you want to slow down. I almost took you for a joy-rider." It is a man's voice. He might be a security guard with too much time on his hands. "Are you lost?"

"No. I'm looking for a . . . for a friend's house."

"I wouldn't recommend you hang around here, Lady. Best you head back the way you came."

"You don't understand. I have to keep going."

I can almost hear him chewing this over as if he wants to phone a friend before making a decision. "Maybe I didn't make myself clear," he drawls.

"But I have to—"

"Keep your hands where I can see them," he says. He's walking around the car, kicking at the tires.

"Please, let me go."

"And what's the big hurry? You in some sort of trouble?"

A wind has come up. Corrugated iron flaps on the ground and I can hear a dog barking. When the man reaches the rear of the car he notices the trunk is popped off its latch. His fingers hook under the lid.

As it opens, I slide my gun through the opening and press it into his groin. His jaw drops open and helps him take a deep breath.

"You are jeopardizing a police undercover operation," I hiss. "Back away from the car and let the lady go."

He blinks several times and nods, before slowly lowering the trunk. As the car pulls away I see his hand raised as if holding a salute.

Moving quickly again, we appear to be circling an industrial estate. Rachel is looking for something. She pulls off the road onto rough ground and stops, killing the engine.

In the sudden silence I can hear her voice but only one side of the conversation. "I can't see any traffic cone," she says. "No, I can't see it." She's growing desperate. "It's just a vacant lot . . . Wait! I see it now."

The door opens. I feel the car gently rock. I don't want her leaving. She has to stay close to me. There is no time to weigh my options. Hopefully, Aleksei and the Russian will have caught up with us and are holding their position.

Easing open the trunk, I roll over the lip and land heavily on the ground, using the momentum to spin away from the light. Then I lie dead still with my face pressed against loose gravel and mud.

Lifting my head I spy Rachel in the beam of the headlights. Ahead of her is a discarded industrial freezer standing upright in the middle of an empty lot. The stainless steel door is pitted and dented by stones, but still reflects the light. Sitting on top of it is an orange traffic cone.

Rachel walks toward it, stumbling over the broken bricks and rubble. Her jeans snag on a coil of barbed wire, half buried in the ground. She twists her leg free.

She's there now, standing in front of the freezer. It's almost as tall as she is. Reaching forward, she grips the handle and pulls open the door. A child's body tumbles forward. Small. Almost liquid. Rachel's arms instinctively reach out and her mouth opens in a silent scream.

I'm on my feet and running toward her. It's the longest forty yards— a horizontal Everest—crossed with my arms pumping and my stomach in my boots. Rachel is on her knees cradling the body. I grab her around her waist and lift her. She's adrenaline light. There's nothing of her. A cloth head lolls backward from her arms, with crosses for eyes and tufts of wool for hair. It's a child-size rag doll with a beige torso and beige limbs and a knobbly bald face, all swollen and worn.

"Listen to me, Rachel. It's not Mickey. It's just a doll. Look! See!"

She has a strange, almost serene look on her face. Only her eyelids are moving of their own accord. Slowly, I pry her fingers loose from the doll and lean her head against my chest.

A note is tied around the doll's neck, threaded with the same blue wool as the hair. Each letter is smeared dark red. I pray to God that it's paint.

Four words—written in capitals: THIS COULD BE HER!

Wrapping my jacket around Rachel, I lead her slowly back to the car and sit her inside. She hasn't uttered a sound. Nor does she respond to my voice. Instead she stares straight ahead at a point in the distance or in the future, a hundred yards or a hundred years from here and now.

I pick up the cell phone on the front seat. Silence. Inside my head I scream in frustration.

They'll call back, I tell myself. *Sit tight. Wait.*

Sliding onto the seat beside Rachel, I take her pulse and tug my jacket tighter around her shoulders. She needs a doctor. I should call this off now.

"What happened?" she asks, regaining some hold on reality.

"They hung up."

"But they'll call back?"

I don't know how to answer her. "I'm calling an ambulance."

"No!"

It's amazing! Although deep in shock there is still one pure, undamaged, functioning brain cell working inside her. It's like the queen bee of brain cells, being guarded by the hive . . . and it's buzzing now.

"If they have Mickey they'll call back," she says. The statement is so forceful and clear that I can't help doing as she says.

"OK. We wait."

She nods and wipes her nose with my sleeve. The headlights still pour white light in a path across the weeds and debris. I can just make out a line of trees, bruised purple against the ambient light.

We messed up. What else could we have done? I glance across at Rachel. Her lips are blue and trembling. With her arms hanging loosely by her sides, it seems only her skeleton is keeping her upright.

The silence amplifies the distant traffic noise . . . and then the phone!

Rachel doesn't flinch. Her mind has gone somewhere safer. I glance at the square glowing screen and take the call.

"Mrs. Carlyle?"

"She's not available."

I could finish a book in the pause.

"Where is she?" The voice is still distorted.

"Mrs. Carlyle is in no condition to talk. You'll have to talk to me."

"You're a policeman."

"It doesn't matter who I am. We can end this now. A straight exchange—the diamonds for the girl."

There is another long pause.

"I have the ransom. It's right here. Either you deal with me or you walk away."

"The girl dies."

"Fine! I think she's dead already. Prove me wrong."

The screen goes blank. He's hung up.

27

The door in my mind is suddenly sucked closed. A feeling of desperation replaces it, along with the sound of the wind. Joe is kneeling over
me. We gaze at each other.

"I remember."

"Just lie still."

"But I remember."

"There's an ambulance coming. Stay calm. I think you just fainted."

Around us the police divers are dragging air tanks from the Zodiacs
and dropping them on the dock. The sound reverberates through my
spine. Navigation lights have appeared on the water and the towers of
Canary Wharf look like vertical cities.

Joe was right all along. If I kept gathering details and following the
trail, something would eventually trigger my memories and the trickle
would become a torrent.

I take a sip of water from a plastic bottle and try to sit up. He lets
me lean on his shoulder. Somewhere overhead I see a passenger jet on
its final approach to Heathrow.

An ambulance officer kneels next to me.

"Any chest pains?"

"No."

"Shortness of breath?"

"No."

The guy has a really thick mustache and pizza breath. I recognize him from somewhere. His fingers are undoing the buttons of my shirt.

"I'm just going to check your heart rate," he says.

My hands shoot out and grip him by the wrist. His eyes widen and he gets a strange look on his face. Slowly, he shifts his gaze to my leg and then to the river.

"I remember you," I tell him.

"That's impossible. You were unconscious."

I'm still holding his wrist, squeezing it hard. "You saved my life."

"I didn't think you'd make it."

"Put paddles on my chest and I'll rip your heart out."

He nods and laughs nervously.

I take a belt of oxygen from a mask, while he takes my blood pressure. The clatter and crash of remembering has ceased for a moment like a held breath. I don't know if I should exhale.

In the spotlights I can see the Thames sliding across the rocks like a black tide. "New Boy" Dave has sealed off the dock with crime-scene tape. The divers are coming back in the morning to continue searching. How many more secrets lie in the silt?

"Let's go home," says Joe.

I don't answer him but I can feel my head shaking from side to side. I'm so close to remembering it all. I have to keep going. It can't wait for another day or be slept on overnight.

Joe calls Julianne and tells her he'll be home late. Her secondhand voice sounds tinny through the cell phone. It's a voice from the kitchen. She has children to feed. We have a child to find.

On the drive away from the river, I tell Joe about what I've remembered—describing the phone calls, the rag doll and the cold finality of the last phone call. Everything had a meaning, a function; a place in the pattern, the diamonds, the tracking devices, the pizza box . . .

We park on the same plot of waste ground, opposite the abandoned industrial freezer. Headlights reflect from the pitted silver door. The rag doll has gone but the witch's hat traffic cone lies among the weeds.

I get out of the car and move gingerly toward the freezer. Joe does his royal consort trick of walking four paces behind me. He's wearing a crumpled-looking linen jacket as if he's going on safari.

"Where was Rachel?"

"She stayed with the car. She couldn't go on."

"What happened next?"

I rack my brains, trying to trigger the memories again.

"He must have called back. The man who hung up the phone—he called again."

"What did he say?"

"I don't know. I can't remember. Wait!"

I look down at my clothes. "He wanted me to take my shoes off, but I didn't do it. I figured he couldn't be watching me—not all this time. He told me to walk straight ahead, past the freezer."

I'm moving as I talk. Ahead of us is a wire fence and beyond that the Bakerloo line. "I heard a young girl crying on the phone."

"Are you sure?"

"Yes, in the background."

The glow of the headlights is fainter now as we move farther from Joe's car. My eyes grow accustomed to the dark but my mind plays tricks. I keep seeing figures in the shadows, crouching in hollows and hiding behind trees.

The purple sky has no stars. That's one of the things I miss about living in the country—the stars and the silence and the frost on winter mornings like a freshly laundered sheet.

"There is a chain-link fence up ahead. I turned left and followed it until I reached the footbridge. He was giving me instructions on the phone."

"You didn't recognize his voice?"

"No."

The fence appears, dividing the darkness into black diamonds with silver frames. We turn and follow it to an arched footbridge above the railway line. A generator rumbles and repair crews are working beneath spotlights.

In the middle of the footbridge, I peer over the side at the silver ribbons curving to the north. "I can't remember what happened next."

"Did you drop the ransom off the bridge?"

"No. This is where the phone rang again. I was traveling too slowly. They were tracking me. The cell phone must have had a GPS device. Someone was sitting in front of a computer screen plotting my exact position."

We both peer down at the tracks as though looking for the answer.

The breeze carries the smell of burning coal and detergent. I can't hear the voice in my head anymore.

"Give it time," says Joe.

"No. I can't give it any more. I *have* to remember."

He takes out his cell phone and punches a number. My pocket vibrates. I flip it open and he turns away from me.

"Why have you stopped? KEEP MOVING! I told you where to go."

The knowledge rises up and breaks soundlessly through the surface. Joe has done it again—helped me to go back.

"Will Mickey be there?" I yell into the phone.

"Shut up and keep moving!"

Where? It's close by. The parking lot on the far side of the station! Move!

Running now, I quickly descend the stairs. Joe has trouble keeping up. I can barely see where I'm going but I remember the path. It curves alongside the railway line, above the cutting. Rigid steel gantries flank the tracks carrying the overhead wires.

A wind has sprung up, rattling fences and sending rubbish swirling past my legs. There are lights along the path, making it easier to see. Abruptly, the footpath opens into a deserted parking lot. A solitary lamppost at the center paints a dome of yellow on the tarmac. I remember a traffic cone sitting under the light. I ran toward it, holding the pizza box under one arm. It seemed an odd place to bring me. It was too open.

Joe has caught up with me. We're standing beneath the lamppost. At my feet is a barred metal grate.

"He wanted me to push the packages into the drain."

"What did you do?"

"I told him I wanted to see Mickey. He threatened to hang up again. His voice was very calm. He said she was close."

"Where?"

I turn my head. Thirty yards away is the dark outline of a stormwater drain. "He said she was waiting for me . . . down there."

Walking to the edge, we peer over the side. The steep concrete walls are sprayed with graffiti.

"I couldn't see her. It was too dark. I shouted her name. '*Mickey! Can you hear me?*' I was yelling into the phone. 'I can't see her. Where is she?' 'She's in the pipe,' he said. *'Where?'* I shouted: *'Mickey. Are you in there?'* "

Joe has hold of me now. He's frightened I might fall over the edge. At the same time he wants me to go on. "Show me," he says.

Set into the wall of the drain is a steel ladder. The rungs feel cold against my fingers. Joe is following me down. I couldn't hold the Glock and carry the pizza box at the same time. I left the gun in its holster and tucked the pizza box under my arm.

" *'Mickey! Can you hear me?'* "

My feet touch the bottom. Against the nearside wall I can just make out the deeper shadow of an access pipe.

She must have been in the pipe. It was the only place to hide.

" *'Michaela?'* "

There was a muffled rumble, like distant thunder. I could feel it through my shoes. I reached for my gun but left it there.

" *'Mickey?'* "

Wind ruffled my hair and I heard a rushing sound, like a train in a tunnel or the thunder of hooves on a loading ramp. My head jerked left and right, looking for her. The sound grew louder. It was coming toward me, coming out of the darkness . . . a wave.

Again the door opens and the world dissolves into noise and movement. Gravity is no more. I am flying, tumbling over and over, as an ocean roars past my ears. Head up, half a breath and I'm underwater, plunging into blackness.

Totally disoriented, I can't find the surface. I'm dragged sideways by the current and carried down a pipe or tunnel. My fingernails are torn and broken as they claw at the slick sides.

Seconds later I tumble into another vertical shaft. Snatching half a breath, I suck in silt and shit and detritus. I'm in a flooded sewer, full of reeking gases and decomposing turds. I'm going to die down here.

There are flashes of light above me. Iron grates. I reach out and my fingers close around the metal bars. The pressure of the water surges against my chest and neck, filling my mouth with foulness.

Holding my mouth and nose above the water, I try to push the grate upward. It won't budge. The force of the water pulls me horizontally.

Through the grate I see lights. Moving shapes. Pedestrians. Traffic. I try to scream something. They can't hear me. Someone steps off the pavement and tosses a cigarette into the gutter. Red sparks shower into my eyes.

"Help me! Help me!"

Something is crawling on my shoulder. A rat digs its claws into my shirt, dragging its sodden body from the current. I can smell wet fur and see sharp teeth, reflected in the square of light. My whole body shudders. Rats are all around me clinging to crevices.

Finger by finger, my hands surrender. I can't hold on much longer. The current is too strong. I think of Luke. He had such great lungs; air-sucking bags. He could hold his breath for much longer than I could, but not beneath the ice.

He was a stubborn little tyke. I used to give him Chinese burns. "Give up?" I'd say.

Tears would be welling in his eyes. "Never!"

"You just have to give up and I won't hurt you anymore."

"No."

In awe of him I'd offer a truce, but he'd refuse.

"OK, OK, you win," I'd say, sick of the game and embarrassed at hurting him.

My last finger surrenders. I roll faceup in the current and take a deep sulfurous breath. Washed into darkness, I tumble over a waterfall and get dragged into a larger pipe.

I don't know where the ransom has gone. Washed away, along with my shoes. And what of Mickey—is she drowning somewhere ahead of me or behind me? I heard a soft cry when I peered into the pipe. Perhaps it was the wind or the rats.

So this is how it ends! I am going to drown in stinking slime water, which is pretty much how I've lived—in a putrid soup of thieves, liars, murderers and victims. I'm a rat catcher and a sewer hunter, a bone grubber and a muck dredger. Poverty, ignorance and inequality create criminals, and I lock them away so that polite society doesn't have to smell them or fear them.

My shoulder strikes something hard and the pressure of the water rolls me over. Gulping a mouthful of air, I flay from side to side, trying to find a handhold as I tumble down a sloping ramp or weir.

Blindly, I plunge into a deep pool. I don't know which way is up. I could be swimming away from safety. My hand breaks the surface but the current won't let me go. A whirlpool drags me around and around, sucking me under. I want the air but the water wins.

The end is close now. I'm inside a narrow pipe, barely wide enough for my shoulders. There is no air pocket. My chest feels like it is wrapped in cables pulled tight with a ratchet.

I need to breathe. Carbon dioxide is building up in my blood. I'm being poisoned from within. The instinct not to breathe is being overcome by the agony of airlessness. My mouth opens. The first involuntary breath fills my windpipe with water. My throat contracts but can't stop water flooding into my lungs. I'm as helpless as the day I was born.

My shoulders are no longer scraping along the walls. A different, slower current has picked me up, turning me over and over like a leaf caught in a gust of wind.

I'm dying but I can't accept it. Above me—or maybe it's below—there is a solid gray light. I feel myself rising, fighting for the surface; climbing one hand at a time as if trying to pull the light toward me like it's a candelabrum at the end of a long table. The last few strokes are impossibly hard.

Breaking free, I vomit water and phlegm, making room for that first breath. A floodlight is blinding me. Something hard hooks my belt from behind and hauls me upward, dragging me onto a wooden deck. My lungs are heaving in their cage like bloated battery hens. Strong hands pump my stomach. Someone leans over me and wipes my chin and neck. It's Kirsten Fitzroy!

I loll back against her arm. She strokes my head, pushing wet hair across my forehead.

"Jesus, you're a crazy bastard!" she mutters, wiping my mouth again.

My stomach is still contracting and I can't speak.

The boat engine is idling in neutral. I can smell the fumes and see a dull light shining in the cockpit. Taking ragged, greedy gulps of air I turn my head and recognize Ray Murphy kneeling next to me, dressed all in black. "We should have let him drown," he says.

"Nobody is supposed to get hurt," replies Kirsten.

They argue with each other but Kirsten refuses to listen.

"Where's Mickey?" I whisper.

"Sshhh, just relax," she says.

"Is she OK?"

"Don't tell him a fucking thing!" threatens Murphy.

A tiny red dot is dancing on his forehead as though bouncing over the lyrics of a song. A fraction of a second later he makes a noise like a popped water balloon and half his head disappears in a spray of fine red mist and shattered bone. One eye, one cheek, half a jaw are suddenly erased from his face.

The sound of the bullet comes a heartbeat later. *Zip!*

Kirsten screams. Her eyes are as wide as a child's. Blood has splattered her cheeks.

Murphy's body is lying across me with his head on my chest. I roll him off me, kicking my legs to get away, sliding on the wet and bloody deck.

Kirsten still hasn't moved, immobilized by the shock. I turn and crawl back toward her.

A bullet enters my thigh. It's only a small hole, no bigger than my little finger, but as it exits it vaporizes skin, muscle and flesh, leaving a wound the size of a pie tin. Part of me is impressed. It's like watching a building getting blown up or a car crash.

Another bullet passes close to my ear and hits the deck near my right knee. Whoever is shooting is above us. I roll sideways, sliding through blood, until I reach Kirsten and pull her below the level of the wooden railings.

A section of the polished wood above our heads disintegrates and a splinter slices into her neck. She screams again.

Unbuckling my belt I lever myself upward and pull it around my upper thigh. I hold one end of the belt between my teeth and pull it tightly, trying to stem the flow of blood. I tie it off with sticky fingers.

Beside me, Ray Murphy flinches as a bullet tears through his thigh and enters the deck beneath him. On the far side, almost touching his leg, is a fisherman's net on a long pole. Lodged within the mesh are four plastic packages. The ransom.

Someone is in the wheelhouse trying desperately to engage the throttle but the mooring rope is still looped through a large silver cleat on the stern. Reaching under my armpit I feel for the Glock and pull it out of the holster. I look at Kirsten. She's deep in shock but listening.

"We can't stay here! You have to get to the wheelhouse. Quickly! Now!"

Kirsten nods.

I push her across the deck, watching her slip and slide through the blood. At the same time I spin around and aim the Glock blindly into the night sky. Nothing happens when I pull the trigger.

Kirsten's body spins and she clutches her side. A fraction of a second later I hear the bullet. Blood flows over her fingers but she keeps moving.

The choice of two targets has distracted the shooter but I have to do something about the floodlight. It's made of brass and chrome and fixed to a pillar in the center of the deck.

I spin the Glock until I'm holding it like a hammer. Using Ray Murphy's body as a shield, I slide across the deck until I'm beneath the light. Reaching up I smash the glass. The bulb flares and dies.

A shadow passes in front of me, tripping over my feet and sprawling on the deck. Gerry Brandt scrambles to his feet and tries to reach the diamonds. Launching a kick at his groin, I send him in the opposite direction. A bullet detonates in the space he left behind. He yowls and gives me a murderous look. I save the arsehole's life and this is the thanks I get.

His face is a pale blankness of shock. A red dot appears in the center of his chest. Even without the spotlight the sniper can still see us. He must have an infrared scope.

Gerry looks at his chest and then at me. He's about to die.

He rolls and the deck splinters beneath him. Over and over, he tumbles, past the netting and the packages. He disappears off the stern but the splash is muffled by the sound of the engine revving at full throttle. I have visions of him falling directly onto the spinning propeller.

Kirsten is in the wheelhouse, opening the throttle. A mooring rope is still looped through a cleat on the stern. The boat dips and sways, going nowhere. The dual engines are pulling us under. Rolling across the deck, I reach up and uncoil the last loop of rope from the cleat, feeling it whip through my fingers. The boat pitches forward but instead of turning away from the bank we steer toward it, colliding heavily against the stonework.

For fuck's sake, what's she doing!

The boat collides with a sunken pylon or another boat, before spinning into open water. There's nobody at the wheel. Where's she gone?

The boat is going around in circles. The shooter is waiting to get another clean shot at me.

Half crawling and half dragging myself across the deck toward the wheelhouse, I brace my back against the outside wall. Reaching up, I hook my fingers over the edge of the porthole, pulling myself upward until my eyes reach the glass window.

There's nobody there. In that same instant a dark stain fills my vision, a spray of blood. My finger disappears along with my wedding ring. It's a neat, clean amputation by a high-velocity bullet. I slide backward, landing heavily on the deck.

The shooter is somewhere high up on a bridge or a building. Now he's aiming at the engines or the fuel tanks. The current is turning the rudder and we're drifting on the tide. Soon we'll be out of range.

I suck the stump of my missing finger. There's surprisingly little blood. Where's Mickey? Was she in the pipe? Is she down below? I can't leave her behind.

I hear another sound—a different engine. With my back against the wall, I lever myself upward again, peering through the shattered porthole. I can't see any navigation lights. Instead I make out the silhouette of a boat. There is someone standing on the bow holding a gun.

I can either stay here or take my chances in the river. It takes less than a fraction of a second to decide.

Then I see Kirsten lying under a tarpaulin against the bow. I don't see her face, just her outline as she tries to stand and falls. She tries again and rolls over the side. I hear the splash followed by the sound of men yelling and bullets hitting the water.

The boat is getting closer. I have one good leg and one leaking. Pushing off the wall, I take two stumbling steps and roll over the railing. The cold comes as a shock. I don't know why. I'm still wet from before.

Kicking with one good leg and whipping my arms across my body, I swim down into the darkness where I'm going to drown or bleed to death. I'll let the river decide.

28

Joe is holding on to me. I'm growing accustomed to his face. He lays my arm over his shoulders and braces his body against mine.

"C'mon, let's get you out of here."

"I remembered."

"Yes, you did."

"What about Mickey?"

"She's not here. We'll find her."

I climb out of the drain and we limp across the parking lot. A pair of teenagers, a boy and a girl, have parked their car away from the light. I wonder what they make of two middle-aged men arm in arm. Are we drunks or lovers? I'm way past caring.

I have remembered. I have waited and hoped for this to happen. I have feared it. What if I shot someone? What if I had Mickey in my arms and lost her to the river? I dreamed the nightmare because I didn't have the truth.

It's almost ten o'clock when we reach Primrose Hill. Yellow light paints the edges of the curtains and a coal fire warms the sitting room.

"You'll stay here tonight," says Joe, opening the door.

I want to say no, but I'm too tired to argue. I can't go home or to Ali's parents' place. I'm like an infectious disease—poisoning those around me. I won't stay long. Just tonight.

I keep getting flashbacks of being under water, unable to breathe. I smell the foulness of the sewers and see the white-green water boiling at my feet. Each time it happens I take a ragged urgent breath. Joe looks at me. He thinks I'm having a heart attack.

"I should take you to the hospital. They could run some tests."

"No. I need to talk." I have to tell him what I remember in case I forget again.

Joe pours me a drink and then moves to sit down. He suddenly freezes. For a split second he looks like a statue, trapped between sitting and standing. Just as suddenly, he moves again as the signals reach his limbs. He smiles at me apologetically.

The mantelpiece is decorated with photographs of his family. The new baby has a moon face and a tangle of blond hair. She looks more like Joe than Julianne.

"Where is your lovely wife?"

"Tucked up in bed. She's an early riser."

Joe rocks forward with his hands between his thighs. I tell him about being washed through the sewers and what happened on the boat. I remember Kirsten Fitzroy wiping vomit from my lips and feeling the dead weight of Ray Murphy slumped across me. His blood leaked down my neck, pooling in the depression beneath my Adam's apple. I remember the sound of high-velocity bullets and seeing Kirsten spinning across the deck, clutching her side.

Memories carry more memories—fleeting images captured before they fade. Gerry Brandt going over the stern, the silhouette of a gunman, my finger disappearing . . . These things have all become substance now and nothing else is real except what happened that night. Even as I try to explain this to Joe I have the horrors of hindsight and regret to contend with. If only I could change what happened. If only I could go back.

Ray Murphy worked for Thames Water. He knew his way through the storm-water drains and sewers because he used to be a flusher and a flood planner. He knew what water main to sabotage to create a flood. The explosion would be blamed on methane or a gas leak and nobody would bother investigating further.

Radio transmitters and satellite tracking devices are useless underground and nobody was likely to make such a journey. Ray Murphy would also have known about the underground river beneath Dolphin Mansions. He and Kirsten provided each other with an alibi on the morning Mickey disappeared. But where did Gerry Brandt come into the operation? Perhaps they needed a third person for the plan.

"You still can't be sure they kidnapped Mickey," says Joe. "There's no direct evidence." A sudden spastic movement of his arm flicks up at my face. "It could still be a hoax. Kirsten had access to Rachel's flat. She could have taken strands of Mickey's hair and counted the money in her money box. If they kidnapped her three years ago, why wait until now to send a ransom demand?"

"Perhaps it was never about a ransom—not at first. Sir Douglas Carlyle said he would do almost anything to safeguard his granddaughter. We know he hired Kirsten to spy on Rachel. He was gathering evidence for a custody battle, but his lawyers told him he couldn't succeed. He might have taken the law into his own hands."

"What about Mickey's towel—how did it get to the cemetery?"

My brain is caught in a vague, desperate pause. Maybe they framed Howard. They put Mickey's blood on a towel and planted it in the cemetery. The police and the courts did the rest.

"You still have no proof that Mickey is alive."

"I know."

Bending toward the fire, Joe asks a question of the flames instead of me. "Why send the ransom demand now?"

"Greed."

At least it's a motive I understand. Joe can have his psychopaths and sadists but give me an old-fashioned everyday motive I can identify with.

"Who did the shooting? Who wanted them dead?"

"Someone who wanted to silence them or punish them," I whisper, rocking forward in the armchair. "It could have been Sir Douglas. If he arranged Mickey's kidnapping he may have been threatened with blackmail."

"Or what else? I know you don't think it's him."

"Aleksei."

"You said he was following you and Rachel that night."

"Following the diamonds."

Joe waits for my explanation. I know he's already there but he wants to hear me lay out the arguments. "Aleksei was never going to stand back and let anyone walk away with two million pounds. Whether they kidnapped Mickey or not, whether she was dead or alive, somebody was going to pay. Look what he did to his own brother."

"Did that include killing you?"

"No. I wasn't supposed to be on the boat. Nobody expected anyone to follow the ransom through the sewers."

"And the attack in the hospital?"

The memory climbs up my throat and hangs there. "I don't know. I haven't worked that out yet. Maybe he was frightened that I'd put the pieces together or perhaps he thinks I saw something that night . . ."

I still can't explain how the diamonds ended up in my linen cupboard. I know they were in the pizza box and I saw the packages on the deck of the *Charmaine*. Most of the facts fit but not all of them.

I have to convince the Met to reopen the investigation. This isn't about Howard Wavell anymore. Yes, he belongs in prison but not for this crime. Aleksei is the true monster.

———

I shudder awake and feel like weeping with tiredness. The day is just be-ginning but I can't tell where the last one ended. All night I have drowned in sewers and watched red dots dancing across the walls.

Julianne gives me a cheery smile in the kitchen. "How are you feeling?"

Five seconds of my life evaporate considering this and I decide not to answer. Instead I gratefully accept a cup of coffee.

"Where are the girls?"

"Joe is dropping Charlie at school. He took Emma along for the ride."

Her pale blue eyes stare at me with the vague, almost accusatory air of someone who has discovered the one true path to happiness—mar-ried life. Wrapped in a crimson skirt and light sweater, she looks beau-tiful as always. I can imagine her walking barefoot along a beach in some warm country, supporting a child on her slender hip. The Professor is a lucky man.

The front door opens. Joe is carrying Emma in one arm and the morning papers under the other. Julianne takes the toddler and kisses her cold nose, running her fingers through her curls.

"Cold nose, warm heart."

Joe opens a paper on the table. "There's a very small piece—just a couple of paragraphs—about a body found in the Thames."

"It's too early. They won't do a postmortem until today."

"What are you going to do?"

"I have to convince them to investigate the shootings. Will you come with me? I need someone to back me up."

"I don't think they'll listen to me."

"We have to try."

On the drive to New Scotland Yard my hands begin to shake. Maybe it's obvious to Joe what I'm going through—the headaches, stomach cramps, the constant churning in my guts. If he *does* recognize the withdrawal symptoms he doesn't say anything.

At the Yard we are made to wait like any other members of the public. My request to see the Commissioner is sent via the public affairs department through various branches of bureaucracy, only to be rejected. I ask to see the Assistant Commissioner. Again the request goes upstairs and is passed around like a problem that nobody wants. Eventually, I'm directed back to Campbell Smith.

We cross the city and cool our heels for another hour downstairs at the Harrow Road Police Station. Joe spends his time studying the missing persons posters as if he's at the National Portrait Gallery. Receptionists, secretaries and uniforms ignore us. A month ago I used to run this place. I gave it my life.

Eventually, Campbell agrees to see us.

Joe limps alongside me down the corridor, our footsteps echoing on the shiny floor. At the far end of the incident room civilian operators sit at a bank of computer screens. The flurry of their keystrokes sounds like rain falling on plastic. Some wear headsets, talking to officers in the field, running checks on names, addresses and license plates.

There's a new head of the Serious Crime Group—DI John Meldrum. He spies me. "Hey, we once had a guy who looked just like you working here. I think he might be dead."

"But not buried," I yell back. "Congratulations on the promotion."

I try to sound genuine but it doesn't work. Instead I feel a juvenile rush of anger and jealousy. Meldrum is in *my* office. His jacket is hanging over *my* chair.

Campbell makes us wait again outside his office. Joe doesn't understand the politics involved. It's not actually politics—it's spite.

Finally we are summoned. I let the Professor walk ahead of me. Campbell shakes his hand and gives him the no-brand smile. Then he studies me for a moment and motions to a chair. Meldrum slides his chair back a few inches, taking himself outside the circle. He's here to watch and witness.

I should be addressing a task force. There should be detectives sitting on chairs and corners of desks—men in gray suits with Father's Day ties and women with sensible hairstyles and minimal makeup. Instead I have to argue my case in front of a Chief Superintendent who thinks I betrayed my fellow officers and jeopardized a murder conviction.

Using a whiteboard, I explain what happened on the river. I write four names across the top: Ray Murphy, Kirsten Fitzroy, Gerry Brandt and Aleksei Kuznet. Ray Murphy is dead. Kirsten and Gerry Brandt are missing.

Taking out the brown envelope, I show him the ransom letters and the DNA reports, before describing the ransom drop and my trip through the sewers.

"I know it sounds far-fetched but I've been down there. I've followed the trail. They were waiting at the other end. Ray Murphy was the caretaker at Dolphin Mansions when Mickey Carlyle disappeared. I saw him shot and killed on the *Charmaine*. They'll match the blood and the bullets to the boat."

"Who killed him?"

"A sniper."

Meldrum leans closer. "And this is the same sniper who tried to kill you?"

"I got in the way."

Campbell hasn't said a word but I know he's struggling to remain composed.

"Kirsten Fitzroy lived at Dolphin Mansions when Mickey disappeared. She was Rachel Carlyle's best friend. I saw her shot on the

Charmaine. She suffered a stomach wound and went over the side. I don't know if she survived."

"Her flat was burgled," says Meldrum.

"Not burgled. It was searched. I think Aleksei Kuznet is looking for Kirsten. He wants to punish the people who sent the ransom demand. I believe they're the same people who kidnapped his daughter."

Campbell scoffs angrily. "Howard Wavell killed Mickey Carlyle."

"Even if you believe that—you have to accept that someone else sent the ransom demand. They included a lock of Mickey's hair and the bikini."

"Neither of which prove she's alive."

"No. But Ray Murphy is dead and Kirsten is in danger. Aleksei Kuznet was never going to let anyone steal two million pounds from him. He organized an execution. Now he's looking for Kirsten and Gerry Brandt—to finish the job."

I make a decision not to mention Sir Douglas Carlyle. Campbell is already on the edge. My only chance of persuading him to investigate is to let him believe the ransom was a hoax. I still can't prove otherwise.

"What does Gerry Brandt have to do with this?"

"He was on the *Charmaine*. I saw him go over the side."

I wait. I don't know if I've done enough.

Campbell has assumed a perfect proprietary air. "Let me get this straight. So far you have mentioned a kidnapping, a revenge killing, a shooting and a ransom demand. I'll add a few to the list: dereliction of duty, crippling a fellow police officer, withholding information and disobeying orders . . ."

A sense of alarm spreads through me. He doesn't understand. He can't see past Howard Wavell.

"We have to find Kirsten before Aleksei does. If she survived she would have needed medical help. We have to search local hospitals and ask doctors to go back through their files. We have to check her bank, telephone and travel records. We need to know her last known movements, possible associations and favorite haunts."

Campbell's look is piercing. "You're using the word 'we' a lot. For some reason you seem to be under the misapprehension that you're still a serving member of the Metropolitan Police."

I'm so angry my vision blurs.

Joe tries to calm things down. "It seems to me, gentlemen, that we're all seeking the truth. DI Meldrum here is investigating the shootings on the river. DI Ruiz is a witness. He's offering to make a statement. He won't interfere with the investigation."

Meldrum nods. Satisfied.

Campbell points his finger at me. "I want you to know one thing, Ruiz. I know the truth."

"Sure you do," I say.

Campbell gives me a triumphant smile. "You're right about Aleksei Kuznet. He's not the sort of man who lets someone take two million pounds from him. He claims *you* stole his diamonds and he's made an official complaint. We're drawing up a warrant for your arrest. If I were you—I'd get myself a lawyer."

Rage quickens my footsteps. Joe struggles to keep up with me as I stride down the corridor and punch through the swinging glass doors.

On the pavement a voice hits me like a cold wind. "Did you shoot him?"

Tony Murphy is asking the question with his entire body. "I had to go to the morgue to identify him. You ever seen a body like that . . . in pieces. And white like a candle melted into a puddle. The police say someone shot him. They got a witness. Is it you?"

"Yes."

He chews the inside of his cheek. "Did you shoot him?"

"No."

"Do you know who did?"

"I don't know who pulled the trigger but I saw him go down. I couldn't help him."

He swallows a lump in his throat. "So I'm looking after Mum and Stevie now. The pub is all we got left."

"I'm sorry."

He wants to do something more but can only stand there, imprisoned by his own misery.

"Go home, Tony. I'll sort this out."

29

Joe is waiting for me to say something. His dark brown eyes are staring at me with a vague sadness and the certainty that he can't help me. Meanwhile, I keep considering what should have happened. Campbell should have set up a task force. There should be two dozen detectives looking for Kirsten and Gerry Brandt. We should have Aleksei under surveillance and be searching his boat.

For one cool precise hour I want to know what to do. I want every decision to be the right one.

We're driving along Euston Road, past Regent's Park.

"So what are you going to do?" he asks.

"Find them."

"You can't do it alone."

"I have no choice."

Joe looks like a man with a plan. "What if we got some volunteers? We could call friends and family. How many people do you need?"

"I don't know. We need to contact the hospitals and doctors' surgeries and clinics. One of them must have treated Kirsten."

"We can use my office," says Joe. "It's not very big but there's the waiting room and the storeroom and a kitchen. There are six phone lines and a fax. We could get some more handsets. I'll get my secretary, Philippa, to start calling people."

We pull up outside his office. "What are you going to do?"

There's a small invisible shock in the air. A decision is made.

"One way or another I'm going to see Rachel Carlyle."

There will be no tennis today. Puddles cover the court and fat drops hang on the net like glass beads. It must be autumn—the rain is colder.

Parked in front of the Carlyle house, I watch the driveway and listen to the radio. Ray Murphy's name has been released but there's no mention of Kirsten during the news bulletin. Campbell won't allow it.

Glancing up at the house, I watch a dark Mercedes glide through the front gates and pause before turning left. Sir Douglas and Tottie are going out.

I give them a few minutes and then approach the house. Soggy mounds of leaves have gathered along the drive, trapped by the hedges. Some have clogged the fountain and the water spills over the side, flooding the footings.

Avoiding the front door, I skirt the building and use a set of stone steps at the right-hand side of the house. I knock four times before it opens. Thomas stands there.

"I need to speak to Rachel."

"Miss Rachel isn't here, Sir."

He's lying.

"You don't have to protect her. I don't want to cause any trouble. If she doesn't want to speak to me I'll leave."

He looks past me into the garden. "I don't think Sir Douglas would approve."

"Just ask her."

He contemplates this and agrees, leaving me waiting on the steps. A fire is smoldering somewhere, turning the air the color of dirty water.

Thomas appears again. "Miss Carlyle will see you in the kitchen."

He leads the way. We pass along hallways lined with paintings of foxhounds, horses and pheasants. The frames are so dark they blend into the walls and the animals appear to be suspended, set in aspic. Above the stairs there are English landscapes of lakes and rivers.

At first I don't realize that Rachel is already in the kitchen. She stands with the stillness of a photograph, tall and dark, with her hair drawn back.

"Your father said I couldn't see you," I say.

"He didn't ask me."

She is wearing jeans and a raw-silk shirt. Her wedge-shaped face is softened by the cut of her hair, which is shorter than I remember, loosely brushing her shoulders.

"I hear you couldn't remember what happened that night."

"Yes, for a while."

She bites her bottom lip and weighs whether to believe me. "You didn't forget about me."

"No. I didn't know what happened to you. I only discovered a few days ago."

Urgency fills her eyes. "Did you see Mickey? Was she there?"

"No, I'm sorry."

She purses her lips and turns her face away. "Losing your memory, forgetting everything, must be nice. All the terrible things in your life, the guilt, the regret, gone, washed away. Sometimes I wish . . ." She doesn't finish. Leaning over the sink, she fills a glass of water from the tap and empties it into a row of African violets on the windowsill. "You never asked me why I married Aleksei."

"It's none of my business."

"I met my ex-husband at a fund-raising dinner for Bosnian orphans. He wrote a very large check. He wrote a lot of very large checks in those days. Whenever I took him to lectures and documentaries about deforestation or animal cruelty or the plight of the homeless—he pulled out his checkbook."

"He was buying your affection."

"I thought he believed in the same things."

"Your parents didn't like him?"

"They were horrified. Aleksei had no equal—anybody would have been better than a Russian émigré with a murdering father."

"Did you love him?"

She ponders this. "Yes. I think so."

"What happened?"

She shrugs. "We got married. For the first three years we lived in Holland. Mickey was born in Amsterdam: Aleksei was building up the business."

Rachel's voice is low and introspective. "In spite of what my father says, I'm not a foolish person. I knew something was going on. Mostly it was just rumors and nervous glances in restaurants. I used to ask Aleksei but he told me people were jealous of him. I knew he was involved in something illegal. I kept asking questions and he grew irritated. He told me that a wife should not question her husband. She must obey.

"Then one day the wife of a Dutch flower grower visited me at home. I don't know how she found my address. She showed me a photograph of her husband. His face was so scarred by acid that his skin looked like melted wax.

" 'Tell me why a woman would stay with a man who looks like this?' she asked me. I shook my head. Then she said, 'Because it cannot be as bad as staying with the man who would do such a thing.'

"From then on I began to discover things. I eavesdropped on conversations, read e-mails and kept copies of letters. I learned things—"

"Enough to get you killed."

"Enough to keep me safe," she corrects. "I learned how Aleksei does business. It is simple and brutal. First he offers to buy a business. If a price cannot be agreed he burns it down. If they set up again he burns their houses down. And if the message still fails to be heard, he burns down the houses of their relatives and the schools of their children."

"What did Aleksei do when you left him?"

"First he begged me to come back. Then he tried to bribe me with grand gestures. Finally he tried to bully me."

"You didn't go back to your family."

Pushing hair behind her ears with both hands, she shakes her head. "I've been running away from them my whole life."

We sit in silence. The warm air rising from the stove lifts loose strands of her hair, suspending them in midair.

"When did you last see Kirsten Fitzroy?"

"About two months ago; she said she was going abroad."

"Did she say where?"

"America or South America; she had some brochures. It might have been Argentina. She was going to send me postcards but I didn't receive a thing. What's happened? Is she in trouble?"

"You met at Dolphin Mansions."

"Yes."

"Did Kirsten ever meet your father?"

"No, I don't think so."

"Are you sure?"

"Please tell me what she's supposed to have done."

"Your father paid her rent at Dolphin Mansions. Later he helped her buy her flat in Notting Hill."

Rachel doesn't react. I can't tell if she's shocked or if she suspected it all along.

"She was keeping watch on you. Sir Douglas wanted custody of Mickey. He had his lawyers preparing an application. They were going to argue you were unfit to care for a child because of your drinking. The application was withdrawn after you joined AA."

"I can't believe any of this," she whispers.

There's more. I don't know how much to tell her.

"On the night of the ransom drop, I followed the diamonds through the sewers. I washed up in the Thames. Kirsten saved my life."

"What was she doing there?"

"She and Ray Murphy were waiting for the diamonds. They organized the whole thing—the ransom demand, the locks of hair, the bikini. Kirsten knew everything about you and Mickey. She counted the money in Mickey's money box. She knew exactly what buttons to press."

Rachel shakes her head. "But the bikini . . . it belonged to Mickey."

"And they took it from her."

Suddenly, she realizes what I'm saying. The sense of alarm spreads through her before the instant of comprehension.

At that moment a door swings open somewhere in the house and the air pressure changes. Sir Douglas comes storming through the main hall, yelling at Thomas to call the police. The butler must have phoned him the moment I arrived.

I lose sight of him for a few seconds and then he appears in the doorway of the kitchen carrying a shotgun. His face is like a warning light.

"You stay here! Don't go anywhere. You're under arrest."

"Calm down."

"You're trespassing on my property."

"Put the gun down, Daddy."

He waves the gun at me. "Stay away from him."

"Please put that down."

Rachel is watching him with a you-must-be-crazy look. She takes a step toward him, distracting him for a moment. He doesn't see me close the final two paces. I seize the gun, twisting it out of his hands and drop him with a punch just below his ribs. I look at Rachel apologetically. I didn't want to hit him.

Sir Douglas takes a long staggering breath. He tries to talk, telling me to get out. I'm already leaving after emptying the cartridges and tossing the gun toward Thomas. Rachel follows, pleading with me to explain. "Why would they do that? Why would they take Mickey?"

Turning back, I blink at her sadly. "I don't know. Ask your father."

I don't want to give her false hopes. I'm not even sure if I'm talking sense. I've been wrong so often lately.

Out of the front door and down the steps, I crunch along the gravel drive. Rachel watches from the steps.

"What about Mickey?" she yells.

"I don't think Howard killed her."

At first she doesn't react. Maybe she's given up hope or she's shackled to the past. This is only for a moment and then she's running toward me. I have given her a choice between hating, forgiving and believing. She wants to believe.

30

"Where are we going?" asks Rachel.

"You'll see. It's right up here."

We pull up outside a cottage in Hampstead; there is an arbor over the front gate and neatly pruned rosebushes along the path. Making a dash through the light rain, we squeeze beneath the overhang until the doorbell is answered.

Esmerelda Bird, a matronly woman in a skirt and cardigan, leaves us waiting in the sitting room while she gets her husband. We perch on the edge of sofas looking at a room full of crocheted cushion covers, lace doilies and photographs of overweight grandchildren. This is how sitting rooms used to look before people started buying up warehouses full of lacquered pine from Scandinavia.

I met the Birds three years ago, during the original investigation. Retired pensioners, they're the sort of couple who clip their vowels when addressing a police officer and have special voices for the telephone.

Mrs. Bird returns. She's done something to her hair, tied it back or perhaps just brushed it a different way. And she's changed into a different cardigan and put on her pearl earrings.

"I'm just making a pot of tea."

"That really won't be necessary."

She doesn't hear me. "I have a cake."

Brian Bird hobbles into view, a slow-motion cadaver who has a completely bald head and a face as wrinkled as crushed cellophane. He rocks forward on a walking stick and takes what seems like an hour to lower himself into a chair.

Nothing is said as the tea is brewed, poured, strained and sweetened. Slices of cake are offered around.

"Do you remember when I last came to see you?"

"Yes. It was about that missing girl—the one we saw on the station platform."

Rachel looks from Mrs. Bird's face to mine and back again.

"That's right. You thought you saw Michaela Carlyle. This is her mother, Rachel."

The couple give her sad smiles.

"I want you to tell Mrs. Carlyle what you saw that night."

"Yes, of course," says Mrs. Bird, "but I think we must have been mistaken. That dreadful man went to prison. I can't think of his name." She looks to her husband who stares at her blankly.

Rachel finds her voice. "Please tell me what you saw."

"On the platform, yes . . . let me see. It was . . . a Wednesday evening. We'd been to see *Les Miserables* at the Queens Theatre. I've been to see *Les Miz* more than thirty times. Brian missed out on some shows because of his heart bypass operation. Isn't that right, Brian?"

Brian nods.

"What makes you think it was Mickey?" I ask.

"Her picture had been in all the papers. We were just going down the escalator. She was loitering at the bottom."

"Loitering?"

"Yes. She seemed a little lost."

"What was she wearing?"

"Well, let me think. It's so long ago now, dear. What did I tell you then?"

"Trousers and a jacket," I prompt.

"Oh, yes, although Brian thought she was wearing a pair of those tracksuit bottoms that zipped up over her shoes. And she definitely had a hood."

"And this hood was up?"

"Up."

"So you didn't see her hair—if it was long or short?"

"I couldn't tell."

"What about the color?"

"Light brown."

"How close did you get to her?"

"Brian couldn't move very quickly on account of his legs. I was ahead of him. We were maybe ten feet away. I didn't recognize her at first. I said to her, 'Can I help you, dear? Are you lost?' But she just ran off."

"Where?"

"Along the platform." Her hand points the way, past Rachel's shoulder, and she nods resolutely. Then she leans forward with her teacup, using her other hand to find the saucer and bring both together.

"I think I talked to you back then about your glasses, do you remember?"

She touches the bridge of her nose self-consciously. "Yes."

"You weren't wearing them?"

"No. I normally don't forget."

"Did she have pierced ears?"

"I can't remember. She ran off too quickly."

"But you did say she had a gap in her teeth and freckles. She was also carrying something. Could it have been a towel?"

"Oh dear, I don't know. I didn't look that closely. There were other people on the platform. They must have seen her."

"We looked for them. Nobody came forward."

"Oh dear."

A teacup rattles against a saucer. Rachel's hands are shaking. "Do you have grandchildren, Mrs. Bird?"

"Oh, yes, dear. Six of them."

"How old are they?"

"They're aged between eight and eighteen."

"And the girl you saw on the platform, she was about the same age as your youngest grandchild is now?"

"Yes."

"Did she seem frightened?"

"Lost. She seemed lost."

Rachel's eyes are fixed with an almost ecstatic intensity.

"I'm sorry I can't remember any more. It's so long ago." Mrs. Bird glances at her hands. "It did look like her but when the police arrested that chap . . . well . . . I thought I must have been mistaken. When you get old your eyes play tricks. I'm very sorry for your loss. Another cup of tea?"

Back in the car Rachel is full of questions, most of which I can't answer. There were dozens of reported sightings of Mickey in the weeks after she disappeared. Without any independent corroboration and given that Mrs. Bird wasn't wearing her glasses, I couldn't rely on her account.

"There must have been cameras at the station," says Rachel.

"The footage is useless. We couldn't even tell if it was a child."

Rachel is adamant. "I want to see it."

"Good. That's where we're going now."

The headquarters of London Underground is on Broadway, around the corner from New Scotland Yard. The Area Commander of the Transport Police, Chief Superintendent Paul Magee, is an old friend. I've known him for thirty years. Back in those days the IRA kept him awake at night. Now it's a different type of terrorist.

His face is thin and shaved. He looks almost youthful, despite his gray hair, which seems whiter every time I see him. Soon he'll pass for blond.

"You look like shit, Vince."

"People keep telling me that."

"I hear you're getting divorced again. What happened?"

"I forgot to put sugar in her tea."

He laughs. Paul is married to a girl he met in grammar school. Shirley is a real keeper, who thinks I'm a bad influence but still made me godfather to her eldest boy.

We're sitting in Paul's office, which has a view over Wellington Barracks. He can watch the "new guard" march out every morning along Birdcage Walk to Buckingham Palace. Rachel is hanging back, waiting for an introduction. He doesn't recognize her name. I tell him we need to see a CCTV tape from three years ago.

"We don't keep them that long."

"This one you kept. I asked you to."

He suddenly puts two and two together and glances back at Rachel. Without another word, he takes us out of his office and down the corridor, tapping security codes into consoles and leading us deeper into the building.

Eventually, we're sitting in a small room, waiting for a video player to rewind a tape. Rachel watches motionless, even her breathing seems suspended. Grainy black-and-white images appear on the screen. They show a figure near the bottom of the escalators at Leicester Square Underground. Assuming it's a girl, she is wearing a dark blue tracksuit and carrying something in her arms. It might be a beach towel. It could be anything.

There were twelve security cameras at the station, each mounted above platforms and escalators. The angles were wrong because they didn't pick up faces. No amount of computer enhancement could make someone look up into the lens.

She pauses at the bottom of the escalator, as though momentarily unsure of where to go. Mrs. Bird comes into view and then Mr. Bird a few moments later, planting his walker and shuffling behind her. Mrs. Bird can be seen saying something to the girl, who turns away, disappearing through an arch onto the southbound platform.

The time and date are displayed in the bottom right-hand corner of the screen: 22:14, July 24, Wednesday evening.

A second camera on the platform picked up the girl again, but from much farther away. She appeared to be alone. A plump, dark-haired woman dressed in a nurse's uniform walked past her.

"So what do you think?" I ask Rachel.

She doesn't answer. I turn to face her and see tears welling up in her eyes. She blinks and they fall.

"Are you sure?"

She nods, still silent.

"But she could be seven or seventeen. You can't even see her face."

"It's her. I know my daughter. I know how she walks and holds her head."

Nine times out of ten I would not believe it was anything more than a mother's desperate desire to believe her daughter is alive. That's why

I didn't show Rachel the tape three years ago. It risked derailing the entire investigation, sending dozens of officers off on a tangent and diverting public attention instead of focusing it.

Now I believe Rachel. I know there isn't a judge or a jury in the land who would accept beyond doubt that Mickey is the person on the tape but that doesn't matter. The person who knows her best is sure. On Wednesday, July 24—two days after she disappeared—Mickey was still alive.

31

The only other person in Joe's waiting room is a middle-aged man in a cheap suit that bunches at his shoulders when he folds his arms. He picks at his teeth with a matchstick and watches me take a seat.

"The secretary went to get coffee," he says. "The Professor has a patient."

I nod and notice him watching me. Finally, he asks, "Do we know each other?"

"I don't think so. Are you a copper?"

"Yeah. DS Roger Casey. They call me the Dodger." He moves a few seats closer and thrusts out his hand, at the same time eyeing up Rachel.

"So where are you working, Roger?"

"Vice out of Holborn."

He's sitting close, feeling a sense of camaraderie. I should probably remember his face but a lot of guys his age have left the service in the past ten years.

"You heard this one," he asks. "How many coppers does it take to throw a man down the stairs?"

"I don't know. How many?"

"None. He fell."

Roger laughs and I offer him a chiseled smile. He lifts an eyebrow and goes quiet.

The Professor's secretary arrives back, carrying takeout coffee and a brown paper bag stained by a pastry. She looks barely out of school and blinks through wire-frame glasses as though she should have known we were coming.

"I'm DI Ruiz. Could you tell the Professor we're here?"

She sighs, "Join the queue."

At that moment the inner door opens and a young woman emerges with red-rimmed eyes.

Joe is behind her.

"So I'll see you next week, Christine. Remember, it's not immodest to wear culottes and it doesn't make you less feminine."

She nods and keeps her eyes down. Everyone in the room does the same apart from Roger who starts giggling. The poor woman flees down the corridor.

Joe gives him an angry stare and is about to say something when he sees me sitting with Rachel. "Come inside, you two."

"The Detective Sergeant was here first," I suggest.

Joe shakes his head and sighs. "Oh dear . . . and you were doing so well, Roger." He turns to his secretary. "For future reference, Philippa, DI Ruiz is a *real* police officer. Not everyone who comes in here claiming to be a detective is a fantasist."

Philippa's cheeks redden and Rachel starts to giggle.

"I'm sorry about Roger," says Joe, as we're ushered into his office. "He pretends to be a police officer and tricks prostitutes into giving him free sex."

"Does it work?"

"Apparently."

"He's a freak!"

Joe looks at me awkwardly. "Well, he's part of our team."

There's a promising start!

Joe has spent the morning calling in favors. So far we have thirteen volunteers including two of my old rugby mates and a snitch called "Dicko" who has a nose for trouble and no sense of smell at all, which unfortunately means his personal hygiene leaves a lot to be desired.

Over the next hour the rest of the "team" arrives. Joe has managed to recruit his brother-in-law Eric and his younger sister, Rebecca, who works for the United Nations. Julianne is coming after she picks up Charlie from school. There are also several patients, including Margaret, who is nursing a torpedo-shaped life preserver, and another woman, Jean, who keeps disinfecting the phones with wet wipes.

Margaret sidles up to me. "I hear you almost drowned. Don't trust bridges." She taps her orange torpedo reassuringly.

When the last of the stragglers arrive, I gather them in the waiting room. It is the strangest collection of "detectives" I have ever commanded.

Pinning two photographs to a corkboard, I clear my throat and introduce myself—not as a Detective Inspector but as a member of the public.

"The two people in these photographs are missing. Their names are Kirsten Fitzroy and Gerry Brandt. We hope to find them."

"What did they do?" asks Margaret.

"I believe they kidnapped a young girl."

A murmur goes around the room.

"We need to discover how they're linked—when they met, where they talked, what they have in common—but most importantly we have to locate them. Each of you will be given a task. You won't be asked to do anything illegal, but this is detective work and has to remain confidential."

"Why don't we just ask the police to find them?" asks Eric, perched on the edge of a desk.

"The police aren't looking hard enough."

"But you're a policeman!"

"Not anymore."

Moving on, I explain that Kirsten was last seen going over the side of the *Charmaine*. "She suffered a stomach wound and may not have survived her injuries or the river but we're going to assume she's still alive. Gerry Brandt is a known drug dealer, pimp and armed robber. Nobody is to approach him."

I glance at Dicko. The flesh around his mouth seems to be moving but no sound comes out.

Addressing him directly, I say, "I want you to talk to anyone who knows him—suppliers, junkies, mules, friends . . . He used to hang out in a pub on Pentonville Road. See if anyone remembers him."

After a few seconds of clicking his teeth, he says, "Might need some readies."

"If I catch you drinking I'll drill a hole in your head."

The women peel their eyebrows off their hairlines.

"Maybe I should go with him," suggests Roger.

"Fine. Remember what I said. Under no circumstances do you approach Gerry Brandt."

Roger gives me a casual salute.

"Philippa, Margaret and Jean, I want you to ring the hospitals, clinics and doctors' surgeries. Make up a story. Say you're looking for a missing friend. Rachel and the Professor will contact Kirsten's family and any former employers. She grew up in the West Country."

"What are you going to do?" asks Joe.

"Gerry Brandt had a former girlfriend, a skinny thing with bleeding gums and blond streaks. I'm hoping she might know where he's hiding."

Hell's Half Mile is a road behind Kings Cross Station where the curbs get crawled and prostitutes hunt in packs. Some of these girls are barely sixteen but there's no way of telling. Even without the scars and bruises, a year on the streets adds five years to the faces.

Very few prostitutes work the streets anymore because the police have chased them indoors. Now they work for escort agencies and massage parlors, or they move around following the political conferences, trade shows and exhibitions. Become a prostitute and see the world!

The walk-up places are open doorways leading to upstairs flats with signs in the windows announcing BUSTY YOUNG MODEL or something similar. Most have a maid, usually an older woman, who takes the money and a small tip.

Apart from the passing trade, they advertise with cards in phone boxes or rely on the patron saint of the horny—the London cabbie.

Cruising the street slowly I try to recognize any of the girls. A pixie with a pageboy cut and a padded bra saunters over.

"You want to ask me something?"

"Yeah, what was on *Sesame Street* this morning?"

Her face flushes. "Piss off!"

"I'm looking for a particular girl. Her name is Theresa. She's about five foot six. Blond. Comes from Harrogate. And she has a tattoo on her shoulder of a butterfly."

"What's this girl got that I ain't?"

"Boobs. Cut the crap. Have you seen her?"

"Nah."

"OK, here's the deal. I got a fifty here. You walk down the street, knock on the doors and ask if any of the girls know this Theresa. You get me the right answer and you get the fifty."

"Are you a copper?"

"No." For once I'm telling the truth.

"Why you want her?"

"She won the bloody lottery. What does it matter to you?"

"I'll do it for a ton."

"You get fifty. It's the easiest money you ever made."

"You reckon! Some of these guys blow just looking at me."

"Sure."

I watch her leave. She doesn't even know how to walk like a woman yet. Maybe it's an occupational trait.

The streetlights are beginning to glow purple as they blink into life. I take a table at a delicatessen on the corner which is doing a roaring trade in takeout coffee and homemade soup served by Czech girls with heavy accents and tight tops. I'm old enough to be their grandfather but that doesn't make me feel as guilty as it should. One of them brings me coffee and a muffin that looks half-cooked inside.

The place is full of pimps and working girls, counting the wages of sin. A couple of them regard me suspiciously, sitting still and very straight like a pair of magistrates.

Pimps don't look the same in real life as they do in films. They're not snappy dressers in long leather coats and lots of gold jewelry. Mostly they're dealers and boyfriends who'd spread their own legs if anyone would pay for the privilege.

The pixie with the pageboy cut has come back. She eyes the large pot of soup steaming on a burner. I buy her a bowl. An older black girl is looking at us nervously through the window. She's dressed in a microskirt and lace-up boots. Her hair is twisted into bangs that run back from her forehead between paler strips of scalp.

"She says she knows Theresa."

"What's her name?"

"Brittany."

"Why won't she come inside?"

"Her pimp might be watching. He don't like her slacking. Where's my fifty?"

She reaches to snatch it out of my fingers. I pin her wrist to the table and turn it over, pulling her sleeve up her arm. Her skin is pale and unblemished.

"I'm not using," she sniffles.

"Good. Go home."

"Yeah, sure—you should see where I live."

Brittany talks to me outside. She has ants in her pants about something and can't stand still. Her jaw works constantly on gum, punctuating sentences with a sucking noise.

"What's Theresa done?"

"Nothing, I just want to talk to her."

Brittany glances down the street, trying to decide if she believes me. Eventually, she surrenders to apathy and a twenty quid note.

"She lives in a tower block in Finsbury Park. She's got a kid now."

"Is she still on the game?"

"Only a few regulars."

Fifteen minutes later I'm climbing to the fourteenth floor of a tower block because the lift is out of order. Various cooking smells mingle in the stairwell, along with the noise from dueling TVs and domestic disputes.

Theresa must be expecting someone else because she opens the door with a flourish, wearing only a black teddy and bunny ears.

"Shit! Who are you?"

"The Big Bad Wolf."

She looks past me into the hallway and then back at me. The penny drops. "Oh, no!"

Turning away from the door she wraps a dressing gown around her shoulders and I follow her inside. There are baby toys scattered on the living-room floor and a monitor hums on top of the TV. The bedroom door is closed.

"You remember me?"

"Yeah." She flicks her hair over her shoulder and lights a cigarette.

"I'm looking for Gerry."

"You were looking for him three years ago."

"I'm very patient."

She glances at a pineapple-shaped clock on the wall. "Hey, I got someone coming. He's my best customer. If he finds you here he'll never come back."

"Married is he?"

"The best customers are."

I push aside a colorful baby rug and take a seat on the sofa bed. "About Gerry."

"I ain't seen him."

"Maybe he's hiding in the bedroom."

"Please don't wake the baby."

She's quite a pretty-looking thing, except for her crooked nose and the junkie hollows beneath her eyes.

"Gerry ran out on me three years ago. I thought he was probably dead until he turned up again during the summer with a suntan and lots of big-shot stories about owning a bar in Thailand."

"A bar?"

"Yeah. He had a passport and a driver's license in the name of some other geezer. I figured he must have pinched it."

"You remember the name?"

"Peter Brannigan."

"Why did he come back?"

"Dunno. He said he had a big payday coming."

"When did you last see him?"

"Three days ago—must have been Tuesday night." She stubs out her cigarette and lights another. "He came busting in here, sweating and yelling. He was scared. I ain't never seen anybody that scared. He looked like the devil himself was chasing him."

That must have been after he crippled Ali. I remember how terrified he looked when he took off. He thought Aleksei had sent someone to kill him.

Theresa dabs at the lipstick in the corners of her mouth. "He wanted money. Said he had to get out of the country. He was crazy, I tell you. I let him stay but as soon as he fell asleep I got a knife. I put it right under here." She points to her septum, pushing up her nostrils. "I told him to get out. If he comes back I'll kill him."

"And that was Tuesday night."

"Early hours of Wednesday."

"Do you know where he went?"

"Nope. And I don't care. He's a bloody nutcase."

The packet of cigarettes is crushed in her hand. Glossy eyes slide over the sofa and the toys before resting on me. "I got something good going here. I don't need Grub, or Peter Brannigan or whoever else he calls himself, to mess it up."

———

Three hours ago it was midnight. The desk lamp in Joe's office casts a circular glow, harsh in the center and soft at the edges. My eyes are so full of grit I can only look at the shadows.

I bought pizzas at nine and the coffee ran out at eleven. The rest of the volunteers have gone home except for Joe and Rachel, who are still hard at work. A large corkboard in the waiting room is plastered with phone messages and notes. Nearby there are box files stacked five abreast beneath the window forming a makeshift shelf for leftover pizza and bottles of water.

Rachel is still on the phone.

"Hello, is that St. Catherine's? I'm sorry to call so late. I'm looking for a friend of mine who has gone missing. Her name is Kirsten Fitzroy. She's thirty-three, with brown hair, green eyes and a birthmark on her neck."

Rachel waits. "OK, she's not there now but she may have needed medical help in the past few weeks. You have a clinic. Is it possible you could check your files? Yes, I know it's late but it's very important." She refuses to lose this battle. "She's actually my sister. My parents are worried sick about her. We think she might have hurt herself . . ."

Again she waits. "No record. OK. Thank you so much. I'm sorry to have troubled you."

They have all worked so hard. Roger and Dicko took a magical mystery tour of London's underbelly, visiting pubs, illegal casinos and strip joints looking for Gerry. Meanwhile, Margaret proved to be a genius at getting passenger manifests out of airlines, ferry and train operators. So far we've established that Kirsten hasn't left the country on any regular transport service.

London's major hospitals and twenty-four-hour clinics have no record of a female shooting victim in the week after the ransom drop. Now we're ringing individual doctors and hospices.

We know more about Kirsten than we did six hours ago. She was born in Exeter in 1972, the daughter of a postman and a teaching assistant. Her two brothers still live in Devon. In 1984 she won a scholarship to Sherborne School for Girls in Dorset. She excelled in art and history. One of her sculptures was accepted in the Summer Exhibition at the Royal Academy in London. In her final year she left the school under a cloud, along with two other students. Drugs were mentioned but nothing went on file.

A year later Kirsten sat A levels and won a place to read art and history at Bristol University. After several false starts, she graduated with a first in 1995. That same year she was photographed at a polo match in Windsor by *Tatler* magazine with the son of a Saudi Minister. Then she seemed to disappear, surfacing again six years later as the manager of the employment agency.

"I spoke to a few people at Sotheby's," says Rachel. "Kirsten was well known among the dealers and salesroom staff. She always wore black to auctions and talked constantly on a cell phone."

"She was bidding for someone else?"

"Four months ago she bid £170,000 for a Turner watercolor."

"Who was the *real* buyer?"

"Sotheby's wouldn't say but faxed me a photograph of the painting. I've seen it hanging in my father's study."

Her eyes, unnaturally wide, flick back and forth between my face and Joe's. Her thoughts are moving at a terrible speed—making her whole body vibrate.

"I still can't believe she could have done this. She loved Mickey."

"What are you going to do?"

"Ask my father."

"Will he tell you the truth?"

"There's always a first time."

Joe's arm twitches as he reaches for a bottle of water. "We're a long way behind. Kirsten's family and friends have been contacted. Some have been threatened. One of Kirsten's brothers was beaten senseless only an hour after he slammed the door on a man claiming to be a debt collector."

"Do you think her family knows where she is?" I ask him.

"No."

Rachel nods. "Kirsten wouldn't put them in danger."

Why is Aleksei going to so much trouble? If he sat back he knows that Kirsten will turn up eventually. They always do, look at Gerry Brandt. This isn't just about the diamonds. It's more personal than that. According to the stories, Aleksei had his own brother killed for dishonoring the family. What would he do to someone who kidnapped his daughter?

Sitting opposite me, Joe continues making notes. He reminds me of my old primary-school teacher, who knew exactly how many pencils, books and paintbrushes were in the storeroom, yet would arrive at school with shaving foam on his neck, or wearing different-colored socks.

Julianne called me. She made me promise not to let Joe drive home. His Parkinson's gets worse when he's tired. She also talked to Joe and told him to look after me.

Rachel begins picking up cups and carrying them into the kitchenette. There isn't much to wash. Jean has been manically cleaning all evening.

Reaching into his pocket, Joe takes out a crumpled page of notes and smooths it on his thigh. "I've been thinking."

"Good."

"I want to forget about the kidnapping question and concentrate on the ransom demand. If you look at the letters there's no indication of psychological looseness or obsession. They asked for a huge ransom but it was a feasible amount for someone like Aleksei to pay or even Sir Douglas. Enough to be worth the risk.

"We know there were at least three people involved. Kirsten was the likely planner. Ray Murphy did the logistics. Intellectually Kirsten is above average. Everything about her typifies carefulness and preplanning. She must have experimented with the packages, getting the right dimensions. She was aware of tracking devices and forensic tests . . ."

The Professor is on a roll. I've seen him do this before—crawl inside someone's head until he knows what they know and feels what they feel. "The ransom plot was clever but overcomplicated. When people are faced with a complex problem they often only consider a certain number of options or scenarios. If there are too many unknowns, they get confused. That's why people plan up to a point or in sections. Sometimes they leave out the exit strategies because they don't consider failure as a possibility.

"Whoever conceived the plan worked everything out but they made it too complicated. Look at all the things that had to go right. The packaging of the ransom had to be perfect, the control of the courier, getting the diamonds to the storm-water drain, detonating the explosives, creating the flood . . . If any one of these things had gone wrong, the plan would have failed."

"Maybe they tested the system first. The voice on the phone to Rachel said, 'Let's do this one more time.' "

Joe nods slowly but isn't convinced. "This is the sort of operation you only mess up once. Given a second chance, you'd want to simplify things."

He begins pacing, flourishing his hands. "Let's assume just for a moment that they did kidnap her. They took her underground, which is also how they chose to collect the ransom. They needed somewhere to hold her. Somewhere that Ray Murphy was most likely to have chosen."

"Not in the sewers—it's too dangerous."

"And taking her above ground meant risking recognition. Her photograph was everywhere."

"You think they held her underground?"

"It's worth considering."

There's someone I can ask—Weatherman Pete. I look at my watch. I'll call him in a few hours.

"What about Gerry Brandt?" asks Joe.

"He had a passport in the name of Peter Brannigan as well as a driver's license. It costs a lot of money to get a new identity and to disappear—even to a place like Thailand. You need connections."

"You thinking drugs?"

"Maybe. According to international directory inquiries there's a beach bar called Brannigan's in Phuket."

"Fancy that. What's the time in Thailand?"

"Time to wake them up."

Rachel has fallen asleep on the sofa in the waiting room. I gently shake her awake. "Come on, I'll take you home."

"But what about Mickey?"

"We'll find her. First you need to sleep. Where do you want to go?"

"Dolphin Mansions."

"Take my car," says Joe. "I've called a cab."

He's still on the phone to Phuket talking to a waitress who doesn't understand English, trying to get a description of Peter Brannigan.

Outside the streets are empty except for a council sweeping machine with twirling brushes and jets of water. I open the car door and Rachel slips inside. The interior smells of pine air freshener and ancient tobacco.

Using a borrowed overcoat as a blanket, she covers her knees. I know she has questions. She wants reassurance. Maybe we're both deluding ourselves.

Headlights sweep across the interior of the car as we drive toward Maida Vale. She rests her head against the seat, watching me.

"Do you have children, Inspector?"

"I'm not a policeman anymore. Please call me Vincent."

She waits for an answer.

"Twins. They're grown up now."

"Do you see much of them?"

"No."

"Why?"

"It's a long story."

"How long can it be? They're your children."

I'm caught now. No matter what I say to her she won't understand. She desperately wants to find her child and I don't even talk to mine. Where's the fairness in that?

She tucks her hair behind her ears. "Do you know that sometimes I think I made Mickey frightened of the world."

"Why do you say that?"

"I kept telling her to be careful."

"All parents do that."

"Yes, but it wasn't just the normal stuff like not patting stray dogs or talking to strangers. I made her frightened of what can happen if you love something too much and it disappoints you or gets taken away. She wasn't always scared to go outside. It only started when she was about four."

"What happened?"

In a forlorn voice she describes a Saturday afternoon at a local park, where she and Mickey would often go to feed the ducks. This one particular Saturday there was an old-fashioned fair, with a steam-powered carousel, cotton candy and whirligigs. Mickey rode all by herself on a gaily painted horse, proud of the fact that she didn't need her mother to sit behind her. When the ride finished, she was on the far side of the carousel. Rachel had been drawn into conversation with a woman from her mothers' group and didn't notice the ride ending.

Mickey stepped off. Instead of circling, she wandered through the forest of legs thinking that surely one of the hands belonged to her mother.

She walked back toward the pond where the ducks had gathered in the skirts of a willow tree. Peering over the low railing fence she watched two boys, no older than eleven, throwing stones. The ducks huddled together. Mickey wondered why they didn't fly away. Then she noticed the ducklings, sheltering beneath a feathered breast and muddy tail feathers.

One duckling—a dark ball of down against the darkness of the shade—separated from the others. It took the full force of a stone and disappeared beneath the surface. Seconds later it reappeared, floating lifelessly on the green scum in that corner of the pond.

Mickey burst into hysterical wailing. Tears streamed down her cheeks into the wide corners of her mouth. Her crying made the boys drop their stones and edge away, not wanting to be blamed for whatever had made her cry.

The howls from the edge of the pond created a strange dichotomy of reactions. Some people almost fell over each other to ignore them. Others watched and waited for someone else to intervene.

The pigeon man was nearest. Grizzled and yellow-toothed, he raised himself up from his bench, brushing pigeons off his lap as though they were spilled crumbs. Shuffling across to Mickey, he hitched up his trousers so that he could kneel beside her.

"You got a problem, Missy?"

"Make them stop," she wailed, with her hands clamped over her ears.

He didn't seem to hear her. "You want to feed the birds?"

"The ducks," she sobbed.

"You want to feed the ducks?"

Mickey howled again and the pigeon man raised his eyebrows. He could never understand children. Taking her hand, he went in search of a park attendant or the girl's mother.

A policeman was already approaching. He pushed through the crowd and took in the scene. "I want you to let her go," he demanded.

"I'm looking for her mother," explained the pigeon man. Spittle clung to his tangled beard.

"Just let the girl go and step away."

By then Rachel had arrived. She swept Mickey up, held her tightly, and the two of them tried to out-hug each other. Meanwhile, the pigeon man had his arms stretched wide on the back of a park bench, while the policeman patted him down and searched his pockets, spilling birdseed onto the grass.

Mickey didn't ask to feed the ducks again. She didn't go to the park and soon she stopped going outside Dolphin Mansions. A year later she saw her first therapist.

The children's book that Timothy found in Mickey's cubbyhole in the basement was about five little ducks who go out in the world and return home again. Mickey knew from experience that not all little ducks come back.

32

Weatherman Pete brushes milk foam from his mustache and motions toward the river with his paper cup. "Sewers are no place for little girls."

His van is parked up on a boat ramp in the shadow of Putney Bridge where eight-oared shells skim the surface of the river like gigantic water beetles. Moley is asleep in the back of the van, curled up with one eye open.

"Where could they have kept her?"

Pete exhales slowly, making his lips vibrate. "There are hundreds of places—disused tube stations, service tunnels, bomb shelters, aqueducts, drains . . . What makes you think he's hiding down there?"

"He's scared. People are looking for him."

Pete hums. "Takes a unique sort of individual to live down there."

"He *is* unique."

"No, you don't get me. You take Moley. If he disappeared down there you wouldn't find him in a hundred years. You see he likes the dark, just like some people prefer the cold. You know what I mean?"

"This guy isn't like that."

"So how does he know his way down there?"

"He's going from memory. Someone showed him where to hide and how to move around. A former flusher called Ray Murphy."

"Saccharine Ray! The boxer."

"You know him?"

"Yeah, I know him. Ray was never really the genuine article as a boxer. He took more dives than Ruud van Nistelrooy. I don't remember him working down the sewers."

"It was a long time ago. After that he worked as a flood planner."

A slow sweet smile spreads across Pete's face like jam on toast. "The old HQ of London Flood Management is underground—in the Kingsway Tram Underpass."

"But there haven't been trams in central London for more than fifty years."

"Precisely. The tunnel was abandoned. If you ask me it was a bloody silly place to have a flood emergency center. It would have been the first place under water if the Thames broke its banks. Bureaucrats!"

The Kingsway Underpass is one of those strange, almost secret, landmarks you find in cities. Tens of thousands of people walk past it and drive over it every day with no idea it's there. All you can see is a railing fence and a cobblestone approach road before it disappears underground. It runs beneath Kingsway—one of the busiest streets in the West End—down to the Aldwych, where it turns right and comes out directly beneath Waterloo Bridge.

Weatherman Pete parks his van on the approach road, ignoring the painted red lines and NO STOPPING signs. He hands me a hard hat and pulls out a construction sign. "If anyone asks we work for the council."

The remnants of the tram tracks are embedded in the stones and a large gate guards the entrance to the tunnel.

"Can we get inside?"

"That'd be illegal," he says, producing the biggest set of bolt cutters I've ever seen. Moley moans and pulls a blanket over his head.

Trying to curb Pete's enthusiasm I explain that Gerry Brandt is dangerous. He's already put Ali in the hospital and I don't want anyone else getting hurt. Once we know he's in there, I'll call the police.

"We could send a mole down the hole." Pete nudges the bundle of blankets. Moley's head appears. "You're up."

Trooping down the ramp we look like a trio of engineers on our way to survey something on a typical Saturday morning. The padlock on the gate looks secure enough but the bolt cutters snap it like balsa wood. We slide inside.

Although I can only see about twenty feet of tunnel it appears to open out and grow wider before the darkness becomes absolute. The most obvious feature is a pile of road signs stacked against the walls—street names, traffic controls, posts and paving slabs. The council must use the tunnel for storage.

"We should wait here," whispers Pete. "No use us blundering around in the dark." He hands Moley what looks like an emergency flare. "Just in case."

Moley presses his ear to the wall of the tunnel and listens for about fifteen seconds. Then he jogs forward silently and listens again. Within seconds he is out of sight. The only sounds are my heartbeat and the throb of traffic forty feet above our heads.

Fifteen minutes later Moley returns.

"There's someone there. About a hundred yards farther on there are two Portakabins. He's in the first one."

"What's he doing?"

"Sleeping."

I know I have to call it in. I can talk directly to "New Boy" Dave and hopefully bypass Meldrum and Campbell. Dave hates Gerry Brandt as much as I do. We look after our own.

But another part of me has a different desire. I can't rid myself of the memory of Gerry Brandt holding Ali against his back, looking directly at me, as he fell backward, crushing her spine. This is just the sort of place I wanted to find him—a dark place, with nobody around.

The police will come charging in here, armed to the teeth. That's when people get hurt or get killed. I'm not talking conspiracies here, I just know the reality—people fuck up. I can't afford to lose Gerry Brandt. He's a violent impulsive thug who peddles misery in tiny packets of foil but I need him for Ali's sake and for Mickey's. He knows what happened to her.

"So what do you want to do?" whispers Pete.

"I'm going to call the police but I also want to talk to this guy. I don't want him getting away or getting hurt."

The light from the entrance forms a halo around Moley's head. He cocks his face to one side and looks at me with a mixture of apprehension and expectancy. "He did a bad thing, this guy?"

"Yes, he did."

"You want me to take you in there?"

"Yes."

Pete gives it five seconds of contemplation and nods his head. It's like he does this every day of the week. Back at the van I call "New Boy" Dave. Glancing at my watch, I realize that Ali will be in surgery. I don't know the exact details but they're going to insert pins into her spine and fuse several vertebrae.

Weatherman Pete has collected some gear from the van—extra flares and his "secret weapon." He shows me two Ping-Pong balls. "I make these myself. Black powder, flash powder, magnesium ribbon and a drop of candle wax."

"What do they do?"

"Kerboom!" He grins at me. "Nothing but sound and fury. You should hear one of them go off in a sewer."

The plan is simple enough. Moley is going to make sure there are no other exits. Once he's in place, he'll set off the flash-bangs and flares.

"We're going to scare the son of a bitch half to death," he says excitedly.

Pete looks at me. "You got sunglasses—wear them. And don't look at the light. You only have a few seconds to grab him while he's disoriented."

We give Moley a ten-minute head start. Weatherman Pete and I keep on opposite sides of the tunnel, feeling our way blindly along the walls and stepping in oily puddles and nests of leaves.

Slowly the tunnel begins to change in character. The roof slopes down where the roadway above has been cut into the old ceiling. The Portakabins are just ahead of me. I can see the faint yellow glow of the lantern, leaking around the edges of a window that has been covered up or taped over.

Crouching, I wait for Moley. He could be right next to me and I wouldn't know it. My mouth is dry. For two days I've been popping codeine forte and craving morphine, telling myself my leg doesn't hurt and it's just my imagination.

What happens next wouldn't find a place in many training manuals. The explosion of noise is so sudden and ferocious it feels like I've been shot from a cannon. Darkness turns to light, as a flare of brilliant white arcs overhead and lands in the doorway of the nearest Portakabin.

Squinting into the dazzling ivory, my eyes sting. I see nothing but white. Turning my face away, I begin to move, crossing the last ten feet to the door. The second flash-bang explodes and a shape comes bursting out the entrance, with legs pumping in midair as though trying to gain traction. Blinded by the light, he runs smack into the far wall and almost knocks himself unconscious.

I grab him from behind, locking my arms around his waist. He pitches to the left, arms flailing. Both of us crash into a puddle. I don't let go. Pulling his arm behind his back, I try to put on the cuffs. He snaps his head back like he did to Ali but I'm ready.

Keeping behind him, I straddle his torso and twist his arm until he roars. He's fighting blindly, arching his spine to reach me. I wrap my forearm around his neck, cutting off his windpipe. With my arm squeezing his throat, I add more weight, pushing his face into the floor. He can't breathe. His legs are twitching as if he's made of rubber.

I could kill him now, so easily. I could hold on until he suffocates or I could snap his neck. So what if he dies? It's no great loss to humanity. There won't be any grand achievements left unfulfilled or prizes unclaimed. The only mark Gerry Brandt was ever likely to leave on the world was a bloodstain.

My forearm loosens and I let his head drop. It makes a dull noise against the concrete. He's gasping for breath.

Dragging his other arm behind his back, I snap on the handcuffs and roll away. Stumbling to my feet I look down at him for a moment. Dark hair spikes from his head and pieces of crushed glass are stuck to his cheekbone. A thin line of blood trickles past his ear as the burning flares begin to die out.

There are police sirens in the distance. "Come on, let's get him out of here."

"Are we going to get in trouble?" asks Moley, falling into step beside Weatherman Pete.

"You'll be fine. Get to the van and let me do the talking."

We're almost at the end of the tunnel. The gate gives off a hollow clang as it opens. Two armed response vehicles have pulled onto the ramp beside the van. The officers are armed with MP5 carbines. An unmarked police car pulls up alongside them. "New Boy" Dave gets out, along with Campbell who walks like he's got bowling balls down his Y-fronts.

"Arrest him," he yells, pointing at me instead of my prisoner.

Gerry Brandt raises his head. "I didn't mean to do it. I let her go."

"Where is she?"

He shakes his head. "I let her go."

"What did you do with Mickey?"

"You got to tell Mr. Kuznet, I let her go."

A red dot appears on his cheek, just above where he's bleeding. For a moment it catches in his eye, making him blink, and then rises to his forehead. Recognition jars inside me but it's too late. In a fleeting puff of blood and vapor, he spins and falls.

The bullet, fired from somewhere above, has passed through his cheek, down his neck and exited below his collarbone. I can't hold him. He's six one and more than two hundred pounds. He carries me down. I roll away, letting gravity take over, bouncing my head against the cobblestones until I strike the wall.

The ramp is empty. People have scattered like cockroaches. Only Gerry Brandt is unmoved by it all, lying with his jacket half covering his head, slowly soaking up the blood.

There are no more shots. One was enough.

33

According to the experts the world is going to end in five thousand million years when the sun swells up and engulfs the innermost planets and turns the rest of them into charcoal. I've always imagined it more like a dual second coming, where Jesus and Charlton Heston compete to see who gets the final word. I don't suppose I'll be around.

This is what I think about as I sit in the backseat of a police car, watching them photograph Gerry Brandt's body. Teams of armed officers are going door to door, searching shops, offices and flats. They won't find anything. The sniper is long gone.

Campbell has also slipped away, escaping from me. I followed him all the way to his car, yelling, "Who did you tell? Who knew?"

The moment I phoned for backup, somebody put in a separate call, tipping off Aleksei. How else did the sniper know where to find Brandt? It's the only logical explanation.

A dozen police officers walk in single file down the ramp, peering between their polished boots at the cobblestones and sodden leaves. A handful of Camden Council workers watch the proceedings as though they're going to be tested on it later.

This whole business reeks of a setup. The guilty are gunned down and innocent people get caught in the crossfire. Howard might be one of them. I still can't figure out where he fits into all this, but I can picture him, lying on his prison bunk, planning his first days of freedom.

Child molesters sleep the sleep of the damned in prison. They listen to their names being whispered from cell to cell, turning to a chant as the noise rises and becomes a frightening symphony that must open and close their sphincters like the wings of a butterfly.

The SOCO team, dressed in white overalls, has set up arc lights on mobile gantries, casting grotesque shadows against the walls. Noonan is in charge, shouting into a tape recorder: "I'm looking at a well-developed, well-nourished white male. A light purple contusion is visible on the left forehead and another over the bridge of the nose. He may have fallen after the shooting or someone hit him in the face prior to the shooting . . ."

"New Boy" Dave hands me a coffee. It tastes like tar and brings back memories of surveillance operations and endless predawn shifts.

Noonan rolls the body over and checks the pockets and lining. His hand emerges with a small foil packet wedged between his fingertips.

Dave screws up his face. "Well if you ask me, I'm glad he's dead."

I guess that's understandable given what happened to Ali. He doesn't understand why I needed Gerry alive. Dave loosens his tie and undoes the top button of his shirt.

"They say you're trying to destroy the Howard Wavell conviction."

"No."

"They also say you stole diamonds from Aleksei Kuznet. They say you're bent."

"What do you think?"

"Ali doesn't think so."

A double-decker bus rumbles by, glowing red and yellow. Bored faces peer out from the bright interior, heads resting against the glass. London doesn't seem so exciting from this angle. The landmarks are rendered featureless by the gloom and there is no magic in the Monopoly board names.

I am under arrest. Campbell insisted on it. At least Dave hasn't bothered with handcuffs so my past must count for something. I could even handle the police officers staring at me, if one of them was Ali and she'd never been involved in this.

After SOCO has finished at the crime scene, I'm driven to the Harrow Road Police Station and taken through a back door into the charge room. I know the drill. Strands of hair are sealed in plastic. Saliva and skin cells dampen a cotton swab. My fingers are pressed in ink. Afterward I am taken to an interview room rather than a police cell.

They make me wait. I lean forward, with my elbows braced on my knees, counting the pop rivets on the side of the table. This is all part of any interrogation. Silence can be more important than the questions.

When Keebal finally arrives, he carries a large bundle of files and proceeds to shuffle through the papers. Most of them probably have nothing to do with me but he wants me to think evidence is stacking up against me. Everybody is having fun today.

Keebal likes to pretend he's a patient man but it's bullshit. Maybe it's the Rom blood in me but I can sit opposite someone all day and not say a thing. Gypsies are like Sicilians. We can share a drink and be smiling our heads off while out of sight a knife or a shotgun is pointed directly at the other guy's stomach.

Finally he turns on the tape recorder, giving the time, date and names of everybody present.

He pats his coiffed hair. "I hear you got your memory back."

"Can we do this later? You obviously have an appointment at a beauty parlor."

He stops touching himself and glares at me.

"At approximately 1600 hours on September 25, you were given a briefcase containing 965 one carat and above, superior-quality diamonds. Is that correct?"

"Yes."

"When did you last see these diamonds?"

I feel my stomach lurch as if an internal gear has suddenly engaged. I can still picture the packages spilling from the sports bag beneath my linen cupboard. A dry thunder is pounding in my head—the beginnings of a migraine. "I don't know."

"Did you give them to someone?"

"No."

"What were these diamonds for?"

"You know the answer to that question."

"For the benefit of the tape, please answer the question."

"A ransom."

He doesn't bat an eyelid. I'm doing just what he wants—digging myself deeper into a hole. I start at the beginning, recounting the whole story. I have nothing left to lose, but at least I'm getting it down. There'll be a record somewhere if something happens to me. I tell him about the ransom demand, the strands of hair, the bikini and my journey through the sewers.

For the next ninety minutes I relate the details. Hundreds of cumulative hours are condensed and laid out like stepping-stones for him to follow. Even so, it sounds more like a confessional than an interrogation.

Keebal looks like he should be selling used cars or life insurance. "You admit you were present on the boat when Ray Murphy died?"

"Yes."

"And you say the diamonds were in packages on the deck?"

"Yes."

"Was there a tracking device with the diamonds?"

"Yes."

"When you went overboard did you take the diamonds?"

"No."

"You were the last person to see them. I think you know where they are."

"That's an interesting theory."

"I think they're tucked under your mattress at home?"

"Could be."

He studies my face, looking for the lie. It's there. He just can't see it.

"Let me help you out," he says. "Next time you try to steal a ransom, remember to take the tracking device out. Otherwise someone might follow you and realize what you're doing."

"How is Aleksei? How much is he paying you to recover his diamonds?"

Keebal tightens his lips and sighs through his nose like I've disappointed him.

"Tell me this," I ask him. "A sniper put a bullet in my leg and I nearly bled to death. Eight days I lay in a coma. You think I took the diamonds. How? When?"

A sense of triumph is stenciled on his face. "I'll tell you how—they never left your house. You helped set this whole thing up—the ransom letters, the DNA tests . . . you fooled everyone. And the people who know the truth keep dying when you're around. First it was Ray Murphy and then Gerry Brandt . . ."

Keebal can't really believe any of this. It's crazy. I always had him pegged as a fanatic but the man has squirrels juggling knives in his head.

"I got shot."

"Maybe because you tried to double-cross them."

I'm shouting at him now. "You called Aleksei. You told him where he could find Gerry Brandt. All these years you've been persecuting honest cops and now we see your true colors—yellow right through."

In the silence I can hear my clothes creasing. Keebal thinks he knows. He knows nothing.

The Professor collects me just after 5:00 p.m.

"How are you?"

"I still have my health."

"That's good."

I savor the sound of my shoes on the tarmac, pleased to be free. Keebal didn't have enough to hold me and there isn't a magistrate in the land who would deny me bail with my record of service.

Joe's office is still full of our ragtag task force, manning telephones and tapping at keyboards. They're searching electoral rolls and reverse phone directories. Someone has pinned a photograph of Mickey to the window—to remind everyone of why we're here.

The familiar faces acknowledge me—Roger, Margaret, Jean, Eric and Rebecca—along with a few new ones, two of Ali's brothers.

"How long have they been here?"

"Since lunchtime," says Joe.

Ali will have called them. She is out of surgery and must have heard about Gerry Brandt.

Rachel spies me from across the room. She looks at me hopefully, her hands fidgeting with her collar.

"Did you talk to him? I mean . . . did he say anything?"

"He said he let Mickey go."

A breath snags in her throat. "What happened to her?"

"I don't know. He didn't get to tell me." I turn to the others and let them all hear. "It's now even more imperative that we find Kirsten

Fitzroy. She may be the only one left who knows what happened to Mickey."

Gathering the chairs in a circle, we hold a "kitchen cabinet" meeting.

Margaret and Jean have managed to find a dozen of Kirsten's ex-employees. All are women aged between twenty-two and thirty-four, many of them with foreign-sounding names. They were nervous about talking—sex work isn't something you advertise. None of them has seen Kirsten since the agency closed down.

Meanwhile, Roger visited the old offices. The managing agent had kept two boxes of files that had been left behind when the agency vacated the premises. Among the documents were invoices from a pathology lab. The girls were being tested for STDs.

Another file contained encoded credit card details and initials. Kirsten probably had a diary with names matching the initials. I run my finger down the page searching for Sir Douglas's initials. Nothing.

"So far we've called more than four hundred clinics and surgeries," says Rachel. "Nobody has reported treating a gunshot victim but a pharmacy in Southwark had a break-in on September 26. Someone stole bandages and painkillers."

"Call the pharmacist back. Ask him if the police pulled any fingerprints."

Margaret hands me a coffee. Jean takes it away and washes the cup before I can take a sip. Someone gets sandwiches and soft drinks. I feel like something a lot stronger, something warm and yeasty and golden.

Joe finds me sitting alone on the stairs and takes a seat beside me. "You haven't mentioned the diamonds. What did you do with them?"

"Put them somewhere safe."

I can picture the velvet pouches stitched inside a woolly mammoth in Ali's old room. I should probably tell Joe. If something happens to me, nobody will know where to find them. Then again, I don't want to put anyone else in danger.

"Did you know that elephants with their trunks raised are meant to symbolize good luck?"

"No."

"Ali told me. She's got a thing about elephants. I don't know how much good luck it's brought her."

My mouth has gone dry. I stand and slip my arms through my jacket.

"You're going to see Aleksei, aren't you?" asks Joe. I swear to God he can read minds.

My silence responds eloquently.

"You know that's crazy," he says.

"I have to stop this."

I know it sounds foolishly old-fashioned but I'm stuck with this idea that there is something dignified and noble about facing your enemy and looking him squarely in the eye—before you thrust a saber in his heart.

"You can't go alone."

"He won't see me otherwise. I'll make an appointment. People don't get killed when they make an appointment."

Joe considers this. "I'll come with you."

"No, but thanks for the offer."

I don't know why people keep trying to help me like this. They should be heading for the hills. Ali says I inspire loyalty but I seem to be taking kindnesses that I can never hope to repay. I am not a perfect human being. I'm a cynic and a pessimist and sometimes I feel as though I'm locked into this life by an accident of birth. But at times like this, a random act of kindness or the touch of another human being makes me believe I can be different, better, redeemed. Joe has that effect on me. A poor man shouldn't borrow so much.

The phone call to Aleksei is diverted through several numbers before he answers. I can hear water in the background. The river.

"I want to talk. No lawyers or police or third parties."

I can hear him thinking. "Where did you have in mind?"

"Neutral ground."

"No. If you want a meeting you come to me. Chelsea Harbour. You'll find me."

A black cab drops me at the entrance to the marina shortly before ten. I lift my watch and count the final minutes. It's no use being early for your own funeral.

Spotlights reflect from the whiteness of the motor yachts and cruisers, creating pools like spilled paint. By comparison, the interlocking docks are weathered and gray, with life buoys hanging from pylons anchored deep in the mud.

Aleksei's boat, draped in fairy lights, takes up two moorings and has three decks with sleek lines that angle like an arrowhead from bow to stern. The upper deck bristles with radio antennae and satellite tracking devices.

I spent five years mucking about on boats. I know they float and soak up money. People with a highly defined sense of balance are more likely to get seasick, they say. I can vouch for my equilibrium but an hour in rough weather on a cross-channel ferry can still feel like a year.

The gangway has a thick rubber mat and railings with bronze pillars. As I step on board the vessel shifts slightly. Through an open doorway I see a stateroom and a large mahogany dining table with seating for eight. To one side is a bar area and a modular lounge arranged in front of a flat-screen TV.

Descending the steps I duck my head, which isn't necessary. Aleksei Kuznet is sitting behind a desk, his head lowered, reading the screen of a laptop computer. He raises his hand, making me wait. It remains there, suspended. Slowly the hand turns and his fingers wave me forward.

When he raises his eyes he looks past me as though I might have forgotten something. The ransom. He wants his diamonds.

"Nice boat."

"It's a motor yacht."

"An expensive toy."

"On the contrary—it is my office. I had her built to an American design at a boatyard on the Black Sea near Odessa. You see I take the best from different cultures—American design, German engineering, Italian craftsmen, Brazilian teak and Slav laborers. People often criticize Eastern European nations and say they don't do capitalism well. But the truth is that they operate the purest form of capitalism. If I had wanted to build this boat in Britain I would have had to pay award wages, workers compensation, national insurance, design fees and bribes to keep the unions happy. It's the same when you put up a building. At any stage someone can stop you. In Russia or Latvia or Georgia none of this matters if you have enough money. That's what I call *pure* capitalism."

"Is that why you're selling up? Are you going home?"

He laughs mordantly. "Inspector, you mistake me for a patriot. I will employ Russians, I will fund their schools and hospitals and prop up their corrupt politicians but do not expect me to live with them."

He has moved across to the bar. My eyes flick around the stateroom, almost waiting for the trap to snap shut.

"So why *are* you selling up?"

"Greener pastures. Fresh challenges. Maybe I'll buy a football club. That seems very popular nowadays. Or I could just go somewhere warm for the winter."

"I have never understood what people see in hot climates."

He glances into the darkness of the starboard window. "Each man makes his own paradise, DI, but it's hard to love London."

He hands me a glass of Scotch and slides the ice bucket toward me. "Are you a sailor?"

"Not really."

"Shame. With me it's flying. You ever see that episode of *The Twilight Zone* where William Shatner looks out of the window of a plane at 20,000 feet and sees a gremlin tearing off pieces of the wing? They made it into a film, which was nowhere near as good. That's how I feel when I step on a plane. I'm the only person who *knows* it's going to crash."

"So you never fly?"

He turns over both his palms, as if revealing the obvious. "I have a motor yacht."

The Scotch burns pleasantly as I swallow but the aftertaste is not like it used to be. All that morphine has deadened my taste buds.

Aleksei is a businessman, accustomed to cutting deals. He knows how to read a balance sheet, to manage risk and maximize profit.

"I might have something to trade," I announce.

He raises his hand again, this time pressing a finger to his lips. The Russian steps from the companionway looking as if he's been trapped in an ill-fitting suit.

"I'm sure you understand," says Aleksei apologetically as the bodyguard sweeps a metal detector over me. Meanwhile, he issues instructions via a radio. The engines of the boat rumble and the ice shudders in my glass.

He motions me to follow him along the companionway to the galley where a narrow ladder descends to the lower deck. We reach a heavily insulated door that opens into the engine room. Noise fills my head.

The engine block is six feet high with valves, fuel cocks, radiator pipes, springs and polished steel. Two chairs have been arranged on the metal walkways that run down each side of the room. Aleksei takes a seat as if attending a recital and waits until I join him. Still nursing his drink, he looks at me with an aloof curiosity.

Shouting to be heard above the engines, I ask him how he found Gerry Brandt. He smiles. It is the same indolent foreknowing expression he gave me when I saw him outside Wormwood Scrubs. "I hope you're not accusing me of any wrongdoing, Inspector."

"Then you know who I'm talking about?"

"No. Who is he?"

This is like a game to him—a trifling annoyance compared to other more important matters. I risk boring him unless I get to the point.

"Is Kirsten Fitzroy still alive?"

He doesn't answer.

"I'm not here to accuse you, Aleksei. I have a hypothetical deal to offer."

"A hypothetical one?" Now he laughs out loud and I feel my resolve draining away.

"I will trade you the diamonds for Kirsten's life. Leave her alone and you get them back."

Aleksei runs his finger through his hair, leaving a trail in the gel. "You have my diamonds?"

"Hypothetically."

"Then hypothetically you are obliged to give them back to me. Why should I have to trade?"

"Because right now this is only hypothetical; I can make it real. I know you planted the diamonds in my house to frame me. Keebal was supposed to get a warrant but I found them first. You think I saw something that night. You think I can hurt you somehow. You have my word. Nobody else has to get hurt."

"Really?" he asks sarcastically. "Do not attempt a career as a salesman."

"It's a genuine offer."

"A hypothetical one." Aleksei looks at me, pursing his lips. "Let me get this straight. My daughter is kidnapped and you fail to find her. She is murdered and you do not recover her body. Then people try to extort two million pounds from me and you fail to catch them. Then you steal my diamonds and accuse me of planting them on you. And on top of it all, you want me to forgive and forget. You people are scum. You have preyed on my ex-wife's grief. You have taken advantage of my good nature and my desire to make things right. I didn't start this—"

"You have a chance to end it."

"You mistake me for someone who desires peace and harmony. On the contrary, what I desire is revenge."

He moves to stand. The negotiation is over.

I feel my temper rising. "For Christ's sake, Aleksei, I'm trying to find Mickey. She's your family. Don't you want to know what happened?"

"I know what happened, Inspector. She's dead. She died three years ago. And let me tell you something about families—they're overrated. They're a weakness. They leave you or get taken from you or they disappoint you. Families are a liability."

"Is that why you got rid of Sacha?"

He ignores me, pushing open the heavy door. We're outside now. I can hear myself think. Aleksei is still talking.

"You say to trust you. You say trust the deal. You have no idea, do you? Not a clue. You're like the three wise monkeys all rolled into one. Now let me make a deal with you—hypothetically speaking, of course. You return the diamonds to me and then step back. Let people work things out for themselves. Market forces, you see, capitalism, supply and demand, these are the things I understand. People reap what they sow."

"People like Gerry Brandt?" With a flick of my wrist, I grip his forearm. He doesn't flinch. "Leave Kirsten alone."

His eyes are narrow and dark, with something toxic behind them. He thinks I'm some dumb plod, barely off the beat, whose idea of subtle interrogation is a nightstick and a strong right arm. That's how I'm acting.

"You know what a Heffalump is?" I ask.

"Winnie-the-Pooh's friend."

"No, you're thinking of Piglet. Heffalumps and Woozles are the nightmare creatures that Pooh Bear dreams about. He's afraid they're going to steal his honey. Nobody can see them except Pooh. That's who you remind me of."

"A Heffalump?"

"No. Pooh Bear. You think the world is full of people who want to steal from you."

The sky is gray and the evening air damp and heavy. Away from the throb of the engines my headache finds its own rhythm. Aleksei walks me to the gangway. The Russian is close behind him, swinging his left arm a little wider because of his holster.

"Have you ever thought of getting a normal job?" I ask.

Aleksei contemplates this. "Maybe we should both do something new."

Then it dawns on me that he's right, we're not so different. We both screwed up our relationships and lost our children. And we're too old to do anything else. I have spent two-thirds of my life putting criminals away, most of them small-timers and lowlifes. Aleksei was what I was working toward. My ambition. He's the reason I did the job.

As I step onto the gangway the Russian follows, two paces behind. The rope handrails are looped between brass posts. He closes the last step and I feel the warm metal of the gun brush the short hairs at the base of my skull.

Aleksei explains: "My employee will go with you and collect the diamonds."

In the same instant I fall over the side, plunging toward the water. Reaching up in midair, I grab onto the rope railing and hang on as my body swings through an arc, tipping the gangway on its side. The Russian plunges past me.

Swinging my good leg onto the dock, I climb to my feet. Aleksei is watching the Russian flailing his arms as he tries to stay afloat.

"I don't think he can swim," I point out.

"Some people never learn," says Aleksei, unconcerned.

I take a life buoy from the pylon and toss it into the water. The Russian hugs it to his chest.

"One last question: How did you know where the ransom was going to surface? Somebody must have told you."

Aleksei pulls back his lips in a grimace but his eyes are empty. "You have until tomorrow morning to return my diamonds."

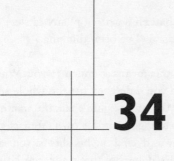

34

Ali is asleep. Tubes flow into her carrying painkillers and out of her carrying waste. Every few hours they add another bag of liquid morphine. Time is measured by the gaps between them.

"You really can't stay," says the nursing sister. "Come back in the morning and she'll be awake."

The corridors of the hospital are almost deserted. I walk to the visitors lounge and take a seat, closing my eyes. I wish I could have made Aleksei understand but his hatred has blinded him. He doesn't believe Mickey is still alive. Instead, he thinks people have taken advantage of him because of his weakness—his family.

I think of Luke and wonder if maybe he's right. Daj is still grieving about her lost family. I'm still fretting about Claire and Michael, wondering what went wrong. Not caring would be so much easier.

My muscles ache and my whole body seems to be fighting against itself. Dreamlike images fill my head; bodies lowered into rivers or washed down sewers. Kirsten's turn is coming.

Darkness presses against the window. I gaze at the street below and feel nostalgic for the countryside. The rhythms of a city are set by pneumatic drills, traffic lights and train timetables. I barely notice the seasons.

A reflection appears in the window beside me.

"I thought I might find you here," says Joe, taking a seat and propping his legs on the low table. "How did it go with Aleksei?"

"He wouldn't listen."

Joe nods. "You should get some sleep."

"So should you."

"You're long enough dead."

"My stepfather used to say that. He's getting plenty of sleep now."

Joe motions to the sofa opposite. "I've been thinking."

"Yeah."

"I figure maybe I know why this means so much to you. When you told me what happened to Luke you didn't tell me the whole story."

I feel a lump forming in my throat. I couldn't talk if I wanted to.

"You said he was riding the toboggan on his own. Your stepfather had gone to town, your mother was dyeing the bedsheets. You said you couldn't remember what you were doing but that's not true. You didn't forget. You were with Luke."

I can see the day. Snow lay thick on the ground. From the top of Hill Field you could see the entire farm, all the way to Telegraph Point on the river and the wind socks on the aerodrome.

"You were looking after him."

He had biscuit on his breath. He sat between my knees, rugged up in one of my hand-me-down jackets. He was so small that my chin rested on his head. He wore an old flying cap, lined with wool that flapped from his ears and made him look like a Labrador puppy.

Joe explains. "When we were in the pub, before we found Rachel's car, I started describing a dream to you. It was *your* dream. I said you fantasized about saving Luke; you imagined being there, riding the toboggan down the hill, driving your boots into the snow to stop him before he reached the pond. That's when I should have realized. It wasn't a dream—it was the truth."

The bumps threw the toboggan in the air and Luke squealed with laughter. "Faster, Yanko! Faster!" He hugged my knees, leaning back against my chest. The track leveled off toward the end where the mesh fence sagged between posts. We were traveling faster than normal because of the extra weight. I put my boots down to stop but we hit the fence too fast. One moment he was in my arms and the next I clutched at air.

The ice broke beneath him. It split into diamonds and triangles;

shapes without curves. I waded in, screaming for him. I went under and under. If I could just feel his hair, if I could just grab his collar, he'd be OK. I could save him. But it was too cold and the pond was too deep.

My stepfather came. He used a spotlight powered by the tractor engine and laid planks across the pond to crawl out. He hammered on the ice with an ax and reached down with his hands, feeling for the bottom. I watched from the bedroom window, praying that somehow Luke would be all right. Nobody said anything. They didn't have to. It was my fault. I killed him.

"You were twelve years old. It was an accident."

"I lost him."

Wiping wetness from my cheeks, I shake my head and curse him. What do other people know of guilt?

Joe is standing, offering his hand. "Come on, let's go."

I don't look diminished in his eyes but it will never be the same between us. I wish he could have left Luke alone.

On the drive to his office nothing is said. Rachel greets us at the door. She's been working all night.

"I might have found something," she explains as we climb the stairs. "I remember something Kirsten told me during Howard's trial. We were talking about giving evidence in court and she said that she once got called as a character witness for a friend who was facing charges."

"Do you know what sort of charges?"

"No. And she didn't mention a name."

I pick up the phone. I'm not owed any favors but maybe "New Boy" Dave will grant me one for Ali's sake.

"Sorry to wake you."

I hear him groan.

"I need your help. I want to cross-reference police and court records for Kirsten Fitzroy."

"It's been done."

"Yes, but you've been treating her as the subject. She might have been a witness."

He doesn't reply. I know he's debating whether to hang up on me. There is no reason to help and a dozen reasons to say no.

"Can it wait till *proper* morning?"

"No."

There's another long pause. "Meet me at Otto's at six."

. . .

Otto's is a café between a betting shop and a launderette at the western end of Elgin Avenue. The Sunday-morning clientele are mainly cabbies and delivery drivers, priming themselves with coffee and carbohydrates for the day ahead.

I wait by the window. "New Boy" Dave is on time, dodging the dog shit and puddles, before ducking inside. His shirt is creased and hair uncombed.

He orders a coffee and pulls a scrap of paper from his pocket, holding it out of reach. "First, you can answer some questions for me. Gerry Brandt had a fake passport and driver's license in the name of Peter Brannigan. For the last three years he's been running a bar in Thailand. The guy's a scrote—where did he get that sort of money?"

"Drugs."

"That's what I figured, but the DEA and Interpol have nothing on him."

"He came back into the country three months ago. According to his uncle he was looking for investors. Ray Murphy's pub was also struggling."

"So that explains the ransom demand. It also got them killed. Ballistics has matched the bullet from Brandt with the one found in Ray Murphy's body. Same rifle."

Dave looks at his watch. "I got to get to the hospital. I want to be there when Ali wakes up."

He hands over the scrap of paper. "Six years ago Kirsten Fitzroy gave evidence at a soliciting trial at Southwark Crown Court. She was a character witness for a Heather Wilde, who was convicted of running an illegal brothel and living off immoral earnings."

I remember that case. Heather ran a swinging club from a house in Brixton. She had a Web site, Wilde Times, but claimed that no money changed hands so it wasn't prostitution.

Where in Brixton? Dumbarton Road.

My memory triumphs again. It's a curse.

35

The single door is set in a whitewashed brick wall with no number or mailbox. Rising three floors, the façade has maybe a dozen windows, each divided by vertical bars and gray with dirt.

I don't know if Kirsten is inside. The place looks empty. I want to be sure but this time I won't be calling the police—not after what happened to Gerry Brandt.

Rain has beaded the hoods of cars parked down either side of the street. Walking along the pavement, I pass bicycles chained to the railing fence and trash cans waiting for collection.

I knock and wait. Bolts slide and a barrel lock turns, before the door opens no more than a crack. An unsmiling, fifty-plus face appears looking me up and down.

"Mrs. Wilde?"

"Do you know what time it is?"

"I'm looking for Kirsten Fitzroy."

"Never heard of her."

Looking past her I see a narrow entrance hall and dimly lit sitting room. She tries to shut the door but my shoulder strikes it first, forcing her backward into a phone table that topples over.

"I don't want to cause any trouble. Just hear me out." I help her right the table and pick up the phone books.

A greasy stain of lipstick smears her mouth and she reeks of damp ash and perfume. Her breasts are squeezed into a satin dressing gown, creating a cleavage that brings to mind honeydew melons. Daj always told me that you could tell if a honeydew melon was ripe if they were whitish in color. See how my memory works?

In the sitting room almost every piece of furniture is covered in sheets except for a wicker chair by the fireplace and an ornate lamp on a trestle table. The table also carries an open book, a cigarette box, a full ashtray and a lighter in the shape of the Venus de Milo.

"Have you heard from Kirsten?"

"I told you I never heard of her."

"Tell her I have her diamonds."

"What diamonds?"

I've sparked her curiosity. "The ones she almost died for."

Mrs. Wilde hasn't offered me a seat but I take one anyway, pulling the sheet from an armchair. Her skin is taut and almost translucent except for her neck and the backs of her hands. She reaches for a cigarette and watches me through the flame of the lighter.

"Kirsten is in a lot of trouble," I explain. "I'm trying to help her. I know she's a friend of yours. I thought she might come looking for you if she needed somewhere to hole up for a while."

Smoke curls in ribbons from her lips. "I don't know what you're talking about."

I glance around the room at the deep velvet wallpaper and baroque furnishings. If there's one place more depressing than a brothel it's a former brothel. It's like they soak up the loathing and disappointment until they feel as tired and worn out as the sexual organs of the employees.

"A long while ago Kirsten told me that she would never cross Aleksei Kuznet or if she did she'd be catching the first plane to Patagonia. She missed her flight."

Aleksei's name has shaken her calmness.

"Didn't Kirsten tell you? She tried to rip him off. You must realize how much danger she's in . . ." I pause, ". . . how much danger you're both in."

"I haven't done anything."

"I'm sure Aleksei will understand. He's a reasonable man. I saw him only yesterday. I offered him a deal—two million pounds' worth of diamonds if he left Kirsten alone. He didn't take it. He sees himself as a man of honor. Money doesn't matter and neither do excuses. But if you haven't seen Kirsten, that's fine. I'll let him know."

Ash falls from her cigarette and smudges her dress. "I might be able to ask around. You mentioned money."

"I mentioned diamonds."

"It might help me find her."

"And I had you pegged as a humanitarian."

Her top lip curls. "You see a limousine parked outside?"

Her eyelids seem to work on wires attached to the top of her forehead. I've heard it called a Croydon face-lift—pulling back your hair so tightly that everything else lifts.

Drawing out my wallet, I peel off three twenties. She counts with her eyes.

"There's a clinic in Tottenham. It patched her up. Expensive. But discreet."

I put another two twenties on the stack. She has the money in her hand and it vanishes down her cleavage as if part of a conjuring trick. She tilts her head as though listening to the rain.

"I know all about you. You're a Gypsy." My surprise pleases her. "They used to say your mother had a gift."

"How do you know her?"

"Don't you recognize a kindred spirit?" She cackles hoarsely, claiming to be a Gypsy. "Your mother told my fortune once. She said I would always be a great beauty and could have any man I wanted."

(Somehow I don't think she was talking quantity.)

Daj had a gift all right—a gift for doing cold readings and predicting the bleeding obvious. She took people's money and tapped their spring of eternal hope. And afterward, having ushered them out of the door, she ran to the liquor store and bought her vodka.

There's a sound from upstairs: something falling. Mrs. Wilde looks up quickly.

"It's just one of my old girls. She stays sometimes."

Her milky blue eyes betray her and her hand shoots out to stop me from rising. "Let me tell you the address of the clinic. They might know where she is."

I brush her hand aside and move up the stairs, leaning out to peer between the banisters above me. On the first landing there are three doors, two open and one closed. I knock gently and turn the handle. Locked.

"Don't touch me! Leave me alone!"

It sounds like the voice of a child—the same one I heard on the phone during the ransom drop. I step away, bracing my back against the wall, with only my hand protruding past the door frame.

The first bullet hits six inches to the right of the handle at stomach height. I sit heavily letting my feet hit the opposite wall, letting out a low groan.

Mrs. Wilde yells up the stairs, "Is that my door? If that's my bloody door you'll be paying for it."

A second bullet rips through the wood a foot above the floor.

Mrs. Wilde again: "Right, that's it! From now on I'm taking a fucking deposit."

I sit quietly, listening to my own breathing.

"Hey, you out there," says the voice, just above a whisper. "Are you dead?"

"No."

"Are you wounded?"

"No."

She curses.

"It's me, Vincent Ruiz. I'm here to help you."

A long silence follows.

"Please let me come in. I'm here alone."

"Stay away. Please go." I recognize Kirsten's voice, thick with phlegm and fear.

"I can't do that."

After another long pause: "How's your leg?"

"Half an inch shorter."

Mrs. Wilde calls up the stairs. "I'm calling the police unless someone pays for my door!"

Sighing heavily, I tell Kirsten, "You can keep the gun if you shoot your landlady."

Her laugh is cut short by a hacking cough.

"I'm coming in."

"Then I'll have to shoot you."

"No, you won't."

I ease myself up and face the door. "Are you going to unlock it for me?"

After a long wait there are two metallic clicks. Turning the handle, I push the door open.

Heavy drapes are drawn and the bedroom is in semidarkness. The room has high ceilings and mirrors on two walls. A large iron bed occupies the center and Kirsten is marooned amid the covers, with her legs drawn up and the gun resting on her knees. She has cut her hair and dyed it blond. It falls in sweaty ringlets down her forehead.

"I thought you were dead," she says.

"I could say the same about you."

She lowers her chin onto the barrel of the gun, staring forlornly into the shadows. The cheap chandelier above her head catches the light leaking from the curtains and the mirrors reflect the same scene, each from a slightly different angle.

I lean against the windowsill letting the curtains sag against my back. I can hear the raindrops hitting the panes of glass.

Kirsten shifts slightly and grimaces in pain. Boxes of painkillers and torn silver foil litter the floor around her bed.

"Can I have a look?"

Without acknowledging me, she raises her shirt high enough to show me the yellowing bandage, crusty with blood and sweat.

"You need to get to a hospital."

She lowers the shirt but doesn't answer.

"A lot of people are looking for you."

"And you get the prize."

"Can I call an ambulance?"

"No."

"OK, we'll just talk for a while. You want to tell me what happened?"

Kirsten shrugs and lowers the gun, resting it between her thighs. "I saw an opportunity."

"To play with fire."

"To make a new life . . ." She doesn't finish the sentence. Dampening her lips, she makes a silent decision and starts again. "It was almost a joke at first; one of those 'what if' ideas that you toss around among yourselves and laugh about. Ray was good at the technical side. He used to work in the sewers. I kept an eye on the little details. At first I thought

Rachel might even play along. We could set the whole thing up and she'd finally get what she deserved from her family or her ex-husband. She was owed."

"She wouldn't play along?"

"I didn't ask. I knew the answer."

I look around the room. The wallpaper has a honeycomb design and within each octagon is the outline of a naked woman in a different sexual pose.

"What happened to Mickey?"

Kirsten doesn't seem to hear me. She's telling the story in her own time.

"We would have been fine, you know, if it hadn't been for Gerry Brandt. Mickey would have made it home. Ray would still be alive. Gerry should never have let her go . . . not alone. He was supposed to take her home."

"I don't understand. What are you talking about?"

A painful smile steals across her face but doesn't part her lips. "Poor Inspector, you haven't worked it out yet, have you?"

The truth grows in me like a tumor with the cells doubling and dividing, invading the empty spaces and the gaps in my memory. Gerry Brandt said he let her go. They were his last words.

"We only had her for a few days," says Kirsten, gnawing at a fingernail. "Then he paid the ransom."

"What ransom?"

"The first one."

"What do you mean, a first ransom?"

"We were never going to hurt her. Once we got the ransom, we told Gerry to take her home. He was supposed to drop her at the end of her street but he panicked and left her at an Underground station. The fucking idiot! He was always a loose cannon. Right from the first day he jeopardized everything. He was supposed to be looking after Mickey but he couldn't resist going back to Randolph Avenue to see the TV crews and police.

"We would never have included him except we needed someone to look after Mickey who she couldn't identify. Like I said, we were always going to let her go. She told Gerry she knew the way home. She said she'd change trains at Piccadilly Circus and catch the Bakerloo line."

This information seeps into my stomach and joins forces with the tepid nausea. My mind is tallying the details. Mr. and Mrs. Bird saw Mickey at Leicester Square. It's one stop from Piccadilly Circus.

"But if you let her go, what happened?"

Her misery is complete. "Howard Wavell!"

I don't understand.

"Howard happened," she says again. "Mickey made it home but she ran into Howard."

God, no! Surely not! It was a Wednesday night. Rachel wasn't home. She was on *News at Ten* making another appeal. I remember watching her on TV at the station. They used footage of the press conference earlier in the day.

"I tell you we didn't mean to hurt her. We let her go. Then you found her bloodstained towel and arrested Howard. I wanted to die."

An image presents itself. I picture a small, terrified child with a fear of being outside, crossing a city alone. She almost made it. Only steps away—not even eighty-five of them. Howard found her on the front steps.

My legs go weak and I struggle to stand. It's as though my insides have become liquid and want to flood out, throbbing and glistening on the floor. My God, what have I done? I couldn't have been more wrong. Ali, Rachel, Mickey—I let them all down.

"You don't know how many times I have wanted to change things," says Kirsten. "I would have brought Mickey home myself. I would have walked her right to her door. Believe me!"

"You were *friends* with Rachel. How could you do that to her?"

For a fleeting moment her sadness turns to anger, but takes too much energy to sustain. She whispers, "I never meant to hurt them . . . not Mickey or Rachel."

"Why then?"

"We were stealing from the ultimate thief—taking money from Aleksei Kuznet, a monster. He murdered his own brother, for God's sake."

"You wanted to take on the biggest bully in the playground."

"We live in a new feudal age, Inspector. We fight wars over oil and we hand out reconstruction contracts in return for political donations. We have more parking wardens than we do police officers—"

"Oh for pity's sake, spare me the speeches!"

"We didn't want to hurt anyone."

"Rachel was always going to be hurt."

She looks at me with wet eyes. I can almost taste the salt in them.

"I didn't mean . . . we let Mickey go. I would never have . . ." She lowers the gun between her knees and her head follows, rocking back and forth. "I'm sorry . . . I'm so sorry . . ."

Her self-pity irritates me. I keep pressing for the rest of the story. Kirsten doesn't look at me as she describes the cesspit in the basement and the underground river. Ray Murphy inflated a boat below ground and drew a map for Gerry to follow. He only had to travel a few hundred feet before bringing Mickey up through a storm-water drain.

"Ray knew a place to keep her. I never went there. My job was to send the ransom letter."

"Where did you send it?"

"Directly to Aleksei."

"What about the bikini?"

"Gerry held on to it."

"What was she wearing when he let her go?"

"I don't know exactly."

"Did she have her beach towel?"

"Gerry said it was like her security blanket. She wouldn't let it go."

I'm struggling now. Of all the scenarios to contemplate I had left Howard out, convinced of his innocence. I had weighed up the evidence and the odds and decided he had been wrongly accused and convicted. Campbell said I was blind to the obvious. I thought he couldn't see anything except his own prejudices.

"Why in God's name did you try for a second ransom? How could you put Rachel through it again? You convinced her Mickey was still alive."

Her face creases as she sucks back the pain. "I didn't want to. You don't understand."

"Then explain it to me."

"When you arrested Howard for Mickey's murder Gerry went off his head. He kept saying we helped kill her. He said he couldn't go back inside—not for killing a child. He knew what they did to child murderers in prison. Right away I knew we had a problem. We either had to silence Gerry or help him disappear."

"So you got him out of the country."

"We gave him double what he deserved—four hundred grand. He was supposed to stay away but he poured his money down slot machines or shot it up his arm."

"He bought a bar in Thailand."

"Whatever."

"And then he came back."

"The first I knew about the second ransom was when Rachel received the postcard. Gerry came up with the idea all by himself. Mickey's body had never been found. He still had her swimsuit and strands of her hair. I went ballistic. His greed and stupidity threatened us all. Ray said he was going to stop Gerry before he gave us away . . ."

"You could have walked away then. Nobody would have known."

"I wanted to kill him—I really did."

"What changed your mind?"

"None of us thought Aleksei would say yes—not after paying one ransom—but then straight off he agreed. I almost felt sorry for him then. He must have really wanted to believe Mickey was still alive."

"He didn't have a choice. Fathers are meant to believe."

"No, he wanted revenge. He didn't care what it cost. He didn't care about Mickey or Rachel. He wanted us dead—that's the only reason."

Maybe she's right. Aleksei has always preferred to dispense his own brand of justice.

Outside Wormwood Scrubs Prison and again at the police station, Aleksei had said, "I don't pay for things twice." This is what he meant. He had already paid a ransom for Mickey and wouldn't easily surrender another one.

"You must have used the same drop procedure. That's how Aleksei found you."

"We didn't have time to come up with a new one. Aleksei figured it out. It's like I said, we didn't expect him to go through with it. We had to scramble to get everything ready. I didn't want to go ahead but Ray needed the money and he said it would be easier second time around."

"You knew I was in the car with Rachel."

"No. Not after we made her change vehicles. And we didn't expect anyone to be foolish enough to follow the ransom through the sewers."

"During the ransom drop, I heard the sound of a child's voice. It was you, wasn't it?"

"Yes."

The room has grown darker and she seems to be turning to shadow. The distance between us has grown wide and cold.

"When the shooting started, I thought it must be the police. Then they just kept firing."

"Did you see the sniper?"

"No."

"Did you see anyone?"

She shakes her head.

Although exhausted she looks almost relieved to be talking. She can't remember how long she spent in the water. The tide carried her east past Westminster. Eventually she crawled onto the steps at Bankside Jetty near the Globe Theatre. She broke into a pharmacy and stole bandages and painkillers. She slept in a shop that was being refurbished, lying beneath painter's sheets.

She couldn't run and she couldn't go to a hospital. Aleksei would have found her. Once he knew who had kidnapped Mickey he was never going to stop looking.

"And since then you've been hiding?"

"Waiting to die." Her voice is so soft it might be coming from another room.

The cloying smell of sweat and infection thickens the air. Either everything Kirsten has told me is the truth or an extraordinarily elaborate lie. "Please move away from the window," she says.

"Why?"

"I keep seeing red dots. They're burned into my eyelids."

I know what she means.

Taking a chair beside the bed, I pour her a glass of water. Her finger is no longer curled around the trigger of the gun.

"What were you going to do with the ransom?"

"I had plans." She describes a new life in America, making it sound almost irresistible—the idea of walking away and never looking back, the romance of the clean slate.

I have thoughts like that sometimes—wanting to be someone else or to start afresh—but then I realize I have no desire to see most of the world and I have enough trouble keeping old friends without meeting new ones. What would I be running from? I'd be another dog chasing its tail.

"We were foolish. We should have walked away and counted our blessings that nobody knew the truth about Mickey. Now it's too late."

"I can protect you," I say.

"Nobody can."

"I can talk to the Crown Prosecution Service. If you give evidence against Aleksei they can put you—"

"What evidence?" she says harshly. "I didn't see him shoot anyone. I can't point to a mug shot or pick someone out of a police lineup. So what if he paid two ransoms—it's not against the law."

She is right. The most Aleksei is guilty of is withholding information from the police about the first ransom demand.

Surely there *must* be something more. A man organizes to have people executed and nobody can touch him.

For the first time in a long while, I have no idea of what to do next. I know I have to call the police. I also have to keep her safe. There are witness protection programs for IRA informers and organized crime witnesses but what can they offer Kirsten? She can't give them Aleksei. She can't link him to the executions or any of his many crimes.

"What if we arrange a meeting?"

"What?"

"Contact Aleksei—organize to see him."

She puts her hands over her ears, not wanting to hear. Her skin is like metal, shining at angles in the light from the bedside lamp.

She's right. Aleksei would never agree.

"You can't save me. If I were you, I'd phone him now and tell him where I am. You might win a reprieve."

"I'm going to call an ambulance."

"No."

"You can't stay here. How long before your landlady gives you up?"

"We're old friends."

"I can see that! How much has it cost you to still be here?"

She holds up her fingers. Her jewelry is gone.

We sit in silence and after a while I hear her breathing find a steady rhythm. She's asleep. Moving to her side, I gently take the revolver from her lap before covering her with a blanket. Then I move to the landing and call "New Boy" Dave. My hands are shaking.

"I've found Kirsten Fitzroy. I need an ambulance and a police escort. Don't tell Meldrum or Campbell."

"OK."

Back in the room Kirsten's eyes are open.

"Are they coming?"

"Yes."

"The cavalry or a hearse?"

"An ambulance."

Gritting her teeth against the pain, she swings her legs off the bed and sits facing away from me. Her black shirt is stuck perfectly to her body with sweat and it looks as though someone has poured oil over her.

"You might be able to protect me today but it is just *one* day," she says, managing to stand and shuffle toward the bathroom. Sensing I'm about to follow, she stops me. "I have to go potty."

I'm expected to wait on the landing, which I do—pleased to escape from the sickroom smell and the hypocrisy. The sheer number of lies and depth of betrayal is staggering. Mickey is dead! I failed. I want to crawl back into the sewer where I belong.

There's a knock on the door downstairs. Mrs. Wilde answers. I look over the banister half expecting to see "New Boy" Dave. It's a courier. I can't make out what he's saying.

Mrs. Wilde turns away from the door holding a bunch of flowers. In that same instant I hear a blunt sound, metal on bone. She topples forward, crushing the flowers beneath her. A motorcycle courier in leathers and a gleaming black helmet steps over her body.

I hit the redial button on the cell phone. Dave's number is engaged. He must be calling the ambulance.

I can hear the courier searching downstairs—kicking open doors. I can imagine him crouching and swinging the gun in a wide arc. He's a professional. Ex-military.

Kirsten flushes the toilet and walks from the bathroom. I signal for her to get down and she drops to her knees with a groan. She sees something in my eyes that wasn't there before.

"Don't leave me," she mouths. I hold my finger to my lips and point above my head.

The courier has heard the toilet flushing and the cistern filling. Now he's at the bottom of the stairs. Turning away from Kirsten I climb to the next landing. Again I hit the speed dial. Engaged.

A floorboard depresses and releases. The noise vibrates through me.

Kirsten fired two shots. Assuming the gun is fully loaded, I have four bullets left.

I should be scared but maybe I'm beyond that. Instead I think of the past three weeks and all those times that Aleksei has toyed with me. I'm not angry or bitter. This is like one of those children's stories, Goldilocks and the Three Bears, where Goldilocks gets chased out of the house for eating porridge and breaking a chair. Only in my new version she comes back with a gun and she's going to make sure she aims not too high and not too low but just right.

"New Boy" Dave answers his phone.

"Code One. Officer in trouble. Help!"

The courier is on the stairs, staying close to the wall to shield himself from above. When he turns onto the landing I should get a clean shot. I wait in darkness, trying to make myself small. A river leaks down my back.

Another step. His shadow appears. He's carrying a fully automatic machine pistol that sweeps from side to side. My finger pulls gently on the trigger, pushing the hammer backward and compressing a metal spring in the handle. A ratchet rotates the cylinder, putting a bullet in the breech chamber in line with the barrel.

He's fully in view—about to turn into the bedroom. I can't see his face behind the visor.

"Police! Put the gun down!"

He drops and rolls, firing blindly up the stairs. Bullets punch tattered holes in the wallpaper beside my head and shatter the banister. A splinter of wood slices into my neck.

The moment I shoot he'll see the muzzle flash and know where I am. I pull the trigger lever all the way back, releasing the hammer.

The bullet enters through his shoulder, angling down into his chest. His head hits the wall. The wide dark visor is staring at me. His finger closes on the trigger again. We fire together and he tumbles backward.

I can taste blood in my mouth where I've bitten my tongue and my lungs hurt like a bastard. Where has all the oxygen gone? I don't know how long I sit on the stairs. There are sirens and screeching tires in the street. "New Boy" Dave comes through the door so fast he almost trips over Mrs. Wilde.

Kneeling on the landing, I put the gun at my side and stare down at my chest. Dave is climbing the stairs, yelling my name. Ripping open the buttons, I press my fingers to my breastbone. A neat depression, still warm from the bullet, lies at the center of the vest.

Well I'll be damned! Ali saved my life.

Looking through the railings I see the courier's body crumpled at the foot of the stairs. Forty-three years in the police force, thirty-five of them as a detective, and I managed not to kill anyone. Another unwanted milestone reached.

36

Four hours ago a warrant was issued for Aleksei's arrest but it hasn't been served. His motor yacht left Chelsea Harbour at midnight on Saturday, only an hour after our meeting. The skipper claimed to be doing a transfer to Moody's boatyard in Hamble on the south coast but failed to arrive by midday Sunday.

Coast guards and lifeboat stations have been alerted and all vessels within a five hundred nautical mile range have been told to report any sightings. Descriptions of the vessel are also being sent to harbormasters in France, Belgium, Holland, Denmark, Portugal and Spain.

I didn't expect Aleksei to run. A part of me still thinks he's going to waltz into a police station with a team of lawyers looking smug and ready to rumble. He knows there is nothing but circumstantial evidence. Nobody can put him at the scene of the murders. If Kirsten dies I can't even prove he paid the first ransom.

Of course, it's not my job to prove anything, as Campbell keeps telling me, as he storms around the hospital, dressed in an overcoat of angry tweed. Every time his eyes reach me he looks away. He was right and I couldn't have been more wrong. Despite all the bloody mayhem of the past few weeks, the facts have remained unchanged—Mickey died three years ago and Howard Wavell killed her.

According to the X-rays my ribs are only bruised and the cut on my neck doesn't need stitches. Kirsten is under guard upstairs. Not even the paramedics knew her name when they delivered her into intensive care.

Tomorrow morning Eddie Barrett and the Rook will argue that Howard Wavell should be released from prison. They will claim that Mickey Carlyle was taken for a ransom and killed by her abductors. The CCTV footage from Leicester Square Underground could be of anyone. The towel found at East Finchley Cemetery was planted there to frame Howard for a murder he didn't commit.

It's a version of events that is far easier to argue than the truth. The police case against Howard was always circumstantial. Evidence had to be laid out piece by piece, showing the jury how it all fitted together. Now it seems more like a house of cards.

Howard will get his retrial and our only hope of maintaining his conviction is if a jury believes Kirsten's story. Defense barristers will be queuing up to dismantle her credibility as a confessed kidnapper, extortionist and manager of an escort agency.

I was wrong about Howard, wrong about Mickey, wrong about almost everything. A child killer is going to walk free. I am responsible.

Things get messy when police shoot people. They get even messier when it's an ex-policeman. There will be an inquest and an investigation by the Police Complaints Commission. There will also be drug tests and psych reports. I don't know enough about morphine to say if the opiates are still in my system. If I test positive I'll be swimming in shit.

The man I killed hasn't been identified. He rode a stolen motorbike and carried no papers. His dental work was Eastern European and he carried a fully automatic machine pistol stolen from a Belfast police station four years ago. His only other distinguishing feature was a small silver cross around his neck inlaid with a purple gemstone, chariote, a rare silicate found only in the Bratsk region of Siberia. Perhaps Interpol will have more luck.

Visiting hours are over but the nursing sister has let me in. Although flat on her back, staring at a mirror above her head, Ali gives me a bigger smile than I deserve. She turns her head, making it only partway before the pain catches in her throat.

"I brought you chocolates," I tell her.

"You want me to get fat."

"You haven't been fat since you were hanging off the tit."

It hurts when she laughs.

"How is it going?" I ask.

"OK. I managed to stand this afternoon."

"That's a good sign. So when can we go dancing?"

"You hate dancing."

"I'll dance with *you*."

It sounds too maudlin and I wish I could take it back. Ali seems to appreciate the sentiment.

She explains that she has to wear a special cast for the next three months and then a canvas brace with shoulder bands for another three months after that.

"With any luck I'll be walking by then."

I hate the expression "with any luck." It's not a resounding affirmative but a fingers-crossed, if-all-goes-well sort of statement. What sort of luck has Ali had so far?

I pull a bottle of whiskey from a brown paper bag and wave it in front of her eyes. She grins. Two glasses are next, pulled from the bag like a rabbit from a hat.

I pour her a glass and add water from a tap in the sink.

"I can't really handle a glass," she says apologetically.

Reaching into the bag again, I produce a crazy drinking straw with spirals and loops. I rest the glass on her chest and put the straw in her mouth. She takes a sip and gasps slightly. It's the first time I have ever seen her drink.

Our eyes meet in the mirror. "A Home Office lawyer came to see me today," she says. "They're offering a compensation package and a full disability pension if I want to leave the job."

"What did you tell them?"

"I want to stay."

"They're worried you might sue them."

"Why would I do that? It's nobody's fault."

We look at each other and I feel grateful and undeserving all at once.

"I heard about Gerry Brandt."

"Yeah."

I watch the subtle change in her, a little shrinking created by a single affirmation. Something shifts inside me as well and I get a sense of how much pain she's endured already and the months of operations and physiotherapy still to come.

A swatch of her hair, shiny black, has come loose from a bobby pin. She drops her gaze and sets her mouth defiantly. "And you found Kirsten. We should drink to that."

She takes a sip and notices I haven't joined her. "What's wrong?"

"I'm so sorry. It was a stupid, foolish quest. I just wanted . . . I just hoped Mickey might be alive, you know. And now look! You're here and people are dead and Rachel is grieving all over again. And tomorrow Howard is going to get his retrial. It's my fault. What I've done is unforgivable."

Ali doesn't answer. Outside the sky is tinged with pink and the streetlights are blinking on. I rock forward and stare into the glass. She reaches out and puts her hand on my shoulder to stop it shaking.

"It hurts all over," I moan. "Why put a child on this Earth and give her seven years if you're going to allow her to be kidnapped, raped, tortured, terrified or whatever else happened?"

"There's no answer to that."

"I don't believe in God. I don't believe in eternal life or Heaven or reincarnation. Will you ask your God for me? Ask him why."

Ali looks at me sadly. "He doesn't work like that."

"Well ask him for his grand plan. While he concentrates on the big picture, who looks after kids like Mickey? One child might seem petty and trivial among a few billion but he could start by saving one at a time."

I down the rest of the whiskey, feeling the alcohol burn my throat. I'm already drunk, but not drunk enough.

A black cab drops me home. Fumbling for the keys, I stagger inside and up the stairs, where I lean over the toilet and vomit. Afterward I splash water on my face, letting it leak down my neck and chest.

Staring back from the mirror is a pallid, leering stranger. In his eyes I see Mickey standing at the bottom of the escalator and Daj behind the razor wire and Luke lying beneath the ice.

I seem to have no other memories. Missing children, abused children and dead children fill my thoughts. Babies drowned in bathtubs, toddlers shaken into comas, children sent to gas chambers or snatched from playgrounds or suffocated beneath pillows. How can I blame God when I couldn't save one little girl?

37

Opposite the Royal Courts of Justice a deliveryman is unloading naked mannequins from a truck. Male and female dummies are frozen in an orgy of plaster, some with wigs and others bare. The driver carries them two at a time, balanced across his shoulders, with his hands between each pair of buttocks to stop them from falling. I can see him laughing as cabdrivers toot their horns and office workers lean out of windows.

I stand and watch. It's good to smile.

The feeling doesn't last. Rachel Carlyle looks up as I approach along the corridor. Her gaze is not quite focused and her smile vague, as though she doesn't immediately recognize me. Light coming through high windows is broken and refracted, dissipating before it reaches the depths of the marble entrance hall.

I take her off to one side, finding an empty conference room. Making her sit down I tell her the same story that Kirsten told me, trying to leave nothing out. When I reach the point about Mickey crossing London alone, late at night, she squeezes her eyes shut, endeavoring to rid herself of the image.

"Where is Kirsten now?"

"She's battling an infection. The next forty-eight hours will be crucial."

Rachel's face is etched with concern. Her capacity for forgiveness is beyond mine. I can imagine her saying a prayer for Kirsten or lighting a candle. She should be railing against her and against me. I raised her hopes and look at us now.

Instead she blames herself. "If I hadn't asked Aleksei for the ransom none of this would have happened."

"No. He was punishing them for what happened to Mickey, not for anything you did."

Her voice drops. "I just wanted her back."

"I know."

I look at my watch. We're due in court. Rachel pauses for a moment, drawing strength, before leaving the room. The corridors and public areas have emptied slightly. The Rook is on the stairs. Eddie Barrett is three steps above him, putting them at eye level. The Rook looks invigorated while Eddie growls and gesticulates, almost eating the air.

Rachel takes my arm to steady herself. "If Aleksei received an original ransom demand why didn't he say anything?"

"I guess he didn't want the police involved."

"Yes, but afterward, when Mickey didn't come home, he could have said something then."

I don't know the answer. I suspect he didn't want to advertise his mistake. He is also conceited enough to believe he could find Mickey before the police. He must have known how close she came to making it home—less than eighty-five steps. How that must have torn him apart.

Lord Connelly keeps everyone waiting. He enters the courtroom at ten minutes past ten and the room rises. Then he carefully places his walnut palm gavel to his right and his glass of water to his left.

Howard emerges from below. He is clutching a Bible with red ribbons marking the pages. His eyes look bruised but defiant. Eddie Barrett shakes his hand and Howard gives him a weary smile.

Fiona Hanley, QC, is already on her feet. "Perhaps I can expedite these proceedings a little, Your Honor. Due to information that has come to light over the weekend, the Crown does not oppose the defense application and are content for this case to be retried at the court's earliest convenience."

There is an audible gasp. Blood surges in the air and eyes shift to Howard. I don't think he understands. Even Eddie Barrett looks amazed.

"My chambers," Lord Connelly says. He exits stage right like a black-caped crusader.

Four of us wait in the outer office. Eddie Barrett and the Rook are whispering in one corner. The Rook is actually smiling, an expression that doesn't come naturally to him. Meanwhile, Fiona Hanley avoids my gaze, wrapping her robe around herself.

Lord Connelly's assistant, a large-breasted black woman, has a brilliant smile reserved only for His Honor. She has been with him fifteen years and we've all heard the rumors.

"He'll see you now," she says, pointing to the door.

Eddie takes a step back and lets Miss Hanley go first, bowing slightly and showing his monklike dome.

There are only three chairs in front of the Judge's desk. I stand with my back to the bookshelves that line the walls. Lord Connelly has removed his wig. His *own* hair is similarly white, trimmed neatly above his ears. His voice takes on a kind of exalted public-school inflection.

"I spent four days writing up this judgment and now you spring this." His gaze settles on Fiona.

"I apologize, Your Honor, I only learned of this late yesterday."

"And whose bright idea was it?"

"Further information has come to light—"

"Which casts doubt on Mr. Wavell's guilt?"

She hesitates. "It creates complications."

"I hope you're not telling me one thing and meaning something else."

Eddie is beside himself with glee. The Judge fixes him with a glare. "And you can keep your thoughts to yourself, Mr. Barrett. I have had a bellyful of you in my courtrooms and I won't put up with it in here."

Eddie's smile is erased.

Getting to his feet, Lord Connelly walks behind his chair and braces his hand on the backrest. His eyes settle on me. "I understand that I shouldn't refer to your rank anymore, DI Ruiz, but perhaps you can enlighten me on what is happening here."

"The police have a new witness."

"A witness or a suspect?"

"Both."

"In your evidence several days ago you expressed an opinion that Michaela Carlyle might be alive. Is that still the case?"

"No, Your Honor."

Sadness flickers in his eyes. "And this new witness has led you to question what happened?"

"She has confessed to the kidnapping of Michaela Carlyle and sending a subsequent ransom demand. She will testify that Mickey was released unharmed after three days."

"And then what?"

"We believe she made it as far as Dolphin Mansions."

The Judge can see where I'm going now. He grinds his teeth as though trying to wear them down. "This is ridiculous!"

Eddie interrupts. "We *will* be applying for bail, Your Honor."

"*You* keep your mouth shut."

I raise my voice above both of them. "Howard Wavell is a child killer. He should stay in prison."

"Bullshit," mutters Eddie. "He's ugly and he's weird but last time I looked that still wasn't a crime. We can both be grateful for that."

"You can both be quiet," says Lord Connelly, wanting to tear strips off someone. "Next person to utter a sound gets locked up for contempt."

He addresses me. "DI Ruiz, I hope you're going to explain to that poor girl's family what's happening."

"Yes, Your Honor."

He turns to the others. "I am going to grant the defense leave to appeal. I am also going to make sure they have plenty of opportunity to examine this new evidence. I want a level playing field. You can make your case for bail, Mr. Raynor, but I remind you that your client has been convicted of murder and the presumption of guilt must remain—"

"Your Honor, my client is gravely ill and requires medical attention he is not receiving in prison. The humanitarian considerations outweigh . . ."

Lord Connelly wags his finger. "Now is not the time or the place. Make your case in court."

The rest of the hearing passes in a blur of legal argument and ill temper. Leave to appeal is granted and Lord Connelly orders a retrial but refuses to release Howard from prison. Instead he orders that he be transferred to a civilian hospital under armed guard.

There is pandemonium outside the courtroom. Reporters yell into phones and jostle to get close to Rachel, shouting questions and answers, as though wanting her to agree.

Her arms are locked around my waist, her breasts against my back. It's like a rugby maul without the ball as we try to cross the gain line. Eddie Barrett, an unlikely savior, takes his briefcase and swings it from side to side like a scythe, clearing a path.

"It might be time to consider an alternative exit," he shouts, pointing to a door marked OFFICIALS ONLY.

Eddie is an old hand at exiting courthouses through basements and back doors. He leads us down corridors, past offices and holding cells, getting deeper into the building. Eventually, we emerge into a cobblestoned courtyard where industrial trash containers await collection and wire netting is stretched above our heads to stop the pigeons from landing.

The gates slide open electronically and an ambulance pulls through them. Howard is waiting on the stone steps, head in hands, staring sullenly at the tips of his scuffed shoes. Police officers and prison guards stand on either side of him.

Eddie lights a cigarette in the hollow of his hand, inclining his head as he does so. The smoke floats past his eyes and scatters as he exhales. He offers me one and I feel an impulse toward comradeship; the solidarity of lost soldiers on a battlefield.

"You know he did it."

"That's not what he says."

"But what do *you* think?"

Eddie chuckles. "You want true confessions talk to Oprah."

Rachel is nearby, gazing toward Howard. The paramedics have opened the rear doors and are pulling out a stretcher.

"Can I talk to him?" she asks.

Eddie doesn't think it is appropriate.

"I just want to ask how he is."

Eddie looks at me. I shrug my shoulders.

She crosses the courtyard. The police officers step aside and she stands beside the stretcher. I can't hear what they're saying. She reaches out and puts her hand on his shoulder.

Eddie raises his face to the square of sky above. "What are you trying to do, Inspector?"

"I'm trying to get to the truth."

He inclines his head, respectful but stubborn. "In my experience almost all truths are lies." His features have softened and his face looks unexpectedly gentle. "You said Mickey was set free by her kidnappers. When was that?"

"Wednesday night."

He nods.

I remember that night. I watched Rachel being interviewed on *News at Ten*. That's why she wasn't there when Mickey arrived home. A detective was posted at her flat but Mickey didn't get a chance to press the buzzer. My mind puts everyone where they should have been. Mentally I lift off the roof of Dolphin Mansions and put people inside or take them out. It's like playing with dolls in a dollhouse. Mrs. Swingler, Kirsten, Ray Murphy . . . I put Mickey outside, walking up the steps.

A piece is missing. Turning away from Eddie I walk across the courtyard toward Howard. The paramedics have strapped him to a gurney and are lifting him into the ambulance.

"What did you do on Wednesday evenings, Howard?"

He looks at me blankly.

"Before you went to prison. What did you do?"

He clears his throat. "Choir practice. I never missed a choir practice—not in seven years."

There is a pause for the information to sink in—barely a heartbeat, even less, the pause between heartbeats. I have been a fool. I have spent so much time concentrating on finding Kirsten that I didn't see the other possibilities.

Moving away from them, I can see myself running into the street, whistling at cabs to stop. At the same time I yell into my cell phone, making no sense at all. I don't have all the facts. But I have enough. I know what happened.

The traces of hair dye on Mickey's towel have bothered me all along. Gerry Brandt didn't dye her hair and why would Howard bother with a detail like that?

"I don't pay for things twice," Aleksei said. I know what that means now. He didn't organize Mickey's kidnapping but like Kirsten and Ray Murphy, he saw an opportunity. He wanted his daughter back—the only truly perfect thing he had ever created. So he paid the ransom in secret.

No police and no publicity. And when Mickey arrived home that night it was Aleksei who intercepted her. He was waiting.

Then he hatched his plan—one that hinged on convincing the world that Mickey was dead. At first he imagined he could blame the kidnappers. He would take some of Mickey's blood or make her vomit, plant the evidence and encourage everyone to think that she had died at the hands of her abductors. Unfortunately, he didn't know who they were. Then something serendipitous happened—a made-to-measure suspect, with a corrupt sexuality and no alibi. Howard Wavell. The opportunity was almost too perfect.

And what of Mickey? He spirited her away—smuggling her out of the country, most likely on board his yacht. He changed her appearance and changed her name.

I don't know what Aleksei thought would happen then. Maybe one day, after enough years had passed, he planned to bring Mickey back to Britain with a new identity or perhaps he always intended to join her overseas.

The plan might have been flawless but for Gerry Brandt, a washed-up, drug-addled chancer, who thought he could steal apples from the same tree all over again. Having squandered the first ransom, he came back to Britain with a plan to do it all again. Mickey's body had never been found and he still had a few strands of her hair and her swimsuit. Kirsten knew immediately that Gerry was back in the country. She talked to Ray Murphy. Gerry's greed and stupidity threatened to expose them.

Unbeknownst to them, he also threatened to destroy Aleksei's grand design. The world believed Mickey was dead. A second ransom demand called this into question. It must also have created a separate, more dangerous doubt in Aleksei's mind. Did these people *know*?

The only way to safeguard his secret completely was to silence them. He would pay the ransom, follow the trail and have everyone killed. I gave him the perfect alibi; he was following me.

These thoughts are coming almost too quickly to put in any order or chronology but like Sarah, Mickey's friend, on that first morning at Dolphin Mansions—"I know what I know."

"New Boy" Dave is on the other end of the phone.

"Have you found Aleksei?"

"His motor yacht arrived in Oostende in Belgium at eleven o'clock on Sunday morning."

"Who was on board?"

"Still no word."

I can hear the rasp of my own breathing. "You have to listen to me! I know I've made a lot of mistakes but this time I'm right. You have to find Aleksei. You can't let him disappear."

I pause. He's still on the phone. The only thing we have in common now is Ali. Maybe that's enough. "You have to check the passenger manifests of every ferry and hovercraft and the Eurostar train services out of Waterloo. You can forget about the airlines. Aleksei doesn't fly. You'll need warrants for his house, office, cars, lockups, boatsheds . . . And you'll want his phone records and details of bank transactions going back three years."

Dave is starting to lose patience with me. He doesn't have the authority to do half of these things and Campbell and Meldrum won't listen to anything I say.

Leaning back, I stare out of the window of the cab not actually seeing anything but I'm turning pages in my head full of notes, diagrams and figures; searching through the past for a clue.

When I did my detective training a guy called Donald Kinsella took me under his wing. Donald had spent years working undercover and wore his hair long, tied back in a ponytail and he had a bushy mustache, which was a trademark for coppers in the seventies until the Village People made it a different sort of trademark.

"Keep it simple," was his motto. "Don't believe in conspiracy theories. Listen to them, work out the odds, and then file them in the same drawer as you put stuff you read in the *Socialist Worker* or on the *Daily Telegraph* editorial pages."

Donald believed the truth lay somewhere in the middle. He was a pragmatist. When Diana, Princess of Wales, died in Paris he rang me. He'd retired by then.

"A year from now there will be a dozen books about this," he said. "People will be blaming the CIA, MI5, the PLO, the Mafia, Osama bin Laden, another shooter on the grassy knoll—you name it. There will be secret witnesses, missing evidence, mystery vehicles, stolen reports, tire marks, poisonings and pregnancies . . . Let me tell you the one thing I can guarantee *won't* be in any of these books—the most likely answer.

People *want* to believe conspiracies. They eat them up and say, 'Please can I have some more?' They don't want to think that someone close to them or someone famous could die a mundane, ordinary, kitchen-sink sort of death."

What Donald was trying to say is that lives are complicated but most deaths aren't. People are complicated but not their crimes. Prosecutors and psychologists care about motives. I care about facts—the how, where, what and when, rather than the why. My favorite is "who," the perpetrator—the face that fills my empty picture frame.

Eddie Barrett is wrong. All truth isn't a lie. I'm not naïve enough to believe the opposite, but facts I can hold on to. Facts I can write up in a report. Facts are more reliable than memories.

The cabdriver is staring at me in his mirror. I'm talking to myself.

"The second sign of madness," I explain.

"What's the first one?"

"Killing lots of people and eating their genitals."

He laughs and sneaks another look at me.

38

Three hours ago I learned that Mickey Carlyle might still be alive. Twenty-four hours ago Aleksei's boat arrived in Oostende. He has a head start but will only travel overland. He might already be there. Where?

The Netherlands is a possibility. He and Rachel lived there and Mickey was born in Amsterdam. Eastern Europe is more likely. He has connections and maybe even family.

I glance around the Professor's office at the dozen people who are manning phones and staring at screens. They have all answered the call again—leaving work or taking time off. It almost feels like a proper incident room, full of energy and expectation.

Roger is talking to the harbormaster at Oostende. There were six adults on board the motor yacht, including Aleksei, but no sign of a child. The launch is now moored at the Royal Yacht Club, the largest marina in Oostende, in the heart of the city. We have a list of names for the crew. Margaret and Jean are ringing the local hotels. Others are calling car rental companies, travel agents and ticket offices for rail and ferry services. Unfortunately, the possibilities appear endless. Aleksei could already have disappeared into Europe.

Without a warrant or a court order, we can't access his bank accounts, post boxes or telephone records. There is no way of tracing regular overseas payments and I doubt if the money would lead us to Mickey. Aleksei is too clever for that. His fortune will be spread around the world in offshore tax havens like the Caymans, Bermuda and Gibraltar. Experts could spend the next twenty years trying to follow that paper trail.

I look at my watch. Every minute puts him farther away.

Grabbing my coat, I give Joe a nod. "Come on, let's go."

"Where to?"

"We're going to look at a house."

Contrary to popular belief, the most powerful man in the cut-flower industry doesn't possess a green thumb or even a greenhouse. The gardens surrounding Aleksei's mansion are rather rustic and overgrown with cedar trees and an orchard.

The electronic gates are open and we pull directly into the driveway, gravel snapping under the tires. The house looks closed up. Turrets of dark slate stand out solidly against the sky as though turning their backs on the city and choosing to gaze instead across Hampstead Heath.

Stepping out of the car, I try to take in the building, swiveling my head upward through the floors.

"OK, we're not doing anything illegal, are we?" asks Joe.

"Not yet."

"I'm serious."

"So am I."

Walking slowly around the house, I marvel at the security. There are bars on the windows, security lights and sensor alarms attached to the exterior walls. A large converted stable block is garage to a dozen cars covered by cloth sheets.

At the back of the house, I notice smoke rising from an incinerator. A gardener with a solid build and a mustache like a hula skirt above his top lip looks up as we approach. He's wearing a tweed coat and trousers tucked into Wellingtons.

"Good afternoon."

He takes off his cap. "Good afternoon to you."

"You work here?"

"I do, Sir."

"Where is everyone?"

"Gone. The place is up for sale. I'm just keeping the gardens tidy."

I notice boxes of leaves and grass clippings.

"What's your name?"

"Harold."

"Did you ever meet the owner, Mr. Kuznet?"

"Oh, yes, Sir. I used to clean his motors. He was very particular about what wax and polish I used, with no abrasives. He knows the difference between a wax and a polish—not many people do."

"Was he a good boss?"

"Better 'n most, I reckon."

"A lot of people were scared of him."

"Yeah, but I can't see why. You hear stories, don't you? 'Bout him killing his brother, burying bodies in the basement and doing them other terrible things. But I say it like I see it. He was always good to me."

"Did you ever see a young girl around here?"

Harold scratches his chin. "Can't say I remember any children. Good house for a kiddie—look at them grounds—my grandkids would love this place."

Joe has wandered off, staring upward at the eaves, as though looking for nesting pigeons. He drifts sideways and almost falls over a sprinkler head.

"What's wrong with your mate—he got the shakes?"

"Parkinson's."

Harold nods. "My uncle had that."

He sweeps more leaves into a mound.

"If you're thinking of buying the place you missed the agent. She was here earlier showing the police around. I thought you were another copper."

"Not anymore. Do you think we could have a look inside?"

"I'm not allowed."

"But you have a key?"

"Yeah, well, I know where she keeps them."

I take a tin of hard candies from my pocket and remove the lid, offering him one.

"Listen, Harold, I don't have much time. There's a little girl who we're trying to find. She went missing a long time ago. It's important I look inside. Nobody is going to know."

"A little girl, you say."

"Yes."

He contemplates this for a moment while sucking on a candy. Having made a decision, he puts down the rake and starts walking up the gentle slope toward the house. The ground levels out on a boggy croquet lawn in front of the conservatory. Joe catches up with us, trying not to get his shoes wet.

The side door of the house opens into a small entrance hall with a stone floor and room to hang coats and deposit boots and umbrellas. The laundry must be close by. I can smell detergent and spray starch.

Harold unlocks the next door and we emerge into a large kitchen, with a central bench and brushed-steel appliances. It opens out through an arch into the conservatory, where the breakfast table could seat a dozen people.

Joe has wandered away from us again. This time he's peering beneath chairs and the table, following the edge of the baseboards. "Have you noticed anything unusual about this place?" he asks.

"Like what?"

"There are no telephone lines. The house isn't even hooked up."

"Maybe they're underground."

"Yes, that's what I thought, but I can't even see sockets in the walls."

I turn to Harold. "Are there any telephones?"

He grins. "He's sharp, your mate. Mr. Kuznet didn't believe in normal phones. I don't think he trusted 'em. We all got one of these." Reaching into his jacket he pulls out a cell phone.

"Everyone?"

"Yep. The cook, the driver, the cleaners, even me—s'pose I'll have to give mine back now."

"How long have you had this one?"

"Not long. He made us swap numbers all the time. I never had the same number more than a month before he changed it."

Aleksei was obviously paranoid about his telephones being tapped or monitored. He must have leased hundreds of cell phones, doling them out to his employees at work and at home, rotating them, swapping his own number among them, making it almost impossible for anybody to keep track of his calls or fix on a particular phone number and trace it back to him. The list of numbers must read like lottery results— all put through the one account.

My mind clings to this idea as if for some reason I know it's important. They say elephants never forget. They remember watering holes hundreds of miles away that they haven't visited in twenty years. My memory is a bit like that. It throws away some things like people's birthdays, anniversaries and song lyrics, but give me eighty witness statements and I can remember every detail.

Here's what I remember now. Aleksei had a phone stolen. He told me about it when we were outside Wormwood Scrubs. It was a new model. He loves his gadgets.

Turning suddenly, I head for the door, leaving Joe scrambling to keep up. He chases me across the gravel trying to hear what I'm saying on the phone.

"New Boy" Dave answers but I don't give him a chance to speak. "Aleksei had a phone stolen a few months back. He said he reported it to the police so there should be a record."

I pause. Dave is still on the line. I can hear him tapping at a keyboard. The only other sound I hear is the soft stirring of every wet thing inside me.

Pacing across the driveway I wander along a path of crushed marble that circles the rose garden. At the far end, beyond an arbor, is a sandstone column supporting a sundial. It has a small plaque at the base. The inscription reads, FAMILIES ARE FOREVER.

Dave comes back to me. "He reported a cell phone stolen on August 28."

"OK, listen carefully. You need to pull up the phone records for *that* number. Look for any international calls made on August 14. It's important!"

"Why?"

Dave doesn't have children. He doesn't understand. "Because a parent never forgets a birthday."

39

Birch and elm trees are etched on the ridges like charcoal drawings and the clouds are white breath against a blue sky. The black Gallant rattles and bumps over the pitted tarmac, sliding through patches of black ice in the shadows.

Our driver wrestles with the wheel, seemingly oblivious to the deep ditches on either side of the road. Two identical black Gallants are following us, being sprayed with mud.

The surrounding marshland has iced over at the edges, forming a fragile layer that creeps toward the center of pools and ponds. A refinery with a flaming orange tower reflects from the oily surface.

On one side of the road, separated by a ditch, is a railway track. A clutch of wooden shacks huddle alongside it, more like woodpiles than dwellings. Icicles hang from wet gutters and mounds of dirty snow are piled next to the walls. The only signs of life are thin wisps of smoke from the chimneys and the emaciated dogs picking through the trash cans.

The blacktop ends suddenly and we plunge into a monochrome forest on a track that snakes between the trees. There are tire marks in the mud. One set. There are no return tracks and no roads other than this one. Aleksei's car is somewhere up ahead.

Rachel has barely said a word since we arrived in Moscow. Sitting beside me in the backseat, she keeps her hands at her sides as though bracing herself for the potholes.

Our driver looks more like a military cadet than a policeman. There appears to be mildew sprouting from his top lip and his cheekbones are so sharp they could have been carved with a scalpel. Beside him is Major Dmitri Menshikov, a senior investigator with the Moscow police. The Major met us at Sheremetyevo Airport and ever since has provided a running commentary as though we're here on a guided tour.

For the past twenty-four hours we have tracked Aleksei Kuznet across Western Europe. After reaching Oostende, he stayed overnight and then caught a train from Brussels to Berlin on Monday morning. He then transferred onto an overnight train to Warsaw, crossing into Poland in the early hours of Tuesday.

That's where we almost lost him. If Aleksei continued by rail the most direct route to Moscow was via Brest and Minsk, but according to border guards who stopped the train in Belarus, he wasn't on board. He might have bought a car in Warsaw, but Russian authorities make it difficult to bring vehicles into the country, forcing delays of up to two days. Aleksei couldn't afford to wait. His other options were to either take a bus or a different train, through Lithuania and Latvia.

"New Boy" Dave came through for me. He found the cell-phone records for the stolen handset. Aleksei made dozens of international calls that month but on August 14—Mickey's birthday—he telephoned a dacha southwest of Moscow and talked for more than an hour.

Dmitri turns in his seat. "And you have no idea who is living in this house?" He speaks English with an American accent.

"Nothing firm."

"Are you even sure this girl is in Russia?"

"No."

"So this is a theory." He nods apologetically to Rachel.

Turning back to the track, he holds on to his hat as we hit another bump. The shadows are impenetrable spaces between the trees.

"And you think you will recognize this girl if she is your daughter?"

Rachel nods.

"After more than three years! Children forget. Maybe she is happy here. Maybe you should leave her alone."

The forest relents for a moment, opening out into a clearing dotted with prefabricated houses, rusting cars and power cables slung from poles. Crows lift off from the ground like scraps of ash swirling from a fire.

Soon the trees blur the side of the track again and the car slides in and out of the ruts. Crossing a narrow bridge over a murky tributary, we come to an open gate across the road. A lake emerges on our left, the dark water broken by a makeshift pier that leans at an angle. Tied to one of the pylons are inner tubes, marooned in thickening ice.

Overnight snow has settled on the newly formed crust, so thin I can see the darkness of the lake beneath it, thick like blood. A shiver runs through me and I imagine Luke's face, pressing up against the ice from below.

The house, screened by ash trees, emerges at the end of a driveway paved with loose gravel. Most of the windows are shuttered and outdoor tables and chairs rest upside down on a paved area within a rose garden.

The driveway runs out at a large rectangular courtyard. A silver Mercedes, streaked with mud, is parked near the doors to a stable. The driver's door is open and Aleksei is sitting on the ground, propped against the wheel. A fine rain is falling, collecting on the shoulders of his overcoat and clinging to his hair. His face is completely white except for a neat black hole in his forehead. He looks surprised, as though he slipped on the ice and is gathering his thoughts before he gets up again.

The black Gallants pull up on the far side of the courtyard. The doors open and guns are pointed across hoods or bonnets or whatever the Russians call them.

A man steps from the door of the house carrying a rifle in the crook of his arm. He is younger than Aleksei but has the same narrow nose and high forehead. His heavy trousers are tucked into lace-up boots and a knife hangs from a sheath on his belt.

Stepping out from behind the car, I walk toward him. He raises the rifle and rests it across his shoulder like a boy soldier.

"Hello, Sacha."

He nods and doesn't answer. Glancing at Aleksei he shows a flicker of remorse in the lowering of his eyelids.

"Everyone thinks you're dead."

"The old Sacha *is* dead. You *von't* find him here."

He has lost almost all trace of his English accent. Unlike Aleksei, Sacha didn't ever try to hide his Russian accent or his roots.

Rachel steps out of the car. She hasn't taken her eyes off Aleksei. It is as if she imagines he is going to wipe the blood from his forehead and stand up, having rested long enough.

The rain has turned to sleet.

"You want to tell me what happened?"

He glances at his boots. "Things have gone too far. He should never have come. He took her away from one home and now he wanted to take her away again. He has caused enough trouble."

A woman appears in the doorway behind him. A young girl is pressed against her.

"This is my wife, Elena," says Sacha.

Her arm is wrapped around the girl's shoulders, shielding her from the sight of Aleksei's body.

"We have taken good care of her. She has never wanted for any-thing." Sacha searches for the words. "She has been like a daughter . . ."

Rachel's hand flutters to her mouth as if trying to stop her breath escaping. She moves forward, past my shoulder, crossing the distance between them.

Mickey is wearing jodhpurs and a riding jacket. Her hair is plaited and rests across her shoulder. Elena has an identical plait.

Edging closer, Rachel drops to her knees. The toes of her boots barely move the frozen gravel.

Mickey says something to Elena in Russian.

"English now," says Sacha. "You're going home."

"But this is home."

He smiles at her gently. "Not anymore. You are an English girl."

"No!" She shakes her head angrily, beginning to cry.

"Listen to me." Sacha rests the rifle against the wall of the house and crouches beside her. "Don't cry. I have taught you to be strong. Remember when we went ice fishing last winter? How cold it was? You never once complained. Nyet."

She throws her arms around him, sobbing into his neck.

Rachel has watched with a mixture of trepidation and expectation. She takes a deep breath. "I've missed you, Mickey."

Mickey lifts her face and smears a tear across her cheek with the palm of her hand.

"I've been waiting for you a long time. I stayed in the one place—hoping I might find you. I still have your room and all your toys."

"I can ride a horse now," announces Mickey.

"Really!"

"And I can ice-skate. I'm not scared of going outside anymore."

"I can see that. You've grown so tall. I bet you can reach the top cupboard in the kitchen, near the window."

"Where you keep the treats."

"You remember." Rachel's eyes are shining. She holds out her fingers. Mickey looks at her tentatively and stretches out her own hand. Rachel draws her close and breathes in the smell of her hair.

"I'm OK now," says Mickey. "You don't have to cry."

"I know."

Rachel looks up at me and then at Sacha, who thumps his chest trying to clear his throat. The young Russian policemen have gathered around Aleksei's body, running fingers over the collar of his handmade shirt and feeling the softness of his cashmere overcoat. Dmitri has unclipped the wristwatch and compares it to his own.

Meanwhile, the snow whispers down, swirling in eddies and whirlpools, turning shades of gray into black and white.

———

Another country. Another mother and child.

Daj is in a wheelchair with me alongside, enduring one of those long silences that other people find awkward. She is wrapped in a white shawl that she holds together with her curling hands as she stares motionless out the window like an ancient malevolent bird of prey.

Behind us a flower-arranging class is setting up on the tables. Blue rinses and gray heads hum, coo and twitter to each other, as they sort through greenery and blooms of different colors.

I show Daj the front page of a newspaper. The photograph is of Mickey and Rachel, embracing for the cameras in the arrival hall at Heathrow Airport. You can just see me in the background, pushing the luggage cart. Perched on the top suitcase is a hand-painted babushka doll.

Joe is in the photograph, too. Standing next to him is Ali out of her wheelchair, leaning on his shoulder for support. She's holding a poster saying, "Welcome home, Mickey!"

"Remember that missing girl, Daj—the one I tried to find all those years ago? Well, I found her. I brought her home."

For a brief moment Daj looks at me proudly, curling her long fingers through mine. Then I realize that she doesn't understand. Her mind is answering a different statement.

"Make sure Luke doesn't go outside without his scarf."

"OK."

"And if he rides his bike make sure he tucks his trouser bottoms into his socks so he doesn't get grease on them."

I nod. She lets go of my hand and brushes a nonexistent crumb from her lap.

From now on I will visit her more often—not just at weekends but in the evening, too. I know that most of the time she forgets I am here. She labors to remember but it's beyond her powers and fading strength.

Villawood Lodge is expensive and most of my savings are gone. For the briefest of moments I contemplated keeping a handful of the diamonds or perhaps giving some of them to Ali as compensation for what she's been through. She wouldn't have taken them, of course, and I can understand why. They're covered in blood.

Harold, the gardener at Aleksei's house in Hampstead, found the stones and gratefully accepted a reward. He was even photographed by the newspapers, leaning on a sundial and pointing to where he discovered the four velvet bags.

Daj turns her head and listens. Someone is playing the piano in the music room. Outside an exercise class power walks through the garden, a platoon of swinging arms and swaying buttocks. The leader lifts her knees and glances over her shoulder to make sure she hasn't left any stragglers behind.

"I can see all the lost children," Daj whispers. "You have to find them."

"I can't bring them all back."

"You haven't tried."

She is looking at me now—recognizing me. I want to hold on to the moment because I know it won't last. Something will stir the breeze and her mind will scatter like dandelion seeds.

I am not a believer in fate or destiny or karma. I don't think everything happens for a reason and that luck evens itself out over a lifetime.
The law and order of the universe is breathtaking—the rising and setting of the sun, the seasons, the positioning of the stars. Without such
certainties the heavens will fall on our heads. Society has laws, too. My
job was always to keep them. I know that's not much of a philosophy
on life but so far it has been enough for me.

Kissing Daj on the forehead, I take my coat and walk down the hard
smooth corridor toward the entrance of Villawood Lodge. In the foyer
there is a public phone that takes plastic. Committed to memory I have
the numbers for Claire and Michael. Some things you never forget.

The receiver feels cold against my neck as I punch the buttons and
listen to the ringing. There have been many lost children in my life. I
may not be able to bring them all back but I have to try.

An excerpt from the forthcoming
Doubleday edition of Michael Robotham's

THE NIGHT FERRY

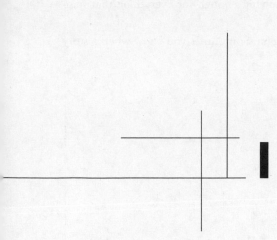

It was Graham Greene who said a story has no beginning or end. The author simply chooses a moment, an arbitrary point, and looks either forward or back. That moment is now—an October morning—when the clang of a metallic letter flap heralds the first post.

There is an envelope on the mat inside my front door. Inside is a small stiff rectangle of paper that says nothing and everything.

> Dear Ali,
> I'm in trouble. I must see you. Please come to the reunion.
> Love, Cate

Sixteen words. Long enough to be a suicide note. Short enough to end an affair. I don't know why Cate has written to me now. She hates me. She told me so the last time we spoke, eight years ago. The past. Given long enough I could tell you the month, the day and the hour but these details are unimportant.

All you need to know is the year—1998. It should have been the summer we finished university; the summer we went backpacking across Europe; the summer I lost my virginity to Brian Rusconi and not to Cate's father. Instead it was the summer she went away and the summer I left home—a summer not big enough for everything that happened.

Now she wants to see me again. Sometimes you know when a story begins . . .

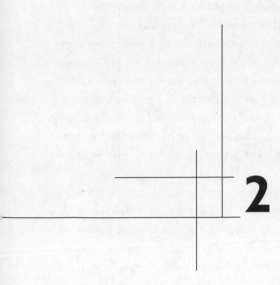

2

When the day comes that I am asked to recalibrate the calendar, I am going to lop a week off January and February and add them to October, which deserves to be forty days long, maybe more.

I love this time of year. The tourists have long gone and the kids are back at school. The TV schedules aren't full of reruns and I can sleep under a duvet again. Mostly I love the sparkle in the air, without the pollen from the plane trees so I can open my lungs and run freely.

I run every morning—three circuits of Victoria Park in Bethnal Green, each one of them more than a mile. Right now I'm just passing Durward Street in Whitechapel. Jack the Ripper territory. I once took a Ripper walking tour, a pub crawl with ghost stories. The victim I remember best was his last one, Mary Kelly, who died on the same date as my birthday, November the ninth.

People forget how small an area Jack roamed. Spitalfields, Shoreditch and Whitechapel cover less than a square mile, yet in 1888 more than a million people were crammed into slums, without decent water and sewerage. It is still overcrowded and poor but that's only compared to places like Hampstead or Chiswick or Holland Park. Poverty is a relative state in a rich country full of people who cry poor.

It is seven years since I last ran competitively, on a September night in Birmingham, under lights. I wanted to get to the Sydney Olympics but only two of us were going to make it. Four-hundredths of a second separated first from fifth; half a meter, a heartbeat, a broken heart.

I don't run to win anymore. I run because I can and because I'm fast. Fast enough to blur at the edges. That's why I'm here now, flirting with the ground while perspiration leaks between my breasts, plastering my T-shirt to my stomach.

When I run my thoughts become clearer. Mostly I think about work and imagine that today someone will call and offer me my old job back.

A year ago I helped solve a kidnapping and find a missing girl. One of the kidnappers dropped me onto a wall, crushing my spine. After six operations and nine months of physiotherapy I am fit again, with more steel in my spine than England's back four. Unfortunately, nobody seems to know what to do with me at the Metropolitan Police. They think I'm a wonky wheel on the machine.

As I pass the playground, I notice a man sitting on a bench reading a newspaper. There is no child on the climbing frame behind him and other benches are in sunshine. Why has he chosen the shade?

In his mid-thirties, dressed in a shirt and tie, he doesn't raise his eyes as I pass. He's studying a crossword. What sort of man does a crossword in a park at this hour of the morning? A man who can't sleep. A man who waits.

Up until a year ago I used to watch people for a living. I guarded diplomats and visiting heads of state, ferrying their wives on shopping trips to Harrods and dropping their children at school. It is probably the most boring job in the Metropolitan Police but I was good at it. During five years with the Diplomatic Protection Group I didn't fire a shot in anger or miss one of the wives' hair appointments. I was like one of those soldiers who sit in the missile silos, praying the phone never rings.

On my second circuit of the park he is still there. His suede jacket is lying across his lap. He has freckles and smooth brown hair, cut symmetrically and parted to the left. A leather briefcase is tucked close to his side.

A gust of wind tears the newspaper from his fingers. Three steps and I reach it first. It wraps around my thigh.

For a moment he wants to retreat, as if he's too close to the edge. His freckles make him look younger. His eyes don't meet mine. Instead he bunches his shoulders shyly and says thank you. The front page is still wrapped around my thigh. For a moment I'm tempted to have some fun. I could make a joke about feeling like tomorrow's fish-and-chips.

The breeze feels cool on my neck. "Sorry, I'm rather sweaty."

He touches his nose nervously, nods and touches his nose again.

"Do you run every day?" he asks suddenly.

"I try to."

"How far?"

"Four miles."

It's an American accent. He doesn't know what else to say.

"I have to keep going. I don't want to cool down."

"Okay. Sure. Have a nice day." It doesn't sound so trite coming from an American.

On my third circuit of the park the bench is empty. I look for him along the street but there are no silhouettes. Normal service has been resumed.

Farther along the street, just visible on the corner, a van is parked at the curb. As I draw nearer, I notice a white plastic tent over missing paving stones. A metal cage is propped open around the hole. They've started work early.

I do this sort of thing—take note of people and vehicles. I look for things that are out of the ordinary; people in the wrong place, or the wrong clothes; cars parked illegally; the same face in different locations. I can't change what I am.

Unlacing my trainers, I pull a key from beneath the insole and unlock my front door. My neighbor, Mr. Mordecai, waves from his window. I once asked him his first name and he said it should be Yo'man.

"Why's that?"

"Because that's what my boys call me: 'Yo man, can I have some money?' 'Yo man, can I borrow the car?'"

His laugh sounded like nuts falling on a roof.

In the kitchen I pour myself a large glass of water and drink it greedily. Then I stretch my quads, balancing one leg on the back of a chair.

The mouse living under my fridge chooses that moment to appear. It is a very ambivalent mouse, scarcely bothering to lift its head to acknowledge me. And it doesn't seem to mind that my youngest brother, Hari, keeps setting mousetraps. Perhaps it knows that I disarm them, taking off the cheese when Hari isn't around.

The mouse finally looks up at me, as though about to complain about the lack of crumbs. Then it sniffs the air and scampers away.

Hari appears in the doorway, bare-chested and barefooted. Opening the fridge, he takes out a carton of orange juice and unscrews the plastic lid. He looks at me, considers his options, and gets a glass from the cupboard. Sometimes I think he is prettier than I am. He has longer lashes and thicker hair.

"Are you going to the reunion tonight?" I ask.

"Nope."

"Why not?"

"Don't tell me *you're* going! You said you wouldn't be caught dead."

"I changed my mind."

There is a voice from upstairs. "Hey, have you seen my knickers?"

Hari looks at me sheepishly.

"I know I had a pair. They're not on the floor."

Hari whispers, "I thought you'd gone out."

"I went for a run. Who is she?"

"An old friend."

"So you must know her name."

"Cheryl."

"Cheryl Taylor!" (She's a bottle blonde who works behind the bar at the White Horse.) "She's older than I am."

"No, she's not."

"What on earth do you see in her?"

"What difference does that make?"

"I'm interested."

"Well, she has assets."

"Assets?"

"The best."

"You think so?"

"Absolutely."

"What about Phoebe Griggs?"

"Too small."

"Emma Shipley?"

"Saggy."

"Mine?"

"Very funny."

Cheryl is coming down the stairs. I can hear her rummaging in the sitting room. "Found them," she shouts.

She arrives in the kitchen still adjusting the elastic beneath her skirt.

"Oh, hello," she squeaks.

"Cheryl, this is my sister, Alisha."

"Nice to see you again," she says, not meaning it.

The silence seems to stretch out. I might never talk again. Finally I excuse myself and go upstairs for a shower. With any luck Cheryl will be gone by the time I come down.

Hari has been living with me for the past two months because it's closer to university. He is supposed to be safeguarding my virtue and helping pay the mortgage but he's four weeks behind in his rent and using my spare room as a knocking shop.

My legs are tingling. I love the feeling of lactic acid leaking away. I look in the mirror and pull back my hair. Yellow flecks spark in my irises like goldfish in a pond. There are no wrinkles. Black don't crack.

My "assets" aren't so bad. When I was running competitively I was always pleased they were on the small side and could be tightly bound in a sports bra. Now I wouldn't mind being a size bigger so I could have a cleavage.

Hari yells up the stairs. "Hey, sis, I'm taking twenty from your purse."

"Why?"

"Because when I take it from strangers they get angry."

Very droll. "You still owe me rent."

"Tomorrow."

"You said that yesterday." *And the day before.*

The front door closes. The house is quiet.

Downstairs, I pick up Cate's note again, resting it between my fingertips. Then I prop it on the table against the salt and pepper shakers, staring at it for a while.

Cate Elliot. Her name still makes me smile. One of the strange things about friendship is that time together isn't canceled out by time apart. One doesn't erase the other or balance it on some invisible scale. You can spend a few hours with someone and they will change your life, or you can spend a lifetime with a person and remain unchanged.

We were born at the same hospital and raised in Bethnal Green in London's East End although we managed to more or less avoid each other for the first thirteen years. Fate brought us together, if you believe in such things.

We became inseparable. Almost telepathic. We were partners in crime, stealing beer from her father's fridge, window shopping on the Kings Road, eating chips with vinegar on our way home from school, sneaking out to see bands at the Hammersmith Odeon and movie stars on the red carpet at Leicester Square.

In our gap year we went to France. I crashed a moped, got cautioned for having a fake ID and tried hash for the first time. Cate lost the key to our hostel during a midnight swim and we had to climb a trellis at 2:00 a.m.

There is no breakup worse than that of best friends. Broken love affairs are painful. Broken marriages are messy. Broken homes are sometimes an improvement. Our breakup was the worst.

Now, after eight years, she wants to see me. The thrill of compliance spreads across my skin. Then comes a nagging, unshakable dread. She's in trouble.

My car keys are in the sitting room. As I pick them up, I notice smudges on the glass-topped coffee table. Looking closer, I can make out two neat buttock prints and what I imagine to be elbow smudges. I could kill my brother!

ALSO BY MICHAEL ROBOTHAM

"Pleasantly creepy. . . . Plotted with precision and narrated with real intelligence." —The New York Times Book Review

SUSPECT

London psychiatrist Joseph O'Loughlin seems to have the perfect life. He has a beautiful wife, an adoring daughter, and a thriving practice to which he brings great skill and compassion. But he's also facing a future dimmed by Parkinson's disease. And when he's called in on a gruesome murder investigation, he discovers that the victim is someone he once knew. Unable to tell the police what he knows, O'Loughlin tells one small lie, which turns out to be the biggest mistake of his life. Suddenly, he's caught in a web of his own making.

Fiction/Literature/978-0-307-27547-9

VINTAGE CRIME/BLACK LIZARD
Available at your local bookstore, or call toll-free to order:
1-800-793-2665 (credit cards only).